ALEXANDER WILSON was a writer, spy and secret service officer. He served in the First World War before moving to India to teach as a Professor of English Literature and eventually became Principal of Islamia College at the University of Punjab in Lahore. He began writing spy novels whilst in India and he enjoyed great success in the 1930s with reviews in the *Telegraph*, *Observer* and the *Times Literary Supplement* amongst others. Wilson also worked as an intelligence agent and his characters are based on his own fascinating and largely unknown career in the Secret Intelligence Service. He passed away in 1963.

By Alexander Wilson

The Mystery of Tunnel 51
The Devil's Cocktail
Wallace of the Secret Service
Get Wallace!
His Excellency, Governor Wallace
Microbes of Power
Wallace at Bay
Wallace Intervenes
Chronicles of the Secret Service

a&b

Microbes of Power

ALEXANDER WILSON

Allison & Busby Limited
12 Fitzroy Mews
London W1T 6DW
allisonandbusby.com

First published in 1937.
This edition published by Allison & Busby in 2015.

A CIP catalogue record for this book is available from
the British Library.

10 9 8 7 6 5 4 3 2 1

ISBN 978-0-7490-1830-6

Typeset in 10.5/15.5 pt Adobe Garamond Pro by
Allison & Busby Ltd.

The paper used for this Allison & Busby publication
has been produced from trees that have been legally sourced
from well-managed and credibly certified forests.

Printed and bound by
CPI Group (UK) Ltd, Croydon, CR0 4YY

CONTENTS

1. A Report from Cyprus   7

2. A Spot of Bother   21

3. The Tale of a Microphone   36

4. Painters' Jackets   50

5. Agent Number Thirty-Three   67

6. Kidnapped in Nicosia   83

7. In Her Country's Service   98

8. Thalia Ictinos   113

9. A Surprise for Shannon   130

10. Thalia is Frank   145

11. Love at First Sight   162

12. A Meeting in the Pincio   181

13. Up a Chimney   199

14. The Amorous Herr Kirche   218

15. Shannon is Trailed—   237

16. And Administers Chastisement   256

17. The Man in the Flat   274

18. Death in a Hypodermic Syringe   292

19. At the Mercy of a Fiend   308

20. From the Flames   324

21. A Gallant Daughter of Greece   341

CHAPTER ONE

A Report from Cyprus

'Good morning, Maddison. Glorious weather, isn't it?'

The speaker, tall, upright, and essentially military-looking, passed into his office followed by the grey-haired, keen-eyed man who had unlocked the door for him.

'Beautiful, sir,' responded the latter. 'I hope you had a pleasant weekend.'

'It was delightful. Possibly the fact that it was the first real weekend I have had for a couple of months helped it to be more enjoyable than it otherwise would have been, but I revelled in every moment of it. The country is wonderful just now. I must confess to a weakness for primroses, and I don't think I've ever seen them growing in such profusion. Wasn't it Browning who wrote, "Oh, to be in England now that April's here"?'

'I believe it was, sir,' smiled Maddison, 'though Cousins is the authority on that sort of thing.'

Major Brien's blue eyes twinkled, he ran his fingers through his fair hair, settled his jacket more comfortably to his shoulders.

'Weather like this is calculated to make him lyrical,' he

remarked. 'If he is experiencing it in the United States, I can imagine him bubbling over with appropriate quotations. And now for work.' He glanced at his desk, made a little grimace at the heap of documents neatly piled in the centre. 'You don't spare me, Maddison, do you?' he grunted. 'If you had a kind heart, you would break me in gradually after a weekend spent trying to forget delicate international situations, foreign intrigues, diplomatic imbroglios, and that sort of thing.'

'I have dealt with the majority of the reports, sir,' the other assured him. 'You will not find more than three, possibly four, that require much attention.'

'Well, that's a relief. I must confess I feel very Mondayish.'

He sat down at the large desk; filled and lit his pipe; then, with Maddison standing by his side like a guardian angel, proceeded to go diligently through the mass of documents. Most of them had marginal notes in the calligraphy of his chief assistant, which he read carefully. In some cases he commented upon them, or asked questions, invariably signifying his approval, and appending his initials. Three were without any annotations. These were placed on one side until the bulk had been dealt with. Brien then drew them before him one by one, reading them carefully and, every now and again, sitting back in his chair, and entering into a discussion with Maddison on some knotty point. At length he made a decision concerning two of them.

'It may turn out,' he pronounced, 'that there is some connection between these affairs. It would be as well if we learn something more definite before putting the matter to Sir Leonard. Is Cartright available?'

'Yes, sir.'

'Very good. Send him to Copenhagen and Brussels, with

instructions to investigate the reports and ascertain, if possible, what relation exists between the two affairs. There are so many points of resemblance that I feel convinced there is a connection. He can fly to Brussels this afternoon, and go on to Copenhagen tomorrow. All being well, he should be able to get back on Wednesday evening. Now for this Cyprus business.'

He read again the decoded report from the Secret Service agent in Nicosia. It appeared to give him a considerable amount of thought for, after he had gone through it for the third time, and had assimilated the information contained therein, he sat back in his chair stroking his moustache and frowning, as though puzzled.

'What do you make of it?' he asked Maddison at length.

'It is difficult to say, sir,' was the reply. 'There seems so very little to go on. On the face of it there is no reason why Plasiras and Bikelas should not visit Cyprus. We know they have many friends there. It is significant, though, that such an effusive welcome should have been accorded them in the light of their present relations with the Greek government, and that their arrival should have been followed by a sense of excitement among the Cypriots. If you remember, there was noticeably a certain amount of unsettlement after their last visit in November.'

'Ah! That's just the point that has occurred to me. We did not take very much notice then, attributing it to the fact that the Greek part of the population was sympathetic with their aspirations. But they failed to overthrow the government in Athens, and everything seemed to have settled down, just as it did after Venizelos failed. Now it looks as though—' He rose to his feet. 'This,' he announced, 'is decidedly an affair in which the chief will be interested. He will probably send someone out. At all events, I'll see him at once.' He took up the report under discussion, nodding at those with which he had dealt. 'You can carry on with that little lot, Maddison, and tell Cartright to see me before he leaves for Brussels.'

He walked along to the office of Sir Leonard Wallace and, knocking, entered to find his chief standing with his back to the fireplace, puffing placidly at his pipe, his hands in the pockets of his immaculate lounge jacket, his whole air denoting thorough ease, if not entire repose.

'Giving your celebrated imitation of a man loitering his way through life, Leonard?' asked his second in command.

'Something like that,' was the response. 'I suppose you have come to interrupt the even tenor of my existence?'

Brien laughed. Knowing Sir Leonard better than anyone else, except possibly his wife, he was never deceived by the air of utter nonchalance with which the famous Chief of the British Intelligence Department invariably surrounded himself. It was not that Wallace's attitude was a pose, nobody realised that better than the man who had known him since they had been little boys at a preparatory school together, but he possesses such an easy-going, unruffled disposition, such an unexcitable temperament and perfect self-control that he is apt to deceive those who do not understand him. Ministers of State, when coming into contact with him for the first time, have often been deluded into regarding him as an unconcerned, inattentive figurehead; they have been persuaded into believing that his fame has been achieved from the exploits of his assistants. They have always been compelled to alter their opinions abruptly and sometimes to their own chagrin. He certainly gives little indication that there are even the elements of adventure and romance in his make-up. Yet in Sir Leonard Wallace are the ingredients which sent those glorious adventurers, Drake, Frobisher and Raleigh out in little cockleshells of boats against seemingly impossible odds. His is the same spirit as that which influenced Nelson to raise the telescope to his blind eye, and thus fail to see the signal of recall at Copenhagen; he is of the breed of men who faced indescribable perils and hardships and, without thought of fame or reward for themselves, built the British Empire into the greatest the world has ever seen.

Those who work with him, and under his direction, are of the same fine calibre. They may not be so cool, so unconcerned, so apparently insouciant, but they are of his quality. How few, who are proud of the might of their country, realise what Great Britain owes to the gallant men of the Secret Service. Their exploits are rarely made public; in fact, to all intents and purposes, the department under which they serve is non-existent. It appears in no reference books, is never mentioned in print, except in very confidential records, yet all the time it is a hive of quiet, efficient, silent work which goes on day and night, never ceasing. The men of the Secret Service have, of necessity, to live their lives on a higher, nobler eminence than those of ordinary individuals. They cannot be influenced by the commonplace, petty things of existence. When at leisure they enjoy themselves as other men do, but that leisure is rare, and cannot be spoilt by the unsavoury incidents that mar most other lives. They have learnt to rise above the little meannesses of life; their training teaches them that only the big things count. Before everything they put the country they serve so selflessly, knowing that at any time they may be asked to lay down their lives for her. That, to them, is the greatest of all honours. They face death, as they face life, with a smile on their lips.

Eyeing Sir Leonard Wallace, as he stood on the rug before the fireplace, Major Brien was conscious of a momentary feeling of astonishment. The years spent in the most exacting profession in the world had left little evidence of strain or stress on the attractive, good-humoured face of his friend. True, there were lines at the corners of his expressive steel-grey eyes, others between his smooth, dark, well-shaped brows; his brown hair was greying a little at the temples, but those were the only indications of the ravages of time. Brien felt that he himself showed far more evidence of tension, and his work was generally confined to the office, while Sir Leonard, on innumerable occasions, had undertaken the most hazardous enterprises, which had often resulted in his being very seriously wounded or injured.

'How old are we, Leonard?' asked the tall, fair-haired man abruptly.

Wallace's eyes twinkled.

'Anyone would imagine we are twins to hear you speak,' he commented.

'Well, we're practically the same age. I was wondering how you manage to look so outrageously young, while I—'

'While you, poor overworked mortal,' interrupted the other mockingly, 'look so aged and senile. One of your vanities, Billy my lad, is your belief that you appear older than I. Well, you're wrong; you don't. Both of us look our ages, which in my case is thirty-eight years and seven months, and in yours is thirty-eight years and two months.'

'You don't look a day older than thirty-two or three.'

Wallace laughed.

'I feel very much flattered,' he remarked. 'I'll return the compliment. You don't look a day older than thirty.'

'Bah! What about my bald spot?'

'What about it? You don't think, do you, that because you're a little thin on top you appear a kind of old inhabitant? What is that you have in your hand?'

'It is a report from Number Thirty-Three,' was the reply. He held the paper out to the chief.

Sir Leonard shook his head.

'Let me hear what you have to say about it first,' he suggested. 'You're an interesting talker, Bill, and I can very often grasp facts better when you put them before me in your usual succinct manner.'

Brien regarded him doubtfully, rather inclined to think that he was jesting. Sir Leonard's face, however, was perfectly serious.

'Aren't you going to sit down?' asked the former.

'No; I'm perfectly comfortable here, thanks.'

'But what's the good of standing there when there's no fire?'

'You know as well as I that it's a favourite position of mine. Hang it all! Can't I do what I like in my own office?'

'Well, I don't see why I should stand?'

'I didn't ask you to do so, did I? In fact, I wouldn't think of it – an old chap like you can't be expected to stand for long. Sit down, ancient! There's a seat behind you nicely upholstered in leather, and thoroughly comfortable. I can recommend it.'

Major Brien grunted something uncomplimentary, and sank into the chair indicated.

'You remember, of course,' he began, 'that, towards the end of last December, Plasiras and Bikelas the Greek ex-ministers, who were members of the government turned out of office in July, made a determined effort to overthrow the present government.' Wallace nodded. 'You probably remember also that in November, that is, about six weeks before their attempted coup, they were in Cyprus and, whether or not it had anything to do with their visit, there was afterwards a good deal of unrest on the island, especially noticeable in Nicosia.' Again Sir Leonard nodded. 'Well, this report from Number Thirty-Three states that they arrived with several other people – the names are given – in Nicosia on Friday afternoon from Smyrna. It seems that their arrival was expected by the population, for they received a most effusive welcome. The streets through which they drove were lined with Cypriots, who cheered them with great heartiness, numerous Greek flags decorated the buildings, and altogether their advent had the appearance of a triumphant homecoming. Since Friday, Nicosia has been in a state of excitement. There has been no disorder or anything of that sort, but the people have congregated continually in the streets and other public places, and an air of tension seems to be prevailing.'

Sir Leonard's manner did not seem to denote that he was particularly interested. He removed the pipe from his mouth; knocked out the dottle into the fireplace.

'The Greek government will be sending a protest, I expect,' he commented, 'at the welcome accorded to the two. They have been declared enemies of the Greek State, and that such a greeting should have been given to them in the crown colony of a friendly country may be regarded as an unfriendly act.'

'You do not regard the matter as particularly important?'

'On the contrary, I regard it as one that merits the fullest investigation. It is significant that they should pay two such visits to Cyprus. There is nothing particularly striking in the fact that they are regarded with sympathy by some of the Cypriots of Greek extraction – we already knew they had warm friends on the island – but it is a trifle ominous that practically the whole population should turn out and give them a demonstrative reception. One would have thought that their dismal failure to snatch power with their followers in December would have put them entirely out of court as likely aspirants for power in the future. I want to know; one: what interest the Cypriots have in them; in other words, what does it matter to the inhabitants of a British colony who is in power in Greece; two: why have Plasiras and Bikelas gone to Cyprus; three: why did they receive such a welcome; four: who accompanied them; five: with whom they are staying and for how long six: has there been any rumour of the coming fall of the present Greek government? I think I can answer number six myself with a fairly decided negative, for if there had been any trouble in government circles we should have known about it. Now, Bill, can you answer the other five?'

'I can answer two of them,' replied Brien, consulting his report. 'I can tell you with whom they are staying and who accompanied them to Cyprus.'

'Doesn't our agent give any explanation of the welcome or of the interest the Cypriots seem to have in them?'

'No; she admits that she is puzzled.'

'But surely, when a whole population is so effusive, someone is bound to divulge the reason for the effusion. You don't mean to tell me that it is being kept a secret by so many thousands. My dear chap, it isn't possible.'

'She thinks that for some reason the Cypriots, at least those of Greek extraction, are antagonistic to the present Greek government. Plasiras and Bikelas are spoken of as deliverers.'

'Ah! Deliverers of Greece, of course – on the surface – but what if deliverers of Cyprus from British rule is really meant?'

Brien whistled.

'Do you really think that the Cypriots would welcome a change of owners?'

'The Greek part of the population would, no doubt. It is possible that Plasiras and Bikelas have hinted that on obtaining power they would work for the cession of Cyprus to Greece. It puzzles me, however, to know what they can expect to gain from such a promise. It isn't as though the Cypriots are in a position to send a naval or military force to their aid.' He walked to his desk, and sat down. Unlocking a drawer, he took out a small, leather-bound book, and commenced to turn the pages. 'Number Thirty-Three,' he murmured to himself, 'Barbara Havelock, teacher at the Nicosia High School for Girls. She's the girl for whose education you took responsibility when her father was killed, isn't she?' Brien nodded. 'She seems to have done pretty good work out there, Bill. Have you ever had any reason to suspect any lack of efficiency on her part since you obtained the job for her?'

'None at all. Why? Aren't you satisfied?'

'Quite. I was only thinking that in a high school her activities are bound to be rather limited. Make a note to get her promoted to an inspectorship of schools, will you? Now for those questions you can answer.' He locked the book away in the drawer again. 'Who accompanied Bikelas and Plasiras to Cyprus, and where are they staying or with whom?'

Again Brien consulted the report.

'General Radoloff, Signor Bruno, Monsieur Doreff, and two secretaries are with them,' he replied, 'and they are the guests of Michalis, the wealthy landowner with whom they stayed before.'

'H'm! Very interesting.' Sir Leonard leant on his desk and regarded his companion thoughtfully. 'The affair begins to have great possibilities. General Radoloff and Monsieur Doreff are Bulgarians, very prominent at the moment, and likely to be important members of the next ministry. Signor Bruno, if I mistake not, is the ambitious Italian who nearly caused an upheaval when he was minister at Belgrade two years ago. He seems to have dropped out of diplomatic circles since, which is not to be wondered at. Michalis is the wealthiest man in Cyprus. With the lot of them in association, the situation is most intriguing. I certainly think we shall have to take a hand. Let me see – Cousins is in the United States, Carter is in Paris, Hill is in Madrid, Willingdon is too inexperienced yet to tackle such an important job, and Shannon deserves a rest after his work in Lucerne. By Jove! We are short-handed at the moment; that is, of experts. Cartright is the only man available for the job, and he doesn't speak Greek, does he?'

Brien shook his head.

'Besides,' he added, 'I am sending him to Brussels and Copenhagen on a rather peculiar affair that I wanted fully investigated before bothering you with it. Of course, if you wish him to go to Cyprus, I'll countermand the order.'

'No; send him to Brussels. It will have to be Shannon.' He pressed one of the numerous buttons under the ledge of his desk. A clerk entered almost at once. 'Tell Captain Shannon I wish to speak to him,' he directed. While waiting for the coming of the man for whom he had asked, he accepted from Brien the report from the agent in Cyprus, and glanced through it. A few minutes later the tall, amazingly broad-shouldered man, who was quite the most powerful individual in the Intelligence Service, entered the office, and walked across to Sir Leonard's desk with that swing which is typical of the well-trained athlete. Although Sir Leonard's comfortable room is large and lofty, he contrived somehow to make it appear of moderate size. He is over six feet in height, but his mighty shoulders cause him to look shorter. One of the most popular as well as one of the most efficient men in the service, he is as capable mentally as he is powerful physically. His clean-shaven face with its determined, almost aggressive jaw, other well-defined features, and clear grey eyes is exceedingly attractive. As he is thoroughly unassuming and possesses a great sense of humour, it is not difficult to understand why everyone who knows him likes him.

'Good morning, sir,' he boomed cheerfully. 'You sent for me?'

Sir Leonard indicated a chair into which Captain Hugh Shannon sank easily.

'I intended giving you a rest after your successful work in Lucerne, Shannon,' observed the chief, 'but I'm afraid Fate has decided otherwise.'

'Thank God for that,' murmured the big man fervently.

Sir Leonard smiled approvingly. The keenness of his assistants, who, as soon as they had accomplished one job, were invariably anxious to be away on another, was one of his greatest delights.

'Perhaps Helen will not feel quite the same about it,' he remarked. 'She will probably think, and quite rightly, that it is time she had you to herself for a while.'

'There's no nonsense about Helen, sir,' returned Shannon. 'She's as proud of the service as I am. She knew very well, when she married me, that she would be called upon to make a lot of sacrifices, and she has kept a firm upper lip ever since.'

'Good girl!' murmured Brien. 'You're a lucky fellow, Hugh.'

'Don't I know it, sir,' agreed Shannon, beaming expansively. 'She's one of God's own. It makes me feel pretty sick sometimes to reflect that, if Sir Leonard hadn't sent me out to India on that Rahtz and Novar business, I might never have met her.'

'Things like that are preordained, my dear chap,' observed Sir Leonard. 'You were intended for each other, and that's the end of it. By the way, I'm glad to see her father has been appointed Home Secretary in the Indian government. A very fine fellow, Rainer. It won't be long before he becomes governor of a province. And now to business. Have you ever been to Cyprus, Shannon?'

'No, sir.'

'So much the better. You will not be known to anyone there. I want you to go out at once. You'd better fly to Athens, and cross from there by boat to Famagusta; thence by train to Nicosia – it's about thirty-six miles, I think. You're to be a thoroughly unobtrusive visitor, but I'll get in touch with the High Commissioner, and arrange for you to be made an honorary member of all the clubs. Your main object is to become acquainted with Mr Paul Michalis, who is the greatest landowner and wealthiest man in the colony. He is entertaining Bikelas and Plasiras, the two Greek ex-ministers, who attempted a coup d'état in Athens last December and failed signally. They have been proclaimed enemies of the state by the present Greek government. Yet they make what practically amounts to a formal visit to Nicosia accompanied by two prominent Bulgarians and an Italian firebrand, and are given an enthusiastic welcome from the people of Greek extraction or sympathies. They must have entered Famagusta quietly and without ostentation of any sort, otherwise steps would have been taken to prevent the public reception accorded them. I want you to discover, if possible, what is in the wind. The report from Number Thirty-Three speaks of an air of tension reigning in the capital, and a vague statement that the Cypriots talk of Bikelas and Plasiras as deliverers. Number Thirty-Three is a teacher in the Nicosia High School for Girls and her name is Barbara Havelock. You will get in touch with her by the usual means, but don't draw her into your activities in any way, or be seen too much with her. It is possible, of course, that there is nothing behind this business, apart from an intense sympathy with Bikelas and Plasiras, but I am of the opinion that there is something much more significant than that in it. This vague talk of deliverers, the fact that they are accompanied by Radoloff, Doreff, and Bruno suggests possibilities which may have tremendous results. We cannot have a Balkan plot hatched on British soil in any case, even if there is no hostile purpose against this country in their scheming.'

A telephone rang. He picked up the receiver of one of the instruments on his desk. 'Yes, put him through,' he directed the operator. 'Read that, and get yourself thoroughly cognisant with the facts,' he added to Shannon, tossing across the desk the report from the secret agent known as Number Thirty-Three. 'Hullo! Yes, Wallace speaking . . . I have just been discussing a report concerning the same affair with Brien . . . Sent in a protest, have they? I thought they would. I'll come across.' He laid down the receiver; smiled at his second in command. 'It was Spencer,' he announced. 'A protest has been received from Greece by the Foreign Office and passed on to him regarding the almost regal reception accorded to Plasiras and Bikelas. I am going round to the Colonial Office.' He turned to Shannon. 'Make your arrangements as soon as possible,' he ordered. 'Maddison will give you all the information you require concerning the people you are going to watch. Keep in touch daily with us from the moment you arrive in Cyprus. If you find it is necessary to put someone into the household of Michalis, cable at once in number four code.'

A few minutes later a slim man of medium height, carefully, almost fastidiously, attired, crossed Whitehall and entered the portals of the Colonial Office. It is doubtful if anybody who had noticed him would have thought that behind his calm, unruffled exterior was the brilliant brain which supplied the forethought, imagination and acute perception upon which Great Britain depends so tremendously for her safety. He looked more like an idler about town than the famous head of the greatest espionage service in the world.

CHAPTER TWO

A Spot of Bother

The Right Honourable Sir Edwin Robert Spencer, Secretary of State for the Colonies, motioned his visitor to a chair. Sir Leonard accepted it, but refused a cigarette.

'I gather,' remarked the colonial secretary, 'that you are acquainted with the rather queer situation that has arisen in Cyprus.'

'I am quite well aware of what has happened,' responded Wallace. 'In what way do you regard it as a queer situation?'

'Don't you? These two ex-ministers of Greece have been exiled from their own country and declared enemies of the State, which means to say that if they set foot in Greece they will be apprehended, tried and probably executed. But the internal affairs of Greece have nothing to do with us. Personally, I consider this protest from Athens exceedingly high-handed. As far as we are concerned, there is no reason why they should not land at Famagusta and stay with a friend at Nicosia and, if a public reception is given them expressive of sympathy, what possible harm can there be in that?'

'You are losing sight of the fact that we are supposed to be on terms of cordial friendship with the present regime in Greece. As

Plasiras and Bikelas are enemies of Greece, and have been received on British soil with every appearance of sympathetic enthusiasm, that, to a sensitive government not too sure of itself, no doubt constitutes an unfriendly act. Thus the protest.'

'All rubbish!' grunted the statesman, who was generally more forcible than tactful. 'I call it behaving in a schoolgirl fashion. It is a pity the Greek government hasn't something better to do. Of course the Foreign Office is making a big thing of it. Of all the old women who sit in the present cabinet, Ainsley is the worst. He is forever on tenterhooks lest we tread on someone's corns. I've been suave and polite, and explained that the reception to the two was in no way countenanced by the Legislative Council; that, in fact, it seems to have originated as a private welcome, and developed into a public affair through the undoubted sympathy which the Cypriots evince for Messieurs Bikelas and Plasiras.'

Sir Leonard chuckled.

'Not very tactful,' he commented.

'Perhaps not,' smiled the statesman, 'but Ainsley can do all the wrapping up he likes. The reply goes from his department, not mine. The reason I wanted to talk to you about the affair is not because I, in any way, regard it as serious, but because Stevenson has sent me such a long note concerning it. Stevenson is the Governor, as perhaps you know. He is one of these over-efficient people, who find specks of dust where there are not any – a splendid man, of course, but fussy. He thinks that there is something serious looming in the background, and asks if he can give Plasiras and Bikelas a hint to move on. How can he do that? It is not a crime to be popular and receive a public greeting, and he certainly seems to have nothing else against them.'

'Nevertheless,' remarked Wallace with quiet emphasis, 'it would be better for Cyprus, I think, if they did move on.'

Sir Edwin Spencer stared at him questioningly for several seconds.

'Do you know something,' he asked, 'that I do not know?'

'Probably. May I see Stevenson's note?' The document was handed to him. He read it through carefully. 'From this report there appears nothing,' he observed, as he handed it back, 'that should have caused him any perturbation. The essential points are missing. They are these: the people who welcomed Plasiras and Bikelas spoke of them, indefinitely it is true, as deliverers. The question, to my mind, is: was the term used because the Cypriots are antagonistic to the present Greek government and consider that Plasiras or Bikelas or both in power would do more good for Greece, or are they, in some manner, hoping that the two are going to encompass their freedom from British rule?

'The second significant point is that the two Greeks are accompanied on their visit to Paul Michalis by General Radoloff and Monsieur Doreff, both very prominent Bulgarians, and Signor Bruno, the fiery Italian, whose excess of zeal over discretion almost caused a war between Yugoslavia and Italy some time ago.'

The colonial secretary pursed his lips in a soundless whistle.

'That does alter the situation,' he commented. 'Radoloff and Doreff have been very conspicuous in Bulgarian politics lately. I wonder what is in the air.'

'That is exactly what I intend to find out. I don't like this talk of deliverers. It may sound rather fantastic to imagine that these ex-ministers contemplate any move against Great Britain, but why should Cypriots, even though they are of Greek blood, be so interested in a change of government in Greece? They are British, not Greek subjects, and whatever happens in Greece can mean absolutely nothing to them. Again, where do Radoloff, Doreff, and

Bruno come into the scheme of things? They are hardly likely to be making a tour for their health in company with Plasiras and Bikelas. You can't very well give instructions to Stevenson to order them to leave the colony without something more definite to go on, but you can order him to see that no further demonstrations take place. No doubt they have called on him by now. I should like to know what they have had to say for themselves. As for the rest, leave it to me. I am sending—' He stopped abruptly; his eyes being fixed on a large painting of Hong Kong harbour hanging on the wall opposite Sir Edwin Spencer's desk. 'I am sending for news,' he ended emphatically.

The colonial secretary frowned as though puzzled.

'What do you mean by—' he commenced.

Sir Leonard placed a finger to his lips to solicit silence. He rose quietly, tiptoed across the room until he was standing directly below the picture; then, drawing up a chair, climbed on it, and lifted the painting away from the wall. A smile flickered momentarily round his lips, though his eyes grew hard in their expression. Resting the heavy frame on his artificial arm, he beckoned to the puzzled statesman, who immediately crossed the room to him. The latter had great difficulty in suppressing an exclamation when he saw that neatly fitted into the wall behind the picture was a microphone. Wallace allowed the heavy frame to fall gently back into place. He signed to Sir Edwin to return to his seat; then sauntered back to his own chair.

'A very interesting document this,' he remarked, apropos of nothing in particular, the comment being made to delude the unseen listener into the belief that he had been engaged in reading some communication or other. 'If you don't mind, I'll take it along to Masterson. There are a few questions about it I should like to ask him.'

'By all means,' returned the cabinet minister, playing up to him admirably.

Wallace leant towards him until his lips were very nearly touching the statesman's ear.

'Carry on as though you did not know that thing was there,' he breathed.

He left the room, and walked along to the office of the permanent undersecretary, Sir James Masterson. There he told a greatly perturbed and indignant individual what he had discovered. Sir James showed signs of an anxiety to rush off, and make drastic investigations – forty years in the calm, unhurried surroundings of government offices had not altered a naturally fiery temperament. Wallace calmed him down.

'We won't find out anything if you dash about like a dog chasing rabbits,' he observed. 'What is behind the wall on which that picture of Hong Kong hangs?'

Masterson thought a moment.

'Why, it must be the room shared by Barton, Marsh and Fellowes, three of the private secretaries,' he declared, and laughed. 'You're not going to suggest—'

'No,' interrupted Sir Leonard, 'I am not going to suggest that one of them has erected a microphone in order to listen in to discussions in the colonial secretary's room.'

'If, as you say, the instrument is behind the picture of Hong Kong harbour, I can't see how anyone can listen in unless he is actually in the secretaries' room.'

'Dear me!' murmured Wallace, 'you're a little bit behind the times, aren't you? I suppose a fellow who is shut within the walls of a government office most of his life does miss noticing progress in the outside world. But they let you out sometimes, don't they?'

Sir James Masterson vouchsafed no reply to such rank flippancy. Indeed his look rather suggested that he was shocked that a man of Wallace's high position should sink so low. Sir Leonard smiled cheerfully at him. 'If you could procure me a plan of this building,' he suggested, 'it would probably save me a good deal of trouble.'

'I have one here.'

'Excellent.'

Sir James went to a cupboard; took therefrom a large plan which he unrolled and spread on his desk. Together they studied it, the undersecretary pointing out the statesman's room and those in its neighbourhood. Before long Sir Leonard gave vent to a soft exclamation. His finger traced a line from the office of the Secretary of State up to the roof.

'An airshaft,' he commented; 'exactly what I was looking for. It's disused now, of course, and probably forgotten, but the enterprising fellow who inserted that microphone found out about it. The wires no doubt run up to the roof, where he sits comfortably and safely listening in to the most private conversations.'

'How could he have obtained access to Sir Edwin's room?' queried the outraged undersecretary.

'That is to be found out. And,' Wallace added grimly, 'I propose to set about the job at once. May I use your private phone?'

'Of course.'

Sir Leonard rang through to his own headquarters, and instructed the operator to connect him with the mess room. This was a large apartment in the basement of the building, comfortably furnished and containing a buffet, reserved as a rule for the use of senior members of the Intelligence Service. It was under the charge of an ex-sergeant of the artillery and a retired policeman, both of unexceptionable characters and records. The latter answered the telephone.

'Is Mr Cartright or Captain Shannon there?' asked Sir Leonard.

'Captain Shannon is, sir.'

'Ask him to join me at once in Sir James Masterson's room at the Colonial Office.'

'Very well, sir.'

In less than five minutes the young giant was shown in. Wallace explained.

'You and I are going to investigate, Shannon.' He added, 'You may have an opportunity to work off a little of your superfluous energy.'

'I suppose the blighter hasn't another microphone connected in this room, sir,' hazarded his assistant.

Sir Leonard shook his head.

'No,' he declared, 'I had a good look round when I entered.'

'Ah!' exclaimed Sir James with the air of a man who has made a great discovery. 'Now I understand why you were wandering about as though looking for something. You got on my nerves a bit I must confess – in fact I thought you a trifle – er – impolite. Sorry!'

Wallace laughed.

'Don't apologise, Masterson. I suppose my conduct did seem a little cool. Now will you go along to the colonial secretary's room, and start a discussion with him about something that sounds important but isn't. I hope to catch the delinquent red-handed.'

The undersecretary nodded, and obeyed. Sir Leonard and Shannon made a further study of the plan, ascertaining the exact position on the roof where the ventilating shaft commenced. They then made their way up the stairs, preferring not to use the lift. On the top floor were two ladders, one at each end of the corridor, connecting with the roof above. They chose that which they had calculated would be farther from the man, if indeed there was anybody up there listening in to the colonial secretary's room. Sir Leonard went first. He raised the trapdoor very gently and, cautiously lifting his head through the opening, surveyed the scene. Close by was a chimney stack, a little farther away was another, in fact it would not be very much exaggerated to describe the roof as a forest of chimney pots, so many were there. He saw no sign of a man or men and, stepping through, motioned to Shannon to follow him.

Presently they stood hidden behind the stack; then, taking advantage of all the cover afforded them, went softly towards the spot where Wallace calculated their quarry should be situated. They caught sight of him at the same time. He was leaning on one of the chimneys in an attitude of ease. On his head was fastened a pair of earphones, the wires connecting them with the microphone below, running into the mouth of a ventilator. He was a big fellow wearing the regulation government uniform. Shannon sighed softly to himself as his eyes fell on him; he was hoping, it must be confessed, that the man would make a fight of it. Something appeared to alarm him, for suddenly he straightened himself and looked round. A cry of astonishment and fear broke from him and, snatching off the earphones, he dashed them on to the roof, and made a desperate rush for the other trapdoor, convinced without doubt that it would be useless to stay and attempt to bluff out the situation. Shannon was after him like a greyhound. Anticipating his intentions, the Secret Service man went straight for the trapdoor; succeeded in cutting the fellow off from his objective. Then commenced a regular game of hide-and-seek round the chimney stacks. Sir Leonard stood and watched, content to bar any attempt the man might make to reach the other descent.

For a while Shannon was quite cleverly baulked. Once or twice they approached perilously near to the edge of the roof, and Wallace was impelled to shout a warning to his assistant. At length the latter feinted to go one way, promptly went the other and, throwing himself forward, tackled his quarry in rugby fashion. He caught and brought him down with a crash, but the fellow had no intention of giving in without a struggle. He resisted desperately with a pluck that was worthy of a better cause; but, although a big man himself, he was not the equal of the young man whose strength was the admiration of his colleagues and the fear of opponents who had, to their great regret, attempted to measure theirs against his. Before long Shannon had rendered his antagonist helpless and very nearly lifeless. He took him by the collar of his coat, and dragged him along to Sir Leonard, depositing him at the latter's feet in the manner of a dog that has retrieved a stick for its master. Wallace looked down at the purple countenance of the gasping victim of a Shannon hug, and sighed.

'Isn't it a pity to think,' he commented, 'that there are, among our own people, a number who are ready to sell their country and their souls for paltry gain. Thank God there are not many of them! This fellow was probably once a soldier with a good record, otherwise he wouldn't have been given a government job. He's allowed himself to be tempted, no doubt, by a worm of a dago, and thrown everything away – pension, job, all. Good work, Shannon.'

'It might have been more interesting, sir,' returned that burly individual. 'Still it wasn't a bad spot of bother, everything considered.'

The man still lay breathing painfully. He was obviously in poor condition, and the treatment he had received had taken all the stuffing out of him. Shannon dragged him to the trapdoor and, letting him down at the full length of his arms, dropped him unceremoniously through. The Secret Service man followed; stood guard over him until Sir Leonard joined him. The chief had stayed behind to examine the earphones and detach the wire. The sound of Shannon's captive being loudly deposited on the floor had brought several clerks, both male and female, from their rooms. Their exclamations and remarks told Shannon that the man's name was Wright, and that he was one of the night watchmen. On Sir Leonard's arrival, he sent the congregation, as Shannon described them, back to their rooms, with the exception of a young man who was dispatched to find a couple of orderlies. The latter, who knew Sir Leonard by sight, choked back the astonished ejaculations that rose to their lips, and lifting Wright between them, at his command, helped the man to a lift, thence along to the room of the Secretary of State. Leaving Shannon outside in charge of the prisoner, Sir Leonard arrived. The statesman and the undersecretary eyed him eagerly as he entered.

'Have you been successful?' asked the former.

Wallace nodded.

'We were lucky enough to catch him at it,' he informed them. 'He is one of your night watchmen, a man named Wright.'

'Good heavens!' ejaculated Masterson. 'He has been here for a considerable time, and I would have said he was a most reliable man. He came to the Colonial Office from the army, having served during the War in the tenth Hants.'

'I thought he probably had,' nodded Sir Leonard. 'He looks like an ex-soldier.'

'What has he to say for himself?' demanded the colonial secretary sternly.

'Nothing at present,' smiled Wallace. 'I am afraid he came up against one of the most powerful men in London, and is taking a little time to recover in consequence.'

Sir Edwin Spencer, who knew Shannon quite well, laughed quietly.

'Do you mean to say,' he asked, 'that he tried conclusions with Shannon?'

'Well, it would hardly be correct to say that he tried conclusions. As a matter of fact, he made desperate efforts to avoid him; they played quite an interesting little game round the chimney pots before Shannon caught him, but Shannon is not only extraordinarily powerful, he is quite the fittest man I know.'

'All you fellows are as hard as nails I should imagine,' commented the statesman. 'I suppose you have to be in your job.'

'We wouldn't last long, if we were not,' returned Sir Leonard a trifle grimly; 'but Shannon surpasses everyone for sheer physical fitness. In fact, he is so fit and strong that it is positively necessary for him to let off energy every now and again. Well, I suppose Wright has recovered sufficiently by now to answer questions. Would you like to hear what he has to say for himself, or will you leave it to me?'

'No; I'd like to know why he has been such a fool. Is he married, Masterson?'

The undersecretary nodded.

'He is,' he sighed, 'and has a fairly large family, I believe.'

'God help them! Why do men do such foolish things when they have families depending on them? He had a good post, with the promise of a pension to follow, and now –' He shrugged his shoulders, and turned to Sir Leonard. 'Tell me, Wallace,' he urged; 'how in the name of all that's wonderful did you know there was a microphone behind that painting?'

'It wasn't very difficult,' replied Sir Leonard. 'Sometimes when a microphone is in an enclosed space or there is something in front of it, sound comes back at one. Have you never noticed it?' Both his companions shook their heads. 'While I was talking to you it seemed to me that there was a faint echo. It puzzled me at first until

I realised what was causing it. If you listen carefully now, you will hear it. Are you listening, Sir Edwin?' he went on, speaking with great distinctness, 'and you, Masterson?'

Sure enough, a faint echo of his voice reached their ears.

'I would never have noticed it,' confessed the Secretary of State, 'if you had not drawn my attention to it.'

'Which goes to prove,' smiled Wallace, 'that you are not observant.' He sank into a chair, and commenced to fill his pipe, using his single hand with almost fascinating celerity and skill. 'Do you mind telling Shannon to bring in Wright?' he asked Sir James Masterson.

The night watchman presently stood, a great, hulking figure, with bent head, before the Secretary of State. Sir Edwin regarded him very sternly, but on the face of Sir James Masterson, who had sunk into a chair on the minister's left, could be seen a certain amount of pity. Sir Leonard Wallace, lounging in an armchair on the other side of the desk, seemed to be the least interested of the three, but his eyes were keenly studying the man.

'I think,' remarked the statesman, 'that your best course, Wright, will be to make a clean breast of everything.'

There was silence for a few seconds; then the fellow raised his head. He looked abjectly miserable.

'I suppose it ain't much good saying I'm sorry, sir,' he muttered huskily, 'but I am. I – I'd never have done it only – only – Well, you see, it was like this; I've always been a – an inquisitive kind of chap, and, when I saw a microphone and headphones in a shop cheap, I bought 'em and set 'em up in various places for fun like. I used to listen in to what other people were saying, not for any bad purpose, as you might say, but out of curiosity. It interested me to use the things and—'

'You are not trying to persuade us into believing that you were operating in the cause of science?' murmured Sir Edwin sarcastically.

Wright looked at him for a moment as though not quite certain how to take the remark, lowered his eyes again and, licking his lips as though they were dry, continued:

'No, sir. I don't know nothing about science, but I'm keen on wireless and loudspeakers and such. I didn't mean no harm. I found out that there was a ventilating shaft running down from the roof to this room, and one night, when I was on duty, I fixed the microphone in here. I only had to take out a couple of bricks what had been put in to close up the hole in the wall and plastered over. I thought I'd like to hear what you gentlemen talk about. I – I'd often wondered. I wasn't going to repeat what I heard.'

'Are you quite sure?' asked Sir James Masterson, who seemed inclined to believe the man.

Wright looked at him eagerly.

'Take my oath, sir,' he replied. 'I would rather have me tongue cut out than give any information to – to unauthorised people about what went on in here.'

'Quite forgetful of the fact,' drawled the Secretary of State, 'that you yourself were an unauthorised person and were committing a very serious breach of discipline as well as betraying trust. You were selected for your post here because your record and character were considered good enough to merit reliance being placed on you. You have repaid the confidence of those who selected you by a rank display of misconduct which merits severe punishment. I have nothing to do with selections or dismissals, but I presume that Sir James Masterson will give the necessary orders regarding your case to your direct superiors. All I wish to say is that you have rendered yourself liable to prosecution under the Official Secrets Act, and, if you are merely summarily dismissed, you can regard yourself as extremely fortunate.'

'I think,' observed the soft-hearted undersecretary, 'that since he has made a clean breast of his – er – unprincipled curiosity, we may waive any consideration of prosecution we would otherwise have had. In losing his post as, of course, he must, without references and no hope of pension, he is perhaps being sufficiently punished.'

Shannon, who was standing behind Wright, caught the expression on his chief's face, and smiled slightly. Sir Leonard removed the pipe from his mouth; rose to his feet languidly.

'I presume, gentlemen,' he remarked, 'that, as you have made up your minds regarding this fellow, there is no more to be said. I will leave him to you.'

'Just a minute, Sir Leonard,' begged the Secretary of State. 'We should like to know, of course, if you have any objection to the procedure Sir James Masterson has suggested.'

A fleeting smile passed quickly across Sir Leonard's face. Abruptly he placed himself directly in front of Wright; his steel-grey eyes bored deeply into those of the night watchman, causing them to drop in confusion, or perhaps it was fear.

'Do you repeat,' he demanded, 'that you bought and fixed up the microphone of your own accord?'

'I do, sir,' came huskily from the other, after a moment of hesitation.

'You were not persuaded, bribed, coerced, or forced to take such an action?'

'No, sir.'

'A certain man or men did not come to you, give you the microphone, and ask you to listen in to conversations held in this room?'

'N-no, sir.'

'You are quite certain that your memory is not misleading you? You did not have a conversation yesterday or the day before with a foreigner who persuaded you into doing this thing? You did not take advantage of the fact that yesterday was Sunday to install the microphone?'

The Secretary of State, Sir James Masterson, and Captain Shannon listened to the battery of questions with great interest. The first two noticed that Wright's face had gone a sickly white. The watchman was visibly agitated; he looked a very much frightened man.

'I tell you,' he persisted, but in a voice that could hardly be heard, 'that I bought the microphone myself, and only put it in because I was inquisitive like, and wanted to hear what was being talked about.'

'Where did you purchase the microphone?'

'In – in a shop in – in Lambeth.'

Sir Leonard looked him up and down, an expression of the greatest contempt on his face. 'You're a liar!' came in scornful, biting words from his lips. He turned to Sir Edwin Spencer. 'I might have been disposed to believe his story,' he added. 'I say "might", because it is unlikely, but, as it happens, I do not believe a word of it. The headphones he was using on the roof are stamped with the name of a firm in Athens. They came from Greece!'

CHAPTER THREE

The Tale of a Microphone

Sir Leonard's announcement was received in varying ways by the men in the room. The colonial secretary's face became harsh and full of contempt as he gazed at the culprit, Masterson appeared shocked, Shannon showed no particular emotion, but edged closer to Wright as though anticipating that the fellow might make a sudden break for freedom. He did nothing of the sort, however; seemed utterly crushed. Wallace eyed his drooping form for some seconds in silence. Then at last he spoke again.

'Do you still hold to the same story?' he asked. There was no answer. 'A few minutes ago,' went on the Chief of the Intelligence Department, 'Sir Edwin Spencer advised you to make a clean breast of everything. You will be wise, if you take the opportunity I am giving you now of renouncing your lies and telling the truth.' Wright continued to maintain a stubborn silence. Sir Leonard slightly shrugged his shoulders. 'Very well, there is nothing for it but trial for you under the Official Secrets Act, with, of course, imprisonment to follow.'

At that the fellow looked up at the slim, upright man facing him.

'Not that, sir,' he pleaded hoarsely; 'for God's sake don't send me to prison. Until now I've been straight, and—'

'Are you prepared to confess?'

Wright was silent for a little while; then he slowly nodded his head.

'Yes,' he muttered, 'if – if you promise not to send me to jail.'

'I make no conditions,' returned Sir Leonard sternly. 'What is done with you is entirely at the discretion of Sir James Masterson, but, if you present us with another bundle of falsehoods, I shall advise your prosecution most emphatically. On the other hand, if I feel you have told the truth, I shall make no objection if he decides to take no further steps against you.'

'Thank you, sir,' muttered Wright. 'What do you want to know?'

'Everything. First of all, tell me: did you serve in Salonika during the War?'

The apparently irrelevant question surprised Spencer and Masterson. Wright, however, did not appear to regard it as inconsequent. He had reached the conclusion that the man examining him had a deadly brain that seemed capable of ferreting out even one's innermost thoughts; it would be useless to attempt to deceive him. He told Wallace, therefore, that he had served in Salonika.

'I thought so,' nodded the Chief of the Secret Service. 'I knew, of course, that your battalion was there. Did you, by any chance, meet your wife there?'

'Yes, sir.'

'Ah! That explains a lot. It was through your wife then, I presume, who is a Greek woman, that you met the man or men who have succeeded in plunging you into this unpleasant situation?' Wright was silent for so long that Sir Leonard repeated the question, adding: 'It is no use your hesitating. Either make a clean breast of the whole business or prepare to stand your trial, when you must expect everything to be dragged from you in open court.'

Wright appeared to have a great fear of imprisonment. The idea of being tried by a judge and jury with perhaps two or three year's hard labour to follow dismayed him. He told the whole story now of his fall from the path of rectitude without faltering. In fact he spoke so quickly that Sir Leonard, who had returned to his chair, had on two or three occasions to pull him up. It appeared that, on his marriage, his wife had presented him with several hundred pounds with which he had bought a house and furnished it. Unfortunately, with the unkind practise peculiar to some women, she had never allowed him to forget the fact that her money had provided the home? As she was also in the habit of inviting compatriots of hers, who happened to be visiting England, to stay at the house during their sojourn, Wright had quickly found that he was more of a lodger, and not a very popular one at that, than anything else.

During the previous year, the house had been visited on several occasions by two men, one of whom was a Greek and the other a Cypriot, who appeared to have a considerable amount of somewhat mysterious business in London. They had arrived again on Saturday evening. Before Wright had started off for his nightly duty, they had taken him into a public house, and had insisted on treating him, behaving altogether as though they were bosom friends of his instead of comparative strangers. The ex-soldier, far from suspecting ulterior designs, was flattered by their attentions, which they had continued on Sunday morning. It was then that they asked him if it were possible for him to listen to conferences or discussions held in the room of the Secretary of State for the Colonies. He had, according to his own story, replied that it was not, and had vehemently asserted that he would not attempt anything of that nature even if it were possible. They had plied him with drink after drink; then had asked him if he could install a microphone in the room, and listen in to conversations from a place where he would be perfectly safe. If he would oblige them in that manner for a week or two, they would pay him three hundred pounds. At this point in his narrative, Wright took pains to make it appear to his listeners that he had time after time resisted the temptation. He had only fallen when the drink and the thought of possessing three hundred pounds, which would mean independence, as he expressed it, from his wife's hold over him, had proved too much for him. He did not explain in what manner the possession of three hundred pounds would render him independent of the woman. Sir Leonard did not trouble to inquire, curtly cutting short the man's efforts to show how he had at first resisted their insidious temptations, and bidding him to continue his story.

Once he had agreed to do their bidding, Wright had apparently entered very keenly into the scheme, though he endeavoured to make it appear that he had continued reluctantly. He knew of the disused ventilating shaft, and it occurred to him as an ideal place in which to fix the apparatus they handed over to him. The only alternative was the chimney. This had a big drawback, for, though April was well advanced and the weather quite warm, there was always a possibility of a fire being lit in the grate. There was no difficulty in obtaining access to the statesman's room and, as he had that part of the building to himself, he was able to arrange his apparatus without fear of interruption. It had taken him a considerable part of Sunday night and the early hours of that morning, especially as he was very careful to leave no trace of his presence in the room in the way of specks of fallen plaster or anything of that nature. He had gone home to breakfast, and announced that the microphone was in place. He had then been paid £100 on account, and given his final instructions. Although off duty, no surprise had been expressed by any of his mates, when he had returned shortly before ten o'clock. It was not unusual for him to appear in the daytime. He had made his way to the roof and, with the headphones in position, had listened to every word spoken in the cabinet minister's room up to the time when he had been discovered.

'Your only reason for committing such an act,' commented Sir Leonard scornfully, when Wright had concluded, 'was, as far as I can make out, a desire to obtain money. You have not even the saving virtue of being confronted by ruin to advance as an excuse, like so many people who get themselves into a similar position. Greed – nothing else but greed – influenced you to become a traitor to your country.'

'Not greed, sir,' whined the man. 'I didn't want the money for itself – I wanted to be able to tell the missus that I had money of me own whenever she nagged me about the house and furniture and all the rest of it. I would have felt independent of her then.'

'Would you!' observed Sir Edwin. 'I very much doubt it. If your wife is the woman you have pictured her, I should imagine she would retort by telling you that you had betrayed your country or your employers to get the money or that her own people had provided you with it. Really, Wright, that's about the weakest excuse for treachery I've ever heard in my life.'

'Was there anything particular you were instructed to listen for?' asked Sir Leonard. 'I mean to say, were you told to take note of all conferences, discussions, or conversations in general or those referring to a particular subject.'

'Those about a particular subject, sir,' replied Wright reluctantly.

'And what was that subject?'

'Well, it was more than one subject in a manner of speaking, sir. I was instructed to listen particularly whenever Greece or Cyprus was mentioned or two Greeks with the names of Bikelas and Plasiras.'

Sir Leonard glanced significantly at the colonial secretary;

turned quickly back to the man he was examining.

'You have the names off rather pat,' he remarked. 'Do you know the men to whom they belong?'

'No, sir.'

Wallace gave him a sharp glance; was satisfied that he spoke the truth.

'How were you going to remember what you heard?' he demanded. 'Were you writing it down?'

'No, sir. It would have been too – too dangerous in – in case of discovery.'

'You'd better search him, Shannon,' directed Sir Leonard.

He was promptly obeyed, the burly Secret Service agent going through the watchman's clothing with the speed and thoroughness of an expert. Everything he found in the pockets was placed on the desk. He even looked in the man's tobacco pouch, opened out all the cigarettes contained in a case, examining the paper for writing. Wright almost forgot the position in which he stood, so fascinated did he apparently become in watching him. The colonial secretary and Masterson were no less interested. They certainly were given a display of a Secret Service man's thoroughness. Shannon was not content in removing and examining the articles in the pockets; there was hardly an inch of Wright's person that escaped the deft inquisition of those expert fingers. At last he turned to Sir Leonard, who was also going through the articles on the desk.

'That's the lot, sir,' he announced. 'Nothing of any significance on him.'

'Not a thing,' agreed Wallace, as he replaced the last article on the table. 'You can put those back in your pockets, Wright.'

The watchman obeyed, glancing a trifle resentfully at the opened cigarettes on a large ashtray.

'Can I have the cigarette tobacco, sir?' he asked. On permission being granted, he poured it into his pouch.

'Now,' demanded Sir Leonard, 'tell us the names of the two men who put you up to this business!'

Wright hesitated.

'Baltazzi and Padakis, sir,' he muttered at last with great reluctance.

'Do you know why they are in England?'

'No; unless it is for the purpose of finding out what is going on over here concerning Greece and Cyprus.'

'What do you mean by "going on over here concerning Greece and Cyprus"?'

'Only that I was to tell them what was said about those two countries in this room.'

'What have they said to you about Cyprus?'

'Nothing, sir. They said that Greece was anxious to make arrangements with England over something or other – they didn't say what it was though.'

Again he was subjected to a searching glance. Sir Leonard was apparently satisfied that he was keeping nothing back, for he nodded.

'What do you know about Cyprus?' he asked sharply.

Wright stared at him as though the question puzzled him.

'Cyprus!' he repeated vaguely. 'It's an island, ain't it? That's all I know about it. I suppose it's got something to do with Greece, as Baltazzi is a Cypriot – leastways that is what he calls himself – and he looks the same breed to me as Padakis.'

'Can you speak Greek?'

'No, sir.'

'Do you think he can speak the language, Shannon?' asked Sir Leonard in Greek.

'No, sir. It is obvious he cannot,' replied the burly man in the same tongue.

The trial was successful. Wright looked vaguely from one to the other as they spoke. It was quite apparent that he did not understand. Neither Sir Leonard Wallace nor Captain Shannon had had more than a very indifferent knowledge of the Greek language a few months previously, but having been brought into contact then with a conspiracy engineered by Greeks, and finding their ignorance a disadvantage, they had since studied the tongue assiduously. A knowledge of Ancient Greek had been helpful, of course, but the ability to master languages quickly and fluently is a necessary adjunct to the Secret Service man's mental equipment.

'Have you any questions you wish to ask this man, Sir Edwin?' Wallace turned to the Secretary of State.

'No; I don't think so,' was the reply.

'Have you, Sir James?'

Masterson shook his head. It was a terrible thing to him that a man in government employ, even though in a menial position, should sink so low as to betray his trust. The affair had thoroughly upset the old civil servant, whose life had become bound in the tentacles of officialdom, but who, nevertheless, had never lost his humanity. Although all his instincts had been outraged by the behaviour of Wright, he still felt a certain amount of pity for the man. It seemed to him that an otherwise honest, though perhaps ignorant and foolish, Englishman had been snared by a scheming wife and her compatriots. If Wright had married an Englishwoman, he reflected, the distasteful situation would never have arisen. He was inclined, rather unfairly perhaps, to place all the blame on an unfortunate marriage, possibly contrived by a designing woman.

'Can Wright be locked up in this building for a few hours?' Sir

Leonard asked him. 'It is essential that he should remain here for the present. Afterwards, if you do not intend to prosecute him, he can go.'

'I daresay it can be arranged,' Masterson assured the Chief of the Secret Service.

'Will you give the necessary orders?'

Sir James left the room, followed by Shannon and Wright. When the door had closed on them, the colonial secretary looked quizzically at Sir Leonard.

'If I ever went wrong,' he declared, 'I should hate to have to face you, Wallace.'

Sir Leonard walked across to the wall on which hung the painting of Hong Kong harbour. Climbing on a chair, he stretched his hand up behind the picture, caught hold of the microphone and pulled it from its position. Returning to the desk, he stood examining it for some minutes.

'Made by the same firm,' he commented, 'and very well made too.' He laid it on the desk, and faced the statesman. 'This business is far more serious than we thought at first,' he remarked. 'The visit of Plasiras and Bikelas to Cyprus must have some very significant reason behind it, since it is considered necessary to send men to find out how the Colonial Office in London regards it.'

'You really think those two fellows are in London for that purpose?'

'Obviously. Messieurs Plasiras and Bikelas have their own espionage department it seems. I suppose they considered it a stroke of great fortune that one of their compatriots is married to an Englishman in the employ of the Colonial Office. No doubt they would have required further and possibly more difficult tasks from Wright before they had finished with him.'

'But why should they be so keen to know what was said in this office about them and their activities?'

'For one thing, they don't know how much is known about the enterprise on which they are at present engaged, and another, they are anxious to discover how their reception in Nicosia is regarded here and if any steps are likely to be taken against them.'

'Do you mean to say that the fellows who bribed Wright have travelled from Nicosia since Friday?'

'No; they could not have done it. I mean to say, they couldn't have been in Nicosia on Friday and in London on Saturday unless they flew all the way. That is most unlikely. Even if they did, it would be an exceptional feat. No; they were already here or within easy reach on the continent. A telegram probably gave them their instructions. It is quite clear that a very big conspiracy is afoot, and that conspiracy involves Great Britain. Shannon is departing for Cyprus today, and I hope he will get to the bottom of it. In the meantime, we'll see if we can get hold of Messieurs Baltazzi and Padakis and make them talk.'

Sir Edwin Spencer made a grimace.

'If you get hold of them,' he remarked, 'I have no doubt you will make them talk. What do you suggest? Shall I give orders to Stevenson to tell Bikelas and Plasiras to move on?'

'Good Lord, no! Let them remain as guests of Michalis until we find out what the game is. Simply acknowledge Stevenson's note. You might add that no particular significance is thought to attach to the welcome accorded Plasiras and Bikelas in Nicosia, though the Greek government has sent a protest.'

The Secretary of State regarded him in astonishment.

'No significance!' he repeated in surprised tones.

Sir Leonard sighed gently.

'It is possible,' he explained, 'that there are spies in Stevenson's household. If they obtain access to your communication, they will report the contents to their masters. The fact that no significance is apparently attached to the affair may lull them into a false sense of security.'

'Oh, I see.'

'That's bright of you,' murmured Wallace sarcastically. Sir Edwin frowned a little; then he sat back in his chair, and laughed.

'You're not very forbearing with us poor cabinet ministers, Wallace, are you? I think you regard us as fools.'

'Most of you are,' retorted Sir Leonard bluntly, 'though you're not as bad as some.'

'Thank you so much,' returned the colonial secretary, sarcastic in his turn.

'Don't mention it,' murmured Wallace with a smile.

Sir James Masterson re-entered the room, followed by Shannon. The former reported that Wright had been locked in a small room in the basement of which he himself had retained the key. Sir Leonard expressed his satisfaction, promising to let the undersecretary know as soon as it was wise to permit the ex-night watchman to depart. Having ascertained Wright's address, the Chief of the Intelligence Department took his leave. He sent Shannon on ahead as he did not wish them to be seen together. There was just a possibility, he thought, that one of the two spies was watching the Colonial Office and might know him. In light of the enterprise Shannon was about to undertake, it would not do for him to be associated in any way with Sir Leonard Wallace. Shannon, in fact, was instructed to walk away from the Colonial Office, and not to return to Secret Service headquarters until he was certain that he was not being followed.

Sir Leonard saw no sign of any lounger, who might be keeping the Colonial Office under observation, as he sauntered back to the innocent-looking building inside which so many tremendous secrets were stored and projects of such worldwide importance planned. He went up in the lift to the floor where his room was situated, but, instead of entering that apartment, walked along the corridor to Major Brien's office. He found his deputy immersed in work, but the soldierly-looking man pushed it aside, and eyed him eagerly. Sir Leonard closed the padded door with his foot and, crossing to the desk, planted himself on it. He told Brien all that had transpired in the Colonial Office, concluding with:

'Jump in your car, will you? And go along to Number Seventy-Two Brook Street, Kennington. Wright lives there, and I want you to get hold of Baltazzi and Padakis, and make them talk, if you can. Take Maddison with you and a couple of the juniors, and be careful not to do anything that is likely to alarm them and enable them to get away. If they're not in, wait for them. Afterwards, take them and Mrs Wright along to Scotland Yard, and ask the SB to take charge of them for a few days.'

'Hadn't I better take them there first, and question them when they're nicely lodged in a place from which they cannot get away?'

Sir Leonard shook his head.

'They may talk more readily in their own quarters. Of course, if they won't, you must do the questioning at Scotland Yard. But don't leave the woman behind. She may be in it as much as the others, and is quite as likely to telegraph the news to Cyprus.'

'What about the children?' queried Brien. 'Didn't you say there is a family?'

'M'm, yes!' Sir Leonard rubbed his chin thoughtfully. 'I haven't any idea how many or how old they are, though. You'll have to find that out, and make arrangements accordingly.'

Brien immediately sent for Maddison; instructed him to choose two of the junior agents, and bring them to his office. The small, keen-eyed man promptly made his choice from the half-dozen eager young fellows who were in the process of winning their spurs in the very exacting and dangerous profession they had chosen, and for which they had been selected, after the most exhaustive investigation into their family history, character and attainments. Willingdon, like several of Sir Leonard's more famous assistants, had graduated from the Special Branch of New Scotland Yard. Foster, the son of a well-known soldier, had himself passed through Sandhurst into the Guards. A spirit of adventure, an amazing aptitude for languages, and a daredevil disposition had presented this old Salopian with an opportunity of which he had quickly and eagerly availed himself. Sir Leonard, standing now on the hearthrug, eyed the two with an air of approval. Jack Willingdon was about Maddison's own height, which was not more than five feet five inches, but he was stockily-built and owned a pair of powerful arms. Dark-haired, dark-eyed, with a slightly Jewish cast of countenance, he was the personification of intelligence. Bernard Foster presented a great contrast. He was tall and thin, fair-haired, pale, and possessed a pair of sleepy blue eyes, which were one of his greatest assets, for they gave him an air of bland innocence. Yet anyone less sleepy than Foster it would be hard to imagine. A small moustache, adorning his upper lip, added to his appearance of harmlessness, while when he wore a monocle, which he did frequently, he looked thoroughly and completely guileless.

Having assured himself that his instructions were quite understood, Brien departed with his assistants. Sir Leonard had a final interview with Shannon before the latter left for Cyprus; then spent the rest of the morning making certain searching enquiries, most of which were connected with the stability of the Greek government and the possibilities of revolution. It appeared that the existing regime was apparently as secure as any in Europe at that time, and though there was a decided tendency in certain quarters to demand the return of the monarchy there was no suggestion of any rising to that end. The ill-fated attempt of Plasiras, assisted by Bikelas, to obtain power in the previous December had, it was confidently asserted, been crushed not only for the time being but for ever. The force of the two ex-ministers had been practically annihilated in an attack on Corinth, which had been followed by imprisonment, trial, and the summary execution of various officials and others of importance known to have been in sympathy with them. The Foreign Office expert on Greece, whom Sir Leonard consulted, scoffed at the idea of the two attempting another coup d'état.

'They are exiles with a price on their heads,' he declared, 'and with no followers to speak of. Orders have been given to the troops that they are to be shot on sight, if they step on Greek soil.' He admitted himself puzzled by the extraordinary reception they had been accorded by the people of Greek extraction in Nicosia, and the fact that they were accompanied by two such well-known and important Bulgarians as General Radoloff and Monsieur Doreff. 'They must be mad if they contemplate causing trouble in Cyprus. What object could they possibly have in antagonising the British government? Personally, I feel certain that the welcome was merely an expression of sympathy for men who, after all, when in power, did do a certain amount of pretty good work for their country. They are not out for trouble, believe me. They probably wish for nothing more than to be allowed to live in peace.'

Wallace made no comment to this. He had different ideas, but he did not feel called upon to expound them.

CHAPTER FOUR

Painters' Jackets

Major Brien and his assistants arrived at the beginning of Brook Street, Kennington, where they left the car in the charge of a police constable whom Foster found in the vicinity, and who, at sight of something shown to him by Maddison, became immediately very attentive and very much on the alert. Brien took a small attaché case from the Vauxhall, and walked along to Number Seventy-Two, the others following some yards behind. He rang the bell of the house, the door being opened to him by a dark-visaged youngster of about ten.

'Is your father in?' asked Brien.

'No; he's out,' was the reply.

'Then may I see Mrs Wright? She will do just as well.' The boy turned away to call his mother, and the Deputy Chief of the Secret Service stepped into the little narrow hall. Almost at once Maddison and Foster entered after him; Willingdon remaining outside to keep watch. They had ascertained that there was no rear exit. A stout, dark woman with sallow skin and black piercing eyes emerged from the nether regions, and confronted them.

'What is this?' she demanded in a shrill voice. 'Who are you?'

'I am an official of the British government,' Brien informed her. 'I wish to interview two gentlemen who, I believe, are staying here. There is some question concerning their permits.'

She had clutched at the banisters of the narrow staircase as though for support; her face had gone pale. For a moment she was obviously very much disconcerted, but she recovered herself quickly.

'Is it usual,' she demanded loudly, 'for officers of the British government to enter houses in a manner so impolite?'

'I do not think we have been impolite, madam,' returned Brien courteously. 'Your small son opened the door, and we entered.'

'My son should not have allowed you to come in. If it was not that he has been ill, he would have been at school with his brother and sister, and I would then have answered the bell. It would not have been so easy for men who may perhaps be thieves to enter. I would—'

'We are not interested in what you would have done,' interrupted Brien, who was becoming a trifle impatient. It seemed to him that she was striving to gain time, and perhaps, since she continued to speak in a loud voice, warn the men he was so anxious to meet. 'You can look at our credentials, if you wish, and assure yourself that we are in fact officers of the government. But I am here to interview Messieurs Baltazzi and Padakis.'

Her manner changed abruptly.

'I am sorry, but there must be a mistake,' she told him. 'There is no one of that name here. Only I and my children and my husband, who is out, live in this house.' Brien signalled to Maddison, who promptly ran up the stairs followed closely by Foster. 'What is this?' she screamed. 'Where are you going?'

'They are going to search the house,' she was informed. 'We know Baltazzi and Padakis are here or, at least, are living here, and we mean to see them. I regret the necessity that forces us to take such a step, but you have compelled it by your attitude. No harm would have come to them or you, if you had behaved in a sensible manner.'

A stream of maledictions in the Greek language poured from her lips, and suddenly she threw herself on Brien, striking at him repeatedly with her clenched hands. He had much ado in avoiding her blows and, at length, loath as he was to grapple with a woman, he grasped her wrists, though that hardly rendered her impotent, for she kicked out at him, catching him painfully two or three times on the shins. To add to his troubles, the little boy, thinking his mother was being maltreated, went to her rescue, and added to the din with his high-pitched voice, while his small fists kept up a continual tattoo on Brien's body. The latter grew tired of the business. He pushed the woman into a tiny little room, furnished most flamboyantly and probably known to the family as the parlour. There he forced her into a chair, whereupon she ceased screaming, and dissolved into tears. He took out a handkerchief and dabbed at his forehead; an expression of embarrassment was on his face. The small boy continued bravely to fight on his mother's behalf, but was presently lifted up, whereupon he kicked and struggled fiercely until he also was planted in a chair.

'You leave my mummy alone,' he cried. 'She ain't done nothing to you.'

'I wouldn't hurt your mummy for the world,' Brien assured him solemnly.

'What was you holding her for?'

'I suppose through a natural objection to being buffeted about. She was a bit rough, you know.'

'So was you; I saw you.'

'That is a prevarication, my son.'

The eyes of the dark-skinned child opened wide.

'What did you say?' he asked in an awed voice.

'Never mind.'

Brien turned his attention to Mrs Wright, who was sobbing and moaning in a lamentable fashion. A few seconds' survey assured him that she was merely acting. There was no sign of tears, and once he caught her eyes glaring malevolently at him from between her fingers. She was simply trying to gain time, while her brain was probably busy thinking out a story to tell him. She obviously guessed that he and his companions were there on a more pressing and serious matter than a question concerning passports. A dangerous woman, he decided, and began to feel a little sorry for the man who had married her. A loud knocking could be heard going on upstairs. Brien concluded that Baltazzi and Padakis had locked themselves in, and were declining to open the door. An unwise proceeding on their part, for it proclaimed guilty consciences.

'If you and those two men had only behaved with ordinary common sense,' he observed to the moaning woman, 'you would have found that everything would have been made easy for you. As it is, you are only heaping up trouble for yourselves.'

She suddenly removed her hands from her face; glared viciously at him.

'Show me your warrant!' she snapped.

He smiled.

'I don't need a warrant,' he returned. 'Whatever I or my men do is done on the responsibility of my department.' He held a card in front of her. 'Read it, and note the signature!' he ordered.

She obeyed, and into her eyes dawned a look of great fear.

'His Majesty's Intelligence Department,' she muttered. 'That is the same as the British Secret Service, is it not? And he—'

'You apparently have heard of the department and – of him,' commented Brien drily. 'Perhaps you will decide now that your attitude is absurd.'

Into the room hurried Foster.

'Mr Maddison believes the two men are in a back room on the first floor, sir,' he reported. 'We heard the door lock as we went up the stairs, but they have not answered our demands to open. I have searched all the other rooms, sir, but they are empty.'

'Give them a minute or so longer to decide,' ordered Brien; 'then break down the door. Wait a minute,' he added, as the young man was about to leave the room again. 'Go and bring Willingdon to me.'

'What have we done,' whispered the woman, 'that you should come into our home like this?'

'You are making it appear as though you and the men upstairs have committed a very serious crime. I came here to ask certain questions. If you had behaved in a sensible manner, you would have answered them and not made all this fuss.'

'I wish my husband was here,' she snapped with a momentary return of her old spirit. 'He would teach you to treat me in proper manner.'

'I don't think you can complain of my treatment of you,' he retorted, 'while on the other hand I might complain quite a lot of your behaviour. However, that doesn't matter. Where is your husband?'

He thought he detected a look of relief on her face.

Apparently she began to feel that her fears that Wright had been discovered at his nefarious work were unfounded. 'He is out,' she replied.

'That is obvious. Where is he?'

'How should I know? He goes out every morning for a little time after his duty is over. He is night watchman at the Colonial Office. Perhaps you know that?'

'Yes; I know that. Is he there now?'

She shot a look full of suspicion at him.

'Why should he be there now?' she snapped.

'No reason at all, as he is a night watchman. I asked you if he *is* there now.'

'No – that is, I do not suppose he is. There is nothing to take him there in the daytime.'

'Not even a little microphone?' he asked quietly.

A cry broke from her; her face turned almost ghastly white. She knew then that it would be useless to pretend innocence any longer. He knew beyond a shadow of doubt that she was involved in the affair as much as anyone. She was not merely a passive spectator; a woman with perhaps a natural desire to protect compatriots of hers from the consequences of acts which she vaguely knew were unlawful. She was in the game of espionage up to the hilt, and likely, he reflected, to be more defiant than any of the others. He judged her to be a woman utterly unscrupulous, greedy, acquisitive, and dangerous. He heard her teeth grinding together.

'Then you know?' she asked after some time.

'Yes. Your husband was caught red-handed. I have come here to discover for what reason he was sent to listen to conversations taking place in the Secretary of State's private room.'

She laughed harshly. The pallor had departed, leaving her expression challenging and hard.

'You will be clever if you discover that,' she declared. 'My husband would have told you, if he had known, for he is a fool, and has no mind of his own, but no others will tell you. No,' her voice rose to a shriek, 'not if you threaten to kill us.'

Brien shrugged his shoulders. He turned to see Willingdon standing in the doorway.

'Keep an eye on this woman while I go upstairs,' he directed. 'Watch her well. You'd better keep the little boy in here also for the present.'

'Very well, sir.'

Willingdon stepped into the room, and planted himself in such a position that it would be impossible for either to make a sudden dash past him. Mrs Wright scowled at him. A glance at his stern young face assured her that he was not the kind of man with whom she could take liberties or from whom she could expect any consideration, if she tried any tricks. To Willingdon an order was an order; there were no elastic sides to it. He obeyed it as it stood.

Brien ran up the stairs, and joined Maddison and Foster outside the door of the back room. The former told him that he had warned the men inside that, if they did not unlock the door within three minutes, it would be broken open. He had received no reply; a minute had passed, and he had uttered another warning. Brien looked around him. There was not much room on that small landing in which to operate, but the door did not look a very strong affair. A few blows should break it in.

'One minute remains,' called out Maddison. 'I will not speak again. You had better unlock the door to save yourselves and us trouble. It will go easier with you.'

There was again no reply. The seconds ticked away one by one as the small, grey-haired man conscientiously eyed his watch. Then, just as he was about to denote to Brien that the time was up, they heard a movement within.

'The first man what break in,' came in a threatening, foreign voice, 'get himself shot. I am holding the gun ready.'

Brien whistled softly.

'The fools!' he muttered. 'They seem jolly desperate. They're asking for it, behaving in this stupid manner. You are very foolish,' he added aloud. 'If you come out quietly, no harm will come to you. You will be asked a few questions, and perhaps detained for a little while; that is all. If you use firearms, you will have to take the consequences, which will be very serious.'

A low laugh could be heard.

'You will ask the questions, and keep us detain,' growled the voice. 'That is all, you say? We not beeg fools like you tink. We know we get shot, if we do come out ourselves. You tink we spies, and Engleesh shoot always men they tink spies.'

'Rubbish!' retorted Brien impatiently. 'English people do not shoot spies, except sometimes when there is a war.'

Again his remarks were answered by a laugh.

'You come and get us – if you can.'

'They've asked for it,' ground out the tall, fair-haired deputy chief. 'Don't kill them, if you can help it. As soon as the door is open,' he added in a whisper, 'drop to the floor behind me and shoot to disable them. Ready?'

Maddison and Foster nodded. In their hands they now held revolvers. Brien also had drawn his. Pushing the others back in order to give himself as much room as possible, he crashed the sole of his foot against the door close to the lock. The whole house resounded and seemed to shake. Again and again he repeated the performance until his leg became numb, but the door resisted the terrific impacts. It appeared to be a stouter affair than he had anticipated. Foster had a turn, but was also unsuccessful. Then he and Maddison tried together. At their third combined attempt, it gave way. They were thrown down by the force of their effort. Brien sprang over their prone bodies, and dived to his hands and knees expecting to hear the sharp crack of revolvers. There was not a sound; the room seemed to be empty. One glance at the bed drawn up to the wide open window, and a great cry of mortification escaped from him. At once he was on his feet; had darted across the room. A sheet, one end knotted to the bedrail, hung out of the window. Two men were clambering over a wall three or four gardens away. Several people were looking out of the back windows of houses opposite, watching their escape with great curiosity and interest.

'Come on!' roared Brien. 'We'll get them yet. You're a hurdler, Foster; those walls will be for easy to you. Down the sheet and after them! You and I will go the other way, Maddison.'

He tore down the stairs followed by the older man. Foster went out of the window without bothering much about the sheet; landed in a heap on the ground below. At once he was up, and gracefully vaulted the wall separating the Wrights' house from the next. Speeding across the narrow gardens, and continuing to vault the walls with ease, he rapidly gained on the fugitives. By that time quite a large number of people were watching the chase, and Foster could hear cries of excitement, but, as luck would have it, there was nobody in any of the gardens, who might have made an attempt to stop the escaping men. Foster had drawn quite close to them when they turned suddenly into a house. He sprang over the one remaining wall and, without hesitation, followed them through the doorway. The house was unoccupied and apparently in the process of redecoration. All the doors and windows on the ground floor were open, but there appeared to be no workmen about. Baltazzi and Padakis had seized a heaven-sent opportunity – it was the dinner hour. Foster hastened from one room to another, but failed to find trace of the fugitives. At last he reached the attic, approached it warily, his revolver ready for action. It was empty! Astonished, he turned, ran down the stairs, and darted out into Brook Street. Maddison and Brien were only a few yards away from him, but he saw no one resembling the two dagoes, as he had mentally dubbed them. He ran and caught up his colleagues, gasping out a hasty explanation of what had happened.

'Good God!' ejaculated Brien. 'Two men in painters' white jackets came out of that house just before we passed – one was carrying a pot of paint too. Where did they go, Maddison? Did you notice?'

That keen-eyed individual shook his head rather dejectedly.

'I was too busy looking for – Damn it!' he exclaimed vehemently. 'Fancy being done like that.'

'It's no use standing here,' grunted Brien. 'Let us look for them!'

It was hopeless, however, as from the start they knew it must be. They only had a vague idea of what the men were like, and it was certain they would quickly discard the white jackets and pot of paint they had so astutely purloined to help them in their escape. Brien, Maddison, and Foster each went in separate directions, but enquiries elicited no information, and eventually they were compelled to give up the search, and return to the house where Willingdon awaited them.

'Lord!' groaned Brien. 'What mugs they have made us look!'

'Damned clever to walk out under your noses like that, don't you think, sir?' asked the tactless Foster. 'The joke was that neither you nor they knew what each other looked like.'

'Your ideas and mine, Foster,' returned Major Brien coldly, 'do not coincide upon the point of what constitutes a joke.' Foster looked suitably subdued. 'I am going to return to headquarters, and tell Sir Leonard what has happened,' went on the deputy to Maddison. 'Take charge here until I return. You had better search the house and particularly the room from where those fellows escaped. They may have left something of interest behind them.'

He quickly traversed the short distance to Whitehall, and went straight to Sir Leonard's office. The latter gathered at once from his expression that all was not well.

'Hullo, Bill!' he exclaimed quietly. 'Has something come unstuck?'

'I should jolly well think it has,' was the disgruntled reply. 'I could kick myself.'

He related the events that had taken place in Brook Street, culminating in the clever escape of Baltazzi and Padakis from the empty house.

'Cute of them,' was Sir Leonard's comment at the conclusion of the recital. 'It's extraordinary,' he went on, 'how often the unexpected element looms up in our game, and spoils things. The presence of that empty house and the fact that it was being redecorated is one of those cursed chances that no one can anticipate. It was a marvellous bit of luck for Padakis and Baltazzi, but I admire their enterprise in grasping the opportunity.'

'Well,' grunted Brien, 'aren't you aching to kick me?'

'Kick you? Good Lord, no! Why should I want to do that?'

'Because I've made such a mess of the business.'

'You haven't made a mess of it. There's no reason at all why you should blame yourself. If anybody is to blame, it is I.'

'You!' ejaculated Brien. 'Why?'

'I should have obtained a full description of Baltazzi and Padakis for you to work on. If you had had it, I don't think you would have allowed them to walk away like that.'

'I daresay we should, at least I should.' Brien was not disposed to spare himself. 'Those white jackets and the pot of paint did me completely. I don't think I even glanced at the faces of the men wearing them.'

'Oh, well, it can't be helped. We'll get a description and circulate it, but I doubt if we'll get them. The pity of it is that they'll warn Plasiras and Bikelas, and show that we are, after all, taking a very active interest in their affairs. I'll come along with you, and have a chat with the lady.'

They returned together to Brook Street in Brien's Vauxhall. The average Londoner has an amazing flair for scenting out anything of a sensational nature. An apparently empty street will fill like magic, if an accident or a quarrel or some equally exciting event is staged in it. Brook Street had quickly discovered that something out of the ordinary was taking place in Number Seventy-Two. Of course, a good many people had viewed the exciting chase over the walls and through the back gardens. Others had not been deaf to the screams of Mrs Wright, which had been heard outside the house. A neighbour had expressed the opinion that nothing more dreadful could have been heard since the days 'when they tortured people with racks and boots and things. 'Orrible days they must 'ave been. I know what pain boots and shoes can give. Only a little while ago my Emmy 'ad a pair of shoes a size too small, and the torture the poor lamb suffered afore I found out must 'ave been 'scruciating.' At all events, Brook Street turned out *en masse* to ascertain, as the dwellers there put it, 'wot was doin' at Seventy-Two.'

Sir Leonard and Brien arrived to find the road completely blocked. A succession of raucous blasts on the horn failed to clear the way through the solid mass of humanity, and they were compelled to leave the car where it was, and force their way through the throng. At first they met with resistance, indignant cries of 'Who're yew a shovin' of?' and, in some cases, a decided show of hostility. As soon, however, as it dawned on the people barring their way that they were connected in some manner with the events that had caused the crowd to collect, it was amazing how quickly and easily a passage was made for them. There were no policemen to be seen anywhere and, as soon as Sir Leonard entered the house, he sent Foster to find a couple in order to move on the assembled curiosity-mongers. He then entered the front room. Mrs Wright was still sitting where Brien had placed her, her vicious face full of sullen anger; the little boy looked extremely frightened, and was crouching in his chair as though terrified to move. Willingdon stood at the door, his good-looking, serious face utterly expressionless. Sir Leonard cast a quick glance round the room, his eyes lingering for a moment on the woman. In that short space of time he summed her up completely; knew that it would be impossible to extract information from her. He found the big, terrified eyes of the child fixed appealingly on him, and smiled reassuringly. That smile should certainly be recorded on the credit side of Sir Leonard's account in the Judgment Book. The small boy, like most children of his age brought up in his surroundings, had read sensational yarns in the cheap magazines for boys of which there are so many; he had heard his mother and father discussing sordid crimes about which they had read in the papers. It was little wonder that the arrival of four strange men in the house, the noise upstairs, and his mother's conduct had frightened him badly. Until the arrival of Sir Leonard he was convinced that the house was in the possession of bandits.

The friendly, altogether attractive smile bestowed on him by the Chief of the Secret Service had gone a long way towards dispelling his terror. Instinctively he knew that here was one in supreme authority and one who would do him no harm. Thereafter his fear turned to curiosity, and he listened to every word, watched every movement with great attention, which as it turned out was perhaps fortunate for Sir Leonard.

Maddison reported that he had discovered nothing in the house of very much interest. Baltazzi and Padakis had, of course, left their belongings behind, but they consisted of two suitcases containing clothing and little else. Wallace was told the story of the locked room again; asked various questions. At first he had been puzzled by the fact that the two men had not made their escape earlier; he had wondered why they had remained in the room after locking the door until Brien and his companions had commenced to batter in the obstruction. Maddison's report that he had found nothing important supplied him with the reason for their delay. Obviously, he thought, the suitcases had contained something which they did not wish to fall into the hands of the authorities. They had been engaged in removing whatever it might have been and destroying it or pocketing it. He sent Brien to the Colonial Office to see Wright and obtain from him a description of the fugitives, afterwards to go to Scotland Yard and put the police on track. He knew very well that the woman would not supply him with an authentic sketch of Baltazzi and Padakis. As soon as his deputy had left the house, he ascended the stairs and himself inspected the room with the battered door. There was no sign of any burnt paper or any other indication that documents had been destroyed. He had not expected to find anything, for Maddison was the most expert searcher in the Secret Service. It was not likely that he would have overlooked anything.

However, Sir Leonard was human enough to feel more satisfied when he had thus assured himself.

He returned to the little sitting room, and turned his attention to the Greek woman. She regarded him with an intense, virulent gaze which rather amused him. At first she refused point-blank to speak to him at all, shaking her head obstinately to everything he said. Then suddenly she let forth a flood of invective which he strove to stop, if only for the sake of the child. It must be said to her credit that, when he reminded her of the presence of the little boy, she promptly ceased. Patiently, and with that firm, inexorable power of interrogation which seldom failed to bear satisfactory results, he questioned her, but she proved adamantine. She quailed certainly under the piercing, steely regard of his grey eyes, but resisted the inquisition in a manner that evoked a certain amount of admiration from Maddison, who had seen strong men wilt under a relentless cross-examination conducted by his chief. Occasionally she answered questions which appeared to have no particular significance, the replies to which she felt could not endanger the people for whom she had been working; once he adroitly steered her into a verbal cul-de-sac, but she realised her danger just in time, thereafter maintaining a sullen, obstinate silence. At length he gave it up.

'I will speak to you again,' he warned her. 'Perhaps in the meantime you will consider the position. It may pay you better to reflect that a lot of time and inconvenience to yourself will be saved, if you decide to answer.'

At that moment Foster entered the room to announce that three boys and a girl, the other children of the house, had returned from school. Wallace walked out into the passage and, smiling cheerfully at the four frightened faces, bade the little ones – the eldest was not more than thirteen – go into the kitchen, assuring them that their mother would soon be with them. They went obediently, accompanied by Foster. Sir Leonard returned to the sitting room.

'I will not detain you any longer,' he remarked to Mrs Wright, 'but I will return. In the meantime you may as well know that this house will be watched. I am warning you lest you think you can communicate with your friends and employers without the fact being known to us.'

He turned away to speak to Maddison. It was then that the fury she had been endeavouring to suppress overcame her. On the table by her side lay a long, thin paper knife fashioned like a stiletto. Snatching it up, she sprang to her feet and threw herself forward with a cry, her intention being to plunge the keen blade into the unprotected back of the Englishman. Her little son, however, who had been watching everything so intently, acted with surprising promptitude.

'Mummy!' he screamed and, springing forward, caught her wrist.

In a moment the woman, now violently hysterical, was disarmed, and thrust back into her chair. She gathered her small son into her arms, as though grateful to him for having prevented her from committing the crime she had contemplated. Sir Leonard stood watching them for a few moments.

'Madam,' he observed quietly, 'I hope you will always be grateful to the little chap. He has saved you possibly from the gallows.'

'Forgive me,' she sobbed. 'I – I went mad.'

'I have nothing more to say except: treat this son of yours well – he deserves it.'

He beckoned to his companions, and left the house, instructing Foster to keep watch on it until he was relieved by a man of the

Special Branch. On the way back to headquarters he was very thoughtful. He did not think the woman would revenge herself on her son; she seemed genuinely grateful to him for his promptitude in preventing her from committing a mad act. Nevertheless, Sir Leonard resolved to keep an eye on the little boy. Little though the youngster realised it then, he had made a very warm and useful friend.

CHAPTER FIVE

Agent Number Thirty-Three

Captain Hugh Shannon had a very fine and speedy journey to Athens, but, after that, due to bad weather and other causes, he was delayed. The result was that he did not arrive in Famagusta until Friday morning, nearly four days after he had left London. It can be imagined that he was not in the best of moods when he arrived at the seaport. He certainly spent no time in gazing at the scenery, but took the first available train on the narrow gauge railway for Nicosia, the capital. There he booked a room, and deposited his bags, at the Palace Hotel, had a much-needed wash and brush-up, and went at once to call on the governor. Sir Gordon Stevenson received him in his private study, shook hands cordially, and invited him to be seated.

'I am afraid, Captain Shannon,' he announced at once, 'that you have had your journey for nothing. I do not, of course, know exactly why you have come to Nicosia, though I have been given confidentially to understand that it was in connection with the visit to this island of Messieurs Plasiras and Bikelas. If it was your intention to interview those gentlemen, that is now out of the question. They departed rather suddenly on Wednesday morning.'

'Departed!' repeated Shannon in a dismayed tone. 'Where have they gone, sir?'

'I am unfortunately unable to tell you. As far as I know, they originally had no intention of leaving so soon. In fact, from enquiries I have made, I think their decision must have been taken almost on the spur of the moment. At all events, they embarked on the Messageries Maritimes steamer which called at Famagusta from Beirut on Wednesday. I reported the fact, of course, to London as I had been in communication with the Colonial Office concerning them. A cable arrived for you yesterday which possibly is consequent upon my report.' He unlocked a drawer of his desk and, taking out a sealed envelope, handed it to his visitor. 'That may tell you something,' he remarked.

Shannon opened it quickly, extracting the message within. It was in code, but a code he knew off by heart. 'Excuse me a moment, sir,' he begged.

Sir Gordon nodded; sat watching while the young man rapidly scribbled a series of letters and figures under those written on the form. At length the Secret Service man had deciphered the communication.

Spare no pains to trace them. If you require assistance, cable. Communicate immediately you have news.

'This was obviously sent as a result of your information to the Colonial Office, sir,' declared Shannon, 'but they do not know the whereabouts of Plasiras and Bikelas. On the contrary, I am instructed by Sir Leonard Wallace to trace them.' He read the decoded message aloud.

'Why are your people so anxious to find them?' queried the governor. 'Now that they have departed from British soil, I should think interest in them would naturally cease, at least until they land on territory under the Union Jack again.'

'Sir Leonard Wallace believes that a conspiracy is afoot. Until he finds out that it does not concern Great Britain or is non-existent, he will not lose interest in Plasiras and Bikelas.'

'It seems to me that your task will prove to be rather difficult.'

Shannon shook his head confidently.

'You have supplied me with a vital item of information; that is, the fact that they departed from here on Wednesday morning by the Messageries Maritimes boat. Would you be good enough to tell me where that vessel goes from here?'

'Constantinople, Naples, and Marseilles,' was the prompt reply.

'When is she due in Constantinople?' asked Shannon quickly.

'I am afraid I cannot say, but we will soon find out. I'll ring up the shipping agents. Are there any other questions you wish me to ask them?'

Shannon thought for a moment.

'Only one, sir, but perhaps you can answer that. Where did Plasiras and Bikelas book to?'

'Yes; I can tell you. They booked to Marseilles.'

'Marseilles!' Shannon rubbed his chin reflectively. '"Curiouser and curiouser" as Alice would say,' he muttered to himself; and aloud: 'Then the only question I want answered, sir, is the time of the boat's arrival in Constantinople.'

Stevenson nodded, and rang up the office of the steamship company's agents. Shannon appreciated the act. Most high commissioners and governors with whom he had come into contact delegated every possible act to their secretaries. It was refreshing to find a man who was so keen and eager to help that he acted himself. The information supplied by the agents delighted the Secret Service man. It was to the effect that the *Ile-de-France* was due to arrive in Constantinople that evening about six o'clock.

'Splendid!' he cried. 'I was afraid that she would have already reached there. May I have a pad of scribbling paper and a cable form, sir? Sorry to give you all this bother.'

'It's no bother, I assure you. I am only too delighted to be of assistance.'

Shannon was supplied with the required articles, and for some time there was no sound in that cool, well-shaded room but the scratching of his pen. At length he looked up.

'Can this cable be sent from here, sir,' he asked, 'and the cost debited to the Foreign Office?'

'Of course.' The governor rang a bell, and an orderly entered almost at once. He was handed the form, and given his instructions. 'Would it be asking too much if I enquired if that was for Sir Leonard Wallace?'

Shannon smiled. He tore into minute pieces the sheet of paper on which he had written the message before committing it to the cable form. The communication from headquarters received the same treatment. He then lit a match and, placing the fragments on an ashtray, burnt them to ashes and crushed them to nothing.

'That message,' he explained, 'was a complaint about the packing of a consignment of perfume, and was addressed to the agent of a well-known firm in Constantinople.'

The governor stared at him.

'Perfume!' he exclaimed. 'Constantinople!'

Shannon laughed.

'Actually,' he told his puzzled host, 'it has informed the agent of the Intelligence Department stationed in Constantinople that Plasiras and Bikelas are on the *Ile-de-France* due there this evening, and asked him to keep trace of them, if they land at that port, and inform me immediately.'

'By Jove!' murmured Sir Gordon Stevenson appreciatively. His eyes travelled from the ashtray, on which the dust of two secret messages lay, to the strong, clear-cut face of his guest. 'That is what I call efficiency. I suppose you will repeat the same performance before the vessel arrives at Naples; that is, if Bikelas and Plasiras do not land at Constantinople?'

Shannon shook his head.

'No,' he replied; 'I shall be there to meet the boat.'

Again the governor's eyes opened wide in surprise.

'But I don't think you will be able to do it,' he objected. 'The *Ile-de-France* will be ahead of any boat you can catch.'

'I shall cross to Beirut, sir,' Shannon informed him. 'There are boats daily, are there not?' Stevenson nodded. 'Then I shall go by train to Damascus where there is an RAF depot, and get a lift to Naples.'

His host laughed.

'I like the lift,' he commented. 'Anyone would imagine you were going to ask someone to give you a ride in a car for a few miles. It will certainly be a lift from Damascus to Naples! But I think I can save you the trouble of going to Damascus. We have an RAF squadron here.'

'How splendid!' exclaimed Shannon. 'Well that is something I did not know, I must confess. I will go and interview the officer in command this afternoon.'

'That is the one thing about you fellows I envy,' declared Stevenson. 'I refer to that possession of yours which gives you a kind of "Open Sesame" to the assistance of whatever authority it is shown in Great Britain or the Empire. But I would not be in your shoes otherwise for anything. Perhaps I value my life and my comfort too highly. Can you ever rely upon a night's rest in your own bed or a feeling of absolute security?'

Shannon smiled.

'Seldom,' he admitted, 'but there's no life in the world like it.'

'Everybody to his taste,' murmured the governor. 'I suppose, since you will be leaving again so soon, you will not wish to be put up for the clubs? I had a communication from your department asking me to do the necessary.'

'It won't be worthwhile, thank you, sir. I'd like a chance of meeting Paul Michalis, however, if that could be arranged in an apparently casual manner.'

Stevenson shook his head.

'I am afraid it is out of the question,' he returned. 'He, too, sailed on the *Ile-de-France*.'

'Did he, by Jove! That's very interesting. I suppose Radoloff, Doreff, and Bruno were also of the party?'

'They were, with Madame Bikelas, and Signora Bruno. In addition there were two secretaries and a young woman who appeared to be companion to Madame Bikelas.'

Shannon grunted.

'The presence of women rather suggests a pleasure trip and nothing else. Perhaps, though, that is the very reason why they are included in the party. I wonder, sir, if you can add anything to my information.'

They compared notes, but Shannon learnt very little more than he already knew. It certainly appeared as though the reception to Plasiras and Bikelas had been a surprise both to them and to

Michalis. The governor had been informed that people had appeared in the streets as though at a prearranged signal. Greek flags had been hung from windows, and a shouting, cheering throng had surrounded the cars. Paul Michalis had appeared very much upset, while the two ex-ministers of Greece had looked startled and angry. The visitors, accompanied by Michalis, had called on Sir Gordon. The Cypriot landowner had explained the exuberant welcome as having been arranged in an excess of zeal by someone; who it was he either would not or could not say. Cypriots as a whole, he had declared, sympathised deeply with the unfortunate men who had once been so prominent in Greece. Altogether Michalis and his friends had been distinctly perturbed. They had tried hard to learn from the governor how he regarded the affair, but, as he explained to Shannon with a smile, he had been entirely non-committal. They had remained quite in the dark concerning his attitude.

'It is worth knowing that they did not desire the welcome,' observed Shannon. 'It may turn out to be one of those queer, unanticipated events which alter the whole course of an apparently well-schemed affair.' He told his interested host of the incident at the Colonial Office, which greatly intrigued him, and caused him to agree that there must be a big conspiracy afoot. 'If I could only get my teeth into something,' went on Shannon. 'At present I'm like a dog that badly wants a bone, but can't get one.'

'Don't be impatient!' advised the other. 'You have only just started.' He eyed the massive shoulders, powerful jaw, and great arms and hands of his visitor; thought the simile of the dog and the bone particularly apt. It was certain, he reflected, that once this young man got a grip on the bone he was after, he would never leave go until he had crushed it. 'I'm afraid you will find out nothing by enquiries among the inhabitants here,' went on Stevenson. 'I have had police mixing among them in plain clothes, but they have not learnt anything of importance except that there is definitely a feeling of sympathy for the two Greeks. You being a stranger, and obviously an Englishman, would have little chance of getting any information out of them.'

'I don't propose to try,' declared Shannon. 'I'm not exactly built for underground enquiries,' he added a trifle ruefully. 'I'm too conspicuous – altogether too outsized. We have a man, called Cousins, who is amazing at that sort of thing. If he hadn't entered the service, he would probably have been world famous as a character actor. He can lose himself utterly in the part he is playing, and can disguise himself perfectly as anything from a marmoset to a Mormon.' He smiled at the exaggeration. 'As he speaks fifteen or sixteen languages fluently, and seems to be able to do anything, you can imagine that he is an asset to the service.'

'He sounds a paragon,' murmured the governor.

'He would be, only he has one vice – a passion for quotations. Still, he's the greatest thing on two legs I've ever met. Unfortunately he's not available, otherwise he'd be here. Give him a day or so to study the breed, and he'd be a Cypriot of the Cypriots. If there is a conspiracy going on, he'd dig it out before long, and appear to be one of the ringleaders.'

'You make me wish I could meet Mr Cousins,' remarked Stevenson with a smile.

'Perhaps you will some day, sir. If you do, cut him short as soon as he commences to spout poetry or reel off wisecracks made by people who are dead and gone and should have known better anyway. But perhaps you like that kind of thing.'

Shannon lunched with the governor and his immediate staff – Sir Gordon Stevenson was not married. He found him a most entertaining host and a thoroughly good fellow. Afterwards he went to the RAF depot with the ADC, and was introduced to the squadron leader in command there. He astonished the latter when he showed his credentials and asked coolly for an aeroplane to take him to Naples, but, as soon as he had recovered from his surprise, the young airman was enthusiastic. There was a flying boat attached to the squadron, he confided, which was kept in a special hangar at Famagusta. He would place that at Shannon's disposal. The latter thanked him warmly.

'It may turn out,' he explained, 'that I shall not have to go to Naples after all, but I shall want it to go somewhere.'

'So long as it's not to kingdom come,' smiled the officer, 'I don't mind. The bus will be ready for you when you want it.'

Shannon returned to his hotel, rested a little while, then had tea. Afterwards he strolled down to the Girls' High School, and asked if he could see Miss Barbara Havelock, explaining that, as he was on the island on a visit, he had called to give her various messages from mutual friends. He was subjected to a somewhat severe scrutiny by a vinegary-looking Cypriot woman, apparently the housekeeper, who grudgingly agreed to call Miss Havelock. Left alone in the rather bare little waiting room for a long time, he grew impatient. Hugh Shannon could never remain still for very long. He rose from the hard chair on which he had been perched, therefore, and commenced to stroll about, gazing abstractedly at the portraits on the walls, mostly of uncomfortable-looking girls in groups. He was regarding one directly opposite the open door with a somewhat pitying smile, when she came. She entered the room quietly, cast a quick, appraising glance at his massive figure, noted the strength of it, reflected that it was probably all muscle with not an ounce of superfluous flesh anywhere. Who on earth could he be, she wondered, and was about to announce herself, when very slightly she started. He was whistling an air which members of the British Secret Service all over the world use to announce themselves. In the glass of the photograph he had caught her reflection as she entered.

'You wish to see me?' she asked.

He swung round to face a small, demure, pretty girl with fair hair and sparkling blue eyes.

'By Jove!' he exclaimed. 'Aren't you like your cousin Mary? I'm Hugh Shannon,' he added, as he held out his hand. 'You've surely heard of me? I've dozens of messages for you.'

'Of course I've heard of you,' she returned, losing her little hand completely in his huge paw. 'How perfectly nice of you to come and see me!'

'It would have been jolly churlish if I hadn't. Besides, I've always heard such a lot about you. Funny we never met before, when we have so many mutual friends. Now what about dinner with me at the Palace, and a dance or something to follow?'

'I should love it,' she replied enthusiastically.

'Right! Then I'll call in a car for you at seven-thirty. That's not too early, is it? We can't rush cocktails, you know – bad for the digestion.'

She smiled.

'You'll get me a very bad reputation,' she declared, 'if you talk about cocktails here.'

'I don't believe it,' he chuckled. 'I'm sure the sweet-faced lady, who admitted me, would never have an objection to a little cocktail or two.' Her brows puckered a little in perplexity, but he had seen an inch or so of dress showing at one side of the door, and had guessed that the housekeeper was standing there listening to the conversation. 'The girls here are jolly lucky,' he went on. 'What with that nice housekeeper and you, I guess they're spoilt. You both look so good-natured. Are the other members of the staff as jolly?'

She did not quite understand, but she responded to his mood.

'We're quite a happy crowd here,' she told him.

'Splendid! Well, cheer-ho for the present, Barbara – I simply have to call you that, everybody talks of you as Barbara at home.'

She felt inclined to laugh outright, but controlled her features to a demure smile.

'Au revoir, Mr Shannon. I'll be ready at half past seven.'

'Good,' he said as they strolled out of the room together; 'but none of that mister business. Since we've known about each other for so long, it's got to be Barbara and Hugh. Don't you think so?' he added to the housekeeper, who was standing close by pretending to arrange flowers on a table.

She actually smiled at him. Barbara was astonished. It was a very unusual event for her to smile at anyone, but Shannon seemed to have captured her imagination. At her request he explained what had prompted his question. She agreed that it seemed very fitting and proper that, since they had so many mutual friends who called them by their Christian names, they should do likewise. She remained chatting with them in the hall for some minutes, then Shannon departed. He returned to the Palace, and went into conference with the maître d'hôtel about a secluded table, flowers, and other important items of a like nature. As soon as he had dressed, he sent for a car, and drove back to the high school. Sir Gordon Stevenson had invited him to dine at Government House, but he had declined, giving as an excuse that he had some important business to do. The governor had naturally not enquired what that business was, but Shannon chuckled to himself at the thought that he would certainly be a trifle puzzled if he saw him dining tête-à-tête with Barbara Havelock.

He found her waiting demurely for him, attended by the housekeeper. In the car she confided that the latter had been very much attracted by him, and, in consequence, had fluttered round her in a most embarrassing fashion; had even offered to help her to dress.

'It was my remark about her sweet face that did it, I expect,' he laughed. 'I knew she was listening outside the door, but I didn't expect her to take what I said seriously. Does she generally hang about like that?'

'Yes; she's a regular nosy parker,' replied the girl. 'Several times I've had my belongings searched. It rather worried me at first, because – well, you know why. But the same thing has happened to all the others, so I don't mind much now. She is not likely to find anything.'

'You're sure of that?'

'Positive.'

'You don't think she suspects you of being – well, not quite what you seem to be?'

She laughed.

'Good gracious, no! Why, most Cypriots are inquisitive like that.'

'How long has she been housekeeper at the school?'

'Oh, not very long. About three months, I should think. She is some sort of relation to Paul Michalis, the landowner, but hates him like poison. I believe she went to him when she was down on her luck, and he refused to help her.'

Shannon became thoughtful. That item of information interested him immensely, but he made no further reference to the housekeeper just then.

'Shall we get over formalities while we are here?' he suggested. 'We cannot be overlooked, which saves the necessity of any sleight of hand.'

She nodded, and from somewhere in her clothing produced her Secret Service symbol which she showed to him, at the same time catching a glimpse of the replica, but with a different number on it, which was cupped in the palm of his hand. Satisfied, those very valuable and secret symbols disappeared again from view.

'That's that,' he observed. 'Now, you and I, Barbara, are going to give ourselves up to enjoyment for a few hours. Afterwards we talk. I understand the band of the Palace is good and the dance floor excellent. When we have dined, we dance, *n' est ce pas*? Don't be terrified! I won't crush you or crash my elephantine hoofs upon your little feet. I may be large, but even my wife admits that I can dance.'

'It will be lovely!' she decided. 'I feel certain I am going to have a perfectly scrumptious evening.'

'Good word "scrumptious",' he commented, 'though for some reason it seems to be reserved for the use of females only. Helen uses it a lot.'

'Who's Helen?' she asked.

'Just my wife!' he told her. 'You must meet her some day. You'll love each other.'

She caught the look in his eyes, and sighed a little. It must be rather wonderful, she reflected, to be loved by a man like the great, splendid fellow by her side, for she had already formed her opinion of him. When a little later they stood together in the lounge, she, exquisitely dainty in a rose pink, daringly low-cut evening gown, which showed off her white shoulders and neck to perfection, her fair hair shimmering in the light, her blue eyes sparkling, he, tall, broad, good-looking, essentially masculine, every inch a man, they felt a great admiration for each other. He never forgot her as he saw her then – his memory appeared to take a photograph that time could not efface.

'Shall we sit?' he suggested, as he relieved her of her cloak.

They lingered over their cocktails, talking frankly and animatedly about a variety of subjects, but never touching on the one that had brought them together. Shannon's conference with the maître d'hôtel had certainly borne fruit. When they entered the restaurant, they were conducted, with every appearance of deference, to a table in an alcove screened by palms, and far enough from the band to render the music delightful. The girl gave a little cry of sheer pleasure, when she saw the masses of blooms tastefully arranged on the table. She buried her face in them, glorying in the perfume. Afterwards she looked up at him with shining eyes.

'It is fortunate you don't come often to Nicosia,' she remarked. 'You would utterly spoil me, which would be exceedingly bad for a hard-working schoolmistress.'

'I don't think it would be possible to spoil you,' he returned soberly.

'How nice of you,' she murmured, 'to say that.'

The dinner had been chosen with care, the wines were excellent, the champagne being of a particularly good vintage and served at exactly the right temperature. Barbara enjoyed herself immensely, though she drank very sparingly. She did most of the talking, Shannon being quite content to listen to her gay, vivacious chatter. He learnt that her father had been an army officer who had been killed during the War, and, although she did not mention his name, he knew she referred to Major Brien, when she spoke of a man who had been a great friend of her father's, and had kept an eye on her since his death.

'I owe so much to him,' she remarked softly. 'Dad left Mother and me rather badly off, and he took full responsibility for my education. It was difficult to persuade him to let me join the SS – that stands for "School Service" in case you don't know –' she smiled up at him – 'but I succeeded in the end, and here I am.'

'And do you like your work?' he asked quietly.

'I love it,' was her enthusiastic response. 'There is not a great deal of scope for one's talents here, but I hope one day to be given a more important post. I have yet to achieve my greatest ambition.'

'What is that, Barbara?'

She glanced round her; then leant towards him.

'I have never met the chief,' she whispered. 'I have not even seen him. I am longing for the time to come, when I shall be able to see him and speak to him.'

'The time will come all right,' Shannon assured her, also in a very low voice. 'Although B. does the actual selecting of agents abroad, and travels round from time to time on tours of inspection, L.W. keeps in very close touch with even the routine work. He generally is too occupied with major matters to have time for tours of inspection, but he carries out surprise visits sometimes. If you are not recalled to fill another post – as I believe you will be – you may be sure he'll turn up here sooner or later.'

'He must be marvellous,' she breathed, clasping her hands together in her ardour.

He smiled at her enthusiasm.

'That's the spirit I like,' he approved. 'He is certainly brilliant, altogether charming and, in many ways, amazing. But, on first acquaintance with him, you'll probably be terribly disappointed.'

'Oh, why?'

'Because he appears so utterly casual and uninterested. He'll make you wonder how the man you see before you can have possibly performed the feats he has.'

'Forewarned is forearmed,' she smiled. 'I know now what to expect, and I *won't* be disappointed. My toes are simply itching to dance, Hugh. Shall we?'

He rose promptly to his feet.

'We certainly shall,' he declared.

CHAPTER SIX

Kidnapped in Nicosia

Barbara Havelock was very nearly in a state of ecstasy for the next couple of hours. She and Shannon danced almost continuously. The band and floor she knew well, having very often danced at the Palace – both were generally considered to be excellent – but Shannon was quite a new experience. She had never possessed a partner of such massive proportions before, and had rather expected her small, slim form to be entirely enveloped by him. She was amazed to find that, instead of there being any awkwardness in their combination, they moved together with ease and in perfect harmony. For such a big man, Shannon was a beautiful dancer; the sense of rhythm was in his bones, and he was astonishingly light and graceful in his movements. Before they had been dancing long, Barbara felt that she had never had such a partner. Being expert herself in her almost ethereal way, she was a very good judge. She was quite content to lose herself in blissful enjoyment, and listen to him now. He talked mostly about his wife, and she grew to admire him more than ever in consequence; began to look forward to meeting one day this Helen of his for whom he obviously had such great devotion.

'Do you know,' he confided once, 'you and she dance very much like each other. You're both fairylike. I have to keep looking down at you to make sure you're there.'

At first the pair had created a certain amount of suppressed amusement among the other dancers in the room. They had appeared ill-matched; he was so enormous, she so small and slender. But, before long, they had become the admiration of the room, and remarks were passed in their hearing which brought a flush of embarrassment to Shannon's face and a smile of frank pleasure to the girl's. It was approaching midnight when, at last, with a sigh of mingled happiness and regret, she declared that she could dance no longer. He procured her cloak, and they wandered out into the beautiful hotel gardens lighted picturesquely by myriads of little lamps hanging from the trees. Finding two cushioned wicker chairs and a table in a secluded spot, they sat down. His order for liquid refreshment was quickly obeyed by an attentive waiter and, with glasses pleasantly tinkling with ice before them, the enchanting perfume of violets and narcissi enrapturing their senses, they spoke for the first time of the matter that had brought them together. There was nobody within hearing, but to make doubly sure they talked in little above a whisper.

She repeated more or less what she had put in her coded report to headquarters, describing more fully, of course, the excitement that had prevailed in Nicosia on the arrival and during the stay of Plasiras and Bikelas.

'Work seemed to be completely suspended by all except the Muslim part of the population,' she stated. 'The people congregated in groups in the streets and public gardens, talking excitedly. As soon as any English people approached, they dropped their voices, looked thoroughly mysterious and rather like a lot of sheepish conspirators. Some of them scowled. I don't think they are very clear themselves what they expect the two Greeks to do for them, but it is quite obvious that they are expecting some great benefit. I am afraid my channels of enquiry have not produced a great deal, but the reason for that is, as I have said, that the Cypriots themselves are so vague about the conspiracy. What it really amounts to is that a report was circulated by some mysterious agency that, if they were prepared to throw in their lot with Bikelas and Plasiras, when called upon, great benefits would be conferred upon them which might include deliverance from the British yoke.'

'By Jove!' exclaimed Shannon. 'That certainly is something to get a grip on, and you say your channels of enquiry have not produced a great deal! I think that's quite a lot myself.'

'But it's so frightfully indefinite, isn't it? After all, nobody apparently knows from where the rumour originated.'

'But the people have obviously taken it seriously.'

'Yes; they have taken it seriously enough. I found out about this, after I had sent in my first report.'

'You sent another, I suppose?'

She nodded.

'Yes; it went on Wednesday. As you probably know, all I was able to say in my first cable was that Plasiras, Bikelas, the two Bulgarians and the Italian had arrived, describe the extraordinary reception they had received, and the tension that was prevailing here. I was also able to state that the people were speaking of the Greeks as deliverers, though I had been unable to find out what they meant by that. As I say, they were, and are, rather uncertain themselves. Now I have been able to add, as I have told you, that they expect great benefits, which might include deliverance from what is called the British yoke; that is, if they throw in their lot with the Greeks.

What the Greeks are intending to do I don't know, and I don't think the Cypriots do either – neither do I, nor they, know what throwing in their lot exactly implies. Most of them think it means an organised rising.'

'And are they prepared to rise?'

'I think they must be – they are so enthusiastic, you see.'

'You mentioned that also in your cable?'

'Of course.'

'Good girl. L.W. will have put the Colonial Office wise by now, and instructions will be received by the governor to make preparations quietly. You have done jolly good work, Barbara, in spite of your assertion that your investigations have not produced a great deal.'

'It seemed so little to me,' she confessed. 'I should have liked to have discovered all that is happening, for there is obviously a great conspiracy brewing.'

'My dear girl,' he laughed, 'don't be greedy! Leave something for me to find out. Are the people who are working for you quite reliable?'

'Quite. They are both Syrians, and entirely devoted to Major B. It was he who sent them here.'

'Oh, that's good hearing. I should hate you to be in danger. You haven't been conducting any investigations yourself, have you?'

She was silent a moment; then she nodded slightly.

'I have been doing a little – when I thought it was quite safe,' she confessed. 'I haven't taken risks.'

'But, my dear girl, you mustn't do things like that. Apart from the danger in which you might involve yourself – that, in our game, doesn't count, of course, if it is necessary – you might render your position here useless. If it was suspected that you were collecting and giving information to the British Intelligence Department, your usefulness would cease at once. Don't let your keenness get the better of your discretion, Barbara. The men placed under your orders must be left to conduct investigations, while you must be content to receive their information, send it home, and give them instructions. Remember always that by keeping in the background you will accomplish the best work and more thoroughly earn L. W.'s approval. Besides, you must not run your pretty little head into danger.'

'Why shouldn't I take my chance of that like you and the rest, who do the big things?' she murmured.

'So you do, simply because you are the SSA here,' he reminded her gently, 'but it is your duty not to do anything that might involve you in discovery. For God's sake, Barbara,' he added hastily as he noticed her woebegone expression, 'don't think I'm preaching. I'm not. I'm trying to be big brotherly, and give you a little advice. I've been in the game for several years now, and you won't resent it, I know. You've done such jolly good work that I don't want you to spoil it by taking needless risks.'

She turned and smiled at him.

'I understand – and thank you. I promise to be more careful in the future, Hugh.'

'Splendid!' he returned, and gave her hand a little pat. 'I suppose,' he asked, lowering his voice again, 'you did not find out where Radoloff, Doreff and Bruno come in?'

'No,' she told him regretfully; 'that seemed to be a puzzle to everybody. It was also a great puzzle why they all departed so suddenly with Paul Michalis on Wednesday. They booked their passages for Marseilles.'

'Yes; I'm aware of that, and I'm hanged if I can guess why. I'll know before morning whether or not they changed their minds and disembarked at Constantinople. If they remained on board, I'll leave here for Naples by air tomorrow, and I shall be on the boat with them to Marseilles.'

'You're leaving – tomorrow?' she asked, and he caught the note of regret in her voice.

'I must,' he declared, giving her hand a brotherly little pat again, 'but I'll be back with Helen before long. I'm due for a spot of leave – we'll spend it here. She'll badly want to know you, when I've told her about you.'

'That will be lovely,' she cried enthusiastically. 'I'm awfully keen to meet her, too. By the way, do you know that Monsieur Bikelas and Signor Bruno are accompanied by their wives?'

'Yes. That seems like a blind to me. They are carting the wives about to give their trip an appearance of innocence. I believe there's a lady companion and a couple of secretaries as well.'

'Yes, but I don't suppose they are connected with the conspiracy.'

'One never knows, Barbara. I've found more than once that the most innocent-looking and innocent-seeming people are the most dangerous. Did you learn the names of the secretaries and companion by any chance?'

'I – I'm afraid I didn't,' she replied, rather as though she thought she had failed to do something she should not have neglected.

'It doesn't matter. I'll find them out soon enough when I'm on the boat from Naples to Marseilles.' He leant towards her. 'You are quite sure,' he asked earnestly, 'that the housekeeper at the school is not watching you for a purpose; that is to say, that she has not been put in by the opposite party, because they suspect you?'

'I am convinced that that is not so,' she assured him. 'Why should I be suspected? Besides, she hates Paul Michalis. She is hardly likely to work on behalf of a cause he supports.'

'The hate may be all pretence – in fact, the whole business, her ill luck, his refusal to help her, may have been arranged for the very purpose of throwing dust in the eyes of others. It may sound imaginative, but in our job, you know, Barbara, we can't afford to take anything for granted. We have to be on our guard all the time, and suspect every darned circumstance and person we come up against.'

'You make me feel a terrible tyro,' she sighed.

'Sorry! I don't mean to. But do be careful of that woman. I hate the look of her. Do your Syrians come to you in the ordinary way of business? I mean to say, have their visits to you the appearance of complete innocence? You don't meet them surreptitiously?'

'Oh, no. One is a laundryman and the other a gardener who looks after the school gardens. As I am in charge of the gardens, any conversation I have with him is a perfectly natural event, isn't it?'

'Quite. Well, that's a relief.'

'Hugh,' she accused him, 'I believe you think I have no common sense at all.'

'Good Heavens!' he returned in a tone of alarm, 'don't get ideas into your head like that. I think you're splendid. And now we're going to have a final little drink before I take you back to the school. Will you have something stronger than lemon squash this time? Can I recommend a gin sling or a horse's neck?'

'Dear me, no!' she laughed. 'I believe I'd like a cup of coffee.'

'What, this time of the night! You won't sleep.'

'I will. Nothing keeps me awake.'

He looked round to find the waiter; suddenly stiffened. In a moment he was on his feet.

'Doesn't seem to be about,' he murmured to Barbara by way of explanation, and in order not to alarm her. 'I'll go and fetch him.'

Standing by a tree a few yards to their rear he had thought to see the housekeeper. There was no sign of the person now, but he walked quickly to the place, rounded the tree, and came suddenly upon a table at which were seated two people, a man and a woman. The woman was the housekeeper at Barbara's school. She looked up at him with easy assurance.

'I was right,' she remarked. 'It was the big Englishman sitting with the little Miss Havelock.'

Shannon gave no indication of his feelings.

'I recognised you standing by the tree, as I rose to call the waiter,' he told her. 'I thought perhaps you might join us, but I see you are not alone. Your pardon, madame.'

She laughed.

'There is not the need to apologise,' she returned. 'I thought it was you, when we took our places here, so I went by the tree to make certain. This is my brother. He called for me to come to the dance. I say I am getting too old, but he insist.'

Shannon bowed to the dark-visaged, oily-looking man sitting by her side. He looked the typical gigolo type, though he certainly lacked the excessive politeness of the breed. He had not even troubled to rise from his chair, when the Englishman addressed his supposed sister. Shannon remained chatting casually for a minute or two; then passed on. He was wholly unconvinced by the explanation of her presence; felt decidedly troubled. He scented danger, and resolved to warn Barbara, even if it meant alarming her. Having given the necessary order to a waiter he found close by, he returned to the table, sat down, and took out his cigarette case with an appearance of smiling unconcern. Eyes, he felt, would be watching him intently. Barbara accepted a cigarette, blew a thin spiral of smoke into the air. At that moment she looked thoroughly happy and content. It was a pity, he reflected, to be forced to spoil her enjoyment.

'Keep on smiling, Barbara,' he murmured, a smile on his own face, 'but I'm afraid I'm going to give you a shock. We are being watched.' Her hand, he noticed, shook a little as she raised the cigarette to her lips, but she gave no other sign that she was startled. 'Your housekeeper friend is seated at a table a little way behind us with a greasy-looking bounder wearing a dress suit that I'll swear was borrowed. She told me that he is her brother, and called for her to come to the dance. Most unconvincing, of course; for one thing it is too much of a coincidence.'

'People like that don't come here to dance,' she whispered. She continued to smile, but he read the trouble in her eyes. 'It was rather an absurd explanation.'

'She had to say something. I must say I admire her *sang froid*. She greeted me in the coolest manner possible, without a trace of embarrassment, and my action in going straight to her must have been a bit of a shock. I caught sight of the woman as I looked round for the waiter. I'm afraid, old girl, that your faith in her will have to undergo revision. I am pretty certain now that she is in league with Michalis and company. Something must have made them suspicious of you, and she was installed in the school to watch.' He saw her underlip tremble, and, in his generous, sympathetic way, took hold of her hand.

'It seems that, after all, I have failed to make good,' she whispered, and something in her tone went straight to his heart. 'Oh, Hugh, I feel awful about it.'

'Don't be silly!' he laughed. 'Because they suspect you, doesn't mean to say that they have anything particular to go on.'

'Even if they haven't, my usefulness here as L.W.'s agent is gone completely. You know it is – you said as much a little while ago.'

They were silent, while the waiter placed his whisky and her coffee on the table. Shannon took such little heed of the amount of soda the man poured into his glass that he was given more than he desired, but his thoughts were very far from whisky and soda at that moment. He signed the chit, and waited until their attendant had departed then:

'I may be altogether wrong,' he pronounced. 'The appearance of that woman here may be quite innocent, and—'

'You know it is not,' she interrupted, 'and I know it is not. I have been too confident, and this is the result. What makes me feel so terrible is that I have not only proved myself useless as a secret agent, but I have brought you under suspicion also. If they think that you are on their track they may – may attempt to kill you.' She shivered slightly. 'Can't you imagine how I feel?'

'You're being a baby now,' he returned, giving her hand, which he still retained, an encouraging little squeeze. 'What I should like to know is what first caused them to suspect you.'

'My own foolishness, I suppose,' she replied bitterly. 'I can see it all now. You know perhaps that Plasiras and Bikelas came to Nicosia last November, a few weeks before they made their disastrous attempt to overthrow the Greek government?' He nodded. 'When they had departed, there seemed a good deal of unrest here, and I tried to find out what caused it. I not only had the two Syrians investigating, but I did a certain amount of private enquiry work myself. I thought I was being very careful and prudent, but I can see now how injudicious it was. It was after that that Madame Malampos was appointed housekeeper.'

'I see,' he nodded. 'Yes; it does look as though you made a mistake then. But don't worry, Barbara; we all make mistakes sometimes. You won't fall into the same error again.'

'I shall not have the chance. L.W. is hardly likely to trust me again.'

'Nonsense.'

'Do you think she has overheard our conversation tonight?'

'Not a chance. I have been on the watch all the time. Nobody could have approached without my knowing. I rather suspect the dear lady was doing her utmost to catch what we were saying when she was standing by that tree. She couldn't have heard a sound, however, which must have riled her a lot. There's another possibility, of which we must not lose sight. On my arrival in Nicosia, I went to call on the governor, and stayed for lunch. Afterwards I was taken to the aerodrome in one of the official cars by his ADC. Perhaps my movements were watched and regarded with suspicion. It is quite likely, you know. In that case it may be I who am bringing danger upon you, by associating with you.'

She smiled at him, and shook her head.

'I believe you are trying to console me,' she declared. 'Englishmen are continually arriving on the island, and calling on Sir Gordon Stevenson. There is nothing strange in that. Neither is the fact that you lunched with him, and went to the air force depot in his car. In fact your movements were calculated to allay suspicion. I quite realise that. Anybody who was taking an interest in you would at once conclude that there was nothing sinister in your appearance here. They would naturally think that a man who was in Cyprus on a mission of investigation would do his utmost to avoid notice. He would not go about in the open manner you have adopted. No, Hugh, I am the villainess of the piece. Mrs Malampos would not be watching you.'

'She might be. Why not?'

She sighed softly.

'You know she would not. Besides, everything points to it. The searching of my belongings, the very fact that she became housekeeper so soon after I had been making my foolish investigations. I know now that I have been living in a fool's paradise. What do you advise me to do?'

He reflected for some moments.

'Carry on with your school work as though your suspicions against her had not been roused,' he suggested at last. 'Do nothing that can in any way be regarded as strange or unusual in a teacher at a girls' school. In the meantime, I'll report to headquarters that we believe your real position here to be known. Then you must wait for instructions from B.'

Tears were not very far from her eyes as she nodded. Nothing he could say was able to comfort her. She could not rid herself of the feeling that she had failed in the duty allotted her. She finished her coffee, and rose to her feet, drawing the cloak closely round her lithe form.

'It is awfully late,' she declared with a heroic attempt at cheerfulness, 'I shall feel like nothing on earth when I take my classes tomorrow, or rather today. It isn't often I am up as late as this.'

He conducted her to the front of the hotel, talking gaily the while. An attentive commissionaire quickly obtained for them a car. They entered, he gave the address, and they were soon speeding rapidly on their way. It was not more than fifteen minutes' run from the Palace hotel to her school, but longer than fifteen minutes went by, and still the driver showed no signs of reducing his headlong pace. They had been so occupied in conversation that she had taken no notice of the direction. Now she gave a little ejaculation of alarm, and clutched his arm.

'Where is he going?' she cried. 'This is the wrong way.'

Most of the houses had been left behind; the car seemed to be heading for the open country. Shannon promptly picked up the speaking-tube; shouted to the driver to stop. But the man took no notice. In fact their speed increased until the motor was tearing along at a reckless pace. The Secret Service man was not given to hesitation. Deciding that an attempt was being made to kidnap him and the girl, he drew the revolver he carried in his hip pocket and, with the butt, smashed the glass partition between the driver's seat and the inside of the car. Some of the splintered glass hit the man in front. They heard him cry out, the motor swerved dangerously; then he applied his brakes, they slowed down, presently stopped.

'What the devil do you think you are doing?' demanded Shannon wrathfully.

The fellow made no reply, sprang out, and disappeared into the night. Almost immediately the darkness was lit up brilliantly in their vicinity. Another car or cars had apparently been following them with dimmed lights, had drawn up behind, and the headlamps had now been switched on. Barbara gave a little cry. He laid one of his great hands reassuringly on hers.

'It looks like a trap, old girl,' he muttered. 'Sit tight, and leave everything to me. We can't be far from Nicosia.'

'We're not,' she told him, and he was glad to note that there was not a tremor in her voice now. 'We're only just outside, but this is rather a desolate spot.'

'Anyhow the sound of shooting here would bring people along to investigate, I should imagine.'

'It might,' she returned doubtfully, 'but I'm not so sure that they would be the people we wanted.'

'Why not?'

'They might be sympathisers of these men.'

'We'll have to chance that. Somehow I don't think they'll shoot. But I will!'

He made her crouch down on the floor of the tonneau, although she pleaded with him to allow her to help him. She carried a little automatic in her bag, and was eager to stand by him, and face the attack they both felt certain would soon be delivered. However, he did not intend to take any risks where she was concerned. She would be comparatively safe on the floor. He told her that, if she had the opportunity, she could fire at their antagonists, but, in any case, was not to rise until he gave her permission to do so.

Several minutes passed by, and still there came no sign from the people in the other cars – a cautious and rapid peep through the little rear window had enabled Shannon to count two pairs of headlights. Two cars probably meant that he would have to deal with eight or ten men; then there was their own driver. If he had been alone, it is quite likely he would actually have enjoyed the situation, but with Barbara Havelock in his care he was not at all happy.

'What do you think they are doing?' she whispered at length.

'Behaving like the cowards they are,' he returned contemptuously. 'They thought, no doubt, we would have stepped into the road to find out what was wrong, whereupon they would promptly have jumped on us. We have perplexed them a trifle by remaining in the car. The idea of being shot at as they try to get us out probably doesn't appeal to them.'

'Do you think there are many of them?'

'Half a dozen perhaps,' he returned in a casual tone. 'Not nearly enough to get the better of us, anyway. I say, I hope you aren't spoiling that frock of yours down there.'

She laughed, and the sound was like music to his ears. She had pluck, and plenty of it; was not the kind to let him down.

'As if a frock counted in a situation like this,' she observed.

'It would be a pity if it was damaged. It's such a topping affair, and suits you—'

A sudden attempt was made to open both doors at once, but as they possessed locks, and he had taken the precaution to fasten them, the result was negative. A shout of baffled fury could be heard.

'Shoot, if anyone pushes in that window,' Shannon ordered the girl. He let down the one on his side of the car. Four men stood close by. He was able to see them perfectly in the brilliant headlights of the cars behind. Three were tough, villainous-looking fellows, the other was quite well-dressed and of a superior class. The Englishman addressed him. 'Look here!' he boomed. 'I don't know who you are or what you want, but I presume you're up to no good. That being the case, I'll start shooting, if you don't clear off in thirty seconds.'

'Come out!' snarled the other in Greek. 'We wish to talk to you.'

'I have too much respect for myself to be seen talking to you,' retorted Shannon. 'That half minute has gone by.'

He suddenly produced the revolver, and fired above their heads but close enough to give them a distinctly unpleasant sensation. At once they scuttled out of sight like a lot of startled rabbits. At the same time a determined attack was made on the other door. The window was smashed in, the glass falling on Barbara, but doing her no injury. Obeying orders, she fired at a man who was endeavouring to wrench the door open. He disappeared from view with a scream of agony.

'First blood to you, Barbara,' commented Shannon.

CHAPTER SEVEN

In Her Country's Service

He stepped over her, and glanced out. Immediately a knife hissed through the air; stuck quivering within a few inches of his head. He withdrew, but not before he had shot the knife-thrower.

'Three shots,' he remarked. 'People in the neighbourhood should be beginning to sit up and take notice by now, unless they sleep very heavily hereabouts.'

Apparently their assailants thought the same. They suddenly launched a determined attack on the car. The saloon shook ominously as they clambered on the roof. Somebody with an axe began to make desperate onslaughts. Shannon looked grave; it would not take them long to break their way in, whereupon he and Barbara would be taken at a serious disadvantage. Better, he thought, under the circumstances to get out into the open, though it would be difficult to protect the girl out there.

'As soon as I open the door and jump out,' he muttered urgently, 'follow and keep behind me. No trying to stand by my side and fight them. Use my body as a buffer – it's big enough – understand?'

'But—'

'Don't argue; obey orders!' he snapped.

Part of the roof came in on top of him, the axe wielded by the man above following it, and swishing past his head. Promptly he grasped the shaft, and pulled. The hand of the fellow was dragged through the gap for a moment before releasing its hold. Shannon transferred his grip with a lightning movement to the wrist, pulled the arm right down, and part of the man's body through the hole with it. He jammed it in tightly causing the wretch to scream with agony, and preventing the others above from getting at Barbara and him. He then unlocked the near door and, suddenly flinging it open, stepped out, revolver in his left hand. Somebody above lunged viciously at him with a knife, but he had anticipated such a move and, avoiding the thrust, caught hold of the man's wrist and dragged him from the roof of the car with such force that he turned a complete somersault before landing on his back some yards away. Barbara had followed Shannon closely. He shepherded her away from the car, continuing to face the lights, and keeping her well protected by his great body. A knife whizzed by his head, and he promptly fired at two men who remained on the top of the car. Whether he hit either or not he was unable to say, as they did not cry out. Both promptly slid to the ground, however, leaving the fellow, whom Shannon had jammed in the smashed roof, to extricate himself as best he could from his exceedingly painful position.

There came a lull in the proceedings, the remainder of their adversaries having collected together behind the car. Four, at least, were out of action. How many remained the Secret Service man was unable to tell. He did not believe there were more than five. Odds like that did not trouble him. He felt sure he would be able to defeat any further attempts they might make, especially as they either did not possess firearms, or hesitated to use them for fear of being heard. He inclined to the former theory, since he felt they would be only too anxious to complete their murderous work and get away, and would no longer shrink from discharging revolvers, as he and Barbara had already roused the echoes with theirs. There were few trees thereabouts and fewer bushes, but the two found cover of a kind in a dip behind a group of shrubs about ten yards from the car.

'Sorry to keep you out of bed so late,' remarked Shannon cheerfully.

She laughed a trifle unsteadily.

'Do you think we'll get away?' she asked.

'Of course. There are not more than five of them capable of carrying on the war. Two have been shot, the one I pulled off the roof has probably broken his spine or his neck or both, and the fellow jammed in will have to be cut out. Everything in the garden's rosy. I'm beastly sorry to mix you up in an affair like this though.'

'*You* mix me up in an affair like this!' she echoed. 'If anyone is to blame, I am. Hugh, they weren't intending to kidnap us. Their object is to kill us.'

'I'm afraid it is, or rather was. I don't see how they're going to satisfy their little craving now. I'm certain of one thing, and that is, you don't go back to the school. You'll stop at Government House tonight, I'll collect your belongings, or we'll send for them, and you'll leave Cyprus as soon as possible. If old Mother Hubbard isn't behind this business, I'll eat my hat.'

'Oh, but will that be necessary,' she protested.

'It will,' he replied in a tone that admitted no argument. 'They're keeping beastly quiet,' he went on. 'I've half a mind to go and find out what they are up to. Can you see their legs? I can't.'

'I think they must have kept the car between themselves and us, and retreated into the shadows on the other side of the road.'

'H'm! That would certainly account for the absence of legs.'

He glanced round uneasily. It had occurred to him that the men could make a detour, keeping well out of the light thrown by their cars, and attack him and the girl in the rear. Behind was pitch-blackness accentuated, no doubt, by the illumination in front. He was unable to see more than a few yards. The position was not as safe as he had thought it. At once his mind was busy trying to think out a scheme which would enable him to place Barbara in absolute safety. At first he was inclined to dash with her to the car, and make a bid to drive it away, but she would be exposed to tremendous peril from those knife-flinging experts, while crossing the unprotected, illumined ground to the motor, and while he was occupied in starting up the engine. Then he thought he saw the way. He and she would retreat into the darkness; they might manage to escape observation if they crawled. Once out of sight they could gradually work their way back to the town, or, at least, to the nearest house. Their chances would not be very great, if the Cypriots discovered they had gone, and started to search for them. She could not walk fast over that difficult ground in dance shoes. He commenced to question her about the country, and learnt, to his chagrin, that the part of the town nearest to them was mostly occupied by sympathisers of Plasiras and Bikelas. That rendered the venture more dangerous, but they could not stop where they were.

'You don't happen to know anybody living near here?' he asked.

'No,' she replied, 'but I should think they are mostly people who would be antagonistic. The fact that nobody has apparently been roused by the shots seems to prove that they are, or else prefer to keep out of trouble. There are one or two farmhouses quite close by. The firing must have disturbed them.'

'It might not have done. This is the time of night or rather morning, when people sleep most soundly.'

'Don't you think it likely we were brought here for the very reason that our assailants knew they were safe from interruption on this side of Nicosia?'

He thought it very likely in the light of what she had told him, but did not say so. The task of getting her to safety began to appear almost insurmountable. His jaw clamped tightly. He meant to do it somehow. He suddenly decided to work his way round to the last car; the enemy would not be looking for him and Barbara there. Perhaps it would be possible to start the engine and get away before they realised what was happening. At all events, he and she must not stop another second where they were. At any moment might come the attack from the rear he was dreading, when Barbara would be placed in deadly peril. He did not like the continued silence from the road; it suggested mischief. He told her his plan, and they started to put it into effect. Crawling out of the dip, they wriggled their way along towards the intense obscurity beyond. There were several yards to traverse before reaching it, and they would be, he knew, visible to anyone who was keeping observation.

Gradually they drew nearer to the welcome opacity. The rough ground made havoc of his suit, ruined utterly her flimsy dress, but neither had any thoughts to spare for such considerations as clothing just then. At last they reached their objective, and he sighed his relief. Standing up, he helped her to her feet, took her arm in his, and led her cautiously forward. It was then that a light was flashed full in their faces, and cries of triumph rose all around them. With an oath he swung her behind him; at the same time raising his revolver and firing, but the glare blinded him. In an instant he found himself fighting desperately with God only knew how many men. Knives seemed to be flashing all around him, but somehow he avoided them, all the time striving to keep the fiends from Barbara. His revolver was knocked out of his hand; then, above the sound of men panting and cursing, there reached his ears a little gurgling sob which seemed to turn his heart to stone, the blood in his veins to water.

He went completely berserk. Utterly careless of knives or any other weapons, he hit out with herculean power all around him. The light went out, but the sudden darkness made no difference to him; one hand felt and clasped a human form. At once he had grabbed it by some part of its anatomy and swung it, screaming horribly, round his head, sending all others, who remained on their feet, toppling to the ground. He cleared a space for yards round him; there seemed no one left to fight. Continuing to swing his human cudgel as easily as any other man would have wielded a truncheon, he presently let it go; heard it crash to the ground sickeningly some distance away. With deadly apprehension holding him in its grip, he knelt down, fumbled in the stygian darkness for Barbara.

His fingers came into contact with a large electric torch. He tried to switch it on, but found it was smashed, and cast it from him. Presently he encountered the body of a man who groaned as he pushed him roughly aside. He found his revolver, put it automatically into his pocket. Then he came to her; a crumpled little bundle of daintiness lying half under the body of another man. With a terrible cry he lifted up the fellow, dashed him violently aside. Gently he raised the girl, as light as a feather to him, and staggered with his precious burden to the ground still illuminated by the headlights of the cars. Every step he took seemed to him to take an age. Careless now whether he was seen or not, his mind prey to dreadful suspense, he placed her gently down on a grassy hillock where the light enabled him to see her clearly. Her eyes were closed, her face ghastly. The breast of her pathetically torn and crumpled dress, originally rose pink in colour, was now stained a terrible crimson. A sob of mingled agony and rage burst from him. Frantically, nevertheless skilfully, he strove to staunch the flow of blood, but it was already ceasing, and a little trickle from the corner of her pallid lips told him the stark, dreadful truth. Her eyelids flickered, and opened. Her blue eyes gazed up at him with the hand of death already beginning to glaze them. She smiled, he saw her lips move, and bent down to listen to what she was endeavouring to say.

'It – was a – glorious – evening, Hugh,' she murmured brokenly. 'I – enjoyed it – so much. Thank you.' She was silent for a little while, and he clasped her cold hands in his. 'I am – sorry I shall – never meet – Helen,' she went on presently in a weaker voice than before. 'God – bless you – Hugh.'

He kissed her very gently. She smiled up at him, a wonderful, brave smile that he never forgot; then her eyes closed, she sighed like a weary little child. Barbara Havelock, like many other gallant souls whose lives were devoted to their country's service, had given her life bravely without complaint. Shannon rose shakily to his feet; the unashamed tears were running freely down his cheeks. As in a mist he saw them approaching, the man and woman responsible for Barbara's death. The man staggered in his walk, he looked as though he had suffered severely, but he held a gleaming knife in his hand. Mrs Malampos gave a triumphant cry.

'The girl is dead – kill the man!' she screamed in Greek. 'Death to all spies!'

A dreadful laugh – icy, terrifying in its timbre – broke from Shannon. He drew the revolver from his pocket, and fired rapidly at them both. The man went down with hardly a sound; the woman gave one piercing shriek then pitched forward, and lay still. Shannon put away his weapon.

'I have avenged you, Barbara,' he whispered, looking down at the still, pathetic little form at his feet.

Kneeling, he gently took possession of the Secret Service emblem which had been her passport of membership; then, wrapping her cloak round her, he carried her to the car that had brought them to that tragic spot. A few minutes later he had driven away, but two cars remained, their glaring headlights revealing, in grim relief, five forms lying grotesquely motionless on the rough ground.

It is doubtful whether Shannon ever afterwards remembered with any clarity his drive to Government House. He sat most of the way like a figure carved in stone, glaring straight ahead of him, his left arm encircling the dreadfully still figure by his side. The gear and brake levers were on the right, a blessing which rendered using his left hand unnecessary. He reached the main gates of the governor's residence to find, as he expected, that they were closed. His summons, however, induced the sentry to call the corporal of the guard, who emerged through the wicket after a delay of two or three minutes. The man flashed a torch on the car, and immediately gave vent to a forcible exclamation. Shannon had quite forgotten the fellow he had jammed in the smashed roof. He was still there, his head, arm, and part of the upper portion of his body hanging downwards inside, the rest lying along the roof. Not a sound came from him; he had obviously lost consciousness.

Sight of the condition of the driver, and the waxen face of the girl held in his left arm, brought more startled exclamations from the corporal, but he was a man of action. On Shannon's demand to be admitted, he wasted no time in protestations he knew would be useless. He gave orders for the sentry to open the gates and call out the guard. Then, with two men standing on the running board on one side and the corporal on the other, the Secret Service man completed the last stage of his sad journey. There was a certain amount of delay in obtaining entrance to the building, but Shannon and the corporal between them overcame the reluctance of the man they had roused. The former carried in the body of Barbara Havelock; placed it reverently on a couch in a small room adjoining the entrance. A message was sent to Major Hastings, the ADC, requesting him to come at once, and to call the governor. The corporal remained with Shannon, but he gave his men orders to extricate the Cypriot in the car from his position. The aide-de-camp arrived within a few minutes clad in a dressing gown, which he had donned hastily over his pyjamas. His eyes immediately fell upon the dead girl, and he started back, his face turning deadly pale beneath its bronze.

'My God!' came from him in a hoarse whisper. 'Barbara Havelock! Is she – is she dead?'

Shannon nodded. He looked like a man carved from marble. The expression of grief on his face, framed as it were in grim, deadly purpose, seemed to have been chiselled there. Hastings turned his eyes full on him and, if possible, his horror increased. The Secret Service man, indeed, was a startling enough object. His clothes were cut and torn, blood was still running from several slashes; his shirt front was stained with large blotches of it; his face alone seemed to have escaped damage. Questions, appalled, urgent questions, were trembling on the ADC's lips, yearning to find expression all at once, but he refrained, waiting for Sir Gordon Stevenson's arrival. The governor was not long in coming. Like Hastings he stood appalled by what he saw; went down on his knees by the body of Barbara; remained there like a man in grief-stricken prayer for some minutes. He and his aide had both known the girl well and had been very fond of her, though neither had known that she had been a member of the British Secret Service. The corporal, with great tact, left the room, indicating to Major Hastings before he went that he would be within call if required. Stevenson rose from his knees; faced Shannon with a white, haggard face. He seemed suddenly to have aged.

'In God's name,' he muttered, 'what has happened?'

'First of all,' replied Shannon, 'in order that you may understand more easily, it is necessary to tell you that Miss Havelock was one of us.'

His two companions looked startled.

'You mean,' asked the governor, 'that she was a member of the Intelligence Service?'

'Yes; she was the resident agent in Cyprus.'

Shannon swayed slightly, and both men showed immediate concern. They started forward to his assistance, but he waved them impatiently, almost roughly away; refused the offer of Stevenson to send for a doctor; declined scornfully the chair pushed forward by Hastings. He would not sit down in the presence of the dead girl. Standing there, swaying occasionally, his voice utterly toneless, the expression on his face never altering, he told them the whole story. It took some time in the telling, for he related nearly every incident that had happened from the moment he had called at the school and introduced himself, until he had killed Madame Malampos and her companion, and driven from the scene of the tragedy. Sir Gordon Stevenson and Major Hastings did not interrupt; in fact they hardly moved, only turning occasionally to cast pitying, tender glances at the form lying so pathetically still on the couch. At the conclusion of the recital, they regarded Shannon with something approaching awe. He had said very little about his own part in the desperate attempt to defeat the Cypriots and save the girl, but he had, of necessity, to speak of the numbers that had attacked them and, judging from his condition, and the fact that he mentioned that seven or eight had been left lying there dead or wounded, it was not difficult to visualise what he had done.

'We shall have to get in touch with the police at once,' declared the governor. 'The question is, Shannon, how much of this must we keep to ourselves?'

'There must be no mention that Barbara and I have any connection with the Secret Service, of course,' returned the other. 'The affair must be given the appearance of an attempt at kidnapping by a gang of bandits. Why, it doesn't matter. I simply have no knowledge of the reason, that is all, and Barbara is dead. The car was obtained for us in the ordinary way by the porter of the hotel – the driver must have been watching and awaiting such a summons. I don't think the porter was in on the plot, but, no doubt, he will be questioned. If I may presume to advise, I suggest that the Chief Commandant of Police be taken into your confidence, and instructed to act accordingly.'

The governor stood thinking deeply for some time, his chin sunk on his breast.

'I daresay it can be arranged as you advise,' he declared at length. 'It is most unlikely that any of the survivors captured will speak. If they know anything, and I doubt whether it will be much, they are not likely to give away the conspiracy. The thing that bothers me most is the position of the woman you shot. The fact that she was housekeeper at Miss Havelock's school, and took part in the attempt against her and you, is bound to cause endless complications.'

'If I may make a suggestion, sir,' put in Hastings, 'I think I see a way by which that can be got over and which will enable us to keep Shannon out of the affair altogether.'

'What is it?' asked Stevenson eagerly.

'It is that Madame Malampos and her companion, who were, we know, at the dance in the hotel, or at least were in the grounds, took Miss Havelock home. That is to say, Shannon's car overtook them, and he offered them a lift, whereupon Miss Havelock told him it was not necessary for him to go on with them, as she would be with Madame Malampos and her companion. Shannon then left the car, and it went on. It was stopped near the Phaneromene Market, which is a lonely spot at night, by a gang of bandits in two cars who forced them to accompany them to the spot where the tragic affair took place. There a quarrel arose between the bandits, during which some were killed and others wounded and, in attempting to escape, the three were killed.'

'Yes,' nodded Stevenson; 'I believe you have thought of the solution.'

'Good God, man!' burst out Shannon, breaking from his icy, dreadful calm for the first time since he had entered the room, 'do you realise that you are whitewashing that fiend of a woman, making her appear a martyr like that poor girl lying there.'

'I know,' agreed Hastings, 'and I understand how you feel about it. I feel the same, so does Sir Gordon. But for the sake of your job, we have to keep you out of this thing as far as possible.'

Shannon, of course, saw the necessity of that himself. The idea, however, that Mrs Malampos, who, he felt, had engineered the whole appalling crime, should be placed on the same pedestal of murdered innocence, as that occupied by Barbara Havelock, was repugnant to him. He was compelled to think of the Service, though; his own feelings, no matter how bitter they might be, must be suppressed. He agreed, therefore, and details were discussed.

Hastings went off telephone to the Chief Commandant of Police, and request him to drive to Government House immediately on a matter of extreme urgency. Stevenson's own body servant bathed and bandaged Shannon's wounds. He had been slashed in more than a dozen places, but none of the cuts were serious, though some were quite deep. He had lost a considerable amount of blood, however, which had weakened even his giant frame. He was glad to sit down in the governor's bedroom, and drink the brandy the latter insisted on his taking. Hastings returned after an absence of ten minutes. He regarded the Secret Service man curiously.

'How did that fellow get jammed in the roof of the car?' he asked.

'Two or three of them climbed on top,' replied Shannon wearily, 'and commenced to smash their way in with an axe. I caught hold of him, and pulled him through the hole he had made, fixing him in it in order to block up the opening, while Barbara and I got out.'

Hastings whistled softly.

'The roof practically had to be demolished to enable the men to extricate him. They have only just succeeded in getting him out. He is dead. A sharp, jagged piece of the broken structure was forced into his body. I suppose his struggles to get away drove it further in.'

A gleam of pitiless joy showed for an instant in Shannon's eyes.

'Another of them,' he muttered. 'Thank God for it.'

Stevenson and Hastings glanced significantly at each other. They understood how the big man was feeling and, if the truth were told, were inclined to reciprocate his sentiments, callous as they might have seemed.

'I have spoken to the men,' Hastings informed the governor, 'and instructed them to keep silent about what they have seen tonight. The corporal will answer for them. Perhaps you will hint to the two indoor servants about the necessity of forgetting all they have seen or heard here tonight, sir. Your word will have greater weight than mine.'

Stevenson nodded.

'They are quite reliable,' he asserted. 'I will speak to them. What are you proposing to do with the man the guard found dead?'

'The corporal himself will drive the car back to the place where the horrible business happened, deposit the body, and leave the car there. He is going to take his bicycle with him, so that he won't have to walk back.'

'He had better take some men with him in case he is attacked.'

'I have told him to go armed, sir. I think it might be injudicious to let too many eyes view the scene before the police get there.'

'Hastings is right, sir,' put in Shannon. 'Besides, there is little danger. I should think the uninjured and wounded have left the place long ago. They are not likely to remain there with the prospect of being arrested hanging over them.'

'I hope you turn out to be correct, Shannon,' returned the governor. 'It would be far better not to have prisoners on our hands. But,' his face grew tense, grimly determined, 'things are going be tightened up in this colony from now on. I'd proclaim martial law, if it were not for the fact that the profession of you and Miss Havelock must run no risk of becoming publicly known.'

'It will be known or, at least, suspected by the people who should not know it,' retorted Shannon bitterly. 'But the pretence must be kept up, I suppose. I think I'd better be smuggled away when I leave. Has there been any reply yet from Constantinople to my cable, sir?'

'Yes. This terrible affair drove it out of my mind until now.' He left the bedroom, returning a few minutes later with a sealed envelope, which he handed to Shannon. 'I hope they haven't escaped you,' he observed anxiously.

Shannon extracted the sheet of flimsy paper and, with the aid of a pencil, spent some minutes decoding the message. At length he looked up, his eyes gleaming.

'They have not disembarked at Constantinople,' he proclaimed. 'I'll meet them at Naples, and go on with them to Marseilles. God grant,' he added, between his clenched teeth, 'that I succeed in getting to the bottom of the infernal plot, and wipe them out. I owe it not only to the country, but to the service and Barbara Havelock. I could not save her life; perhaps I can avenge her fully by bringing to a successful conclusion the investigation she started.'

He was conveyed to a spot not far from his hotel in the car in which he and Barbara had been trapped. It was not a very difficult matter to reach his room unobserved. It was on the ground floor at the side of the building facing the gardens. Dawn had not yet broken, though its coming was imminent, and darkness reigned supreme. There was not a light to be seen anywhere, though no doubt the night porter and the watchman were about. Inside his comfortable apartment, Shannon drew the thick curtains well across the windows before switching on the light. He quickly disrobed, and packed away his ruined clothing at the bottom of a bag, after which he spent nearly an hour writing a report in cypher for Sir Leonard of all that had happened. That done, he threw himself on the bed with no expectation of being able to find solace in slumber. But the weakness caused by loss of blood, combined with the mental and physical strain he had undergone, came to the rescue. In less than five minutes his eyes had closed, and he slept the sleep of utter exhaustion.

CHAPTER EIGHT

Thalia Ictinos

He awoke to find the curtains drawn back, one of the French windows wide open, the sun streaming gloriously into the room. The deep perfume of violets, allied with a more elusive but equally attractive scent, pervaded the atmosphere. From outside came the glorious song of the birds raised joyfully, as though in praise to heaven. But there was no response to their bliss in the heart of Hugh Shannon. With his awakening had come a vision of Barbara Havelock standing in the lounge the evening before, looking so fresh and exquisitely dainty in her rose pink dress, a delightful smile upon her face, her blue eyes sparkling with enjoyment. Then the vision faded to give place to another of that same face, white with the pallor of death, a terrible crimson stain mocking at the delicate pink of the dress. Involuntarily he groaned. Almost at once a hotel valet appeared from the dressing room. Obviously a Frenchman, he had the gay, debonair aspect of the Parisian.

'Good morning, m'sieu,' he bowed. 'It is a delightful morning, this – a morning made for the happiness. Monsieur has slept late, but no doubt he found the dance tiring. I have laid out your clothes, and will now prepare your bath, if monsieur permits.'

'Yes, yes, get it ready at once,' returned Shannon, who was in no mood to listen to gay chatter.

The valet's eyes opened a little wider than usual, the brows were raised slightly. These Englishmen, he thought, drank too much of the spirits. It caused them to be heavy, lethargic, and irritable in the early morning. Now if they confined themselves to the light wines of his beloved France, or even of this island of Cyprus, all would be well with them.

'Monsieur will take coffee?'

Monsieur would, and the Frenchman hastened away to give the order. Relieved to be alone, Shannon sprang out of bed. He was annoyed with himself for having slept so late. It was close to nine o'clock. He strolled to the window, and gazed out on the trim, well-kept lawns, the flower beds a riot of delicious colour, the little wicker tables and chairs dotted about in the distance. From where he stood he could see the table at which he and Barbara had sat. What a delightful companion she had proved! What a friend she would have made for his own Helen! A deep sigh, redolent of the sorrow and bitterness which filled him, broke from his lips, and he stood there stiffly erect, paying a little tribute of silence to the memory of a brave, uncomplaining soul and a fellow member of the British Secret Service. The coniferous tree with dark foliage shading the table at which he and she had sat caught his eye. He recognised it as a Cypress, and started slightly. Was not a branch of such a tree regarded as a symbol of mourning? How tragically significant! But he had work to do, vital, exigent work; there was no time for sorrow in his life.

He turned from the window, drank the coffee brought to him by an attentive waiter, and proceeded with his bathing and shaving.

The valet was dismissed before he commenced to dress. Shannon had no desire for the man to catch sight of the numerous bandages on his arms and body. He had almost finished a meagre breakfast, when a message was brought to him that Colonel Cummings, the Chief Commandant of Police, and Major Hastings, the governor's ADC, wished to see him. He found them awaiting him in the lounge, two grave-faced, bronzed, soldierly-looking men. Major Hastings quickly performed the introduction.

'Colonel Cummings has received the entire confidence of His Excellency,' he told Shannon in a low voice, 'and everything has passed off as we arranged. There is a place over there where we can talk without being overheard.'

He indicated a lounge seat standing in a remote corner of the large hall in the midst of a group of palms in pots.

'Wouldn't you rather come to my room?' asked the Secret Service man.

'No; it is better to remain here. Our conversation will not be heard, and it will not have an appearance of secrecy. The news has got about and, of course, it is known here that you dined and danced with Miss Havelock last night.'

Shannon noticed, as they strolled to the seat, that curious glances were cast at them by the members of the hotel staff present in the lounge and some of the guests.

'Would you mind giving a display of startled surprise as we talk to you?' suggested Colonel Cummings, as they sat down. 'We want those who are watching to get the impression, Shannon, that you are hearing the news for the first time.' The young man nodded. 'By the way,' pursued the colonel, 'how do you feel today? I understand you were pretty badly injured.'

'Oh, I'm all right, sir,' was the response.

'You'll have to have those wounds properly dressed,' put in Hastings. 'Sir Gordon has directed me to tell you that he insists on it. The Chief MO has been requested to call at Government House at eleven for the purpose.'

'Very well,' acquiesced Shannon impatiently, 'but it wasn't necessary. As I tell you, I'm quite all right. May I know what has been done?'

Colonel Cummings nodded. He at once proceeded to tell Shannon that, after he had been made acquainted with the facts by the governor, he had called out the Senior Superintendent of Police and a body of men, and had driven to the scene of the tragedy. There they had found the car with the damaged roof. Inside it lay Miss Havelock – Hastings had followed the corporal of the guard in his own car, conveying the poor girl back to the place where she had met her death. After placing her in the vehicle which had originally taken her there, he had driven back. Close by lay the man who had died while jammed in it and, in various spots in the vicinity, lay four men and the woman also dead. Four had been shot, the fifth had a broken neck. A short distance away, not far from a group of bushes, was another man who apparently had died of strangulation, though several bones in his body were also broken. As he announced this item, the colonel and Major Hastings both looked at Shannon as though tremendously impressed.

'I gather,' declared the former, 'from the medical evidence, that he lost his life very much as though he had been hanged. You told Sir Gordon and Hastings that you used a man to clear a space by swinging him round you. Have you any clear idea how you grasped him?'

'Not very,' admitted Shannon, who had not had any difficulty in obeying the injunction to look startled and horrified as the colonel spoke. The tragedy of Barbara's death had still too real a grip on his mind. 'I think I went a little mad when I heard the cry which told me she had been hurt. I grabbed the fellow by the shoulders and neck I believe.'

Colonel Cummings nodded.

'That would account for it,' he agreed. 'His neck had certainly been held in a terrible grip. God! I shouldn't like to be on the opposite side to you in a fight.'

'Was there no one left alive?' demanded the Secret Service man.

'No; not there. Somebody survived, of course, as the two cars had one when we reached the place. The man with the broken neck turned out to be the fellow who had driven you and Miss Havelock. He wasn't – er – quite dead when we picked him up! I have his dying confession here.' He looked significantly at Shannon as he spoke. 'Would you like to see it?'

The young man nodded, and accepted from the commandant a sheet of foolscap paper. On it was penned the following:

I, Michael Doberinas, wish before I die to make full confession of my part in the attempt to kidnap Miss Barbara Havelock. I was engaged by Stanislas Mowitz, who knew she had accompanied a young Englishman to the Palace Hotel, to arrange that my car was to be hired by them for the return journey. I succeeded in my design, though it was nearly one o'clock before they left the hotel. My instructions were that I was to stop at a certain place in the Phaneromene quarter as though I had engine trouble. Mowitz and his men would then be in waiting, overcome them, and give me further instructions. Soon after leaving the hotel, we overtook a man and lady walking. The Englishman told me to stop, and offered a lift to the woman who, it appeared, was Madame Malampos, the housekeeper at Miss Havelock's school. The Englishman left the car, as he was assured that the two ladies would be perfectly safe. I drove on, stopping as arranged near the Phaneromene market. Two other cars were in waiting, containing Mowitz and eight or ten men, who quickly overcame the two women. I was then told to turn and drive to Evrykhou. A little way beyond Nicosia, on the Evrykhou road, a dispute arose, and I was ordered to stop. The men got out of all the cars, and a violent quarrel took place, some siding with Mowitz and others taking the part of another man whose name I do not know. Weapons were used, and a bad fight took place. Madame Malampos attempted to get away and was shot, and Miss Havelock was stabbed as she tried to get from the car. I saw Mowitz fall dead, and that is all I know, for two men sprang on me. One caught me a terrible blow in the back of my neck, and I lost consciousness until the police came and revived me. I believe that the reason Stanislas Mowitz tried to kidnap Miss Havelock was because he wished to marry her, and she would not have anything to do with him. The quarrel arose because another man wanted to obtain possession of her. That is all I know.

The document was signed in scrawly, practically undecipherable letters. Shannon shuddered as he handed it back.

'Do you know if that is anything like the fellow's signature?' he asked.

'No, and it hardly matters,' replied the colonel. 'A man with a broken neck could not be expected to write legibly. His hand would have to be guided. Nobody is likely to come forward and dispute either the statement or the signature.'

Shannon bent forward, and covered his face with his hands for a few moments. Here was no acting. For the time being he was genuinely overcome at the necessity for such subterfuge.

'It's all so horrible,' he groaned. Then he looked up. 'Tell me the rest,' he urged.

'The bodies of the six men were removed to the mortuary,' the colonel told him. 'Those of Miss Havelock and the woman Malampos were conveyed to the school and, after the news had been broken to Miss Pritchard, the headmistress, were taken in and left there. You are entirely out of the affair, Shannon. The story will appear in full in the papers with a reproduction of the statement made by Doberinas. It is quite natural that I should interview you, as you spent the evening with the girl. I have already questioned the porter who called the car. I am convinced he was not in the plot. He, of course, said you had gone with Miss Havelock, but I let him know that you left the car, when Madame Malampos was invited to enter it, and returned to the hotel.'

Shannon clenched his hands until the knuckles gleamed white.

'God!' he ejaculated in a low, fierce undertone. 'I'd give almost anything if the necessity hadn't arisen to make that woman appear an innocent victim.'

Colonel Cummings gave a short, grim laugh that had nothing of mirth in it.

'I don't think she'll appear innocent for long,' he commented.

'What do you mean?' demanded Shannon eagerly.

'The man Stanislas Mowitz was the fellow she introduced to you as her brother. It was known that she was at the dance with him. It is also believed that he was her lover – you probably guessed the brother yarn was – well, just a yarn. Do you imagine she will be regarded as innocent, when the whole story, as we tell it, is out? Why, even a child will suspect that she was only kidnapped by necessity, because she happened to be in the car with poor Barbara. Mowitz would hardly want to take along his mistress, when he was abducting a girl he proposed to make his wife. A good many people will decide in their own minds that she started the supposed row. Quite a number will believe that Doberinas, either by accident or by design, made a misstatement, and that actually she stabbed Barbara herself in a fit of jealousy. What is believed matters nothing to us. We have got to the bottom of the business as far as all practicable purposes are concerned, and the police will endeavour to find the scoundrels who got away. We won't find them, and don't want to, but nobody knows that but the superintendent and I. Like you, I also hope her name becomes anathema.' He rose, and held out his hand. 'That's all there is to the business as far as you are concerned, Shannon. All that remains for me to do is to wish you – good hunting!'

'Thank you, sir,' returned Shannon gratefully, giving the commandant's hand a grip that caused the colonel to wince.

'Good Lord!' exclaimed the latter, 'I thought that arm was pretty badly cut about.'

'So it is,' Hastings put in. 'It seemed to me to be almost in ribbons.'

'Well, I hope I don't have to shake hands with Shannon when it's fit.'

He nodded, and marched briskly across the lounge, and out of the hotel. The manager was standing a few yards away. Major Hastings caught his eye, and beckoned to him. The immaculately attired and popular man hastened up to them.

'Mr Shannon,' the aide-de-camp told him, 'has had a very bad shock, as you, no doubt, will have gathered. He is a friend of Miss Havelock's relations, and only called at Cyprus to convey their greetings and get to know her. It is rather early, I know, but I think a good stiff dose of your best brandy will help to steady his nerves.'

'I'll give orders myself, Major Hastings,' the manager assured him, and added to Shannon: 'Please accept the very deep sympathy of myself and my staff, Mr Shannon. We all knew and liked Miss Havelock, and the affair has been a tragic shock to us.'

The Secret Service man thanked him, and he hurried away to give orders for the brandy.

'That completes everything I think,' murmured Hastings. 'I don't see how you can now figure in the matter at all, except very incidentally.'

Shannon expressed his gratitude for the manner in which anything suggestive of political intrigue or Secret Service work had been entirely eradicated from the tragic affair. He drank the brandy when it arrived, afterwards driving to Government House with the ADC. There his wounds were dressed, it being found necessary to insert stitches in several. The medical officer, who had been admitted to the governor's confidence, was rather doubtful about the wisdom of allowing his patient to travel for a day or two.

'Who will remove the stitches?' he demanded.

'Oh, I'll find a doctor in Naples,' returned Shannon carelessly. 'The consul there will see to that.'

'Don't forget,' urged the Chief of the Medical Service; 'and for goodness' sake don't do anything to break open those wounds again. It is all very well your calling them scratches. I don't.'

Shannon's report to Sir Leonard Wallace was despatched, but the young man decided, not only for the sake of appearances but because of his own inclinations, to remain in Nicosia for Barbara Havelock's funeral, which took place early the following morning. He calculated that by driving to Famagusta by car directly afterwards – instructions having been given for the flying boat to be ready to start on its journey immediately when he arrived – he could still reach Naples a considerable time before the *Ile-de-France* was due there. A suggestion, emanating from the school, that Madame Malampos and Barbara Havelock should be accorded a joint funeral, was promptly vetoed by the governor, who did not consider it necessary to give Miss Pritchard his reasons for interfering. The poor girl, known in Secret Service records as Number Thirty-Three, was followed to her grave by practically the whole British population of Nicosia, all the girls of her school, and a great concourse of other Nicosians. The governor himself attended, walking directly behind the hearse with Major Hastings on one side of him and Captain Shannon on the other, his commissioners and members of the Legislative Council following directly behind him. Shannon's last tribute, a beautiful wreath composed entirely of violets, had on it the simple inscription: 'To Barbara from Helen and Hugh'. He was almost the last to leave the graveside, but, as he stood there erect without movement, it is unlikely that any of the others, except the governor, the Chief Commandant of Police, Major Hastings and perhaps the chief medical officer, realised that he was paying the silent tribute of respect, as representative of his department, to a member who had given her life in its service.

On returning to Government House, he bade farewell to Sir Gordon and Major Hastings, and left at once in an air force car for Famagusta. Every precaution had been taken to ensure his leaving the capital unobserved, and, in addition, a devious route chosen to throw off any attempt on the part of interested people to trail him. Shannon was able to assure himself fairly confidently, before he had gone far, that he was not being followed. His thoughts were too deep to allow him to take much interest in the scenery, though, probably at any other time, he would have been absorbed in the tract of treeless plain, known as the Messaoria, through which the car passed. It is here that a large portion of the cultivated area of the island is situated. In summer and winter it presents an appearance of barren desolation, but now was at its best. Fields of barley gloriously green gave a perfect background to others rich in irises, poppies, narcissi, anemones, marguerites, ranunculi, and gladioli. To the north was the imposing skyline of the Kyrenia mountains, relieving the flat monotony of the plain. Cyprus has been described by people who have only travelled from Famagusta to Nicosia in the winter, or the latter part of the summer, as barren and desolate, but, like many another country, it presents an entirely different aspect in spring and early summer.

Famagusta appeared to Shannon to be a town of ruins, which indeed it is. Inside its Venetian walls are the remains of nearly a dozen churches dating back to the Lusignan period and even further. The mosque of St Sophia, once the cathedral of St Nicholas, towers over all and, with its beautiful architectural style, of one period only, is most impressive. The car passed slowly through the town, as though the driver thought his passenger would not wish to be hurried through a place with such a chequered history, which had during the fourteenth century, in fact, been of such importance as to merit the title of 'Emporium of the East'. Shannon, however, was eager to be in flight for Naples. He urged the mechanic driving him to go faster. There was an extraordinary contrast between the calm, lazy silence typical of the sabbath in the Christian part of the town and the noisy bustle of the Muslim districts. It was almost as though the one was deliberately doing its utmost to defy the other. The car stopped in the centre of the town near the ruins of Palazzo del Provveditore, and a young flight lieutenant saluted Shannon and entered.

'There is a party of ladies and gentlemen at the Savoy,' he announced, after he had introduced himself, 'who are anxious to see the boat. We thought that, if you went on board with them, sir, as though you were one of the party, you would not be noticed. When they leave, you can stay there. Your bags will be taken on by the driver when he has dropped us at the hotel.'

'Good idea,' approved Shannon. 'When do you think you'll be able to get away?'

'At noon, and I promise to get you to Naples for about seven.'

The car was driven to the Savoy Hotel, where Shannon and the flight lieutenant descended. It then went on to the little dock where the flying boat lay. The Secret Service man was introduced as a visitor touring Cyprus to half a dozen people who had evinced a desire to see the great aeroplane.

'He's another person keen to see the inside of a flying boat,' declared the officer. 'Well, if you're ready, ladies and gentlemen, we'll be off. I can't give you long, as I am due out on a run to Malta at noon. There's no lie in that,' he added in a whisper to Shannon; 'I have orders to go there tonight after dropping you at Naples.'

'I suppose you can't take a passenger?' queried a pretty girl, 'because I should very much like to come with you.'

'Passenger!' He raised his hands in mock horror. 'Why, my dear Miss Molesworth, I should be court-martialled, shot at dawn, and suffer every other unpleasant penalty to be found in regulations, if I dared do such a thing.'

The party, talking merrily, went along to the harbour, and was rowed across to the anchorage of the flying boat which, by that time, had been towed from her dock. She looked beautiful, as she lay there gleaming brightly in the sun like some great silver-grey seabird about to spread her wings in flight.

'There she is,' exulted her pilot. 'Isn't she a beauty? Fifteen tons of Blackburn Perth plane with three Rolls-Royce Buzzard engines, each giving eight hundred and twenty-five horsepower. She can do a hundred and twenty-six miles per hour with ease.'

'Anyone would think you were proud of her,' smiled Miss Molesworth.

'Proud! I'm crazy about her.'

During the inspection Shannon, with the assistance of a smart-looking sergeant wearing a pilot's wings, contrived to get lost, a difficult operation for a man of his bulk, and was hidden away. The uncomfortable attitude in which he was forced to crouch gave him cramp, and it seemed to him an interminable time before the visitors took their departure. At last they went; he rose to his feet with a sigh of relief and stretched himself. Fifteen or twenty minutes passed before the flying officer in charge returned, accompanied by a junior.

'Sorry to keep you crouched up in there for so long, sir,' he grinned, 'but they seemed to want to see everything twice over.'

'Don't apologise!' returned Shannon. 'After all, their anxiety to see over the boat enabled me to come aboard as an innocent sightseer and, therefore, without causing any particular interest. Did the rest wonder what had become of me?'

The young airman nodded.

'They were quite concerned until I told them a message had been sent after you, and you had gone ashore again.' He sighed with mock sorrow. 'I have always been fairly truthful, having been taught at my mother's knee, as the storybooks have it, but it's hard not to be a confirmed liar in the RAF. Still it was in a good cause on this occasion. It's twenty to twelve. We'll leave now, if you're ready, sir.'

'The sooner the better,' returned Shannon.

'Right ho! If you'll keep out of sight until we're up aloft, I don't think anybody but a professional nosy parker will know you're aboard.'

Five minutes later the great flying boat was skimming over the calm surface of the sea to rise presently without any apparent effort, though she carried an extra heavy load of petrol, and soar into the cloudless space above. Not a more glorious day could have been chosen for such a trip. There was a slight following breeze, visibility was excellent, conditions altogether were ideal. At one o'clock a picnic meal was brought to Shannon who enjoyed it immensely. He suddenly realised that he was very hungry, having had breakfast at an early hour before departing from the Palace Hotel and going to Government House. The funeral of Barbara Havelock had taken place at nine o'clock. Less than two hours after leaving Famagusta, the seaplane passed over Rhodes Island at a height of four thousand feet. Thereafter Shannon found a great fascination in gazing down at the Cyclades, the town of Milos, shimmering in the sunshine, presenting a particularly entrancing spectacle. Soon after half past three they passed over Morea, and the officer in charge, having relinquished control to his junior, joined Shannon to tell him in triumphant tones that they were exceeding all expectations. They had tea together, during which they discussed the landing in Naples Bay. It had already been decided that Shannon should pose as a senior officer of the Royal Air Force going on leave, having availed himself of a flying boat, proceeding under orders from Cyprus to

Malta, after obtaining permission from higher authorities for the machine to take the devious route. Wireless communication was established with the authorities in Naples, the matter explained, and permission obtained for the seaplane to alight in the harbour, and disembark its passenger.

The great Blackburn Perth machine maintained its speed, and at half past six, six hours and three-quarters after leaving Famagusta, it was circling over Naples preparatory to alighting. Shannon delighted in the experience of looking down on one of the most charming views to be found in the world. The pleasure of regarding from above Naples and her perfect bay, beautiful Sorrento, lovely Capri in the distance, and Vesuvius is not to be enjoyed by everyone. He, a man not given to rapturous ecstasies over scenery, found the panorama inspiring, and was conscious of a feeling of regret when the flying boat alighted perfectly in the harbour. The port officials were quickly on the scene. Shannon found himself greeted with the utmost courtesy; passport and customs formalities were rapidly conducted, and he was permitted to land. Several Italian flying officers came out in a motor launch to greet the British flying officers, and were greatly disappointed when they learnt that the men in charge of the seaplane could not accept the invitations showered on them, because of the necessity of leaving at once for Malta. Shannon, rather to his dismay, found it incumbent on him, as a supposed senior officer of the RAF, to call on the Italian commandant and accept the very warm invitation to dinner. He thanked the men who had brought him with such speed from Cyprus, and bade them farewell; then went ashore in the motor launch. He spent an exceptionally pleasant evening with the Italian officers, but was rather glad when he was reluctantly permitted to return to the Hotel Vesuve, where he had booked a room. He possessed a fairly intimate knowledge of aircraft; could fly his own machine, but he knew that, if he had not pretended an ignorance of Italian, he would have been lost. On several occasions the airmen seemed eager to enter into highly technical discussions, which they were forced to abandon on account of his supposed lack of knowledge of their language and their indifferent acquaintance with his.

The *Ile-de-France* was due into arrive at Naples at the early hour of six on the following morning, and depart again at ten. Shannon found awaiting him, on his return to the hotel, a sealed envelope in which was enclosed a ticket for Marseilles with the compliments of the British consul. He had telephoned the latter whilst dressing for dinner, and had been informed then that a note would be left for him at the hotel. He smiled to himself at this further example of the efficiency of the Intelligence Department. Before leaving Nicosia he had asked the governor to send by special cable another communication in code to headquarters, in which he announced his intention of meeting the *Ile-de-France* at Naples and sail on her to Marseilles in company with the people he was after. Headquarters, in order to prevent any hitch due to his late arrival, had promptly communicated with the consul in Naples, and arranged everything for him. All had taken place between the hours of ten in the morning and six in the evening – and on a Sunday!

Monday morning dawned wet and dismal, but Shannon was down at the docks long before the Messageries Maritimes steamer was warped alongside her jetty. He had obtained a picture of Paul Michalis while in Nicosia, and on it he depended to pick out the Cypriot and the other members of his party. He had never met or seen photographs of any of the others. Wrapped up in his raincoat, and holding a borrowed umbrella well down over his head, he watched the large vessel with its black hull and funnel and white superstructure draw in to her berth. He had taken up his stand behind a railway van, and was confident that even his great bulk would pass unnoticed, while he was in a position to observe all that went on. He had no great expectations of seeing any of the men he was so anxious to watch at that hour of the morning; had met the boat more as a precaution than for any other reason. There was a possibility that, despite the fact that they had booked to Marseilles, they might land at Naples. He had no intention of taking the risk of losing them.

There was a great deal of bustle and clatter round him as cargo and baggage was discharged from the ship. Close by, an optimist with a guitar, scornful of the rain, sang and strummed Neapolitan airs, though the few passengers to be seen were busily preparing to disembark. They were certainly not likely to spare time to listen to and award largesse to a wandering minstrel. A group reached the head of the gangway, and commenced to descend. Shannon's sharp eyes became fixed on the third person, a short, rotund man with a fat, flabby face in which small piglike eyes were set over a broad nose. It was Michalis – he was certain of it. He had studied the photograph in his possession too often to be mistaken. They were disembarking then. People bent merely on a sightseeing tour did not carry suitcases and impedimenta of that nature. With Michalis were seven men and three women, the identical number Shannon expected. Then he gave a great start, and slipped farther out of sight, his eyes riveted on one of the women.

'Good Lord!' he muttered to himself. 'It's Thalia Ictinos!'

CHAPTER NINE

A Surprise for Shannon

Shannon had vivid recollections of his previous dealings with the girl; had spent too much time in her company to have made an error in identity. Besides, he felt, there could not be two women in the world with that glamorous, fascinating beauty – a beauty which he mentally and cynically decided came from hell rather than heaven, and was calculated to lead men to ruin. Thalia Ictinos was a great and unexpected danger. She would recognise him at once. Her father, ruthless and a fiend, had been engaged with others in a plot to steal and sell international secrets. One of his accomplices, a man with a wonderful power of disguise, had actually impersonated Shannon in order to lure another Secret Service man to destruction. The plot had almost succeeded, but Sir Leonard Wallace, partially by taking advantage of the fact that Shannon had been impersonated, had turned the tables. Ictinos had escaped death on the gallows by dying of pneumonia brought on by wounds and exposure, three of his accomplices had been hanged for murders they had committed, and the gang had been completely broken up. Thalia Ictinos had apparently taken no active part in the conspiracy, though she had shown a vein of cruelty that could only have been inherited from her father. She had, however, made a desperate attempt to save him from Sir Leonard; had afterwards threatened the Chief of the Secret Service. When Stanislas Ictinos had died, she had disappeared from England, and had not been heard of since. That was more than a year ago. It was disconcerting to find that she was connected with the conspiracy Shannon was now bent on unravelling. It meant that he would be gravely handicapped, for, all the time, he would run the risk of being recognised.

Grudgingly he admired the feline grace of her walk, which even a mackintosh could do nothing to hide, as she passed on with the others towards the customs shed. She was wearing a little hat drawn low over her forehead, but he caught a glimpse of the long, curling eyelashes shading her great, slate-blue eyes, her rather long but perfectly shaped nose, the deep scarlet of her exquisite lips, rendering even more noticeable the flawless complexion entirely devoid of colour. Despite his feelings, Shannon gasped. She was so utterly beautiful, quite one of the loveliest women he had ever seen. It was hard to believe that within her beat a heart that was entirely callous and cruel, but he knew her, and he frowned more deeply, as he reflected again on the difficulties that would now beset him.

Taking advantage of every vestige of cover, he followed the party to the customs shed, where their baggage was strictly examined. Perhaps the officers resented having to be on duty at such an early hour, and consequently revenged themselves on the passengers. Whatever the reason, they searched the luggage with the most extreme care, but Shannon was indebted to their meticulous thoroughness for the fact that he obtained an important item of information. The people he had under observation were joined by another man, who seemed as though he also was connected with the party, though he made it consist of one more than Shannon calculated there should have been. He was a man of middle height, thin almost to the point of emaciation, with the stoop of the scholar. He possessed a sallow, cadaverous face in which a long-pointed nose predominated. His eyes were curiously magnified by his glasses and, as he had extremely arched eyebrows, his face wore a permanent expression of almost childlike surprise. A small, thin-lipped mouth completed a countenance which Shannon found interesting. He was engaged in an argument with a customs official, when the Englishman's attention was first drawn to him. The latter managed to approach close enough to get a view of the article that was apparently causing the dispute. It was a large wooden case, fitted to contain the numerous bottles, retorts and burettes with which it was packed. Michalis and two other men, who were looking on and listening, appeared greatly concerned. Eventually a senior officer was called to give his verdict. He questioned the owner of the case very closely about the contents. Shannon was not able to hear much of what was being said until they all raised their voices.

'I am a chemist,' cried the central figure of the controversy in passable Italian; 'these are merely various samples of drugs and gases which I need for certain experiments I am conducting.'

'But, signor,' came firmly from the senior official, 'it is necessary for you to have a permit to land such commodities. You should have obtained it from the Italian consul at the port where you embarked.'

'I did not know. These matters are beyond my understanding.'

'You should learn to understand,' retorted the other drily, 'if you wish to carry articles of this nature about with you.'

One of the others, a stocky, thickset man with a hooked nose and aggressive jaw, stepped forward. He said something to the other rapidly, but not loud enough to enable Shannon to hear. The officer listened attentively; then smiled, and shook his head.

'I know you, of course, by name, Signor Bruno,' he replied, 'nevertheless, I am unable to accept your assurance on behalf of this gentleman. However, you may be able to arrange for the necessary permit. In the meantime, we will be compelled to retain the case.'

'But we are not remaining in Naples,' protested the owner angrily. 'We are going to Rome.'

Shannon gave a little inward sigh of satisfaction. It was something to know their destination.

'Allow me to advise you,' suggested the customs official suavely. 'Go to Rome, and as soon as you arrive obtain the permit. I will see that the case is sealed and sent to Rome by boat today. On its arrival, you will be able to claim it. You will, of course, have to pay the cost of transport.'

With that they were compelled to agree, though the man, to whom the case belonged, showed a good deal of reluctance in letting it pass out of his care. It was closed, locked, and sealed. All other baggage having, by that time, been passed, the party prepared to depart. Three taxicabs were engaged, and Shannon managed to get close enough – always keeping a wary eye on Thalia Ictinos – to hear that the drivers were directed to proceed to his own hotel.

He allowed them to go without following, feeling as certain as he reasonably could be that he had succeeded in remaining unobserved. His visit to the docks had not been wasted. It is true the obtaining of his ticket for Marseilles had turned out to be unnecessary, but that did not matter. He had learnt the destination of the party and, having made a careful study of each member, was assured that he would know them all again. The only fly in the ointment of his complete satisfaction was the appearance of Thalia Ictinos among them. It meant that he would be compelled to ask for the assistance of someone whom she did not know. With that thought in his mind he drove to the British consulate. There he had a chat with the consul who, he discovered, had already risen. In ten minutes a transcontinental telephone call had been put through to the Foreign Office, and extended over the private line to Sir Leonard Wallace's house in Piccadilly. Shannon spoke in guarded terms to the chief. Anyone listening in would have been left with the belief that the conversation was not of any particular importance, but Shannon conveyed to Sir Leonard the news that the people he was watching were bound for Rome whither he would follow them. He also informed Wallace that Thalia Ictinos was of the party, and that it would be necessary for him to keep in the background to a great extent, in consequence. In equally guarded manner he received the congratulations of Sir Leonard on his success in getting in touch with them, and was informed that a man would be sent at once to assist him.

'The Splendide is an excellent place,' remarked Wallace finally, from which Shannon gathered that he was to watch out for his assistant at that hotel in Rome.

He returned to the Vesuve, taking precautions to enter unobserved. He went straight to his room, and packed his belongings, a task that was quickly accomplished. Then, descending, he made his cautious way to the coffee room. Michalis and the whole party were there. Thalia Ictinos and two sleek young men were at a table alone, the rest being seated at two tables drawn together to make a long one. There were few other people in the large room and, at first, Shannon was disinclined to enter, but he espied a vacant table behind a pillar which he could reach without being seen. He walked to it, and sat down. It was in an ideal spot, for he was enabled to keep observation without any possibility of the eyes of the twelve people in the remote corner of the apartment falling on him, except when they passed on their way out. He ordered breakfast, and sent for a newspaper.

'You have a large party over there,' he remarked casually in English to his waiter, when the man came hurrying up with the second course.

He knew that nobody was more qualified to give information regarding hotel guests than an Italian waiter. It was true that Paul Michalis and his companions had only recently arrived, but the man would have already discussed them with his fellows and possibly other members of the hotel staff. Shannon's presumption proved correct.

'Yes, signor,' replied the waiter, who spoke perfect English, 'they arrived on the Messageries Maritimes steamer this morning. They have come here but to rest and take their meals. This afternoon they depart for Rome.'

He was even able to give the time of the train, though that was not of much importance, as Shannon had no intention of allowing them far from his sight. He finished his breakfast before they had concluded theirs, and wandered out to the lounge where again he found a secluded spot which commanded the main doors of the hotel, the lifts, and the staircase. His newspaper proved exceedingly handy as a screen whenever any of them approached, which was not often. Michalis, Bruno, and a grey-haired, soldierly-looking man with a bristly moustache and complexion the colour of mahogany, sat together most of the morning, smoking, and drinking wine. Occasionally one or two of the others joined them for a short period. Shannon saw nothing of Thalia Ictinos or of the other two women. They had apparently retired to a more secluded apartment. The chemist also was conspicuous by his absence. The Secret Service man was rather puzzled by the connection that existed between the conspirators and the scientist. The combination seemed curious to say the least. The latter was hardly the type of individual to further the schemes they had afoot. Yet from the anxious expressions on the faces of the others, when the dispute concerning the case containing the chemical apparatus had been at its height, Shannon had judged them to be as concerned as he. Where had he joined them? There had been no mention of his having been a member of the party that had left Nicosia and sailed from Famagusta so hurriedly. He may, of course, have joined the boat independently of them. The Englishman was rather inclined to believe that he had. He certainly had the appearance of being a Cypriot.

Bruno and Michalis left the hotel shortly after noon as though going for a walk. Shannon followed them. He did not like to be out of touch with, at least, some of them, and the grey-haired man, who, he had concluded, was General Radoloff, had disappeared up the staircase. However, they only went to Detken and Rocholl, the booksellers in the Piazza del Plebiscito, where they spent some time selecting and purchasing a very modern and expensive atlas. Afterwards they returned to the hotel, where the whole party united again for luncheon. Shannon's curiosity had grown. He was still exceedingly puzzled by the chemist and his chemicals. The purchase of the atlas added to his interest. It seemed a strangely innocent article, and yet it suggested possibilities that he found intriguing.

When the Rome Express drew out from Naples that afternoon on its four and a half hours' journey to the Eternal City, Shannon was the sole occupant of a compartment in the rear of the train. The twelve people he was shadowing had entered the first coach, the restaurant car being the third. There was little likelihood, therefore, of any of them appearing at his end of the train. However, he continued to use newspapers to screen himself from the view of anybody passing along the corridor, and ordered tea to be brought along to his compartment.

Rome has only one terminus which, situated as it is in a district suggestive of a conflict between the ages, plunges the visitor at once into the real, vital Rome. No sooner does he leave the station than he finds himself surrounded by an amazing mixture of the ancient and modern. There before his eyes are the Baths of Diocletian, dating from the fourth century AD, and a remnant of the Wall of Servius constructed in the fifth century BC. The church of St Maria degli Angeli, one of the works of Michael Angelo, and dating from the sixteenth century, towers amidst them, while, at the beginning of the Via Nazionale, the Roman architecture of today is represented by a crescent of white buildings. In the open space in front of St Maria degli Angeli also there stands the memorial of the Great War. Even the lovely fountain, one of the many in Rome, with its sparkling column of water, is suggestive of the new and old. The water flows from the Sabine Hills, along an aqueduct that was built in 146 BC, while the fountain with its gods and naiads is entirely modern. Altogether the city of the Romans seems to possess a startlingly anachronistic character, which is heightened by the sight of posters of films pasted against walls that Julius Caesar's eyes may have regarded on his return to Rome from one of his conquests.

Shannon had spent prolonged periods in the Italian capital, which in consequence was a very familiar city to him, but apparently some of the people he was following had never been there before. Signor Bruno, with the pride of the Italian, stood outside the station expatiating on the glories to be seen before their eyes for a considerable time, before at length taxis were called, and the party drove away. Shannon in another was never far behind. Their course from the station, carefully noted by the Englishman, went along the Piazza delle Terme, to the left along the Via Venti Settembre, across the Via Quattro Fontane until the Quirinal was reached, when they turned into the tunnel running under the palace and gardens. No taxi driver in Rome ever seems to neglect an opportunity of taking one through that tunnel. He will often go out of his way in order to enter it. Shannon strongly suspected that it was because of the noise. Romans, he knew from experience, seem to love noise. Motor cars hoot incessantly, tramcars clang and clatter their way along, while there is no apparent rule of the road, drivers depending on arrogant movements of their hands or heads to indicate their direction. Someone once said that in Rome the past is always present, which perhaps accounts for the sense of independence and individuality possessed by the Romans. Pedestrians never seem to hurry out of the way of traffic, and yet are not run over in that paradox of a city, which possesses so many roads apparently constructed for pigmies and palaces built for giants.

Emerging from the tunnel, they eventually reached the Piazza di Spagna, the cars ahead coming to a stop outside an apartment agency. Shannon halted his taxi a little way ahead outside an antiquity shop. The fact that Bruno and two of his companions had entered the agency suggested that their stay in Rome was to be prolonged. It appeared that they were about to engage a house or flats. If their intention had been to remain only for a short time in the city, they would surely have taken rooms in a hotel. Nearly half an hour passed by before the men emerged; then they were accompanied by a smartly dressed man whom Shannon recognised as a house agent he had once met. Again he took up the chase, which eventually ended outside a block of expensive flats in the new Ludovisi quarter. Bidding his driver wait round an adjacent corner, the Englishman watched from behind a tree as all but Thalia Ictinos and the two secretaries, or rather the two men he judged were the secretaries, entered the building. Again there was a delay; then Bruno came out with the house agent with whom he shook hands, before the latter drove away in one of the cars. The drivers were paid off, and the secretaries, assisted by Thalia Ictinos and servants, who emerged from the block, carried in the baggage. Bruno and his party had gone into residence.

Shannon remained in the vicinity for half an hour; then drove to the Splendide, where he engaged a room. It had been his intention to visit the house agent, but business hours had passed, and, though his one previous meeting with the man had been at a club, he wished to see him at his office. It had occurred to him that, if he could engage a flat in the same block for the man who was coming to Rome to assist him, it would be a step in the right direction. The danger of recognition was too great to allow him to take the risk of living there himself. However, there would be time enough if he went to the agency in the Piazza di Spagna in the morning. He unpacked, dressed for dinner, and descended. The lounge was crowded with a gay, chattering throng in which Americans almost seemed to predominate. Everywhere he turned he heard English spoken. There was nothing very strange in that. The language is heard sporadically all over Rome, while it can be said to be spoken in the Piazza di Spagna, which is a favourite meeting place for Americans and Britons, and hotels like the Palace, Grand, and Splendide more even than Italian.

He dined at a small table from which he had an excellent view of the crowded room. Possibly nowhere in the world can be seen a more cosmopolitan collection of human beings than in a big Roman hotel, if the Italian and French rivieras are excepted. Relaxing from the strain of the last few days, Shannon found a good deal of amusement in studying his fellow guests. It seemed to him that few races were unrepresented; he even saw a Chinaman eating solemnly in company with a Hawaiian. He had finished his meal, and was lighting a cigar, wondering lazily whether he should take his coffee there or in the lounge, when the event happened which he had been carefully avoiding all day. He blew out the flame as two men and two women passed, one of them brushing by and knocking the match out of his hand. He looked up quickly; the movement had seemed to him deliberate. Shannon is a man of iron nerve, but at that moment he received a shock that shook him badly.

Glancing down at him insolently, her scarlet lips curved a trifle mockingly, was Thalia Ictinos. She gave no other sign of recognition; might have been merely showing the coquettish interest of a woman in a stranger she found attractive. Though his spirits fell several degrees, Shannon returned her look with an air of curiosity, as though he had never seen her before and wondered who she was. She passed on, creating quite a sensation in that great dining room, where many of the women were beautiful. Clad in a backless evening gown that showed off to perfection her slim, marvellous figure, she walked with a grace that was wholly fascinating. Her dress was black, unrelieved by any colour, except that of the pink rose at her waist and the string of pearls round her exquisite neck. Her glossy black hair was drawn back, exposing to the full her tiny shell-like ears, in each of which glistened a diamond. Her attendant cavalier was the soldierly-looking man, while the other was Bruno. The lady accompanying him, stout, dark, and black-eyed was, no doubt, Signora Bruno. They disappeared into the lounge, and Shannon vented his feelings in a deep sigh.

It was rank bad luck, he thought, that after the precautions he had taken all day to escape observation, particularly from her, he should thus be caught napping. Yet he could hardly blame himself. Before entering the dining room, he had given it a careful survey to assure himself it contained nobody who might recognise him, though he had hardly expected to find her there. She and her companions must have been hidden from his view behind one of the many groups of palms with which the room was adorned. Nevertheless, he was quite certain that they had not been in his part of the room. By one of those congestions that so often take place in a crowded dining room, they must have been forced to make a circuit; had thus come upon him. What a pity, he reflected, that he had been caught in an unguarded moment. However, it could not be helped. As far as he was aware, she had no reason to suspect that he was watching her companions and herself. For all she knew he might be in Rome on one of many duties. At the same time she would naturally tell her companions who he was. He rather wondered why she had not indicated him to them before leaving the room. He gathered she had not, as none of them had looked round and, as far as he had been able to judge, she had not spoken between the time she had looked at him and the moment she had disappeared from view. Another thought perturbed him greatly. He was in a foreign country, and she knew his profession. She had but to make public the fact that he was a British Secret Service agent to render his position distinctly uncomfortable, if not dangerous.

He waited three or four minutes; then strolled casually into the lounge. Admiring glances were cast in his direction, as he stood looking for a seat and also for Thalia Ictinos. In his well-cut dinner suit, his tall, powerful form looked at its best, while his bronzed, good-looking face and somewhat unruly, curly brown hair caused the hearts of more than one woman there to beat perhaps a little faster than usual. It was some time before he saw the Greek girl. She was at the far end of the room, lying back in a deep chair gently fanning herself, while her companion was bending towards her with every appearance of being greatly interested in her. Shannon wondered if General Radoloff, if indeed he were the Bulgarian, was smitten with her charms. There was a vacant table almost opposite where they were sitting. The Secret Service man deliberately sauntered towards it and, sinking into a chair, ordered coffee. Thalia cast a quick glance in his direction, but gave no sign of recognition. He began to wonder if, after all, he had been mistaken. Was it possible that she did not know him? Reflection put any hope that may have risen in his mind, however, out of court. His was hardly a figure, he thought a trifle ruefully, that anyone would have forgotten, and he had been in her company under circumstances which would have left an indelible impression on her memory.

Signor Bruno and his wife seemed to have departed, at least they were not to be seen anywhere. Perhaps Thalia had told the Italian about him, and he had gone at once to warn his companions, though that hardly seemed likely. There could be no hurry, for Shannon was certain they had no reason to think he was in Rome for the purpose of watching them; could not know he had followed them to that city. A British Secret Service man might be in the capital of Italy for several reasons unconnected with their presence there. Bruno, however, was an Italian; had been a member of the diplomatic service. Thalia's announcement of Shannon's profession might have sent him off to pass on the information at once to the authorities. The girl could hardly have been presented with a better opportunity of exacting the vengeance she had threatened to take on one of the men who had encompassed the ruin of her father.

He watched her covertly, but, after her first quick glance in his direction, she did not look at him again. She appeared wholly absorbed in her cavalier, who was entirely monopolising the conversation. From time to time she blew spirals of smoke ceilingwards from the cigarette in the long holder she held to her lips, the occupation apparently giving her a childlike pleasure, particularly when she succeeded in blowing rings. More and more, as he observed her, Shannon wondered how so much beauty and daintiness could cloak the cruel, callous nature which he knew she possessed. It was a million pities, he thought; she might have made a wonderful wife for some man, if she had had the heart and soul of a normal woman. Her companion did not once look at the Englishman, though he could have done so without appearing to be interested in him. He had not even looked across, when Shannon had first taken his seat. Everything seemed to indicate that Thalia Ictinos had made no mention of him at all, but, although he earnestly hoped such was the case, he felt it most unlikely. In any event, even if Bruno had not gone to warn the authorities of his presence in Rome, and did not know who he was, Shannon's activities had received a setback. Thalia Ictinos knew he was there; she was certain to keep a lookout for him, which would cause him to remain very much in the background in all future investigations. It was fortunate indeed that he had asked Sir Leonard Wallace for assistance.

Shannon lingered over his coffee until it had grown cold; ordered another cup and a liqueur. They had hardly arrived when the couple opposite rose to depart. The man placed the cloak round the girl's shoulders almost as though caressing her, an attention which she did not seem to welcome, for the watcher observed a quick little frown appear on her white brow. A group of people talking and laughing obstructed the way. General Radoloff bowed politely, and asked them to make room, which they promptly, and with many apologies, did, but Thalia Ictinos had already encircled them; was squeezing between them and Shannon's table.

'Please do not go,' he was astonished to hear her whisper. 'In half an hour I will return. I must speak with you.'

She passed on, smiling with great charm at the people who were still apologising for being in the way. She took Radoloff's arm, and the two were quickly lost from view. Shannon continued to gaze in the direction they had taken for some time after he could no longer see her. He was almost inclined to believe that she had not spoken to him; that he had imagined it. Why on earth did she want to speak to him, and why had she been so secretive about it? Was it a trap of some kind? Thinking it over, he came to the conclusion that she was intent on finding out his reasons for being in Rome, though it perplexed him to know why she wished to do so without the knowledge of her companion. However, only she could answer the question that was troubling him. He sat awaiting her return in a state of curiosity not unmixed with suspicion.

CHAPTER TEN

Thalia is Frank

A little more than half an hour had passed, when he saw her again. This time she was wearing a magnificent ermine coat, the great collar of which was raised, almost hiding her head from view. Instead of walking up to his table, however, she went on towards the elevators but, as she passed, looked full at him, her lips framing the word 'Upstairs!'. Feeling more mystified than ever, Shannon, who had risen at her approach, sauntered after her. He reached her side as she was about to step into a lift; walked in behind her. Two other people were there, who announced that they wished to go to the fourth floor. Thalia Ictinos asked for the third, Shannon doing the same. On arrival she stepped out, and walked away along a corridor, the Englishman walking after her. There was nobody else about, and presently she waited for him to catch up with her.

'You have a sitting room – yes?' she asked urgently, without bothering to utter either explanation or greeting.

'I am afraid I have not,' he returned, his surprised gaze boring deeply into her wonderful eyes.

She smiled, showing two perfect rows of little, white teeth.

'Then it must be in your bedroom where we will talk,' she decided. 'Is it on this floor?'

'But, mademoiselle—' he commenced to protest.

'Captain Shannon,' she interrupted hastily, 'this is no time for a foolish regard of the convenances. You are a gentleman. Please, you will take me to your room.'

He shrugged his shoulders, and turned away.

'It is on the second floor. Shall we descend by the stairs?'

She nodded, and they walked on together. She was tall, but appeared short by his side. The stairs and the corridor below were deserted. He had his key with him and, opening the door of his room, stood aside for her to enter. She walked in without any trace of embarrassment and, as soon as he had entered, and had closed the door, took off her coat, throwing it on the bed. Her eyes caught sight of the pyjamas laid out for him. She smiled.

'You wrap yourself in silk when you sleep,' she commented. 'You are wise; it helps slumber. I also wear silk.'

He flushed a little.

'I presume,' he observed, with a somewhat laboured attempt at sarcasm, 'that you did not come here to discuss my pyjamas – or your night attire?'

She laughed – a delightfully silvery ripple of sound that thrilled him, despite his repugnance for her.

'No; you are right,' she admitted. 'I came to talk to you of a matter that is very serious, because I begin to feel it is too great for me.'

She sank gracefully into an armchair. Shannon felt curiously uneasy. Her glamorous, fascinating personality was beginning to draw him under its magnetic spell, and it troubled him. He called to mind deliberately his conception that her beauty was of hell, calculated to drive men to ruin. Perhaps it was because of that that his face became grim and a little fierce as he looked down at her. He was resolved that she would not bewitch him.

'What is this serious matter?' he demanded.

She looked up at him lazily, her long lashes half-veiling her slate-blue eyes.

'Captain Shannon,' she murmured, 'I believe you are afraid of me. Is it that my presence in your bedroom shocks your narrow English susceptibilities? Please think of me not as a woman, but as just a human being who is in distress and wishes for your aid.'

The idea of being able to regard her as anything but a woman, and the most alluring of her sex, struck the Englishman as amusing. He laughed, and thereafter the tension was relaxed slightly. She drew her long cigarette tube from the handsome evening bag she carried. He hastened to offer her a cigarette, which she took with a little nod of thanks, asking him to smoke with her.

'Isn't it rather curious,' he said, as he held a lighted match for her, 'that you should ask for my aid?'

'You mean,' she returned, watching the smoke spiral into the air, 'that you are suspicious of me. You do not think I can come to you, but for some purpose not for your advantage?'

He found her slight foreign intonation of the English words wholly attractive, but was fearful of allowing the admiration for her, which he could not suppress, get too strong a possession of him. He retreated to the bed, and sat on it.

'You and I were not exactly friendly last time we met,' he remarked frankly. 'Under the circumstances you cannot expect me to regard this visit without suspicion.'

She sighed.

'What can I do to remove it from your mind?'

He shrugged his shoulders.

'That is for you to decide.'

'It seems that my task will be more difficult than I anticipated,' she complained. 'When I saw you sitting eating your dinner all alone, I thought that perhaps there sat the man who might help me. That is why I have come to you, mon ami. Try to believe, will you not, that my motives are without guile? I am in difficulties, Captain Shannon – you see I have not forgotten your name. Have you forgotten mine, I wonder.'

'No; I have not,' came the uncompromising reply. 'I remember you as the cruel daughter of a callous, unscrupulous scoundrel, who escaped death on the gallows by the sheer good fortune that pneumonia stepped in and carried him off.'

Shannon felt a brute as he spoke, but he was anxious to cast off the spell her personality was casting upon him. He also wished her to realise the opinion he had of her. If she had shown an inclination to dissolve into tears, or expressed outraged indignation, he would probably have decided she was acting. She did neither. For a few moments there was silence between them; then she looked him full in the face.

'You speak of me as cruel,' she remarked quietly at length, 'but have I, to your knowledge, ever said or done anything so cruel as that which you have just said to me?' He felt a trifle ashamed, but made no reply. 'Listen to me, Captain Shannon,' she went on; 'perhaps you will not believe me, perhaps you may. I hated my father. You smile, but it is the truth. It is not nice for a daughter to say a thing so terrible, but I had much reason. When I was a little girl, too little to know much, my beautiful mother died, and I was left to the care of my father. For two years he permitted me to remain at the convent where I was educated in Vienna; then he took me away, because he thought I would be of use to him. You have perhaps noticed I am beautiful?' The question was asked quite simply, without a touch of coquetry in it. Shannon's nod was just as simple, and she continued: 'Well, my friend, he decided my beauty would help in his schemes. We travelled much, and he taught me to regard cruelty and wickedness as very ordinary things – he made me become not any more like my mother, but like him. Of course I admit that in me there must be a little of his nature, for sometimes I felt pleasure in hurting others, but all the time I rebelled against it and, as I rebelled, so I grew to hate my father. But I also feared him. That is why, when I chained up Monsieur Cousins – that so nice little man – I was cruel sometimes to him. I called him my little pet dog-man. I made him to suffer – oh, so very much – but I was always hoping to save his life. When my father killed people in his anger, I dared not tell him what I felt, so I pretend it is nothing – I do not care.' She leant forward earnestly. 'When I found Sir Leonard Wallace in my father's study, did I shoot him? No; and I am a good shot, Monsieur Shannon. He put out the light by shooting that was marvellous, and I also fired, but I took care to miss him. I wanted him captured for the sake of my father, but not killed. I admit I have taken pleasure in cruelty sometimes, perhaps again I may feel the same, but I hope I will not. I have his blood, you see. That I cannot help, but I am not all wicked, as I know you think me.'

Shannon eyed her steadily. Inclination made him long to believe her, knowledge of her dragged him to the other extreme. She was, he felt, trying to influence him for some purpose she had in mind.

'Do you remember when your father was in the hands of the police in Sir Peter Nikoleff's house?' he asked.

'It is something I shall never forget,' she told him.

'You ran down the stairs, and clasped him in your arms, as

they were taking him away. During that short space of time you succeeded in transferring to him a revolver. If it had not been for the skill of Sir Leonard Wallace, Stanislas Ictinos might have killed two or three men in attempting to escape. How does your action on that occasion accord with your assertion now that you hated him?'

'He was my father,' she returned simply. 'Whatever my feelings towards him were, the fact that I was his daughter remained. They were taking him away, perhaps for the terrible punishment of execution. What would you have done, if you had been in my position? Would you not have given your father a chance to escape?'

The question was a poser, which Shannon felt he could not answer.

'What about our threat?' he asked hastily. 'You told Sir Leonard Wallace he would be sorry for that night's work; told him that, if your father died, he would die also.'

'Was that not also natural? Was not the horror of the fate I knew my father deserved enough to cause me to offer threats to the man who had caught him? They were but empty, nevertheless. That happened a year ago. Have I ever attempted to harm Sir Leonard?'

'Not to my knowledge,' admitted Shannon. 'How am I to know that your present visit to me is not connected in some manner with those threats?'

'Is Sir Leonard Wallace here?' she asked in surprise.

'No; but I am. I took part in the capture of your father.'

'I did not threaten you, did I?'

He shook his head.

'I didn't hear you mention me by name, but your vitriolic outbursts in the room in which we kept you were threatening enough.'

'I was very much angry. If I had not been, would you not think I was strangely made?'

Shannon sighed. A voice seemed to be whispering to him to accept her as she now presented herself. Could it be that, after all, she was not the wicked woman he had imagined her? Resolutely he put the thought out of his mind, closed his ears to the insinuating little voice which, he felt, must belong to the devil himself.

'Tell me why you have sought this interview with me,' he demanded gruffly.

'You spend a great deal of your time in Rome, Captain Shannon, do you not?'

He smiled cynically. It was as he had thought. She was there to ferret out his reasons for being in the capital of Italy. He was soon to find that he was wrong.

'Why do you ask that?' he queried.

'Because I find you here now. When the man, who impersonated you at the order of my father, made the study of you for his purpose, it was here you were living. You have a connection with the British embassy, have you not?'

Shannon suppressed the sigh of relief which rose involuntarily to his lips. Was it possible that she did not think he was there in the usual capacity of a Secret Service agent? He surveyed her long and thoughtfully. There was no suggestion of mockery in her face, though he realised she would be far too clever to allow him to catch a glimpse of her mind, if she were not being entirely honest with him.

'Does it matter why I am in Rome?' he asked.

She laughed.

'Oh, la, la! How cautious you are, mon ami! Very well, I will not embarrass you with questions which you do not wish to answer.'

That surprised him. He asked her a question more to cover his own confusion than for any other reason.

'How did you know I was staying here?'

'I did not until I saw you dining; then I did not know you were living here. It was as you sat opposite me and my companion that I found to my satisfaction that you were. You see you signed for the things that you ordered. Only residents do that, Captain Shannon. But how interested you were in me! All the time you watched me and the man who was with me. Why was it? Because I had made you aware of my presence in the dining room, and you were curious?'

Shannon suddenly felt rather helpless. After her first look at him in the lounge, he had been convinced that the girl had not glanced in his direction again. Yet she had been watching him all the time apparently, and not only that but knew he had been observing her.

'I naturally wondered why you had attracted my attention,' he confessed. 'Considering our – er – previous encounter, I thought it unlikely you would feel very friendly disposed towards me.'

'That was entirely wrong of you. My disposition to you is of the most friendly; it is you who are full of suspicion and distrust of me.'

'Need we enter into that again?'

'No, if you do not wish it. I attracted your attention purposely in the dining room, for I wanted you to notice me. At once, when I saw you, I felt perhaps you would help me. This time, Captain Shannon, our interests are not in antagonism. I think, when I have told you why I wish to speak to you in private, you will feel that you and I can work with one another.'

He began to grow very much interested.

'I am afraid I don't understand,' he told her.

'Of course you do not, but I will quickly explain. Will you please look out of the door to see that no one listens? I do not think I was watched and followed, but one does not know. It is possible I have been unfortunate.'

Shannon obediently crossed to the door, opened it suddenly, and looked up and down the corridor. There was no one in sight. He returned and assured the girl of that fact.

'I happen to know,' he added, 'that the rooms on either side are empty, so whatever you say can be said with perfect safety here.'

'So! That is excellent. And, Monsieur Shannon, you will give me your word that, if you cannot help me, you will not betray me?'

He frowned.

'I can hardly do that without knowing what it is,' he protested.

'Oh! So cautious you are!' she cried half irritably. 'Never mind, I will put my faith in you, as you do not put your faith in me. I know, you see, that the assistants of Sir Leonard Wallace are men of honour.'

'That is where you are at an advantage,' he retorted drily.

A spasm that almost looked like pain flashed across her face.

'Must you persist in being cruel, m'sieu?' she asked.

'If you are going to take me into your confidence, Miss Ictinos,' he suggested, 'perhaps you will come to the point. It is getting late.'

She removed the cigarette from the holder; crushed it into the ashtray he had placed by her side.

'I have a profession now,' she told him quietly. 'It is like yours. My life, Captain Shannon, is devoted to my country, as your life is devoted to the service of England. I am in the Secret Service of Greece!'

He looked at her with incredulous eyes.

'Are you serious?' he demanded. 'You are not joking?'

'On the contrary, m'sieu, I am in very deep earnest. When my father died, I offered myself. I thought that my knowledge of people and languages would be of use to Greece. I was correct. My offer was accepted. For some months I was on – what do you call it?'

'Probation?'

'Yes; I was on probation, but now I have been entrusted with a task of importance very great.'

In his astonishment he almost gave his knowledge away.

'I thought you were—' he began; stopped abruptly as he was about to add, 'a lady's companion.'

'You thought I was what?' she asked curiously. He recovered himself admirably.

'I thought you were engaged to the gentleman with whom I saw you tonight. His attentions rather suggested—'

She laughed scornfully.

'Oh, Captain Shannon!' she protested. 'You do not flatter me. Do you think I would have a lover so old? I am only twenty-three; he, I think, is nearly sixty.'

'Stranger things have happened,' he murmured.

'Perhaps, but not with me. Possibly some day I will love, but it will not be an old man. You do not by chance know the man with whom I sat?' Shannon shook his head. 'That, my friend, was General Radoloff. He is a Bulgarian who has much power. He is with the people I have been told to watch. You see how I am trusting you.'

Shannon had great difficulty in preventing the interest he felt from showing in his face.

'Why are you telling me this?' he asked. 'It is hardly usual for the Secret Service agent of one country to announce herself so openly to an officer of another country.'

'I know,' she nodded, her beautiful eyes fixed on his with an expression in them which had nothing of duplicity in it. On the contrary, she looked utterly frank, almost childlike in her eagerness, as she went on. 'But, you see, m'sieu, as I have already tried to explain, I am beginning to fear that my work is too great for me. When I saw you in this hotel tonight, it was as if my prayer for guidance had been answered by the good God. I knew that if I could obtain your help all would be well. I must be quite candid with you – Captain Shannon, I am afraid!'

'Afraid!' he echoed. 'Of what?'

'Listen! As you put it in English, I am placing all my cards on the table. At the end of last year, two very clever countrymen of mine who had, at one time, been in power, made a most desperate bid – I think that is the correct word, no?' He assured her that it was, and she continued: 'They made a bid to overthrow the government, and obtain once more the power. You may perhaps know of their – bid? I am talking of Messieurs Plasiras and Bikelas.'

'Yes,' he replied; 'they came rather a bad cropper.'

The music of her silvery laugh filled the room for a moment.

'The word cropper is amusing,' she declared, 'but it is very much apt like all English and American slang. You are quite correct, mon ami; they came a bad cropper. Their followers were destroyed, and they only escaped very narrowly. But it seems they were not satisfied. Information came that again they were plotting. Then it became known that Madame Bikelas wished for a companion. I knew her well. My father was at one time a friend of her husband. But she and Monsieur did not know I was now of the Greek Secret Service. Nobody knows that but the head and one or two others of the department, and now you. You, of course, understand that such things are kept very much confidential. I have much money, but I go to Madame Bikelas, and tell her I am very lonely and have nothing to do. I ask her if she will have me for her companion. She is delighted. She thinks to herself: "this is someone we know. She will be reliable." Her husband thinks the same thing, and I am

engaged. But I go to her to find out what it is Messieurs Bikelas
and Plasiras are doing, and to keep my chief informed. Alas! Since
February I have been with them. Now April is nearly finished, but
I have not found out very much. With them is General Radoloff,
of whom we have spoken. There is also Monsieur Doreff who, like
the general, is a Bulgarian, and Signor and Signora Bruno who are
Italian. With them also are Messieurs Michalis and Kyprianos who
belong to Cyprus. Always they behave with great secrecy. They lock
themselves often in a room, and talk together for hours. There is a
great plot going on, of that I am certain, but I have not been able
to find out what it is.'

She paused, and looked at Shannon anxiously.

'Go on,' he urged.

'You are interested?'

'Very; though I must confess that I do not understand yet why
you are telling me all this.'

'It is because I am in need of help or, at least, advice. First
we met General Radoloff, Signor Bruno and Monsieur Doreff in
Smyrna. Afterwards we all went together to Nicosia in Cyprus,
where we stayed in the house of Paul Michalis. There Monsieur
Kyprianos came often secretly to the house, and there were long
private discussions. I tried very hard to find out what they were
about, but always I met with failure. Kyprianos is a strange man
whom I do not like at all. He looks at me sometimes in a manner
very strange.'

'Perhaps he is in love with you.'

She shook her head.

'No; one cannot mistake the eyes of love. Often I have seen the
look which tells me men desire me, but he does not look at me like
that. I am afraid of him. I wonder if he suspects me, though I am

sure there is no reason why he should. In Nicosia, when we arrived, there was much excitement. The people gave a great welcome to Messieurs Bikelas and Plasiras, which angered them greatly. It was then, for the first time, that they put aside the mask. They blamed Monsieur Michalis for the greeting they received. In his house they spoke in great indignation, and said their plans would be wrecked. He told them that he did not know anything about the welcome; he even swore that he had only mentioned their coming to Monsieur Kyprianos. When Kyprianos arrived, they asked him if it was he who had arranged the welcome. He said "Yes". Then they became angry with him. He also grew angry. He told them he would not help them, if they behaved to him in such a manner. My friend, it was strange how quickly they changed after that. It was like many nurses trying to soothe and comfort a crying child. I could not hear more of their conversation, for they took him away into the private room of Monsieur Michalis; the door was shut, and outside stood the secretary of Bikelas. It is always the same. When they hold their meetings, the secretary of Bikelas, or the secretary of Plasiras, stands on guard. I am always – baulked – is that the right word, Monsieur Shannon?'

'Yes, I think so,' nodded the Englishman. 'Then you think this Kyprianos holds the key to the situation?'

'I think he does. They do not dare to anger him. There is just one thing I have discovered, though at present it does not seem to me of importance. Kyprianos is a scientist; he has a reputation as a man of much skill with chemicals. Madame Bikelas told me that her husband and Monsieur Plasiras were expecting great help from him in order one day to return and regain their power in Greece.'

'Ah!' Shannon was unable altogether to suppress the exclamation, though he succeeded in rendering it fairly moderate. He had been given an item of information which he felt was of the utmost importance, if indeed it were genuine. Still very much on his guard, he kept the possibility in mind that everything he was being told was said with the purpose of entrapping him in some way. 'It certainly appears,' he agreed, 'that you are correct in assuming that there is some plot afoot against the present government of Greece. Have you been unable to pump Madame Bikelas? I mean to say,' he added with a smile, 'women talk confidentially to their companions, and I should have thought she could have told you a great deal.'

'Mon Dieu!' cried the girl in exasperated tones. 'I have squeezed her as one squeezes a lemon, but she knows nothing. Of that I am convinced. Her husband tells her nothing. We are said to be on a tour of pleasure. I suppose Signora Bruno and Madame Bikelas are with the party for the purpose of giving such an impression. They believe it, poor dears. I could not be a wife of that type, Captain Shannon. If I had a husband who treated me in the manner one treats a doll, I should leave him. I would wish to be a real companion to him, and in his confidence. I know there must come times when a husband cannot confide altogether in his wife, but to be kept, as a man might keep a mistress, just for pleasure and for no other reason is, I think, degrading. Do you not agree?'

He smiled.

'To a certain extent, yes. When did you arrive in Rome?'

He watched her keenly, as he asked the question, alert for any sign that she was aware he already knew. But she returned his regard quite frankly, and replied at once.

'Only today. It was said that we were to stay in Cyprus for some weeks, but we left suddenly, as though there had been a happening which made it necessary to leave the island at once. There was much agitation to be seen on the faces of the men, but I could not find out what it was that caused it. We all left with much abruptness on the Messageries Maritimes ship which was going to Marseilles. Kyprianos pretended that he was not of the party. He travelled separately to the port of Famagusta, and joined the rest of us on the boat. Our tickets were for Marseilles, but we disembarked at Naples early this morning, and came here by train. Is it not significant that we had tickets for one place, and landed at another?'

'It certainly would seem so. What hotel are you residing at?'

'We are not in a hotel, m'sieu. Signor Bruno possesses a very luxurious flat in the Ludovisi quarter. On our arrival in Rome we drove to the agent, who came with us. Through him we have engaged three flats in the same building. There are many vacant. Monsieur and Madame Bikelas, his secretary, and I are in one flat; Messieurs Doreff, and Plasiras and his secretary are in another; the third is occupied by General Radoloff, Messieurs Michalis and Kyprianos.'

'They are to remain in Rome for at least a month then?'

'It would seem to be the case. There is now anxiety because the customs at Naples would not let through a box belonging to Kyprianos. I heard him say that without it he could do nothing.'

'Do you know what is in the case?'

'It contains many bottles and jars filled with liquids. There are also measures and retorts.'

'I see. It appears that he is engaged on some chemical experiments in which they are all interested.' She nodded. 'How can those experiments be connected with your theory that Plasiras and Bikelas are plotting against Greece?'

'I do not know, and I—' she paused, and looked up at him with eyes in which seemed to lurk the shadow of a great fear. 'Monsieur

Shannon,' she cried impulsively, 'I am in much anxiety. I am afraid to permit myself to think, for it is in my mind that Kyprianos has devised some terrible poison gas which it is intended to use in order to obtain great power.'

A similar theory had been vaguely exercising Shannon's mind all day, ever since he had observed the anxiety with which Kyprianos and his companions had regarded the refusal of the customs authorities at Naples to pass the case. Her frankness seemed to him proof positive that she was genuinely seeking his advice. There may have been reason of a treacherous nature for divulging her other items of information, but there could be no object antagonistic to him in the betrayal of a secret that she and her companions would wish to remain hidden under all circumstances. She may, of course, have been purposely misleading him suggesting an explanation of Kyprianos' connection to his mind in order to divert it from any possibility of hitting on the correct reason. Shannon was worried. If he felt he could rely on this girl, he would have a helper whose position in the household would render her a most valuable assistant in his investigations. She had apparently been so honest with him that he was by that time more than half inclined to trust her. Everything she had told him coincided with his own knowledge. There had not been one item which had, in any way, clashed with the information he had acquired. Yet the memory of her father, of her own part in the events of a year before, persisted. He, like his colleagues, had formed his opinion of her then. It seemed to him that, in order to believe in her now, he must accept the incredible fact that there had been a complete *volte-face* in her character. She startled him by putting his thoughts into words.

'You are thinking,' she declared, 'that it is impossible to alter the opinion of me you had formed, is it not so? You are wondering how it can be that I, whom you judged so wicked a woman, could be now any different, and if there is any motive antagonistic to you in my visit. Oh, Captain Shannon, why cannot you try, at least, to believe in me? What possible purpose could I have in coming thus to you at risk so great to myself and confiding these things to you? Even if they are untrue, as perhaps you think, what object can be behind lies so useless? You are not fair to me, mon ami. You have no right to judge by the circumstances in which you first met me. I was then not my own mistress. I was under the influence of a man who though, as you say, a scoundrel was, after all, my father. You say in English that blood is thicker than water. Perhaps I was not very reluctant to be with him, for there is no doubt a cruel streak in my nature – I do not try to deny it, though I think I have suppressed it – and I love the excitement. But, when he died, it was as though I had been released from captivity. Since then I have striven to lead the life which my mother would have approved. Now I am happy in working for my country's welfare in the same way as you are working for England. Will you not give me the chance to prove myself? Will you not try to trust me?'

Her appeal went straight to his heart. Despite his misgivings, he felt inclined to cast, at least, some of his prejudices aside. He was about to reply, when abruptly the silence was shattered by a loud knocking on the door. At once they were both on their feet, eyeing each other in a startled fashion; he again suspicious, she with the hint of terror in her great lovely eyes.

CHAPTER ELEVEN

Love at First Sight

A quiet which, to his mind, seemed pregnant with danger followed the knocking. Had she, after all, betrayed him? Was Signor Bruno outside with officials anxious to question a British Secret Service agent about the reason for his presence in Rome, or had it been arranged between her and her companions that he was to be caught in a compromising position with her for some ulterior purpose? She silently answered his thoughts herself, gliding to his side, and taking his arm as though seeking protection. The faint elusive scent which clung to her threatened to intoxicate his senses, he felt her tremble slightly. Looking down at her, he saw that she was really startled, unless it was that she was a consummate actress. There was no suggestion of hysterical fear, which would immediately have convinced him of its insincerity. She was alarmed, but calm, exactly as he would expect the daughter of her father to be; exactly as the Thalia Ictinos he knew would be expected to face an unpleasant emergency. He knew she possessed great courage. She was not the kind to whimper with fear or lose her head. She did neither now, and consequently his faith in her grew stronger. Suddenly, however, he gripped her by both shoulders; gazed deep into eyes that returned his burning, questioning gaze unflinchingly.

'If this is a trick, Thalia Ictinos,' he whispered tensely, 'God help you. Do you know who is outside?'

'No, Monsieur Shannon,' she murmured, 'I do not, but I fear it may be that I was watched and followed. If so, it is I who am in danger, not you.'

Her words made him feel a trifle ashamed of himself. Releasing her from a grip that he realised then must have hurt, though she had made no protest, he picked up her cloak, and handed it to her.

'In here!' he ordered, opening the door of the wardrobe.

She obeyed at once, while he removed his dressing gown from a peg and, tearing off his dinner jacket, donned the other garment. The knocking was repeated. He threw the jacket on a chair, closed the wardrobe, and sauntered across the room. Opening the door slowly, he confronted the individual standing outside. Immediately a great wave of relief surged through him. The man regarding him with a broad smile was Hill, one of his own colleagues, variously known as 'Tubby', 'Ray', or 'The Doc'. Raymond Hill had qualified brilliantly as a doctor, but his spirit of adventure, a knack of picking up languages, patriotic instinct above the ordinary, and a first-class detective sense had shaped his career otherwise than had been the intention. He was now one of the men Sir Leonard regarded as his experts. About medium height, he was slightly inclined to corpulency. He was fair-haired, had a pair of ingenuous blue eyes, and a fresh, clear skin that would have been a credit to a certain excellent soap which, we are assured, helps people to obtain and retain schoolgirl complexions. Hill was subject to a great deal of chaff from his colleagues on account of his fresh, boyish face, but he took it all in good part. He possessed a sense of humour and a jolly personality, which helped to make him extremely popular.

'By all that's wonderful!' exclaimed Shannon. 'I'm jolly glad to see you, Tubby. But where have you blown in from? I thought you were in Madrid.'

'So I was – returned yesterday. The chief gave orders this morning that I was to join you, and here I am; flew over to save time. Aren't you going to ask me in?'

Shannon pushed him hastily away from the door; stepped outside, closing it behind him. Thalia Ictinos must not catch a glimpse of Hill, since the latter was to help him in his investigations.

'What's the big idea?' queried the ex-doctor, and, grinning broadly, added: 'You're not carrying on an intrigue, are you? She was only a landlady's daughter—'

'Tubby, you've a coarse mind,' interrupted Shannon, 'There is a lady in my room I must confess, and thereby hangs a tale with which I shall thrill your ears anon. At present make yourself scarce; whatever happens she mustn't see you. Come back in about half an hour. She'll have gone by then.'

'Tut! Tut!' sighed Hill. 'A lady in his room at this hour of the night! Hugh, I should be shocked to the marrow – if one could be shocked to the marrow – if I didn't know you.'

'Then it is fortunate you do. I couldn't bear to shock you, Doc.' Hill chuckled. He had a way of chuckling in a manner which can only be described as comfortable. 'Beat it!' ordered Shannon. 'I'll look out for you later.'

Hill obediently departed, and Hugh returned to his room, taking care to close the door tightly when he had entered. Thalia was still in the cupboard. Opening it, he bade her step out.

'It is quite all right, Miss Ictinos,' he assured her. 'Our fears were groundless. The mysterious knocker was merely a friend of mine.'

She stepped forth with a sigh of relief.

'Mon Dieu!' she exclaimed. 'I must admit that I had very much what you call the wind-up. It is a great easement to my mind to know that there was, after all, nothing to fear.' His smile, she thought, was more friendly than it had yet been. 'You were also glad to see it was but a friend, I think. For a little time you were very fierce with me.' She lifted a beautiful white hand, and caressed her shoulder rather ruefully. 'Your fingers are too strong, Captain Shannon; they hurt.'

He eyed the bruise on the satiny flesh with an air of dismay.

'Good Lord!' he ejaculated. 'Did I do that? I'm awfully sorry.'

'It is nothing,' she returned, smiling up at him, 'and I will consider it worthwhile, if now you have learnt to trust me a little.'

He regarded her in silence for some moments, rubbing a great hand reflectively to and fro on his powerful jaw.

'I'm not going to be a hypocrite,' he told her at length, 'therefore, I will not pretend that my misgivings have been entirely eradicated. There is a possibility remaining in my mind, that for some reason, I cannot fathom, you have come to me with this tale – I mean a reason quite different from the one you have given me. But it is there now merely as a possibility. I am casting aside some of my prejudices regarding you, and am endeavouring to trust you. I warn you, however, that I remain on my guard.'

'That is natural,' she conceded. 'It is something to know that you are trying to trust me and, for the future, will not be too prejudiced against me. And you will help me?'

'In what way do you think I can be of assistance?' She sank into the armchair again; accepted the cigarette he offered her.

'Is it too much to ask you to – how would you put it? Ah! Take a hand in the game?'

'I am not a free agent,' he reminded her. 'If I were, I should not hesitate at all.'

'It is nice of you to say that,' she returned gratefully. 'Can you not spare a little of your time? If that is too much for which to hope, will you please advise me? I am obstructed all ways. There are seven men I am observing, and I am but one woman. They are so cautious that I am compelled to be so very, very careful. Is there anything else I can do to obtain the information I need that I have not done?'

'What have you done?'

'What have I not done?' she retorted wearily. 'I have pumped – that is the word, I think – I have pumped Madame Bikelas and Signora Bruno until I am assured they know very little. I have done the same thing with the two secretaries, but have failed. They are stones, not men,' she added in disgusted tones. 'I have tried to flirt with the others – ah! It was distasteful. Messieurs Bruno and Bikelas are either too full of their affairs or afraid of their wives to have much to do with me. Plasiras, Michalis, and Kyprianos have returned my smiles with looks I do not like, especially the scientist who I think is a devil – he frightens me. Sometimes he looks at me but I have told you that. Monsieur Doreff is a weakling; I do not think he is of much account. My hopes rest on General Radoloff. He is perhaps in love with me. I am trying to be very, very kind to him, because, if I let him make love to me, he may talk. It is what you call a forlorn hope, though. Never can I listen at doors or by windows to their discussions, for they guard themselves too well. It is all very difficult, m'sieu.'

'It certainly sounds like it,' agreed Shannon. 'Look here, Miss Ictinos, I promise you this. I will think things over, and, if I discover a way of helping you or advising you, I will let you know somehow. Could you manage to see me again?'

She looked dubious.

'I took a great risk when I came here tonight,' she declared slowly. 'Perhaps another time I might not be so fortunate, but, of course, I will endeavour to see you – I must, if you are to help me.'

He sat on the bed; contemplated his shoes thoughtfully. Presently he looked at her.

'I suppose you sometimes go out for a walk by yourself?' he asked.

'But of course,' she laughed. 'I am not a prisoner. Often I walk alone.'

'Well, take a stroll in the Pincio Gardens at sunset tomorrow. I also will walk there. I shall keep to the path at the edge of the hill, until I come to the terrace over the Piazza del Popolo. From there I shall contemplate the view. If you arrive on the terrace, and are assured you have not been followed, you will come and speak to me. If you do not, I shall know that you are being watched, and shall ignore you if I see you. In that case, you must send a message here appointing a fresh rendezvous. How will that do?'

'It is excellent,' she proclaimed, rising to her feet. 'And are you still Captain Shannon in this hotel?'

He smiled, and nodded.

'I am,' he told her, as he helped her on with her coat, adding with a laugh: 'English officers very often visit Rome, you know.'

She held out her hand, which he grasped readily enough.

'You have relieved my anxieties very much, m'sieu,' she declared. 'When the time come that I know you trust me wholly, and have forgotten what is past, I shall be very happy. Goodnight, Captain Shannon, and thank you very much.'

He opened the door, glancing out to make certain there was no one about; then, assuring her the way was clear, let her out.

He watched her go along the corridor, admiring her graceful figure as she tripped daintily away into the distance. When she had disappeared from view, he re-entered the room and, crossing to the armchair, threw himself into its well-upholstered depths, filling and lighting a great briar he took from his pocket. Thereafter, puffing away placidly, he gave himself up to deep thought.

Thalia descended the stairs in preference to taking one of the elevators. She had almost reached the ground floor, when a young man came running up. They both moved the same way, as people often will to avoid one another; then promptly veered in the other direction. At that, both stood still and laughed, and, for a moment, gazed into each other's eyes. An expression of frank admiration came into the man's face; the girl thought how attractive he was.

'I beg your pardon, signor,' she apologised in silvery tones that sent a thrill through Dr Raymond Hill.

He did not recover himself and his manners until she was passing on.

'Forgive me, signorina,' he stammered. 'I – I am afraid you – you will think I am very rude.'

'Not at all, signor,' she replied sweetly. 'It was one of those droll situations which one cannot avoid.'

She smiled and, with a little nod, went on her way. Hill stood where he was, gazing after her until she was out of sight; then he turned, and continued the ascent, but this time did not hurry.

'Gad!' he muttered to himself. 'What a stunning girl! Her Italian was perfect, but I don't think she hails from these parts. Her beauty is more Grecian than Italian.'

He sought his room, still thinking of her, as a result of which he entirely forgot what he had gone there to seek. At the expiration of the time indicated by Shannon, he knocked at the door of the latter's room, and was immediately admitted.

'Jove, Hugh!' he exulted. 'I saw a perfectly topping girl ten minutes ago. I don't think I have ever seen anyone more beautiful.'

Shannon eyed him with an air of surprise. Hill was not given to going into rhapsodies over the other sex.

'Didn't know you were impressionable,' he grunted. 'Take a pew, and have a cigarette.'

'Prefer a pipe, thanks.' Hill took the armchair. 'She has glossy black hair, a marvellous complexion, wonderful mouth, the pearliest of teeth, and her eyes! Oh, boy, if you could only have seen them!' He sighed deeply. 'To think I shall never see her again,' he groaned.

Shannon laughed.

'As bad as all that,' he chuckled. 'Perhaps you will see her again. This is a small world.'

'Don't be so horribly trite! It isn't a small world, when you're searching it for the one girl who matters.'

'You don't mean to tell me this houri has actually captured the cold, self-centred heart of our tubby little doc!'

'I am not tubby,' protested Hill vehemently. As it was the first time Shannon had ever known the ex-doctor resent the word, he concluded the affair was serious. 'My heart is neither cold nor self-centred,' went on Hill, 'and you know it. Women simply haven't interested me before.'

The burly man sank rather weakly on the bed.

'Are you really trying to tell me,' he demanded, 'that you are in love, and with a girl you've only met today?'

Hill scratched his head with the stem of his pipe.

'It sounds darn stupid,' he admitted, 'but I believe I am. If I were in the habit of falling in and out of love like Tommy Carter, I wouldn't take any notice of it, but honestly there is nothing more I desire at this moment than to meet her again.'

'Who is she?'

'Haven't the foggiest. Dash it all! I only saw her for a moment on the stairs. We almost collided. All we have said to each other were apologies, though why she apologised to me, I don't know – it was my fault.'

'There is no such thing as love at first sight,' declared Shannon sententiously. 'Her beauty gave you a jar, that's all. It will wear off.'

'What? The beauty or the jar?' asked Hill sarcastically.

'Both,' was the reply, 'especially if she obtains the beauty from a jar.'

'Hugh Shannon,' protested the other, 'this sad and solemn moment is not the time to give expression to your extremely low sense of humour. And let me tell you that love at first sight is the only real and genuine love. Dash it all! I wish I hadn't gone up those stairs.'

'Why not? You wouldn't have met her, if you hadn't.'

'That's just it. If I hadn't met her, I should not now be suffering the pain and torment of a love that is bound to be unrequited.'

'May I remind you that you are here on duty, and not on pleasure?'

Hill nodded gloomily.

'You're right,' he agreed. 'That girl has so taken possession of my senses that I nearly forgot. We'll put her from our minds.'

'You mean you'll put her from your mind. She's not in mine. There's another girl occupying my mental equipment to the exclusion of all else.'

'You mean Helen?'

'I do not mean Helen. Even she must take a back seat just now. I refer to the lady who was here when you first called.'

'Oh, yes. Tell me about her.'

'That is exactly what I propose to do. You never met Thalia Ictinos, did you? Of course you didn't, or the chief wouldn't have sent you out.'

'I didn't meet the lady,' returned Hill, ruefully fingering a scar in his neck, 'but I have a good deal of reason for remembering her father. Sir Leonard told me the fair Thalia was with the party you are after. By Jove!' he exclaimed suddenly, 'you don't mean to tell me she was the woman here – in your room?'

'I do,' returned Shannon. 'It was Thalia Ictinos, my lad. She came to ask for my help.'

'Great Scott!' Hill's innocent blue eyes were open to their widest extent. 'Ask your help!' he echoed. 'You mean she has tumbled to your game, and is brewing something of her own?'

'I don't think she is,' replied Shannon slowly. 'She has almost persuaded me that she is genuinely in need of assistance. But light that pipe of yours – you've wasted half a box of matches on it already – and give me all your attention. I have a tale to unfold.'

Hill dutifully lit his pipe, a task he had already essayed half a dozen times only to interrupt himself. Shannon waited until the tobacco was glowing evenly.

'How much do you know about this affair?' he asked then.

'Pretty well all up-to-date I should think,' was the reply. 'Sir Leonard sent for me directly after he had been speaking to you on the telephone, and gave me the lowdown, as the Yankees call it. Of course I don't know the details of that tragic business in Cyprus. The chief and Major Brien are terribly cut up about it, especially Brien. He was almost a second father to her, I believe.'

Shannon nodded. Reference to the death of Barbara Havelock had caused his face to become grim and hard. He told Hill the full story of the events leading up to the tragedy, the fight, and the manner in which all reference to the British Secret Service had been suppressed. His own efforts to save Barbara were glossed over, but the doctor knew his colleague, and guessed a lot. Shannon then took him step by step through subsequent happenings, concluding with the coming of Thalia Ictinos to his room and the conversation he had had with her.

'What do you think?' he asked finally. 'Has she some deep and sinister motive in coming to me, or has she been entirely genuine and truthful?'

Hill pulled his right ear, a habit of his when deep in thought or perplexed.

'I find it difficult to express an opinion,' he replied. 'After all, I have never met her. You fellows, who have, always seemed to be pretty certain she was a beautiful devil with no suggestion of the angel about her anywhere, though Jerry Cousins has declared that there was a good side to her character. He, you remember, suffered rather severely at her hands.'

'Yes, and I'd back Jerry's judgment against most other people's. Personally, Tubby, I'm inclined to believe she is sincere.'

'I can't see what motive she could possibly have had in coming to you, and telling you things which you know to be true, unless she is. If she had spun a yarn which your knowledge proved to you was false, it would have been a different matter. All the same I should go warily, old chap. Remember her previous threats and expressions of hatred.'

'Aren't you helpful?' scoffed Shannon. 'You don't think I have forgotten, do you?'

'No; but it seems to me the young siren has bewitched you slightly. She must be marvellous to do even that with our Hugh.'

'She is marvellous,' Shannon retorted. 'I don't think I have ever seen a woman more beautiful, glamorous, or magnetic.'

'Coming from a man who, the whole world knows, thinks there is no woman on earth like his wife,' laughed Hill, 'that is complete evidence that Miss Thalia Ictinos is a unique being.'

'So she is. One can't get away from it. Helen is lovely, Lady Wallace is a beauty, but Thalia, in some ways, stands alone. I suppose it is her allure – she is fascinating beyond description.'

'Ha! A siren indeed. But you haven't seen the girl I met on the stairs. You wait until you do; then, believe me, Thalia Ictinos will pale into insignificance.'

'I thought you didn't know where to find her.'

'I don't.'

'Then it seems to me,' observed Shannon drily, 'that my wait will be a long one. But this isn't a discussion on the beauty of women. Listen, Ray, while I propound a scheme I have in mind. You speak German like a native, and would pass anywhere as an Austrian, even in Vienna. My idea is this: tomorrow morning I shall take you along to the house agent in the Piazza di Spagna, and introduce you as an Austrian friend of mine who has come to Rome for two or three months to study Roman art. Savvy? You will announce that you wish to rent a furnished flat, and that the block in the Ludovisi district has taken your eye.'

'Supposing it does not contain a vacant flat?' objected Hill.

'It does, my son. Thalia told me there are several vacant ones there. I will leave you to his tender mercies. No doubt he will take you round, you can find out where the others are grouped, and choose one near by. Once installed, you ought to find some means of listening in to conversations. You and I don't find guards and watchdogs a bother as a rule.' He grinned, and Hill indulged in one of his comfortable chuckles. 'You'll have to be circumspect of course,' went on Shannon. 'They're bound to regard any newcomer with suspicion, but, if you show no apparent interest in them, I don't see why you shouldn't pass muster. How does the idea appeal to you?'

'It's better than any I can think of at the moment,' was the frank reply. 'What are you going to do? Play possum?'

'No; I am going to meet Thalia in the Pincio tomorrow evening, and I shall tell her I am at her disposal. If she plays me false, it won't matter, because you will be running your show separately, and can carry on without me.'

'I can also get you out of the mess you get into I suppose?' commented Hill drily.

'Not on your life,' boomed Shannon. 'If I come to grief, you're not to interfere understand? Your job will be to find out what game those blokes are up to. It would be damn silly, if you gave yourself away by trying to rescue me. Hang it all! You know the rule of the service. Failure must not be risked, because I get in a jam.'

Hill nodded.

'No; I suppose not,' he returned, 'but you're taking a hell of a chance, old chap.'

'To hear you speak,' scoffed Shannon, 'one would imagine that was something rather unique. I am not worrying. I have a notion Thalia is playing a straight game this time. If she is, I'm all for her. If she is not,' he shrugged his shoulders; 'then I'm very much afraid someone will get hurt.' Suddenly he laughed. 'That reminds me, I'm sewn up in various odd places. Would you mind removing the stitches?'

'Let's have a look at you!' commanded Hill tersely.

Shannon removed his upper garments. The other gave vent to an exclamation, as his eyes fell on the numerous bandages. When he had removed the dressings, his ejaculations were even louder and more forcible.

'They certainly cut you about,' he remarked. 'Great Scott! Anybody else, but you, would have been in bed at least a week with wounds like these. Yet, except that you're a bit paler than usual, you don't look much the worse!'

'Rot! They're only scratches,' retorted Shannon scornfully; then he sighed deeply, and his eyes became sorrowful. 'I wish to God,' he murmured, 'that poor Barbara had escaped as lightly.'

Hill nodded.

'I'll leave the stitches in until tomorrow,' he announced, bandaging the wounds again. 'I'll also put on fresh dressings. I have a surgical case with me.'

'Do you ever travel without it?'

'Seldom. It often comes in useful, and, although I have renounced the profession of doctor, I like to keep my hand in.'

'It's nice to have a tame medico knocking about,' chuckled Shannon. 'It saves answering awkward questions.'

After breakfast the following morning, Hill accompanied the burly Shannon to the house agency in the Piazza di Spagna. The latter, who was thought by the head of the firm to be a member of the British Diplomatic Service and connected with the embassy, introduced Hill as Herr Kirche, explaining that the supposed Austrian and he had become friendly while he was attached to the British Legation in Vienna. Shannon's assurances of the integrity of his companion were good enough for Signor Bonella. He personally took Herr Kirche to view the flats in the block which the latter declared had attracted him. Shannon did not accompany them. He paid a duty call at the embassy in the Via Venti Settembre, where he was a well-known and popular figure.

It is not usual for a Secret Service agent to visit his embassy or legation in a foreign capital when engaged on any confidential duty. Secret diplomacy is a strange game. The men who play it, those particularly who run the risk of capture and imprisonment, perhaps death, have to act entirely on their own. If they are caught, they cannot, and do not, expect the governments of their countries to intercede or interfere on their behalf. They know they and their actions will be repudiated. Success brings little or no reward, failure utter and complete ruin. It has its sordid, unpleasant side this great game, but the men and women who play it are usually actuated by the noblest of all motives. Shannon, as yet, was conducting no enterprise that could in any way reflect on the British government. There was no reason, therefore, why he should not call at the embassy. Sixteen or eighteen months previously he had been stationed there as an extra attaché. The ambassador had fallen foul of a certain section of the Communists in Italy, who had threatened him. Shannon's post, as a kind of official watchdog and investigator, had become almost a sinecure, owing to the very excellent precautions taken by the Italian authorities. As he had complained to his colleagues on recall, he had not even had an opportunity of hitting someone.

He was greeted warmly, but no questions were asked concerning the reason for his presence in Rome. It is always wiser not to enquire too closely into the motives underlying a Secret Service agent's arrival in any particular place. Under certain circumstances it is necessary for them to communicate with their embassies and keep in touch with them, but unless they do, they are never questioned. Shannon was invited to stay to luncheon, but declined. He was anxious to return to the Hotel Splendide, and discover if Hill had succeeded in obtaining a flat that would be suitable for his purpose. He was sitting in the lounge when the ex-doctor strolled in. Shannon watched him approach, but gave no sign of recognition. Men who daily carry their lives in their hands are rendered extremely cautious by the very nature of their hazardous profession. There was a possibility that Plasiras and his companions had had their suspicions roused, and had set a watch on Hill with a view to ascertaining if he were actually the man he represented himself to be. However, there seemed no grounds for caution on this occasion to judge from the manner in which the fresh-faced man conducted himself. He walked up to Shannon in a perfectly open manner, smiled cheerfully at him, and threw himself into a chair at the same table.

'I'll have a Bronx, Hugh, thanks very much,' he announced.

Shannon gave the order to a waiter hovering by.

'You're sure you haven't been followed?' he asked.

'I was followed by a thin, haggard caricature of a human being, who seemed to wear a perpetual look of surprise,' was the calm reply.

'The deuce you were. What have you done with him?'

'I took him to the Grand, and lost him there by the simple expedient of dismissing my taxi, going up in an elevator as though I owned the hotel, descending by a service staircase, leaving by a back entrance, and driving here. I even drove round half of Rome to make assurance doubly sure. Frightfully untidy place, Rome.'

'How do you mean?'

'The Romans leave their ruins about so, don't you agree?'

Shannon laughed.

'S'sh!' he hissed. 'A remark like that is sacrilege in the Eternal City. I deliberately went to the Colosseum once, and smoked a pipe there. I'm not the only one who has done that of course.

There must be nearly enough cigarette ends in the place to rebuild it. I merely wanted to do my little bit towards the anachronism that is Rome.'

'I like the notion of rebuilding the Colosseum with cigarette ends,' chuckled Hill. ''Tis a quaint conceit, my Hugh. Ah!' The exclamation was in greeting to the cocktail at that moment placed before him. 'Cheer ho!'

He drained the glass, and recalled the waiter.

'Mine's a dry Martini,' Shannon told him in response to his question.

Hill gave the order.

'Dry Martinis,' he shuddered, 'are suggestive of the catacombs and gloomy people.'

'Why?'

'I don't know, unless it is because I do not like them.'

'As a doctor,' remarked Shannon severely, 'you should realise that a dry Martini is a good deal better for you than a Bronx. But we mustn't waste time on airy persiflage. It is not safe to sit here together too long. You may have shaken off Kyprianos – obviously it was he – but if some of them came here for dinner they might just as likely come for luncheon, and it would be as well if you were not seen. You are not registered as Herr Kirche remember.'

'I am not forgetting,' returned Hill complacently. He seemed to be bubbling over with an emotion he was endeavouring to suppress. Shannon did not question him, feeling sure he would be told before long. 'I have obtained what the ladies would call a perfectly ducky flat,' went on the other. 'What is more, my son, it is on the second floor at the end of a hall. And – listen! – It is flanked by the flat occupied by Doreff and Plasiras on one side, and by that occupied by Radoloff, Michalis and Kyprianos on the other. Furthermore, on the other side of the wall of my sitting room is the sitting room of Radoloff and company, while the sitting room of Doreff and Plasiras is beyond one of the walls of my bedroom.'

'By Jove! That is great,' exulted Shannon. 'How did you find that out?'

'By my well-known and infallible methods of question and deduction,' grinned Hill. 'I also discovered that Bikelas and his wife occupy a flat opposite Bruno's on the floor below. I rather wondered why they didn't take mine but dare not be too nosey about them. There's a ladies drawing room on that floor, and I presume that's the reason.'

'Did you see any of them?'

'Only the fellow you call Kyprianos. He poked his head out of a door, and watched. His Christian name, if he has one, must be Suspicion, I think. His long, pointed nose indicates it.'

'You don't think he followed you because he had any grounds on which to base his suspicion?'

'Not on your life. He's just naturally curious. He'd probably follow the Pope, if he saw him inspecting a flat near one he occupied.'

'Beware of him, Ray,' warned Shannon. 'I am inclined to believe he constitutes our greatest danger.'

'He is ticketed, numbered, and ear-marked,' declared Hill. 'I had already sensed that he was not nice to know. I do hope he is enjoying himself at the Grand. Now for my surprise.'

'Yes; get it off your chest, or you'll burst.'

'How did you know there was anything else?'

'I'm not blind. What is it?'

'I've seen *her* – my girl of the stairs. She was walking near the block when I left. I couldn't stop, because I knew Kyprianos was in a taxi behind. She was attired in a neat, tailor-made suit that seemed part of her, and a little hat, nevertheless I recognised her, even though last night she wore an ermine coat and no hat.'

'What's that?' suddenly boomed Shannon, raising his voice much louder than he intended. 'Did you say she wore an ermine coat last night?'

'Yes,' nodded the surprised Hill. 'Why? Do you know her?'

'Describe her,' snapped his companion.

'I did last night.'

'I wasn't taking much notice then. Do it again!' Hill obliged, and, despite the numerous superlatives, gave the other a very good and unmistakable description of Thalia.

'And so that is the girl with whom you have fallen in love!' commented Shannon, laughing in a manner Hill thought distinctly queer.

'Do you know her by any chance?' he asked.

'I certainly do,' came the grave response. 'She, my dear Tubby, is Thalia Ictinos!'

CHAPTER TWELVE

A Meeting in the Pincio

Hill's head went back with a jerk, and he blinked rather like a man who had received a blow in the face.

'You're joking,' he gasped

'I certainly am not. Your description was rather flowery, and perhaps a little exaggerated, but it fits Thalia perfectly. The fact that she was here last night, wore a magnificent ermine coat, and would have been descending the stairs at about the time you met the lady, removes any doubt that may otherwise have lingered in my mind. I was a fool not to have guessed it before, but, as I remarked, I did not pay any particular attention to your previous description of her.'

Hill tugged at his ear.

'The situation requires a good deal of thought,' he murmured.

'It does. The question we have to consider is: how will she react to your arrival in a flat above the one in which she is living?'

'Goodness knows. She'll probably think I followed her, found out where she resided, and took a flat in the same building to be near her.'

'I hope that is all she does think. On the other hand, she may gather that you are in some way connected with me, and that I have sent you there to watch her and her companions. If her game is treachery; then, in that case, you are going to be in danger, and your chances of making any discoveries absolutely nullified. She is bound to know you are there. When you apologised to each other last night, what language did you speak?'

'Italian.'

'Well, that's one blessing. She, therefore, has no reason to suspect you of being English, and your pretence of Austrian nationality might stand. She's very clever, however, and is quite likely to connect you with the man who knocked at my door and who I told her was a friend. I can't say I like the position, Ray. More than ever seems to depend now upon whether she is playing straight with me or not. If she is not—' he stopped, and shrugged his huge shoulders significantly. 'When are you taking up your residence in the flat?' he asked.

'This afternoon,' returned Hill. 'Oh, Lord!' he groaned, 'I can hardly believe that lovely girl can be the devil you fellows have painted Thalia Ictinos.'

'Perhaps our painting was a bit lurid,' remarked Shannon in soothing tones. 'I am inclined to believe, from my impressions of her now and her apparent honesty to me, that it was. At the same time, you and I cannot afford to lose sight of the fact that she is Stanislas Ictinos' daughter, and that she was concerned with him in his operations.'

Hill drained his glass; rose to his feet.

'Go up to your room,' he bade the other abruptly. 'I will be along there in a few minutes to dress your wounds.'

He walked away, Shannon watching him go with sympathy shining from his eyes. He had not taken seriously before his colleague's assertion that he had fallen in love with the girl he had met on the stairs. Now he felt he could no longer doubt it. The expression on Hill's face, his demeanour, was that of a man who had been badly hit. He had gone away as much to be alone for a few minutes and attempt to adjust himself to this new situation as to obtain the instruments and dressings necessary to enable him to attend to Shannon. The latter followed him presently, a thoughtful frown on his broad forehead, his jaw appearing perhaps a little more aggressive than usual. Hill did not make his appearance in his companion's room for nearly half an hour. He removed the stitches, and put fresh bandages on the wounds in silence, not uttering a word until he had finished.

'There, that will do,' he grunted. 'They're healing beautifully, but don't attempt to throw people about for a few days or you'll open them again.' He packed up his neat case of instruments. 'Now, Hugh,' he demanded, 'what about it?'

'What about what?' asked Shannon.

'You know what I mean,' he said impatiently. 'Am I to carry on as per your previous instructions, or have you thought out a fresh scheme?'

'I did consider taking your place in the flat,' admitted the other, 'but I don't think it would be wise. Thalia may, and will, I hope, consider that your personal interest in her has led you to engage a flat in the same building. She may even regard it as coincidence, but that is rather too much to expect. My advice to you is to cultivate her society as a man does cultivate the society of a girl who attracts him. It might even be wise to confess to her, when you get to know her a little better, that you followed her on account of the interest roused in you at your first meeting, discovered that there were some vacant flats adjacent to hers, and took one to be near her.

An appearance of frankness is more disarming than any amount of subterfuge.'

An expression of distaste crossed Hill's face.

'But telling her I had followed her and all the rest of it is subterfuge,' he protested. 'Damn it all, man! Can't you see what being in daily contact with her will mean to me? I am not the type of man that falls in love easily. It sounds darn ridiculous to you, I suppose, that I can possibly be in love with a girl whom I only saw for about a minute. It seems absurd to me, but there it is. I hadn't a notion before that love could grip with such an intensity of longing. I'd give my soul to marry her, and that's no jest. The fact that she is proved to be Thalia Ictinos makes no difference to me at all. It has given me a nasty jar, but it hasn't altered my feelings for her. If I am in constant contact with her, the longing for her will become intensified. What then?'

'You and I cannot put personal feelings before our job, Tubby,' replied Shannon quietly. 'It is part of the price we have to pay for playing the great game that we are compelled to make sacrifices. I know exactly how you feel, at least I think I do. But, if in the interests of the service and the country you are compelled to sacrifice Thalia and your newborn love for her, you will do it. That goes without saying.'

Hill nodded. His face was very pale; in his eyes an expression of pain.

'You're right, of course,' he murmured. 'It seems that I am to be brought up hard and grimly against one of the realities of our profession. It is a pity in a sense I was not called upon to make a sacrifice before. I am not well prepared.'

'You sacrificed a brilliant and promising career as a doctor, didn't you?'

'Was it a sacrifice? Not a bit of it. The chance came. It was an opportunity I grasped eagerly with both hands. No, old chap; there was no sacrifice in taking up the greater work and dropping the lesser. Now things are different. The possibility of seeing Thalia crushed into ruin with others through my handiwork is not nice to – to contemplate.'

Shannon's hearty laugh boomed through the room.

'Hang it all!' he exclaimed. 'What a couple of dismal jimmies we are becoming! What about the other side of the picture, Ray? If Thalia is now what she has represented herself to be, what then? You and I will be working with, not against her. You will not be attempting to bring the girl you love to destruction; you will be assisting her to achieve a great triumph. After that – well, if she reciprocates your love, what more natural than that you and she should marry?' His eyes shone. 'Jove, old lad! The thought even thrills me. To be loved by a girl like Thalia would be marvellous I think.'

'Marvellous indeed,' agreed Hill, 'but as though Thalia Ictinos would fall in love with me! The idea is ridiculous.'

'Why on earth is it?'

'What is there in me to appeal to her? I can't think of a single thing. I'm nothing to look at – I'm rather inclined to embonpoint, and—'

Shannon interrupted him with another laugh. 'You told me last night you were not tubby, Tubby,' he reminded him. 'What's the matter? Has love had the effect on you that it is usually supposed to have on most men. Has your red blood turned to water in your veins?'

He slapped the other on the back with such heartiness that he almost sent him headlong to the floor. 'Go in and win, old man.'

'And if she proves to be still the Thalia Ictinos of London?' questioned Hill soberly.

'We won't think of that. At least we'll keep the thought in the background until we can bury it for ever.' He held out his hand, which Hill gripped firmly. 'Good luck, Tubby,' he murmured quietly. 'May she prove true blue for all our sakes, but particularly for yours.'

'Thanks, Hugh.'

The ex-doctor left the room, and Shannon descended to lunch.

No finer view of Rome can be obtained than that from the Pincio. It is a favourite rendezvous at sunset and, as Shannon strolled towards the terrace over the Piazza del Popolo, he found himself in the midst of a gay and happy crowd of people of all ages and callings. Bands of seminarists, with varied splashes of colour on their soutanes, according to their nationalities, passed and repassed. Elegant young Romans stood or sat in groups discussing the events of the day. Nurses chatted, whilst their olive-skinned charges played merrily round them, and foster mothers lovingly tended their babies. Here and there lovers met happily, wandering away arm in arm to find sequestered spots where they could tell that age-old story, which can never die, to each other in comparative privacy. A band was playing beneath the trees, an appreciative throng surrounding it and applauding enthusiastically its tuneful melodies. As a promenade and park, the Pincio can surely have few superiors in Europe. There is no place more perfect for repose and rest in hot weather, no place more ideal in which to walk in the cold weather.

Shannon gazed appreciatively at the ilexes above and the pomegranates under the wall below, as he sauntered along; stood for some minutes regarding the skilfully tended gardens stretching away beyond the pomegranates. He came at length to the terrace, and an involuntary gasp of admiration broke from his lips, even though he had often viewed the same scene before. Sunsets in Rome can be very wonderful; this one was particularly gorgeous. Shannon looked, and understood now why someone had said that sunset in Rome was 'stained with the blood of martyrs.' The city from that viewpoint was sublime, impressive, serene. St Peter's towered over all in its immensity, with half a dozen, at least, smaller imitations of it showing in various districts. The dome of the Pantheon, the Courts of Justice, the great Vittorio Emmanuele II monument stood as striking landmarks, and the Englishman noticed how the horizon seemed to cut in two the Archangel Michael on his Castello. He amused himself in idle pleasure by picking out the Colosseum, the Forum, the Palatine and other famous buildings, of which he was able to catch a glimpse. He was thus engaged when a hand lightly touched his arm. He swung round to confront Thalia, looking delicious in a well-cut suit of a crushed-strawberry colour with a close fitting little hat to match. Her lips opened in a smile, her great grey-blue eyes sparkled merrily.

'Am I to believe,' she questioned, 'that this giant of a man, who I hope is going to be my friend, has a soul which appreciates the beauty he sees around him?'

'You are,' asserted Shannon. 'I may not look it, but I am a great admirer of the beautiful.'

Her creamy skin flushed slightly at the obviously implied compliment. She looked frankly pleased. Turning towards the city she gave a deep sigh; spread out her hands in rapturous enjoyment.

'Is it not wonderful?' she murmured. 'Were there ever sunsets to be compared with these of Rome? I have watched the sun sinking to his rest from the Olympieion in Athens, behind the pyramids in Egypt – oh! In many places – but never, I think, is the sunset more impressive than here in Rome. Does it not even make you feel insignificant, my friend, to look on this age-old city, and reflect on the glory that has dwelt here? I! I always feel myself to be a mortal of the puniest.'

He eyed her thoughtfully as well as with a great sense of appreciation. Here was no lovely shell – a woman without a soul. Her half-open lips, her glowing eyes, the joy in her face spoke eloquently of the deep love that was in her for the beautiful. She continued to speak almost in rapt tones of the wonders of Rome. Shannon discovered that she had an intimate knowledge which he could never hope to acquire. Of Michael Angelo, Bernini and, above all, Raphael, she spoke in the voice of one worshipping at a hallowed shrine, and in the few minutes they spent together on the terrace of the Pincio she did more to eradicate the distrust in his mind than any protestations and avowals she could ever have uttered. No woman with her sensibilities could be really wicked, he decided; there was bound to be good of the most intrinsic worth in a soul with such appreciative and delicate sentience. She could not be cold, or cruel, or hard at heart. Through her veins flowed warm, red, pure blood, and fortunate indeed would be the man who could rouse in her the powerful, ardent devotion which Shannon now instinctively knew lay latent in her. She was a woman who, once her heart had been touched, would bestow a priceless love on the man of her choice. 'God!' reflected the big Englishman involuntarily, 'how she would love!' His thoughts went immediately to Raymond Hill, and with them went a devout hope that his friend might find with Thalia Ictinos a great, imperishable happiness. She turned impulsively to him, a little spot of colour in each alabaster-like cheek testifying to the fervour and enthusiasm which had been roused within her.

'Your pardon, mon ami,' she begged. 'I fear I have let my feelings run away with me. Things that are beautiful have always that effect on me. I think, perhaps, you are bored; yes?'

'Good Lord, no,' he assured her earnestly. 'It has been a delight to listen to you. Probably, as a result, I shall feel a greater appreciation of the art that is in Rome in the future. And, of all the artists who built up her imperishable glory, you consider Raphael the greatest?'

'Who does not?' she returned. 'Is not the couplet on his tomb, which was composed by the Cardinal Bembo, truly appropriate and descriptive? You know it?'

'I have read it,' he confessed, 'but cannot call it to mind at the moment.'

'I can never forget it. Listen! In English it goes:

Nature, who feared the unequal strife
With Raphael in his glorious life,
Was smitten with a deeper dread
That she might die when he was dead.

Is it not beautiful?'

'Very,' returned Shannon soberly.

They stood silent for some moments; then she took his arm.

'Come!' she bade him reluctantly. 'We must leave the things that are sublime, and discuss matters that are sordid. I wish it could be otherwise, for, after thinking of things of such great nobility and purity, it is like a sacrilege to speak of – those others. Standing there has made me feel very much sad, Captain Shannon, because of the cruel and wicked things I have done. Come!'

They walked away quietly together until they came to a vacant seat standing alone amidst the trees. There they sat side by side, each feeling that in some subtle manner a camaraderie had been born between them.

'You are quite sure you have not been followed?' he asked.

'I am certain,' she assured him. 'I took precautions of the most vigilant. And now what have you to tell me? Can I hope that perhaps you have decided to help me?'

He looked at her to find her great eyes fixed anxiously on his face. He smiled, and nodded.

'Yes, Miss Ictinos,' he told her, 'I have resolved to do all I can to help you. It is fortunate,' he added, feeling a trifle ashamed, but showing nothing of his inner thoughts in his face, 'that my duties in Rome are not onerous, and will allow me to devote practically all my time, for the present at least, to your service.'

She gave a little cry of pleasure, which sounded thoroughly genuine.

'But this is wonderful!' she exclaimed. 'I did not hope for so much. You trust me then, and we are to be comrades?'

'Comrades by all means,' he rejoined, 'and I think that even my suspicious nature is lulled to sleep as far as you are concerned.'

'God be praised!' she cried fervently. 'I am indeed fortunate beyond my deserts. Tell me: have you thought of a way by which we can find out what those men are plotting?'

'Do you think it would be possible for us to insert a microphone in the room which is used most for their discussions?'

Remembrance of the manner in which the agents of Plasiras and Bikelas had endeavoured to obtain information from the Colonial Office had recurred to him on the previous night. It would be rather apt, he thought, if he could return the compliment. She frowned a little.

'A microphone!' she repeated. 'Even if it were possible to put in place such an instrument, how could you or I listen to what was happening?'

'That would be the least difficult part of the undertaking. Tell me how the flats are situated.'

She gave him the information which he had already obtained from Hill.

'At the end of the hall on the second floor is another flat,' she added, 'which I thought perhaps you might occupy, but today it has been let.'

'Do you know who has taken it? Is he someone connected with your people?'

She shook her head.

'I only know that he is an Austrian gentleman by the name of Herr Kirche,' she replied. 'I am quite certain he is not known to the men I am observing. In fact, I heard Monsieur Kyprianos grumble about his coming. He said it was a great pity that a stranger should have come to live there, and that they would have been better advised to have rented that suite of rooms as well. You see, Monsieur Shannon, the rooms occupied by General Radoloff and Messieurs Kyprianos, and Michalis are opposite those of Messieurs Doreff and Plasiras. The flat of the Austrian gentleman is at the end of the hall adjoining both. It might have been very useful for you.'

Shannon nodded.

'Perhaps it would have been,' he agreed; 'yet I think, after all, it would be better if I did not live there, I do not wish to be seen particularly. Have you met the Austrian?'

'No, but no doubt I will. You are interested in him?'

'I am interested in everyone in that part of the building. Of course, you do not know which room is most likely to be used for conferences; that is hardly to be expected.'

'But I do,' she cried triumphantly. 'All the time my ears are very wide open—'

'They are not very big,' he commented, glancing appreciatively at the one little shell-like appendage within his view.

She laughed.

'Not very big – no, but they hear well,' she declared. 'I learnt through these ears that are not big that the room of Monsieur Kyprianos is the one chosen for the discussions they will have. The bed has been removed, and in its place has been put a chair which becomes a bed at night. The room is now being fitted like a laboratory.'

'H'm! They're wasting no time. Did Kyprianos receive the case of which you told me?'

'He obtained the permit yesterday through the influence of Signor Bruno. This afternoon the boat arrived from Naples, and he went with the two secretaries to obtain the box.'

'I see. I suppose you haven't been able to obtain a glimpse of Kyprianos' apartment?'

'No, but mine is directly underneath, and I believe is the same.'

'Is it, by Jove! Then, Miss Ictinos, I think I see a way.'

'Do you?' she asked excitedly. 'Please tell me! But, first, would it not be nicer for you to call me Thalia now we are comrades?'

He smiled.

'Thalia it shall be,' he agreed. 'My name is Hugh.'

'I know. I heard that it was when – but I wish to forget that time. Will you please continue – Hugh.'

'My idea all depends on the size of your fireplace and chimney. Is it one of the large kind one sees in so many houses in Rome?'

'Yes; it is very big, and very ornamental.'

'Good. Then tonight at midnight I will come to the building, if you will give me the address. Will you meet me outside, in order that I may know if the way is clear, and lead me to your room?'

She looked quickly at him in a half-startled fashion.

'Lead you to my room!' she echoed.

'Yes; you're not afraid of me, are you, Thalia?'

She laughed.

'But no; of course I am not. But why do you wish to enter my room?'

'I will bring with me a microphone and connections. Once in your room, I shall climb up the chimney, and fix the microphone in position adjacent to the room of Kyprianos. Then you and sometimes I will be able to listen to the conversation.'

'How splendid!' she cried; then looked him up and down dubiously. 'But I doubt very much that you can climb up even that wide chimney – you are so big.'

'I think I can manage. If not, we shall have to think of some other way. Will there be much risk to you in admitting me?'

'We cannot bother about the risk,' she retorted. 'Entering from the outside hall there is a passage. The sitting room, which is also a dining room, if it is necessary, comes first; then is my bedroom. Beyond it is the room occupied by Madame and Monsieur – a very large room that. At the end of the little corridor is the apartment of the secretary, and next to it the bathroom. To come to you I will not have to pass by the other rooms, you will see, so there is not so much danger as there would be, if mine were at the end.'

'Is there a hall porter?'

'Yes; but only in the daytime. At night his little glass room is empty.'

'You are sure of that?'

'But certainly. Did I not pass by last night? It was locked up.'

'Everything seems to be arranged to suit my purpose,' he commented. 'Then tonight at midnight! If you do not come to me, I will conclude there is danger, but I will wait for an hour. If you have not come by one o'clock, I will go away, and return again tomorrow night. Is that understood?'

'Yes; I will come, unless they are about and make it impossible.'

'You must not take any risks. Remember that everything depends on your remaining unsuspected, besides we must ensure that you do not run into danger.'

'That is nothing,' she remarked simply, 'so long as my country does not suffer.'

He made a note of her address, though, of course, he already knew it. Then they parted. He watched her as she walked away, her elegance once again charming him. Every movement Thalia Ictinos made was graceful, and yet all were eminently natural. There was nothing studied or artificial about her at all, a fact which undeniably added to her charm. Shannon found it increasingly difficult to realise that she was the same girl who had taken a delight in keeping his colleague Cousins chained to a wall, and had heaped humiliations upon him. It seemed ridiculous to think of the Thalia Ictinos who had just left him as the same Thalia Ictinos who had apparently been so entirely cruel-minded and callous. He came to the conclusion that she had spoken nothing but the truth in attributing her character, as he had previously known it, to the influence of her father. In her was undoubtedly a streak of the ruthlessness and cruelty of her parent, who had taken care to nourish and sustain it. Freed from his sway, she had reverted to her real self, the self Shannon had discovered in this new acquaintance with her. He began to feel sure of her; yet his natural caution, and the great issues which depended so much on him, compelled him to remain on his guard. If he had been helping her, as he firmly believed she thought, simply because she had appealed to him, it is certain that he would by then have cast all prejudices against her finally aside, and entered into his association with her eagerly and wholeheartedly.

He left the Pincio and, walking along until he came to the famous Spanish stairs, glowing warmly yellow in the dying light, descended the hundred and thirty-seven to the Piazza di Spagna below. The flower-sellers had not yet left their stations, and the whole place looked a mass of blossoms. Here and there still lingered a few artists' models, hopeful of obtaining employment for the morrow, the men conspicuous by their picturesque hair and of course, the inevitable umbrellas. Shannon went on until he came to the Rome agency of the famous Parisian firm of *Lalére et Cie*, whose perfumes are world famous. It was beyond business hours, and most of the employees had departed, but the manager, an Englishman of the name of Tempest, was still on the premises. Shannon announced that he wished to see him about an order he had recently given, and sent in his name. Almost at once he was shown into the agent's sanctum. A tall, keen-eyed man rose and greeted him.

'What can I do for you, Shannon?' he asked.

The burly Secret Service man glanced round the cosy office.

'Are we quite safe here?' he asked.

'Perfectly. This room, as I think you know, has been constructed with a main regard to my principal object in being in Rome. Have a cigarette?'

'Thanks. Well, Tempest, old boy, I want a microphone, and extra long connections. And I want it before eleven tonight. Can do?'

Tempest nodded.

'Yes, I think I can manage that OK. What's going on? Anything in my line?'

Shannon grinned.

'His eyes gleamed with the blood lust, he sniffed the air as though scenting battle from afar. That about describes you, my lad.'

'Are you quoting from something?' asked Tempest suspiciously.

'Heaven forbid. I leave that sort of thing to Cousins. It sounds like a quotation, though, doesn't it?'

'It does. Last time Cousins was in here he spouted reams of quotations until my brain had become a kind of poetical cocktail, in which the chief ingredients were spirits of Shelley, essence of Keats, a few drops of Byron and Tennyson, and bitters of Pope.'

Shannon laughed.

'That's about how the old lad makes me feel.'

'Well, you haven't told me,' persisted Tempest. 'Is there anything doing in my line?'

'No, my boy; do you think I dare drag a respectable agent of *Lalére et Cie* into my sordid affairs? You supply the microphone, that's your pidgin.'

'I am growing fat and lazy running this show,' complained the other. 'I wish Sir Leonard would give me a chance to show my paces.'

Shannon eyed his spare, lean form and chuckled.

'I am glad you told me you were growing fat,' he commented. 'Concerning your second remark, it seems to me you've shown your paces often enough. You have one priceless gift which I wish

I possessed; I mean your ability to lip-read. Perhaps I may need to make use of it before I'm through with this business. Listen, and I'll put you wise.'

He spoke earnestly for nearly half an hour, the interested Tempest listening without interruption; then Shannon rose to depart.

'That's that,' he remarked finally. 'If Hill and I disappear you'll know where to direct whoever comes after us to commence investigations. How will you send along the microphone?'

'In a box, well labelled,' grinned Tempest. 'Everyone will think you're giving your best girl a specially large present. How is Mrs Shannon by the way?'

'Fine. Well, cheer-ho, old son. Don't forget – the Splendide, room one, two, four!'

They shook hands, and Shannon walked out. Although the actual name of the firm of *Lalére et Cie* is slightly different, the great and prosperous business exists. Its headquarters is in Paris, from where it is directed by the genial Monsieur Lalére himself. It has branches or agencies in all the big capitals, and the managers and agents have their offices, attend to the business affairs which grow greater year by year, and draw their salaries. But it was originally founded by money supplied by Sir Leonard Wallace, and the ladies and gentlemen who represent it are members of the British Secret Service.

A box, well pasted with labels, on which the name of *Lalére et Cie* stood out in bold letters, duly arrived at the Hotel Splendide addressed to Shannon. It was taken to him by a smart pageboy, who smiled knowingly as he handed it in. Inside was the microphone, carefully wrapped up, with connections, which the Secret Service man was satisfied were amply long for his purpose. A pair of headphones completed the equipment. At the bottom of the box was a large bottle of scent of a kind much favoured by his wife, with a card attached bearing Tempest's name and the written message: 'With compliments to Mrs Shannon.' Hugh smiled at the thought which had prompted the gift.

'Good old Tempest,' he murmured, 'bully for you. And now to wait for the witching hour.'

CHAPTER THIRTEEN

Up a Chimney

Thalia Ictinos returned home after her meeting with Shannon, and entered the main doors of the great elegant building in the Ludovisi quarter, quite unaware that Fate in the person of a blue eyed, boyish-looking man with fair hair and a jolly face was awaiting her there. She was walking towards the stairs, thinking it was hardly worthwhile going to the first floor in an elevator, when she heard hurried steps descending; looked up to see the immaculately-dressed man of whom she had thought more than once since the night before. He stopped two steps from the bottom; she stood where she was, and gradually a vivid blush stole up from her peerless neck until it had suffused her face. Hill's heart gave a great bound within him. He did not know much about women, but surely, he thought, that blush meant something in the face of a girl who looked as though blushing were not a habit with her. He took off his hat, which had previously shaded his eyes, and Thalia recognised in them something that spoke directly to her heart, something that she could not mistake.

'Signor!' she faltered.

'Signorina,' he returned in unsteady, husky tones, 'this is wonderful! It seems that we are fated to meet on stairs, though you are not actually standing on them. Ever since last night I have thought of you as "My lady of the stairs".'

'That is nice of you, signor,' she replied, smiling gloriously at him.

'It is nice of you,' he corrected gently, 'not to be angry with me for my presumption in daring to think of you under such a title.'

'Why should I be angry?' she asked. 'Perhaps I, too, have thought with amusement of the manner in which you and I strove to pass, and could not.'

'With amusement only?' he queried, a note of reproach in his voice.

'Were you not amused?'

'I was angry with myself for my clumsiness. Yet, if I had not been clumsy, I should not have had the delight of hearing your voice.' He came down the remaining steps; stood facing her. 'The memory of it has remained with me ever since,' he told her. 'I think stairs will always be associated in my mind with what was a wonderful experience to me.'

She laughed softly. The blush had gone now, leaving her satiny skin looking whiter, more alabaster-like than ever.

'And now,' she commented, 'that experience has been nearly repeated, but perhaps it is not so wonderful this time.'

'If possible, it is more wonderful,' he breathed.

'You have the trick of making compliments like an Italian,' she remarked, 'but I do not think you are an Italian. Am I not right?'

'I am an Austrian, signorina. May I present myself? My name is Kirche – Raymond Kirche.'

'I am very pleased to know you, Herr Kirche,' came quickly from her in perfect German. 'I am Thalia Ictinos, and I am of Greek blood.' He bowed. A sudden light of understanding flashed into her eyes. 'Are you the gentleman,' she asked, 'who has today taken the vacant flat on the second floor?'

'I am, Fraulein.'

'But how extraordinary it is. I – I mean,' she added in dainty confusion, 'it is strange, is it not? That last night we should meet on the stairs of the Hotel Splendide, and today you rent a flat in the building where I live.'

Hill's eyes were lowered. He hated himself for the lie he was about to tell her. Better that, however, for everybody's sake, than that she should grow suspicious of him.

'Signorina,' he confessed, reverting to Italian, 'I fear that there is much I am about to beg you to forgive. Perhaps you will not be able to find it in your heart to forgive, but I should hate myself, if I were not honest with you.'

How he wished he were in a position to be really honest with her! This second meeting had consolidated already the love he felt for her. At that moment he was in peril of risking all by a declaration from his heart of the whole truth. He mastered his inclinations with a great effort. His words had startled her a little. He looked up to find her great slate-blue eyes gazing at him with something approaching trepidation.

'I do not understand,' she murmured. 'What can I have to forgive you, when you and I are strangers?'

'Were strangers, signorina,' he corrected. 'I hope that that word can, after this, never be applied to us again. Last night I knew that I could not feel any peace unless I met you once more, at least. I took the unpardonable liberty of following you. I found that you lived here. This morning I went to the agent, and enquired about flats in this building. To my joy, I found there were several. I took the vacant one on the second floor. I wished so much to be near you. Signorina, I beg of you not to be angry with me because of my presumption. Will you forgive me, and grant me the great privilege of your friendship?'

Thalia was thoroughly startled now; not only that, but he thought to see the shadow of fear in her eyes. Possibly, he reflected, she was worried at the idea that she had been thus followed from the Hotel Splendide, when she had taken precautions to avoid such a contingency. Also it was likely that she feared his coming would be misunderstood by her companions. If she had been honest with Shannon, she might anticipate that Hill would be regarded with suspicion by the people she had asserted she was watching, and any association with him bring danger on her. Whatever was in her thoughts, the startled look presently passed away, and she favoured him with one of her glorious smiles.

'I suppose,' she pronounced, 'that I really should be very angry with you, but, as you have been so candid with me, I do not think I can be.' He commenced to speak, but she raised a gloved hand with a little imperious gesture. 'I am flattered, signor, that I should have made such an impression on you that you desired to be near me. Alas! I fear, however, that friendship between us is impossible.'

'Oh, but why?' he demanded.

'I am not my own mistress, otherwise I should be honoured. I also will be frank. I know you to be a gentleman – I think I am a good judge – and your interest in me to be due to no ignoble motives. If circumstances were different, it would give me much pleasure to accept your friendship, and give you mine. But I am merely the companion to a lady who is staying here.'

'What does that matter?' he asked eagerly. 'It makes no difference to me what you are.'

'What would you say, if I told you I was a scheming, perhaps wicked woman, who had been mixed up in sordid intrigue, even in crime?'

'I would say that you were either not being truthful, or that you were not responsible for being concerned in anything of a sordid nature. I would swear that your character was pure, even if circumstances proved the reverse.'

Her eyes glistened. He wondered if the tears were near; then the music of her laugh floated round the hall.

'You are very daring to take me on trust in such a manner,' she observed lightly.

'Am I not asking you to take me on trust?' he demurred.

She shook her head.

'I do not mistake integrity when I see it so openly before my eyes,' she contended. 'But we are talking like old friends not new acquaintances. I must go, Signor Kirche.'

'And is that friendship, for which I ask, quite impossible?'

'I do not know – I fear it is,' she replied in troubled tones. 'You must let me think. There are other circumstances, besides my employment, which may prevent it. I will talk to my employer about this ardent, young man who has come so suddenly into my life.'

Her smile, as she made the last remark, was full of a tenderness he found irresistible.

'I pray,' he murmured, 'that I may stay in your life.'

'Hush!' she chided. 'For an Austrian you are very impetuous, my friend. Has the air of Italy already had its influence on you?'

'Not the air of Italy, signorina, but a daughter of Greece who is ornamenting the Eternal City.'

'You must not say things like that. Rome is noble, sublime. To speak of me in such a manner is desecration to this wonderful city.' She made as though to pass on, but he stayed her. 'Please let me go. I must not stop here.'

'Can you not give me hope that you and I will be friends?' he urged.

'I have told you, I must think. Afterwards I will tell you. Sometime we will meet.'

'Sometime!' he echoed in dismay. 'That sounds dreadful. Please make it more definite than that.'

'Very well,' she smiled. 'Tomorrow morning at eleven I will walk on the terrace of the Pincio. Perhaps Signor Kirche may also be there – who knows? If so, it is possible we may meet.'

His eyes shone, a happy smile lighted up a face that had been gloomy far longer than was its habit.

'I will live for tomorrow morning, Signorina Ictinos,' he vowed.

'There is one thing I must ask you,' she whispered seriously. 'You are a man of honour; you will promise me. Please do not at any time mention to a soul that we first met on the stairs at the Hotel Splendide. Let it be thought, if you wish, that we first met here and today. Will you promise this to me?'

'Assuredly, signorina; you have my word.'

'You do not wish to know why I ask this?'

'It is not my business.'

'Thank you very much, signor. I am very grateful.'

'You have no objection to my remembering in my secret heart that it was on the stairs of the Splendide that we met?'

She smiled.

'I cannot prevent your doing that, can I? I also will never forget it – in my secret heart,' she added in a murmur that was the sweetest of music to his ears.

She passed on, and he watched her go, his very soul in his eyes for all the world to see. At the top of the great staircase she bent over the banisters, and smiled down at him. He turned rather like a man bemused to walk out of the building; found the caretaker in his little glass enclosed nook regarding him with a broad smile.

'The signorina is very beautiful,' the man observed as Hill approached.

'She is perfect!' declared the young man with ardent emphasis. 'The most wonderful of women.'

'Ah! I think that the signor has something of the warmth of Italy in his blood.'

Hill passed on. He almost felt that the doorkeeper was right. Thalia had roused in him an ardour and élan that he would, at one time, have considered foreign to his nature.

It was exactly midnight, when Hugh Shannon, carrying a parcel, and attired in a dark suit with a soft hat pulled well down over his eyes, arrived in the vicinity of the building wherein he felt so much that was mysterious and sinister was going on. It was a dark night, but the road was well-lighted, while a glow of illumination was diffused before the entrance by an artistic electric lamp. He had not long to wait. A figure emerged from the half-open door, and flitted like a shadow towards where he had taken up his stand.

'I saw you pass under one of the lights, Hugh,' whispered Thalia. 'Come quickly; all is well at the moment, but, if we delay, there may be interruptions.'

He followed her without a word, both of them taking care to avoid the light as much as possible. They crept into the dimly-lit hall, she preceding him to make certain there was no one about. A pause of a few seconds occupied in listening, and they ascended the broad, artistic staircase. At the top she bade him wait a little while, and left him. In a few moments she was back and, taking him by the hand, led him to a door standing ajar. Pushing it open, they entered, and he found himself in a well-lit but narrow corridor. Almost opposite was a room into which she quickly guided him. He glanced appreciatively round the dainty apartment, which, though she had occupied it for so short a time, seemed to contain the indefinable atmosphere of her personality. She closed and locked the door, sighing her relief.

'It was a little trying to the nerves,' she confessed in a whisper. 'Please remember to speak in a very low voice, for beyond that wall is the room of Monsieur and Madame Bikelas. Madame is, I think, yet awake.'

'Awake!' he murmured. 'Wasn't it rather risky to fetch me under the circumstances?'

She shrugged her shoulders which gleamed entrancingly under the glare of the electricity. She was clothed in a lace evening gown of aquamarine blue which suited her to perfection; over one arm she carried a black Spanish shawl; a diamond necklace that must have been very valuable hung round her neck. As usual her almost blue-black glossy hair was brushed lightly back, displaying her little white ears, in each of which shone a diamond. If possible she looked more alluring, more captivating than ever.

'I had no choice,' she told him. 'A party of us went to the opera. Afterwards the men went together to the room of Kyprianos. They may be there for a very long time. I think tonight they have a most important conference. I heard Monsieur Bikelas inform Madame that he would be late, and she must go to bed. If I had waited, the danger would increase, for at any time he and his secretary might come down. I thought it would be safer for you to come while only Madame was here.'

He nodded.

'You are right.' He smiled at her. It seemed to him that there was something different about her. The slight suggestion of hardness in her face was gone completely. He thought to see a new gentleness there that he had certainly not noticed before. 'Thalia,' he told her candidly, 'you look bewitching tonight. You are always beautiful, but tonight you are more wonderful than ever.'

She smiled up at him gladly.

'Perhaps it is that I am very happy,' she murmured. 'Something has come into my heart that I do not understand, but it is very nice. It makes me feel – oh, I cannot explain, and I must not think of it, because of the duty which must occupy all my attention. You have the microphone in that parcel?'

Shannon nodded, and proceeded to unwrap it, wondering all the time what it was that had come into her heart that had made her very happy, and which she did not understand.

'Did your gallant cavalier, General Radoloff, accompany you to the opera?' he asked.

She made a sound expressive of disgust.

'Yes; and tonight I found his attentions most distasteful to me. Before, I did not mind very much, but all seemed so different tonight. I think he is a beast, that man. All the time he bends over me, and looks at me with eyes that seem to gloat, as though I were a very choice morsel of food that he was about to eat. I know what it is he is thinking, and it is not nice, my friend. Tonight I felt that his presence – what is it I wish to say?'

'Sullied you?'

'Yes, sullied me.'

'Beast!' growled Shannon.

She quickly put a white, shapely hand over his mouth.

'S'sh!' she warned. 'Your voice is like yourself, Hugh; very, very big. Oh! What is that?'

He withdrew from the parcel a suit of overalls with which he had thoughtfully provided himself. He explained, quickly donning it over his clothing, while she curiously examined the microphone. Shannon's thoughts were busy, and not altogether with the work in hand. He was wondering if Thalia had again met Hill, and if she also had been attracted to him as he had been to her. That would certainly account for the softness in her face, and that something in her heart which she said she could not understand. It would also explain her sudden repugnance for Radoloff's attentions. He wished he could have asked her, for he was very keen that his friend's sudden devotion for her should end in happiness, but of course it was out of the question. He abruptly put all thoughts of a sentimental nature aside, and turned his attention to the matter on hand.

'It is lucky,' he commented, remembering to keep his voice very low, 'that it is too warm for fires. That certainly would make our project impossible.'

He walked to the huge ornamental fireplace, which had been designed in imitation of the work of Bernini. Stretching his great bulk underneath, and looking up, he was gratified to find that he would be able to negotiate the chimney. It would be a tight squeeze, but it could be done. Bars of iron, placed at uniform distances apart, would make the ascent fairly easy. Pushing the microphone into his pocket, he handed Thalia the headphones, arranging the flex in such a manner that it would run out evenly as he ascended, and not jerk the microphone out of his possession.

'Be careful not to make a noise,' she warned him. 'It is possible that they may hear you.'

'They will think it is a mouse,' he grinned.

She laughed softly.

'Oh, but what a very great mouse!' she exclaimed.

He commenced the ascent, and was soon in an atmosphere of soot that threatened to choke him. The chimney had not been swept at a very recent date, he reflected ruefully, and wondered if he would cause the soot to fall and make a mess of Thalia's neat room. He just fitted in, and that was about all. If he had been two or three inches more in girth, it is probable that he would have been unable to make the ascent. Slowly he went up, taking care not to make a sound, and endeavouring to refrain from dislodging the thick masses of carbon deposit he found all around him. In this he was not altogether successful, as he could tell by the chunks which he could hear softly falling. It seemed a long way up, the rooms of the building were extremely lofty, but at last he came to a turn in the chimney, and knew he was close to the fireplace above. Here it narrowed, and he found it impossible to squeeze his broad shoulders any farther up. That was a poser, and he remained where he was, wondering what to do.

It was while he was stationary that he became aware of the murmur of voices. He decided that he must be directly behind the fireplace. A few inches higher, and he ought to be able to hear the conversation. He reached up a hand, and presently felt what seemed to be a ledge. If he could succeed in jamming the microphone there, it would be an ideal spot. Wriggling desperately, keeping his hand up and one shoulder higher than the other, he succeeded in gaining at least half a foot, but he was now fastened in so tightly that he was helpless. The voices, however, were quite distinct, and he remained in his desperately uncomfortable position listening intently. Someone, speaking in the Greek language, was apparently giving a long technical explanation of a chemical formula, which was gibberish to Shannon. Presently he caught the word plague; then typhoid and cholera, and became at once intensely interested.

'Are you quite certain you can do this?' asked an eager voice.

'Of course I am,' came the quick reply of the man who had already been speaking. 'Paul Michalis and you, also, Plasiras, have observed what I can do. It is only the difficulty of making enough to enable you to commence operations. When you dictate your terms, it is necessary that you give evidence that your threats are not empty. You can only do that by having a sufficient supply at hand. Is it not so?'

'But it is amazing. I did not realise that your research work had taken you so far forward. Actually then it would be possible to declare our intentions almost at once.'

'Yes. It is only that there must be a good supply in reserve.'

'And the antidote?' queried another man. 'It is quite certain?'

'Absolutely. Listen, my friends, I have not told you this before – only Michalis knows. I experimented on myself.'

There were mingled exclamations of horror and excitement.

'It was terrible,' declared a deep, vibrating voice. 'I, Paul Michalis, give you my word that I was terrified. I strove to dissuade Kyprianos, but he was so certain that he could not fail. In the cause of science and our great schemes, he took the risk, while I stood by and watched him. As you will gather, it was entirely successful.'

Murmurs of admiration reached Shannon's ears.

'When can the demonstration be arranged that you promise us, Kyprianos?' asked someone, after a short silence.

'In two or three days I will tell you. It is a great pity that we had to leave Cyprus so hurriedly. I had selected Troödos for the experiment on the first grand scale. All of our people would have been warned to leave. There are not many. Muslims and Armenians and some English would remain – to die.' His voice contained a soft, horribly gloating note. 'A few pints of my preparation in the water supply and, in less than a week, the inhabitants would have been stricken with a mysterious disease which could not have been combated. The bacteria have been interbred in such a manner that the drugs administered to prevent the spread of one branch of the disease would simply encourage another. You see, gentlemen, drugs which kill some species of microbe organisms feed others, and it was with that idea in my mind that I experimented. The result has been successful beyond my dreams. No one who is infected can be cured, and once an epidemic commenced it would spread with the greatest rapidity.

'Think of the power which is in your grasp. You, Plasiras and Bikelas, will be dictators of Greece; General Radoloff and Doreff of Bulgaria; Bruno of Italy; Michalis of Cyprus. When you have obtained the power in your own countries; then you can combine to become masters of Europe – of the world. There is no limit to the possibilities which my brain has conceived for you. And you, Plasiras, with Bikelas had visions of making one more attempt to overthrow the present Greek government in a similar manner to that which ended so disastrously in December. You plotted with the general to obtain the help of Bulgaria, and held out the promise of Western Thrace in return. Signor Bruno was admitted to your counsels in the hope of his being able to rouse the sympathy and perhaps the help of Italy. Then Michalis was to raise an army of Cypriots of Greek extraction in return for which Cyprus would be annexed by Greece – that is the Greece under Plasiras and Bikelas. Were there ever ideas of such foolishness? But I, my friends, I, Nicholas Kyprianos, have made them not only possible but certain.

With the help of Bulgaria would you have conquered Greece? No – I tell you, you would not. If you had tampered with Cyprus, down on you would come the British navy and army. Of all your mad plans, that I think was the worst. What Signor Bruno could have done, when he is out of favour with his own government, I do not know. But now because you have allied yourselves with me you can all benefit beyond your wildest dreams.

'You need no army, you need no navy. All that is necessary is for you to express your demands, and give an unmistakable demonstration of your powers. General Radoloff and Monsieur Doreff are men of importance already, yet they are, after all, but two in a government, with no promise of anything greater. Now supreme and unlimited control looms before them. Western Thrace – bah! Bulgaria, under them, can have any seaboard she wishes to take that does not interfere with the Greece of Messieurs Plasiras and Bikelas or the Italy of Signor Bruno. The people themselves will quickly decide for you. Threaten to wipe them out with a strange contagious disease; show them how with one small proof, and quickly they will destroy the existing governments and bend the knee to you. Are you not glad you took Paul into your confidence, gentlemen, and were told by him of me? It is good that he is to have Cyprus. Great Britain will not dare to refuse, when she knows what refusal will mean to her people. He is popular, and will make a good ruler.'

His harangue was followed by a buzz of excited chatter, but of too confused a nature for Shannon to follow clearly. He had forgotten his painful cramped position. If he had not already been practically unable to move, he would have been frozen into a condition of horrified immobility by what he had heard. He had little thought, when ascending the chimney, that such a diabolical scheme was afoot. The thought of it made him feel physically sick. Kyprianos must be a monster, when his brain could conceive a plot so vile, and experiment until the means were at hand to exploit it. No less fiends than he were the others who could countenance, for one moment, a way so utterly inhuman of forcing themselves into power. All the time the Cypriot had talked with the fanaticism of a cold-blooded scientist, whom no scruples of humanity could deviate from a course which the cleverness of his brain had opened up. Shannon became acutely aware of the pain in his arm and neck, but was too eager to listen to all it was possible to hear to descend a little for relief. One of the men put a question to Kyprianos, when the babble had subsided, which had occurred to the Englishman.

'You have spoken much of what we obtain through the brilliance of your experiments, friend Kyprianos, but what is your reward?'

The Cypriot could be heard to laugh.

'That I will tell you afterwards,' he replied, 'when your plans have succeeded. It is at present a secret in here.' Shannon concluded he had indicated his head or heart. 'You will not deny it to me. Of that I am quite certain. You will, in fact, be eager to grant me my wish.'

The listener thought there was something sinister in his observation. Apparently the other men were of the same opinion, for there was a silence, suggestive of unease, lasting for several seconds. 'Why not tell us what it is now?' asked one.

'Because it is something I prefer to keep to myself. Afterwards you will know. I shall not forget.'

Again there was a silence, broken at last by the deep voice of Michalis.

'Once an epidemic of this terrible disease has been started,' he observed, 'it appears to me that it will be difficult to stop it.'

'The antidote I have contrived is all that can stop it. That is why I have said that you cannot commence operations until the supply is enough. In these bottles is a sufficient quantity of interbred bacteria to send the disease raging through the whole of Europe, but only this large green one contains the antidote. How far would that go, do you think, gentlemen, to put an end to a devastating contagion that spreads hourly? Large quantities must be made. You will have to supply me with a bigger laboratory than this. During the next month I will be at work, and can promise you that by the end of that time there will be two dozen large bottles like this full. Perhaps you may think such an amount will suffice. If not, then you must arrange for a proper laboratory and assistance.'

'Would it not be dangerous for you to have people to assist you?'

Kyprianos laughed.

'They would not know what they were doing. I would take care of that. We should select students who do not know much, and the two chief components would be inserted only by me, and without the knowledge of anybody.'

'Where do you keep the formula?' came in a voice Shannon had not heard before.

'Why do you wish to know, Signor Bruno?' snarled Kyprianos savagely and suspiciously.

'I merely asked out of curiosity.'

'Well, it is a question I do not like. But, in order that you may not waste your time prying for it, I will tell you where it is. It is in my head. I do not think anyone could steal it from there. When my experiments had been conducted with entire success, I studied the formula until I knew it by heart word for word, measure for measure. Then I destroyed every scrap of memoranda I possessed regarding it.'

'It seems,' remarked another voice, 'that you, Nicholas Kyprianos, hold the ultimate power.'

'Is that not as it should be, my friend? I do not trust anybody, and, therefore, must take precautions to protect myself. And in order that you may not be disappointed I will add, for your benefit, that analysis of the antidote will not reveal the vital constituent that renders it potent. It becomes utterly lost, leaving only its effect on the other constituents.'

'Kyprianos, you are a devil,' declared one of his companions.

The Cypriot laughed as though at a compliment.

'Are not we all, Monsieur Bikelas? This is, I think, a meeting of devils, and I am the supreme devil, is it not so? Perhaps it would be well, if that fact was not forgotten.'

'If you are attempting to threaten us,' snapped Bikelas, 'you had better learn now that I, for one, will not allow myself to be threatened.'

'I do not threaten. I but desire to protect myself for, as I have told you, I trust no one. Is it not natural?'

'Well, you can protect yourself as much as you like, so long as it is not at the expense of my friends or me. Threats from you will mean that I instantly withdraw from any further part in the scheme.'

'You cannot withdraw now – none of us can,' declared another. 'We are in far too deep. One withdrawing would immediately constitute himself a danger to the others. It would, therefore, be incumbent on the others to destroy him.'

'What do you mean by that, general?'

'Exactly what I have said, no more and no less. I think it is plain enough.'

Again the voices became confused as a heated argument

ensued. Shannon by that time found that it was absolutely essential that he should seek relief, at least for a little while, from the terribly cramped position in which he was jammed. It was not as easy as he had expected, however. He had forced himself up, but, wriggle as he would, he was unable for some time to descend. Matters began to look serious; he did not wish to use too much exertion for fear of dislodging bricks and, in consequence, causing a noise that would be heard. He rested from his efforts, and heard one of the men asking anxiously if the bottles containing the deadly bacteria were securely sealed.

'There is no reason why you should have fears, Monsieur Doreff,' returned the suspicious Kyprianos, 'if you do not try to investigate when I am not here. The bottles are very safely sealed. Of course, if any are knocked over and broken, the consequences might be deplorable, but in the case as they are they cannot be damaged.' He laughed. 'I do not think, Signor Bruno, that even you could have obtained for me the permit, if it had been thought what was in those bottles.'

'Surely the glass is of a thickness that renders breaking impossible,' persisted Doreff.

'Unlikely but not impossible. Even very thick glass sometimes, under certain circumstances, is liable to become broken.'

Suddenly Shannon felt himself sliding. At last he had succeeded in releasing himself, and threatened to go down rather abruptly, especially as his foot missed the iron rung. However, by pressing his knees hard against the walls, he prevented his further descent. His foot sought for and found a bar, and he rested. The arm that had been above his head was absolutely numb, and he decided that there was nothing for it but to return to Thalia's room. He would never be able to get the life restored to it in the close confines of the chimney. He continued to descend, therefore, and was not very far from the bottom when he stopped abruptly. The sound of voices reached his ears, and it was coming from the girl's bedroom. His teeth clenched, and his lips drew tightly together. To whom was she talking? It could only be one of the people with whom she had come to Rome. A dreadful suspicion that she had, after all, played him false entered his mind, and persisted. Heavens! What a trap! They would wait for him at the bottom, and he would be captured without being able to make the slightest attempt at resistance. Strangely enough his deepest emotion at that moment was a feeling of sorrow for Hill. What a terrible disillusionment for the man who loved Thalia Ictinos!

CHAPTER FOURTEEN

The Amorous Herr Kirche

He remained where he was for some minutes, wondering what he was to do. The voices continued, and before long he decided that they both belonged to women. That brought a slight renewal of hope. Thalia's visitor must either be Madame Bikelas or Signora Bruno; more probably the former. Anything, of course, might have been responsible for the employer visiting her companion, even at that late hour of the night, or rather early hour of the morning. Perhaps his thoughts of treachery on the part of the girl were unjustified, though he was inclined to think that she had called in whoever was with her. Reflection, however, quickly decided him that it was most unlikely, whereupon his feelings almost completely veered to the belief that she was innocent of the betrayal he had been so ready to impute to her. If she had intended treachery, she would have sent for the men, or at least Madame Bikelas would have done so, and the discussion above would certainly not have continued so complacently.

A great deal easier in his mind, Shannon strained his ears in an endeavour to hear what was being said. Then a worse feeling of perturbation than before seized him. His hat had been left on a chair in the room; then there was the soot he must have caused to fall and the headphones. No doubt the person with Thalia had been disturbed, had demanded admittance, and was now engaged in questioning the girl. Poor Thalia, thought Shannon, he had involved her beyond hope of explanation. It would not be possible for her to clear herself of the suspicion that the man's hat, the headphones, and the soot were bound to bring upon her. Somehow he must endeavour to save her. One girl had lost her life while in his company, and acting with him. He made a resolve that he would not allow Thalia to share the fate of Barbara Havelock. He was half-inclined to go down at once, and protect her, but the hope that she had possibly found some way out restrained him. The voices ceased. Several anxious moments went by; then came floating up to him:

'It is quite safe, Hugh. You can come down.'

He was conscious of a feeling of surprise. How had she known he was close by? Descending to the bottom, he emerged from the fireplace to receive another surprise. Gone from her person were the necklace and earrings, while her hair was ruffled and a beautiful silk kimono was wrapped round her slender form. He noticed also that the bed had been rumpled as though it had been slept in. A soft little gurgle drew his attention back to her. She was endeavouring to stifle her laughter; something about him was obviously causing her amusement, which was not lessened by the questioning look he shot at her. She took him by an arm, and drew him before a mirror. He understood then why she was laughing. His face had a startlingly piebald appearance, while his hair and overalls were black with soot. He grinned at his reflection in the glass, but immediately afterwards glanced down at the carpet with dismay. It had been thoughtless of him to walk across the floor, leaving the impression of his feet and dropping a little heap of soot at every step. Hastily he returned to the fireplace.

'Do not worry, Hugh,' she murmured, interpreting the reason for his action. 'I will clean it before the morning.' She had suddenly become very grave. 'I have had a visitor,' she announced. 'You heard us talking?'

'Yes. Who was it?'

'Madame Bikelas. All the time you were in the chimney that black stuff was falling, but without any noise. A little while ago, though, there came down a great deal together which made a loud sound. I was listening by the wall, and I thought I heard Madame move. Quickly I made my hair untidy and the bed to look as if I had been sleeping there. Then I put on this kimono, hid away your hat and the paper, and put in the chimney the instrument for the ears with the wire that could be seen. I was only just in time, for I heard her door open, and at once came a knock on mine and her voice asking if I was awake. I told her I was very much awake, and was feeling dismayed, for there had been a fall of soot in my room. I let her in, feeling all the time very much anxious in case you came down, but it was all I could do to make certain she would not be suspicious.'

'It was exceedingly quick-witted of you, Thalia,' he approved feeling greatly ashamed of the thoughts he had entertained regarding her.

'Madame told me she had heard the noise and it had worried her. She is a very nervous woman. She was relieved that it had but been caused by soot, and promised to see that the chimney is swept without delay. Then it was that I became full of fear, for I saw your foot. Fortunately Madame then was not looking at the fireplace, and I spoke loudly in the hope of giving you warning. To my great relief you did not come down any farther.'

'No; I heard. But what a fool I was not to have thought that my feet might be seen! I have a lot to thank you for, Thalia.'

'You have a lot for which to thank me!' she echoed. 'It is I who owe you thanks for what you are doing for me. I think, Hugh, that the microphone will have to come down. If it is left there, it will be found when the men come to sweep the chimney. I am sorry that—'

'It is not there,' he told her. 'I stood listening to the conversation, and my right arm and shoulder became so numbed that I could do nothing. I came down to get life back into them, and intended ascending again.'

'You were away a long time, and I was very much anxious.' She inserted a cigarette in her long tube and lit it. 'You will have one?'

'Please.'

She selected, and lit it for him. She saw his eyes on an ashtray filled with cigarette ends.

'You think I smoke too much; yes? It is good for the nerves to smoke, I think. You were up there so long that my nerves became not good. Did you hear anything of importance, Hugh?'

'I have discovered everything, Thalia,' he informed her grimly. 'The plot being hatched is about the most diabolical it is possible to imagine.'

'Oh, what is it? Tell me!'

'I don't think I had better stop now. Perhaps you will meet me somewhere during the morning, and I will then tell you all. It would be unwise to stop longer. Bikelas and his secretary and Bruno might descend from above at any moment. Madame might even bring her husband to see the soot.'

'I think perhaps you are right. I will pour you some water to wash.'

'No, don't do that. I will have a bath when I get back to the hotel.'

'But what of your face? It will be seen.'

He laughed softly.

'I don't think so.' Quickly he stripped off the overalls. 'The microphone is hardly necessary now,' he went on. 'I have heard all that is worthwhile hearing, and we can hardly learn much more. Now we will have to discuss the matter, and decide what to do. It is absolutely essential that we must act at once. If you like, I will leave the microphone with you, and come tomorrow night to fix it. But, when you hear what I have to tell you, I think you will agree with me that we can dispense with it.'

'Perhaps it will be better if you take it with you. There would then not be the risk of them finding it. I do not think it is likely, but perhaps my room and my things sometimes get searched.'

He nodded. Retrieving the headphones, and winding up the flex, he wrapped up the microphone and its connections in the overalls, packing them in the paper in which he had brought them.

'Is that which you heard very terrible, Hugh?' she questioned, her great eyes fixed on his.

'Devilish,' he returned succinctly.

'I shall be in much suspense until I hear from you what it is. It is dangerous for my country?'

'Very, and not only for your country, but for others as well. Now will you please see if the way is clear?'

She nodded, and quietly opened the door, Shannon having first taken the precaution of switching off the light. The narrow corridor outside was still brilliantly illumined. He could see her as she crossed to the entrance door, and a feeling of deep anxiety took possession of him. At that moment she was taking a tremendous risk. What could she possibly do to explain herself, if Bikelas and his secretary suddenly appeared? He wished now that he had not asked her to look out for him; he felt he was involving her in a danger that she should never have been called upon to face. It was with a feeling of intense relief that he saw her turn and come back to him.

'It is all right,' she whispered. 'Go quickly, Hugh. I will shut the door after you.' He muttered a hurried goodnight, was about to hasten quietly away, when she caught his arm. 'You have not said where I am to meet you,' she reminded him.

'Oh, no! It's lucky you remembered. The same place where we previously met – on the terrace of the Pincio between ten and eleven. Will that suit you?'

She nodded. It was only after he had gone that she recollected another appointment she had on the terrace of the Pincio at eleven. A little smile played softly round her lips.

Shannon passed out of the flat safely, and the door closed behind him. He hurried quietly to the stairs; suddenly stopped dead. The sound of voices had reached him from above. Apparently the meeting in Kyprianos' room had terminated; Bikelas and Bruno would be coming down. As the light on the first floor was full on, Shannon knew he could hardly hope to descend the stairs without being seen by the men as they came down the upper flight. Yet there was no place capable of hiding him. If he switched off the light, they would be certain to grow suspicious; plotters of their kind were bound to be always on the *qui vive*, always distrustful of every incident, no matter how small or trivial it might have appeared to others. The Secret Service man momentarily felt he was in a hole, but, always resourceful, a way out occurred to him. It had nothing to recommend it; he would not have attempted it except under the score of expediency. He walked along the corridor, to the end where the twin elevator shafts were situated. If one of the lifts was in position on that floor, it would be a simple matter to hide inside, unless the doors made too much noise when opening. On the other hand, if, as he expected, neither was stationed there, he would swing himself down the shaft, neither a pleasant nor easy job when both arms were damaged. The partially healed wounds, from which the stitches had so recently been drawn, were likely to be opened again. He already felt that he had torn one when climbing the chimney. However, his was a position in which account of such things could not be considered. He was unable to use an elevator because of the hum of the machinery. The men above still lingered talking, which was fortunate.

Glancing through the glass-panelled doors he saw, as he had anticipated, that neither elevator was there. He hoped that both were higher up. As they were worked by automatic means, it was likely they were. People ascending would naturally leave them at the floor to which they had taken them. By gradual degrees he opened one of the doors. It swung back silently, greatly to his relief, and he looked down. The roof of the lift was below him. That meant he would not be able to get out by that shaft; he must try the other. He was turning away, when there came a click and the little cabinet began to move upwards. He started back. He had not considered the possibility of the men coming down from the floor above by lift. If he had only known, he could have descended the stairs safely, and been well away by that time. Now he ran quietly back to the stairs, gave one sharp glance upward to make certain that he was unobserved, and went down. He had reached the bottom, was crossing the hall, when he heard the hum of the elevator descending, but it was coming right down. There was no doubt of it. Hastily he looked round for a place in which to hide. There were several lounges, great palms, and chairs placed in various positions and, selecting one of the former, he went down behind it just as he heard the lift stop and the door open.

The sound of people talking in whispers reached his ears, and he wondered at the secrecy. What were they doing? When he heard footsteps moving across the hall with measured tread, as though carrying something heavy, his curiosity got the better of him, and he glanced cautiously out. A muttered exclamation broke from him at what he saw. Four men, two of whom he recognised as Radoloff and Bruno, even in that dim light, were carrying the inert body of a fifth. They placed it down near the porter's little glass-enclosed office, and stood talking in whispers. Then one of them went out, returning after several minutes, and nodding to the others. The body was lifted again, and carried through the front entrance. Inclination urged Shannon to follow, caution bade him remain where he was. It was well he did so. In rather less than five minutes the four returned, and walked slowly in his direction on their way towards the stairs.

'It was well we knew in time,' Bruno was saying as they approached. 'I hope Kyprianos is right, and that he will be found to have died of heart failure, and nothing else.'

'Kyprianos does not make mistakes,' declared another softly. 'For a long time I have suspected that secretary of mine of being a traitor. Now his treacherous days are ended. Are you quite sure yours is trustworthy, Bikelas?'

'I would answer for him with my life,' came the reply from the man addressed as Bikelas.

'I hope, my friend, that you are not compelled to do so,' commented General Radoloff.

'He has been with me for seven years and I knew him before that for—'

The remainder was lost to Shannon as the four passed on. He had squirmed his way round the lounge seat, as they went by, in order that he would not be seen by any who chanced to look back. Waiting until they had ascended the stairs, and disappeared from view, he rose, and hurried out of the building. Quickly withdrawing from the circle of light cast by the lamp over the entrance, he effaced himself in the darkness, his eyes searching for the form of the man who had been killed, and who would be found to have died of heart failure. But although he knew it could not be far away, he realised that the task of searching for it would probably take a long time in that darkness. He went on his way, therefore, reflecting on the fate that had overtaken the poor fellow, every thought causing him to understand the more what deadly peril Thalia Ictinos was in. Plasiras, Bikelas, Bruno and the rest were desperate, as was only to be expected of men who were nursing and guarding such a terrible secret. If suspicions, even of the slightest, were raised in their breasts against the girl, her life would not be worth a moment's purchase. Already she had spoken as though she thought Kyprianos had doubts of her. It was his devilish ingenuity which had brought about the secretary's death, making it appear, if Shannon had heard correctly, that it was due to natural causes. If one such death could so easily be contrived, another could take place with the same appearance of innocence.

Shannon succeeded in entering the hotel, and reaching his room without being seen by any members of the night staff. He locked away the parcel containing the overalls and microphone, had a bath which he felt he needed badly; then, attired in pyjamas and dressing gown, filled and lit his pipe and, sinking into the armchair, gave himself up to meditation. In a sense he felt triumphant at having stumbled upon the details of the conspiracy, but the cold-blooded inhumanity of the scheme so revolted and appalled him that he had little time for personal congratulations. One thing was apparent; it was that the scoundrels who intended grasping dictatorial powers in their respective countries by means so horrible must be checkmated at the earliest possible moment. The question only remained concerning the best and safest manner to accomplish such a purpose. As the Greek government was most directly concerned, Shannon thought that representations could best be made to the authorities at Rome from Athens. However, Sir Leonard Wallace was the best judge of that, and a report must go through to him at once. On reflection, Shannon decided to telephone through from the British embassy early in the morning. He could then receive instructions without delay. He sat down, and wrote a complete account of his discoveries up to date, including the part Thalia Ictinos was taking in the affair, and the manner in which she had sought his help. This he put into code ready to dictate through the telephone. He knew it would be taken down at the other end, and decoded as he spoke. Having assured himself that the cipher was correct, he tore up the original into minute scraps, and burnt them in the fireplace.

Soon after nine o'clock the following morning, he entered the British embassy, and obtained an interview with the ambassador himself. A transcontinental official telephone call was put through to the Foreign Office in London from where, at the mention of a certain word, connection was obtained with Secret Service headquarters. Shannon was delighted to find that Major Brien was already in his office. He indicated that he had an urgent report to make and, after a short delay, during which he envisaged the deputy chief sending for Maddison, and the latter positioning himself at the desk with pad and pencil – a little flight of imagination that brought a smile to his face – he was told to proceed. Carefully, assuring himself that every word was correctly received, he dictated his report. Maddison was the most expert code man at headquarters. Shannon was not surprised, therefore, when his voice came through almost directly after the message had been received to announce that it was complete – and understood. He was told to hold on, and he smiled to himself again presently when he heard faintly a long-drawn whistle. Someone, probably Major Brien, he reflected, was registering astonishment. There was a distinct click which the listener took to indicate that the latter was communicating with Sir Leonard Wallace. Five or six minutes went by; then Shannon heard the chief's well-known voice.

'Great work, Hugh,' he applauded without appearing to be in the slightest bit enthusiastic. 'Before action, the contents of that case must be rendered innocuous or removed, otherwise anything might happen when K. is cornered. Do you think you and H. can manage without causing a stampede? You must not fail.'

Shannon thought rapidly.

'Yes, sir,' he replied. 'Can do, I think – even if it means a hurried exit for K.'

'Exactly; there must be no scruples. Ring through every morning at this time to let me know how things are going. Don't undertake the job until everything seems auspicious, and use T. and one or two of his men if necessary, but don't drag him in unless you must. Finally, beware of T. I. I hope she is all you think her. It seems that she must be, but don't trust her too far. If she is doing the job she says she is, you must acquaint her with what you've heard, in order that she can send her report, but tell her to wait until you give her permission. Is that understood?'

'Yes, sir.'

'Right. Keep your eyes open for two men called Baltazzi and Padakis. They got away from London – due to them others left Nicosia of course. Any indication that your lot have heard what happened there?'

'Not as far as I am able to tell. T. I. knows nothing.'

'Excellent. Well, good luck!'

The telephone became silent. Shannon put down the receiver, contemplating it with a whimsical smile. The chief had given him a job after his own heart. To beard Kyprianos in his own den, if necessary, was the kind of thing which appealed to him, and he knew Hill would also appreciate the opportunity that had come their way. The burly Secret Service agent decided to walk to the Pincio. He always found that he could think better when walking, and there was a great deal of thinking to be done. Sir Leonard Wallace had paid him the compliment of leaving ways and means to him. The question was: how were the cultures to be removed or rendered innocuous without Kyprianos being aware of the fact? Such a feat appeared impossible. The only way appeared to be to remove Kyprianos with them. A grim smile flashed into Shannon's face. If the Cypriot were removed, there would be no need to bother about the case. The others would not dare to do anything without him. Obviously Sir Leonard wished the affair to be managed, if possible, without the rest of the band taking alarm, in order that they could all be apprehended together when the time came. It was a pretty problem.

Shannon had traversed the Via Bon Compagni, and was approaching the church of St Trinità dei Monti when he suddenly remembered the fact that Hill was a doctor – he had also specialised in bacteriology. Would it be possible for him to inject some drug into Kyprianos which would render *him* innocuous! The thought sent a glow of excitement through Shannon. If they could only kidnap the scientist for a short while! He must get in touch with Hill, and discuss the matter with him at the earliest possible moment. He swung away from the Via Sistina, and climbed to the Pincio at a pace that would have made most people gasp; it was as though he felt he had to keep up with the thoughts which were racing through his brain. He reached the terrace to find that Thalia had not yet arrived. That was rather a relief, as he wished to attune himself more to the mood in which he had been on the preceding night, after he had listened to the discussion which he had found so appalling. It would not do to give her an inkling of the plans which were being hatched in his mind. It was shortly after half past ten when she came to him, looking as wonderfully fascinating as ever in an ankle length spring creation in flowered silk, a large hat of soft delicate straw shading her face from the sun which, even at that hour, was very powerful. Shannon reflected that she showed common sense as well as exquisite taste. The morning was definitely very hot. He removed his hat, and bowed low over the hand extended to him in greeting.

'My friend,' she smiled, 'you look very warm.'

'I am,' he admitted, 'I have been walking fast.'

She raised her delicate eyebrows.

'Walking!' she echoed, 'on such a morning? But I forget, it is one of the madnesses of the English to walk, is it not? Come! We will find a seat in the shade where we can talk. I have news also for you. Something has happened which puzzles me very greatly.'

He guessed what it was.

'Tell me!' he begged, as they came to an unoccupied seat, and sat down.

'This morning early the secretary of Plasiras was found dead in the road a little way from the building. His hat and coat were lying near, and it seems that he was returning home from the theatre, where Plasiras said he had gone, when he was taken ill and died. Two doctors who came said at once that he had died of heart disease. His body has gone already for – what is it?'

'An autopsy?'

'Yes; that is it. But the doctors say there is no doubt. It must be done for the matter of form. Oh, Hugh,' she added, looking at him as though uneasy, 'I do not understand this at all. I am sure that he was up there – in the flat – when the conference was going on. I know, I am sure, that one secretary is on guard inside, and one outside – always that has happened.'

'And no doubt it happened last night,' he observed quietly.

'What – what do you mean?'

'I hope you have not said anything of your thoughts to anyone?' he asked anxiously.

'I am not a fool, my friend. Tell me why you said that?'

'That man was murdered, Thalia. Apparently they have suspected him. Probably they caught him listening at the door last night. At all events, they overcame him, and Kyprianos injected, or forced him to swallow, a drug which killed him and left the appearance of heart disease. Come to think of it, they would be too wise to inject – a hypodermic syringe leaves a mark – no; whatever it was, they forced him to drink it.'

'But how do you know this?' she asked in profound surprise.

He told her. She listened quietly, even smiled a little, as he impressed upon her the necessity of being more careful than ever in her dealings with the people with whom she was connected. She begged a cigarette, inserted it in the inevitable holder, and raised it to her lips with a hand that was as steady as a rock.

'I am always careful, mon ami,' she assured him.

'Remember, though, that they are desperate men,' he urged, 'and have proved that they will stick at nothing. They would remove you, Thalia, with as little compunction as they have removed that poor fellow.'

'I know,' she admitted soberly; 'I realise that – oh, very well indeed. A little while ago I would not bother, I would have shrugged my shoulders and said, "What does it matter?" But everything has changed. I have no wish to die, Hugh. Something has happened to me, which is very nice, but very strange.'

'What is it?' he asked.

'Presently I will tell you. First, can I hear what it was you heard when you were in the chimney?'

Without preamble or preface, he went straight to the point, repeating the conversation almost word for word, for it was as though it had been burnt into his brain. She was a good listener; did not make a sound, but her hand fell on his arm, as he spoke of the deadly disease which it was proposed to threaten to spread among innocent people.

'Oh, Hugh,' she cried, when the recital had ended, 'how diabolical! It is inconceivable that men like General Radoloff and Signor Bruno could associate themselves with a scheme so wicked. I do not think even my father would have stooped to a thing so vile.'

'You will realise now, more than ever, why you must be careful. May I give you some advice?'

'But, of course. Have I not asked for it?'

'Then do not do anything but that which an ordinary lady's companion would do. Discontinue all your investigations completely!'

'How can I do that. My country expects me to accomplish that for which I am with these people. I must do my duty.'

'You have done it admirably. Now leave everything to me. Will you promise this?'

'You mean you will also report to my government?'

'No; you will do that, but not now. The time is not yet ripe. As soon as it is, I will tell you, and you will immediately communicate with Athens. At the same, I will inform my department in order that Italy can be warned of the manner of people she is nursing unconsciously in Rome. Please promise to leave everything to me henceforth. I will keep you informed of what I am doing and, if necessary, will ask your assistance.'

She smiled up at him.

'You are very good to me, Hugh, and I was once so wicked. I do not deserve this wonderful kindness. Very well, since you ask, I promise.'

'Splendid!' he ejaculated. 'You are sure you were not followed here?'

'Oh, perfectly. They were all too busy pretending to be so sad about that poor man. But I looked and watched, and went three different ways in three taxis. Oh, I was very much careful.'

'I am glad to hear it. Now, Thalia, tell me what has happened to you which is strange but very nice.'

Her eyes dropped until the long, curling lashes hid them completely from him. He was interested to observe the colour stealing slowly into her cheeks. For some moments she remained silent.

'It is very difficult for me to speak of this,' she murmured at length, 'but it is good to have a friend in whom to confide. I have no mother or sister or even a brother. I think, Hugh – I am not sure, but I think love has come to me.'

'By Jove!' he exclaimed softly, as though he had not already guessed. 'This is fine, Thalia. I hope he is worthy of your love.'

'Worthy of my love!' Her voice contained a harsh note, and she turned to look him full in the face, her eyes flashing fire. 'I am sure of him – I know, I feel he is a very good, a very honourable and noble man. It is that I fear I am not worthy of his love. What will he say; what will he do, when I tell him I am the daughter of Stanislas Ictinos, and have myself been a woman so bad?'

'You will tell him of the past?'

'But, of course,' she replied simply. 'Otherwise I would live a lie, and I could not do that, Hugh.'

'No,' he agreed; 'I don't think you could. You are sure he loves you?'

She laughed.

'Oh, you will think it very silly. You will be amused. Do you know, I met him for the first time on the stairs of the Splendide, when I was coming from your rooms. He was running up in a great hurry, and almost we bumped. He was very much apologetic, and we did not speak more than half a dozen words, but we looked at each other, and I think I knew then that for me he was different from other men. Yesterday, when I returned after speaking to you, I met him in the house where I live, and again on the stairs. We speak to each other for a little while, and he is very frank. He tells me he followed me, and takes a flat there to be near me.'

Shannon pretended alarm.

'Do you not think he may be engaged to watch you?' he asked.

'No, no, no!' she cried vehemently. 'Of that I am most certain. It is because he – he loves me that he takes the flat.'

'Did he tell you so?'

'No,' she laughed; 'he is impulsive, but that would be too

sudden, would it not? But he has eyes that are very honest. As he looked at me I knew, because his heart spoke to me from his eyes.'

Shannon pondered. It was extraordinary that love for each other should come to two people in such a flash, he reflected. He knew Hill was in love with Thalia; he felt there was no mistaking that she reciprocated that love. It must be confessed that the news delighted him, not only for the sake of his friend, but because it helped to remove all remaining shreds of doubt in his mind concerning Thalia. He would have liked to have taken her entirely into his confidence; to have told her the real truth concerning his presence in Rome; that he was not working so much to assist her as to carry out instructions given to him by his own department. A man who hated playing a deceitful role, Shannon felt more regretful now than before that circumstances compelled him to delude the girl.

'You think all this is very foolish; yes?' she asked.

'By no means,' he assured her. 'It certainly strikes me as very wonderful. I have never heard of a more striking case of love at first sight. My wishes, Thalia, are that the affair will progress, and end for you in great happiness.'

'Oh, thank you,' she cried. 'You are so good that it is difficult to express my gratitude to you. Do you remember I told you that an Austrian gentleman had come to live in a flat on the second floor of the house?' He nodded. 'Well, my friend Hugh, it is he, and we meet together on the terrace this morning. He will be waiting. Come with me please! I wish so much for you to meet him.'

He murmured something about being very delighted. They rose, and strolled back to the terrace. Hill, carefully dressed, and carrying in his hand a beautiful bouquet of flowers, which he had purchased from one of the saleswomen at the base of the Spanish stairs, was there.

'Oh! For me?' cried Thalia, as he swept off his hat, and presented her with the flowers. 'This is delightful. Herr Kirche, I wish you to meet my very dear friend Captain Shannon. I think you will like each other very much.'

Not a sign of recognition passed between the two men as they shook hands, but both felt as though they were behaving like cads. Shannon remained talking to them for a few minutes; then took his leave.

'Perhaps you will give me the pleasure of your company at lunch in the Hotel Splendide, Herr Kirche,' he invited before he went; 'that is, unless you and Signorina Ictinos are lunching together?'

'Can you?' asked Hill, devouring the girl with his eyes.

She shook her head regretfully.

'It is impossible,' she returned. 'My employer will expect me. Perhaps I may be able to arrange another time, but not today.'

'Then, signor,' declared Hill to his colleague, clicking his heels together, and giving the typical little bow of the Austrian, 'I will be delighted to accept your invitation.'

'I will await you at one o'clock in the lounge,' Shannon told him, and departed.

CHAPTER FIFTEEN

Shannon is Trailed—

Hill arrived promptly to time, swinging his stick jauntily, his whole air proclaiming the man who had much about which to be glad. Shannon, from the table he had chosen at one end of the lounge, watched his approach with a smile. He stood up to indicate where he was, as his position had been chosen with an eye to seclusion, and was surrounded by palms. The ex-doctor took some time to find him, but eventually his eyes fell on the mighty figure in the corner. He made his way across the crowded room, and sank into a chair by Shannon's side.

'For a man who is not particularly anxious to draw attention to himself,' commented the latter drily, as he beckoned to a waiter, 'you are not a success, my dear Tubby. You are bubbling over with bliss to such a degree that everyone is compelled to look at you.'

'What did you expect me to do,' grunted Hill; 'slink in like a whipped dog?'

Shannon ordered cocktails.

'Not exactly,' he returned, as the waiter hurried away. 'Still, perhaps a little less advertisement might have been more becoming.

The way you swung that cane about sent shivers down my spine. I expected every moment to hear indignant and outraged cries from someone who had been hit. You missed the red-hot momma over there in the tulle creation by the merest fraction. She's casting languishing glances this way, as though she is longing to cart you back to Philadelphia with her – I bet that's where she came from. How do you do it?'

'Do what?'

'Draw all these females after you.'

'Don't be an idiot, Hugh. No girl ever bothers to look at me. If she does, it's because she's wondering whether I'm a schoolboy dressed up, or a walking advertisement for somebody's complexion cream. It's sickening. You're the bloke who causes female hearts to work overtime. Wherever you hulk that out and outsized figure of yours, it's always followed by eyes popping out of female heads in adoration. And you know it, you old fraud.'

'God forbid!' returned Shannon fervently. 'I imagine, though, from your expression, that you and Thalia understand each other. Have you proposed to her?'

Hill's eyes and mouth opened wide.

'Pro-proposed to – to her!' he stuttered. 'What in the name of all that's wonderful do you mean?'

'Tut! tut!' murmured Shannon mockingly. 'Are you as inexperienced as all that? To propose to a girl is to gaze tenderly into her eyes, clasp her hand – if she'll let you have it – and ask her if she'll take the risk of marrying you.'

'Don't be an ass! I know what to propose means.'

'Go on! You amaze me,' murmured the other.

Hill laughed.

'You can be delightfully idiotic at times,' he commented. 'What surprised me so much was the coolness of your question. Have I proposed to her! Dash it all, man. I'd give my soul to dare it, of course, but considering I've only known her for less than two days, you can hardly – well, I doubt if I'll have enough courage to do it after a year, if I meet her every day, and she's always as perfectly wonderful to me as she was this morning. Oh, Hugh, she's a glorious girl, and how you blokes could ever have mistaken her for the she-devil you all agreed she was, beats me.'

The cocktails were placed before them. Shannon raised his.

'That is over and done with. I agree with you, she's wonderful, and if you don't bowl in and propose as soon as possible, thus making yourself happy and her as well, all I can say is you're a darn fool. Here's to her.'

The toast was drunk solemnly. Then Hill put down his glass firmly.

'Look here, old chap,' he demanded, 'what are you getting at? Why all this talk about proposals? It is true I'd give almost anything for the chance of hearing her say she'll marry me, but there isn't a chance. Besides, even if there was, it isn't usual to propose on such short acquaintance. Why do you keep harping on about my proposing?'

'Simply because I'm fool enough to have a certain amount of affection for you, and am keen to see you happy. I am also keen now on Thalia obtaining happiness – she can't have had much, if any, in her life, and she deserves it.'

'But, if I proposed to her, that wouldn't give her happiness. Why, she would laugh at me.'

'I'm darn sure she wouldn't. If I'm not mistaken, she'd be very, very glad.'

'You're fooling.'

'I'm not. I mean every word of it.'

'But why should she be glad?'

'Because, my son, she loves you.'

Hill's previous surprise was nothing to that which overcame him now. He sat for some moments as though he had congealed, his blue eyes opened to their widest extent, his mouth gaping ludicrously. Once or twice it closed as though he were about to speak, only to expand to the same extent again. At length, with a great effort, he succeeded.

'Don't be a rotter, Hugh,' he muttered huskily.

'I'm not. I repeat again; she loves you.'

'What – what makes you say that?'

'The fact that she told me so. As she put it, she has no mother, brother, or sister to confide in, so she paid me the compliment of making me her confidant. I feel rather as though I am betraying a secret, but she did not tell me to keep it to myself, and I have a sentimental desire to help you all I can.'

Hill gripped his arm convulsively.

'You – you are sure she meant it.'

'Absolutely certain. Steady on with that hand. You are gripping one of my pet wounds.'

The ex-doctor muttered an apology; relaxed his hold. He looked like a man dazed. Suddenly he pulled himself together, and he laughed, joyously, happily.

'Lord!' he cried. 'I'm hanged if I can believe it. Hugh, you old ruffian, I could hug you.'

'Don't you dare!' returned Shannon in mock alarm. 'Keep all your hugs for Thalia.'

'Hug Thalia!' repeated Hill, as though in horror.

'Yes; why not? Dash it all! You speak as though you think she would break. Now perhaps you understand why I say, propose to her. The result ought to be satisfactory to you both. Now, having played the part of a fairy godfather, I suggest we go and eat.'

'Wait a minute. What is yours? This calls for something special.'

'It calls for nothing – at present. Take a cinch on yourself, and remove that grin from your face. You look so positively beatific that I shall burst into tears of joy presently.'

It was all Shannon could do to keep his jubilant guest in a reasonable state of mind during the service of luncheon. He succeeded at length by questioning him closely about his manner of reaching the hotel, to ascertain whether he had been followed.

'I kept a sharp lookout when I left the two of you on the terrace of the Pincio,' he whispered, 'and feel sure nobody was watching you there, but it is possible you were picked up. You are in such a state of fatuous imbecility that you probably wouldn't notice if a whole crowd of people, interested in your movements, was surrounding you.'

'You must take me for a fool,' grunted Hill. Reference to the reason for his being in Rome sobered him down. 'I can assure you that I was very much on the watch. I have been in the service far too long to let my attention wander. You can put your uneasy old mind at rest – nobody picked me up and followed me from the Pincio or anywhere else.'

'One thing worries me,' confessed Shannon. 'It's about you and Thalia. If Plasiras and the rest notice your association with her, do you think it is likely to rouse their suspicions against either you or her or both of you?'

Hill shook his head confidently.

'She and I have talked it over,' he told his colleague. 'Yesterday she wanted to insist that friendship was impossible between us, first because, being a lady's companion, she was not her own mistress.

When I told her that made no difference to me, she hinted that there were other circumstances which might make it impossible. But she arranged to meet me today. After extracting a promise of secrecy from me, she told me that she was employed by the Greek government to watch the people with whom she is associating. I gave the promise, feeling a bit of a rotter as you can guess – God! How I longed to tell her the truth! Anyhow we discussed the matter from every angle, and eventually agreed that the more openly we associated the less likelihood there was of suspicion against either of us being roused. She has already spoken to her employer of the "nice" young Austrian gentleman she met on the stairs.' Hill grinned, 'She proposes now to introduce me to Bikelas and his wife.'

Shannon grunted in a non-committal manner.

'I suppose it will be safer to be quite open,' he agreed. 'It is quite evident, though, that Thalia Ictinos is not an ideal secret agent. She has a lot to learn. The idea of confiding in a man, she has only just met, such intelligence concerning herself strikes me as amusing. She must be very much in love, and consider herself a supreme judge of character, to do that. The sooner you marry her, old chap, and take her away from espionage altogether, the safer for her. Drink your coffee, and come upstairs with me. We have a lot to discuss.'

When they were in the confines of Shannon's bedroom, Hill regarded his host rather dolefully.

'I'm afraid I've nothing to report at all yet, Hugh,' he observed. 'I have an idea there was a conference or something on last night, but, bless you, they stuck a johnny outside the door like a sentinel. I got into conversation with him in good polite Austrian fashion, but he was most unresponsive. There was absolutely no means of listening. I stuck my ear to the wall, but of course heard nothing. I'm wondering if I—'

'You can stop wondering, and listen to me instead,' interrupted the other.

He plunged into an account of his expedition up the chimney, and repeated once again the conversation he had heard. Hill became profoundly interested and, of course, appalled; his only comments being exclamations of abhorrence. Shannon then went on to tell him that he had reported to Sir Leonard, and carefully repeated the instructions he had received. At the end, Hill whistled thoughtfully.

'It's rather annoying to me,' he declared enviously, 'that you were able to accomplish all that, while I was more or less sucking my thumb in exasperation. I heard them whispering together, when they must have been removing the body, but though I glued my ear to the front door I couldn't make out what it was all about. I also heard the lift go down. The shaft stands a few feet in front of my flat. It seems to me Sir Leonard has set us a bit of a problem. Obviously he wants to make no move against the conspirators, until he is sure that Kyprianos cannot revenge himself by sowing this disease of his broadcast. How can we render his cultures innocuous without his knowing it, and alternatively, if we find a way, how can we manage in such a manner that he is unaware of the fact. Euclid, my dear Hugh, would say it is impossible.'

Shannon, who was sitting on the bed, a favourite spot when he had a visitor, leant forward.

'If Kyprianos disappeared,' he observed tensely, 'none of the others would dare touch anything.'

'No; perhaps not, but they might take alarm and disperse.'

'There is a chance that they would not, but I have an alternative. What do you say to kidnapping him for an hour or so, and in that time rendering him incapable of doing anything? A temporary derangement of the mind for instance?'

Hill looked startled; then he slowly shook his head.

'A man in that condition would possibly be obsessed with the thoughts which had been uppermost in his mind before his reason left him. It is quite likely that Kyprianos would be more dangerous than ever then.'

'Well, what do you suggest?'

Hill eyed him thoughtfully.

'You are suggesting that I use my knowledge and whatever skill I possess as a doctor to do something antagonistic to medical principles.'

'Do you object?'

'No; I don't exactly object. As a member of the Secret Service I am all for it; nevertheless, medical ideals persist in me a little.'

'If they do,' declared Shannon bluntly, 'you should be the more eager to use your skill to keep this infernal scoundrel from spreading the disease he has concocted among a host of innocent people. If a raid is made, before anybody could get at him, he could do unthinkable harm. He is probably prepared for an emergency. It is absolutely essential to render him harmless and, at the same time, keep the whole gang from getting the wind up and dispersing before they can be apprehended.'

'You're right of course. Let me think it over for an hour or two, and I'll hit upon something. How do you propose to get hold of him?'

'That shouldn't be difficult. If it wasn't for the fact that he shares his flat with Michalis and Radoloff, we could do a little burglary and hold him up. However, that's out of the question. He'll have to be watched, and the opportunity taken when it comes. You'll have the task of keeping your eye on him. I'll spend most of my time in the hotel so that I'll be at hand, if you telephone through. There is bound to come a time when Radoloff and Michalis are out, leaving the way clear. Kyprianos, I should imagine, will spend most of his time in the laboratory he is fitting up.'

'That will mean that the job will have to be done in the daytime.'

'We can't help that. We've done jobs in the daytime before. When do you think you will have come to a decision?'

'I'll ring you up about six. That do?'

'Splendidly. We mustn't rush the affair. It has got to be done properly when we do it.'

'He deserves to be finished off altogether. It would be poetic justice, were he found to have died of heart failure.'

'It certainly would, but my squeamish soul would revolt, I fear.'

Shannon was sprawling inelegantly in his armchair, smoking a pipe, and reading a book at six o'clock, when the telephone rang exactly on the stroke. He took up the receiver.

'Herr Kirche speaking,' announced Hill's voice with a hint of laughter in it. 'I have to thank you once more for the enjoyable lunch party, and more especially for the news you gave me. I have been presented to Monsieur and Madame Bikelas who know Vienna well. It was good to discuss the beautiful city together, and we all went into ecstasies. My friend, it was very touching. I have been received as a very nice friend for Thalia to know. We go to the opera together tonight. The others are not going out.'

Shannon chuckled softly. Hill had conveyed one item of information neatly.

'I am glad things are progressing so well with you, Herr Kirche. Am I to congratulate you yet?'

'My friend, you must think I am a monster devouring without thought. When a dish of such exquisite daintiness is before one, it is necessary to approach it with reverence and care. In spite of your words, I am very nervous, and fear it may elude me. I am here in the wonderful shop of Messieurs Lalére et Cie, purchasing a little present for the divine Thalia.'

Thus Hill conveyed the information that he was ringing up from Tempest's office, which again proved his wisdom. Steps may have been taken to listen in to any telephone calls he put through from his flat, and it was essential that the conspirators should not become interested in Shannon.

'You are a man of sense, Herr Kirche,' approved the stalwart Secret Service agent. 'There are no perfumes more delicately fragrant and, therefore, more fitting for Thalia than those of Lalére. Please convey my compliments to the manager, who has often supplied me with various requisites.'

'I certainly will. It will please you to know that the little matter is all arranged, that we spoke of. I have prepared the gift for our friend with the long name. It will please him very much, I think, for it will enable him to have a rest from his labours. It only remains now to choose the time for the surprise.'

Shannon expressed his gratification in similar terms, and Hill rang off. It is quite certain that, if anybody in the hotel had been listening to the conversation, he would have received an entirely erroneous idea concerning its purport. Shannon decided to give himself a night off. He dined at the Hotel de la Minerve then went on to the opera. He caught sight, soon after he entered, of Thalia and Hill sitting in a box. Thereafter he often glanced in their direction to find always that they were more absorbed in each other than in *Il Trovatore*, despite the fact that the singing was, as it ever is in Rome, glorious. Thalia looked marvellous, and Shannon thought, as he looked round him, that, though there were many beautiful women present, there was not one to compare with her. Raymond Hill was, he decided, the most fortunate of men.

Several days went by, and the opportunity did not come for which Shannon and Hill were waiting. It almost seemed as though, expecting some attack to be made on Kyprianos, his companions were guarding him. Always one or more seemed to be with him. Hill pointed out that it was more likely that they were so distrustful of the Cypriot that they were keeping a watch on him. Shannon was disposed to agree. When listening to the conference they had held, he had sensed that the rest were more or less frightened of Kyprianos. His refusal to tell them what he hoped to gain from their operations, and the sinister manner in which he had assured them that they would immediately grant whatever he asked had been somehow deadly significant. The Englishman thought that, whilst they might be aspiring to dictatorial powers in their respective countries, he was possibly anticipating hovering in the background, and becoming dictator over all.

Every morning, as arranged, Shannon spoke to headquarters in London; was commended for not taking risks. After the first day, Sir Leonard did not speak to him personally, but Major Brien apparently approved rather than disapproved of the inaction. Sir Leonard seemed to be quite content with the waiting game that was being played. Shannon himself was chafing against the delay. His whole nature rebelled against idling away his time as he was doing. He spent hours in his bedroom, sometimes with Hill, planning and scheming. They were even prepared to kidnap Kyprianos when he went out, but unfortunately, on the rare occasions when he emerged from the seclusion of his flat, he was always accompanied by one, at least, of his friends. Thalia began to show concern. Twice she met Shannon on the terrace of the Pincio, and the second time enquired anxiously when she was to be permitted to communicate with her government. He succeeded in soothing her, not without a certain amount of difficulty. She explained that she was very eager to be finished with the affair, and he understood that her impatience was due chiefly to her association with Hill. They spent a considerable amount of time in each other's company, and their demeanour was now wholly that of lovers, though Raymond, brave to the point of recklessness otherwise, could not succeed in getting up sufficient courage to propose.

Five days after Shannon's adventure in the chimney, his telephone rang, and he took off the receiver, eagerly expecting and hoping that his caller was Hill with the announcement, at last, that Kyprianos was alone. He was disappointed and a trifle perturbed when he heard Thalia's voice. She declared urgently that she must see him; asked if she could come to the hotel, and straight to his room, assuring him that she was quite certain she was unobserved. She was telephoning from the post office. Rather reluctantly he agreed. Ten minutes later he opened the door to her knock. She entered hurriedly and, when it was closed, crossed to the armchair, and sat down. She looked upset; accepted the cigarette he gave to her with a little nod of thanks.

'What's the trouble, Thalia?' he asked, taking up his usual perch on the bed.

'I wish to ask you first, Hugh,' she declared, blowing a cloud of smoke into the air, 'whether it is true that you have been in this affair almost since the beginning and, if it is so, to warn you that you are in great danger.'

He started.

'Tell me why you ask this question?' he demanded.

'This morning there arrived from Cyrpus two men – one is a Greek called Padakis, and the other is a Cypriot by name of Baltazzi. Ah! I see you know them!' His involuntary exclamation, though suppressed almost at birth, had not escaped her. 'You perhaps also know that they are spies of Plasiras. They were in London, and there tried to do something which was found out. They had to run away and, from Paris, they communicated with Plasiras who was then in Cyprus. That is why, I think, we all left in a hurry. It is a British island, and it was feared the British authorities knew too much. Baltazzi and Padakis were told to go quickly to Cyprus, and watch with another spy, a woman called Malampos. As soon as they arrived, they discovered that Madame Malampos and several others had been killed in a terrible fight. These people had tried to capture and murder an English girl, who was thought to be a British espionage agent, and a man of giant stature, who was with her, and also suspected. The two spies received that information from one of the survivors. There were only two – two from nine men and a woman! Three had got away, but one had since died. The Englishman's name was Shannon. It was said that he had enormous strength, and had fought like six men. Only you could do that, Hugh. The Mr Shannon and the Captain Shannon I know are the same person, are they not?'

'Yes, Thalia, they are,' he admitted. It would have been useless to have attempted to deny it.

'Oh, Hugh,' she cried passionately, 'why could you not confide in me, and trust me? Have I not shown that I am worthy of your trust now?'

'You have,' he replied promptly, 'but please try and realise, Thalia, that I am not my own master. When I am told to do a thing, I have to do it without confiding in anyone. I was sent to Cyprus to investigate. Miss Havelock and I were trapped through the wiles of that woman Malampos.' A tinge of sadness entered his voice as he added: 'Miss Havelock was killed – even with all my strength I was unable to prevent that.'

'I heard, too, that she was dead. Poor girl! I am so sorry.'

'I traced your party to Rome, and that is practically all there is to tell.'

'Then it was not to help me you have done so much.' She spoke in sorrowful tones. 'I was so happy, Hugh, because I thought that your eagerness to assist me showed that you believed in me. But it was done not for me, but for your own country.'

'It was done for both,' he insisted earnestly.

She shook her head.

'I know now,' she declared, 'that you must have had greater distrust of me than ever I imagined. I thought I was telling you what you did not know, when I confided in you, but you already knew everything, and finding me with these people—' she shrugged her dainty shoulders. 'What else could you think, but that I was one of them?'

'I did believe that,' he confessed. 'I admit it, and I thought you were attempting to trap me. When I first saw you, I guessed that you would recognise me, and I took care to avoid you, while I kept watch on you. When you passed my table in the restaurant, and looked at me, I was very much perturbed. I thought you would be certain to tell your companions who I was. I continued to distrust you a little after you had come to me. But you soon destroyed all suspicion, which after all was not personal suspicion so much as suspicion engendered by my profession. Now I can honestly say that I am proud to be associated with you, and your friendship is very precious to me.'

'Do you mean that – really mean it from your heart?' she asked eagerly.

'From my soul, Thalia.'

'Then I am not sad any more. I understand it all and do not blame you. But listen, Hugh, you are in danger. One of those men – Baltazzi I think – saw you in London. He again saw you this morning near the British embassy. He tried to follow you, but fortunately for you, he missed you in a crowd of people. They will be looking for you everywhere.'

'Dash it! That's a nuisance,' exclaimed Shannon, more in annoyance than concern. 'I wonder when the fellow saw me in London.'

'That I do not know.'

'How did you hear all this?'

'I was out with Herr Kirche, but returned earlier than I had expected. He spends very much time in his flat – I think he is making notes about Rome in order to write a book or something of that sort.' The idea of Hill writing a book made Shannon feel inclined to smile, but he refrained. 'When I entered, voices came to me very loudly from the sitting room – it was because they were so noisy that I was not heard I think. Plasiras and Bikelas were there with the two men and the secretary. I listened. Madame had gone with Signora Bruno to the Vatican, and it was known that I was out. They, therefore, thought they were quite safe. When I had heard all I have told you, I crept out again like a mouse, and shut the front door with the key in order that there would not be a sound. For a little while I walked, looking back many times to make sure I had not been heard and followed. Then I took a taxicab to the Pantheon and, from there, another to the Piazza Colonna. After that, I walked to the post office, and telephoned you.'

'I am very grateful to you, Thalia. It is certain that, without the aid you have given me, I should have failed altogether in this business. Now that Baltazzi and Padakis are in Rome, I suppose they will be delegated to search for me.'

'Without doubt. Plasiras and Bikelas are very much disconcerted. The presence here of the man who was in Cyprus will have caused them great concern. I could not stop to hear more than I have told you, for I would have been discovered, if I had. Then perhaps I would have died of heart disease, and you would have known nothing.' Her lips curved in a smile, but the expression in her eyes was very grave. 'I do not wish to die, Hugh – not now.'

He rose; stood towering over her.

'Please don't talk like that,' he begged. 'God! How I hate you to be in that flat. I shall hate it more than ever now, for they will be on the alert so much more. You can't manufacture some excuse for leaving?'

She shook her head.

'I cannot leave until my work is done,' she reminded him quietly. 'I think you must allow me to send in my report to Athens.'

'Wait just a day or two longer. I promise that within forty-eight hours you can do it. It is essential now that I act at once.'

'What are you going to do?'

'I don't know yet. I shall have to think.'

'You mean,' she flashed, rising to her feet, 'that you yet do not trust me.'

'I mean nothing of the sort,' he returned promptly, and with emphasis. 'I do trust you, and it is quite true that I don't know what I am going to do. I will tell you this much: it is essential that, before any steps are taken officially against the conspirators, I must make certain that Kyprianos cannot perform some dreadful revengeful act with those cultures of his. How to do that is a problem, but it must be done.'

'Of course – I did not think of that before. Forgive me, my friend, because I was hasty. Tell me what I can do to help.'

'Nothing – absolutely nothing,' he declared emphatically. 'Already one girl, in association with me, has met her death. I do not intend to allow you to come to any harm.'

She smiled; took his hand with a caressing gesture, and raised it to her cheek. A hot flush surged to his face. At that moment all her glamour, fascination, and magnetism seemed to hold him in thrall.

'My big Hugh,' she murmured softly, 'you are very charming to me – like a great, loving brother. But, because we are working together, I must do my share. It is my duty, and my country expects it. Besides, my friend, I do not intend any more to let you face all the danger by yourself.'

He strove to persuade her to allow him to work alone, but she was gently insistent. He succeeded, however, in getting her to be content with the promise that he would ask her assistance, when he had made his plans and was ready to act. Secretly he vowed that her aid would consist in going somewhere where she was out of danger. He discovered, on questioning her, that she had had no communication with the Greek embassy in Rome, and advised her to prepare her report; address it to the ambassador with instructions that it was to be telegraphed to Athens as soon as she gave the word. That pleased her; it meant that the step she was anxious to take would be well on the way towards accomplishment. She declared she would return to the flat, and write it at once, whereupon he pointed out the unwisdom of such an act. She could hardly choose more dangerous surroundings.

'Is it to be sent in code?' he asked.

'Yes; but the code I know by heart.'

'Excellent. Then, why not write it here? I will descend to the lounge while you are engaged. As soon as you are finished, you can destroy the original and all paper you use in translating it into cipher. Lock the door, and I will return in about three-quarters of an hour. Will that be enough?'

'You will not leave the room, Hugh,' she declared with a glorious smile. 'It is unnecessary. You will not seek to learn the secrets of the code – you are a gentleman.'

'Thank you,' he acknowledged simply.

He provided her with paper and a fountain pen, whereupon she sat at the desk with which the room was provided, and commenced her task. Shannon lounged in the armchair smoking his pipe, and turning over in his mind the very disconcerting news she had brought to him. It took her nearly an hour to complete the work on which she was engaged. He was able to produce the sealing wax she requested, and turned away, as she drew from the bosom of her dress the emblem of her service, with which she stamped the hot wax. Returning the symbol to its tender resting place and the letter with it, she gathered up the sheaf of now unnecessary papers and burnt them carefully in the grate.

'It is done,' she announced triumphantly.

He crushed the ashes underfoot, until there was practically nothing left of them.

'One can't be too careful in our job,' he commented.

'When this business is finished,' she declared, 'I will ask you to give me lessons, in order that I may become a good agent of the espionage.'

'When this business is finished,' he retorted, 'I hope I will receive an invitation to your wedding.'

She blushed hotly, while a tremulous little smile played round her lips.

'Oh, you confuse me,' she protested. 'I think perhaps never will that happiness come to me.'

'I am sure it will. Why don't you help Raymond to obtain courage to ask you the question he is yearning to ask?'

'I! Mon Dieu! How terrible you are. Perhaps he does not desire to ask me that question.'

'He does, and you know it, Thalia.'

'I must go,' she pronounced hastily; looked him gravely in the face. 'Be advised by me in one matter, Hugh,' she urged earnestly. 'Do not go near the British embassy. I think they will watch for you there. Also please change from this hotel, and take another name. It will be easy for them to find you by enquiring at all hotels until they know where a gentleman whose name is Shannon is registered.'

'You are right. I shall have to make a move at once. I'll let you know, through Herr Kirche, my new address.'

He opened the door, and looked cautiously out. At once he had closed it again.

'There is a man standing a little way along the corridor,' he announced. 'His back was turned luckily. Will you take a peep to make certain that you do not know him?'

She did so with extreme caution. Like him, she quickly shut the door again; gazed up at him with fear in her eyes, her face even whiter than usual.

'It is too late for you to go, Hugh,' she whispered. 'They have found you. It is Baltazzi!'

CHAPTER SIXTEEN

And Administers Chastisement

It was with an emotion, which was almost pride in her, and certainly admiration, that Shannon heard her words. There was not a thought for her own extremely dangerous position; apparently she was entirely unconcerned about herself. Yet, unless they could think of some means to cause Baltazzi to go away, it was certain that her association with him would become known, and mean death for her; death without compunction or mercy.

'I'm not worrying about myself,' he murmured. 'The only question that concerns me is to get you away from here. If Baltazzi goes back, and reports that you are here with me, it will be fatal for you. On no account must he be allowed to do that.'

'I do not see how it is to be prevented,' she returned calmly. 'Now he has found you, he will keep watch until he sees you. I think he is waiting to make sure. He is not to know that the gentleman with the name of Shannon, staying in this hotel, is the right one. I suppose there are others with your name, Hugh.'

'Many,' he smiled. 'You are quite certain, I suppose, that he hasn't traced you here?'

'Oh, I am quite sure of that. Also I am certain none of the hotel staff saw me come to this room.'

'Good. Then I think I see a way out for you.'

'For me! But what of yourself?'

'My dear Thalia,' he declared, 'I am perfectly capable of looking after myself. Don't worry about me!' He glanced at his watch. 'Good Lord! It is nearly six, and we haven't had any tea.'

She laughed.

'How funny you are! You English are very strange about afternoon tea. Here we are beset by a very difficult and dangerous situation; yet you think with regret of the tea you have forgotten.'

'Don't you like your afternoon cup?'

'Sometimes I do, but to me it is not of great importance.'

'You don't mind missing it then?'

'No, no, of course not.'

'Well, listen! I am going out. Baltazzi will be sure to follow me. Wait for five or ten minutes; then go. Make quite certain first that the way is clear.'

'But I do not like it, Hugh. He may attempt to do you harm.'

'Let him try,' returned Shannon grimly. 'I guarantee he will be very sorry.'

'You will not go anywhere where it is dangerous; I mean to a place where there are no people, and you can be attacked?'

Her question gave him an idea.

'It might be a good notion,' he replied slowly, 'to go where he would be likely to attack me. The danger of Baltazzi might then be removed.'

She eyed him anxiously for a few moments; then gradually a smile replaced the trouble in her face.

'I do not think he could succeed in doing you harm,' she

decided, 'but be careful, my friend, men of his kind do not fight with fairness. They are full of much treachery.'

'I know, but I shall have one advantage, Thalia. He will not think I am aware he is trailing me.' He picked up his hat and stick. 'Now don't leave this room until you are perfectly certain the way is clear.'

She promised and, with a smiling word of farewell, he went out, closing the door firmly behind him. The man, thin, olive-skinned, and dark-eyed, was still in the corridor, this time only a few yards away. He turned sharply as Shannon approached; pretended to be looking for a room. The Englishman passed him by without apparently taking any notice of him, descended in an elevator and, crossing the lounge, left the hotel. He walked along until he came to a shop, the window of which, containing material of a dark hue, caused the glass to make an excellent mirror. At first he saw nothing of Baltazzi, but presently, to his satisfaction, he caught sight of the man standing a few feet away, and with him was now another. The newcomer was a stranger, and Shannon came to the conclusion that he must be Padakis. Two of them! That rather suggested they had orders to attack him, if the opportunity presented itself. Excellent, thought Shannon; he would provide them with the opportunity. He continued on his way, occasionally stopping to glance in the glass of a shop window to make sure they were following.

He reached the Piazza del Popolo and, turning into the Via Fernando di Savoia, came to the Ponte Margherita over the Tiber. Here he remained for some time leaning on the parapet, and gazing down into the river below. From the corner of his eye, he saw Baltazzi and his companion, a man of about the same height but stouter. They had stopped some distance away and, like himself, were apparently engaged in studying the water. There was an unusually chilly wind blowing in from the sea, and the hint of a storm – a sudden change after the extremely hot weather Rome had been experiencing. The bridge was almost deserted, and Shannon reflected that here was a splendid opportunity for the two men to attack him. A sudden stab in the back, as they passed their unsuspecting victim, and their chances of being observed, that is, if they chose the moment well, would be practically nil. A car travelling in the direction of the Via Cola di Rienzi sped swiftly by, a farm cart going in the opposite direction rattled noisily past; then, as far as Shannon was able to observe, the bridge was empty, except for himself and his two trailers.

They left their post, and walked quickly in his direction. Immediately he prepared himself, the stick slipping as though unheeded to the ground. Baltazzi, who was walking slightly ahead of his companion, drew closer. The distance between him and the Englishman rapidly diminished; four or five yards separated them, two, one! Then Shannon swung round at the identical moment that Baltazzi sprang forward, a gleaming stiletto upraised viciously in his hand. The Secret Service man neatly sidestepped, and crashed his right fist full into the other's face with all the power of his mighty body. There was a sickening crunch, a half-stifled cry, and his assailant went down as though he had been poleaxed. At the same time, and with a cry of rage, the second man sprang forward. Shannon went down promptly on one knee and, catching the fellow by the waist, sent him flying over his head and the parapet down to the river below. He was up in time to see him strike the water with a tremendous splash. Presently he rose to the surface, and struck out awkwardly for the bank. It was evident that he was not an expert swimmer, but there were boats about. He would undoubtedly be picked up, which, reflected Shannon, was, on the whole, rather a pity. He turned, and contemplated Baltazzi for a moment. The fellow lay stretched on his back quite unconscious, his face in a deplorable state. The bridge was still deserted and, picking up his stick, the Englishman set off rapidly along the way he had come. He had no desire to be involved in an investigation, and was relieved when he reached the Via Cola di Rienzi without meeting a soul. There he took a taxi, and was driven back to his hotel. He packed at once, paid his bill, announcing that he had been called away, and drove to the railway station. From there he took another car, the driver of which he instructed carefully. He was conveyed across Rome, coming at length to the Ponte Garibaldi, thence to Trastevere. Not far from the Porta Portese, in the vicinity of the church of St Maria dell' Orto, was the house of an English widow, whom he knew well. There he obtained rooms.

As soon as he could do so, he went out again, and telephoned Hill. Speaking German, he announced himself as a friend from Vienna, giving a name which he and Hill had agreed he should use in case of emergency. An arrangement was made to dine together in a restaurant near the university, one simple little word from Shannon warning his colleague to take special precautions not to be followed. Hill found him standing by a taxi in which he was at once invited to enter. They were driven rapidly to the Via Garibaldi, from where they walked to Shannon's new abode. To all of Hill's interested questions he turned a deaf ear, until they were sitting together in the seclusion of his sitting room.

'If I have been traced now,' he declared with a smile; 'then Plasiras and the rest must have supernatural powers. We are dining here, Tubby, and I can promise you a meal which will make you think you are back in London. But the greatest advantage is that we can talk without restraint. Mrs Herbertson is the widow of a man who was in the Diplomatic Service, and died of enteric here. Perhaps that's why she settled down in Rome. She is absolutely reliable, knows quite a lot about my wicked ways, and will ensure that once we have dined, nobody will come anywhere near us. I'm rather sorry now that I didn't come here in the first place.'

'But why all this sudden secrecy?' demanded Hill.

Shannon ignored the question for the moment.

'I'm sorry I haven't the doings for your particular brand of cocktail, Tubby,' he apologised, 'but I can give you a gin and It, pink gin, mixed vermouth, or a gin and french. What is it to be?'

Hill chose a mixed vermouth, while Shannon prepared a Gin and Angostura for himself. Then he sat down, and narrated all that had happened, from the time he had received Thalia's telephone call until they had met near the Pantheon. Hill showed a good deal of concern at the information that Baltazzi and Padakis were in Rome, had discovered Shannon's presence there, and traced him to the Hotel Splendide. He laughed with sheer delight, however, at the description of the chastisement that had been meted out to them on the Ponte Margharita. Over dinner they discussed the situation intermittently, continuing it afterwards more intensely and gravely, when there was no longer any possibility of their being interrupted. Hill was, of course, full of admiration and acclamations for Thalia. He contended that, after the service she had performed for Shannon, the latter could not possibly harbour any doubts concerning her. Hugh told him, at once, that his suspicions had long since been dispersed. He spoke, in fact, as enthusiastically of her as his companion, much to that young man's gratification.

'Tomorrow morning,' he declared, 'I shall ask to speak to the chief himself when I ring through. I shall tell him, of course, what has happened, laying stress on the part she has played, and ask if, under the circumstances, we can take her altogether into our confidence. If he agrees, as I think he will, you will be able to tell her who you really are.'

'What a relief that will be!' commented Hill with feeling. 'I have never hated anything in my life as much as I have hated this necessity of keeping up the pretence to her of being what I am not.'

'By the way,' remarked Shannon drily, 'en passant, Tubby, let me tell you that I am tired of acting as a benevolent matchmaker. When are you going to ask her to be your wife?'

'God knows,' groaned Hill. 'I don't seem to have the nerve. Several times I have been on the point of attempting it, only to back out. Hang it all, Hugh! It seems such a colossal cheek to propose to a girl I have known little more than a week.'

'Rot! You're chicken-hearted,' jeered the other. 'She loves you – you love her. Why, dash it! I'll do it for you, if you don't get a move on.'

'I almost wish you would.'

Shannon stared hard at him; then laughed.

'I'm inclined to believe you mean it. But there's nothing doing, old son. That's a job a man ought to do for himself, especially if he wishes to retain the respect of the girl. Go for it – you've nothing to fear. I guarantee that. Now back to our discussion. We've got to act at once now that the blighters know there is someone here on their trail. My treatment of the two spies will put the wind up them more than ever. I suppose you haven't noticed any signs or portents suggestive of the fact that they are about to go elsewhere?'

Hill shook his head.

'All my efforts at watching them end in dismal failure,' he grunted. 'I've been as much use in Rome as an attack of measles. It's perfectly sickening the way Kyprianos is guarded. How on earth can we get at him, when there are always others with him?'

'We'll have to make a way now. We can't possibly wait.'

They sat silently turning over the problem in their minds for some time. At last Shannon turned to Hill, his eyes gleaming.

'The stuff is quite ready you say?'

'Yes; has been for days – all in a hypo, ready for injection.'

'And the effect is general paralysis – he won't be able to move a limb or cry out?'

'No; his body will be more or less dead for a few days, though his mind will remain active enough. The sensory and motor functions of the nerves will be quite lost for at least a hundred hours. After that he will recover, but by slow degrees.'

'In what part of the body must the injection be made?'

'In the spine. Why all this questioning?'

'Because I'm going to get into that flat tonight,' was Shannon's quiet reply. 'I gather that Kyprianos occupies the room he has turned into a laboratory alone, the others I presume have each one of the bedrooms. Between two and three in the morning they all ought to be asleep, and perhaps I can do the job without disturbing Radoloff and Michalis. I'll take the hypodermic syringe with me and, if you show me the exact spot where the needle must be stuck, I'll—'

'Here, steady on, Hugh. Where do I come in?'

'You stop out. If anything goes wrong, I'll want someone on the outside to notify headquarters. We mustn't risk both of us being done in and spoiling the show altogether.'

Hill protested vehemently, but he might as well have attempted an argument with a brick wall. Shannon had made up his mind, and he refused to give way, even on the smallest point. He did not mention that another reason why he had determined to act alone was because of the love between Thalia and his colleague. He had no wish to run Hill into danger, which might easily end in the loss of his life, when he was on the verge of experiencing a great happiness. There is no time as a rule for sentiment in the lives of the men of the Secret Service, but occasionally it is permitted to creep in. Shannon knew very well that, if he had hinted at his secondary reason for undertaking the venture alone, Hill would have been immensely indignant, and refused point-blank to agree to the scheme. Apart from that, Hugh honestly felt he could manage by himself, and that it was necessary to have an unsuspected assistant to inform headquarters, and carry on in the event of failure. He made Hill show him very carefully the exact spot in the spine where the needle of the syringe was to be inserted. The ex-doctor made one last effort to dissuade him from his purpose.

'Is it worthwhile doing this now?' he asked. 'Won't they guess that Kyprianos' condition is not accidental or natural, since they know you are in Rome and very much on their track. You can't expect them to imagine that they and their whereabouts are unknown to you, especially as you have shown so pointedly that you are aware of the existence of Baltazzi and Padakis.'

'I don't see why they should suspect that I have entered the flat and drugged Kyprianos. They won't gather the point of that action, and I shall certainly leave no evidence of my presence behind. The very fact that they will be almost sure to decide on secret departure from Rome, now they realise I'm busy here, makes it urgent that something must be done, *and tonight*. Be ready for me at two, Ray.'

Hill departed reluctantly, and with a great deal of misgiving concerning the outcome of the desperate venture on which Shannon had set his heart. On one point he was determined; that was, if Shannon did not reappear after a reasonable interval, he would immediately ring up Tempest who, fortunately, possessed a flat over his place of business, and go himself to the rescue. He drove to the Ludovici quarter, and was so deep in thought that he had arrived at his address before he was aware that he was anywhere near it. To his surprise and delight, he found Thalia reclining on a lounge in the great entrance hall. She was in a dark evening gown without ornament of any sort, while her face, under the artistic, subdued lighting, looked paler even than usual. She greeted him with a glad smile, her eyes brightening as though she were greatly relieved to see him. He eagerly accepted her invitation to sit by her side.

'You have been dining out?' she asked.

'Yes,' he returned. 'I – I met a friend at the Pantheon Restaurant. Have you been out?'

She shook her head.

'The storm has passed. It is very nice in the air, and I would like to walk in the gardens. Will you escort me?'

He rose eagerly, and they walked out together. In the gardens she took his arm, sending a great thrill through him. There was no moon, but a wonderful array of stars dotted the heavens with a myriad points of light. For some time she was silent; then she spoke in a low tone that was little above a whisper.

'Raymond, I can trust you implicitly, can I not?'

'Of course – absolutely,' he responded, wondering what was coming.

'I knew I could, but it was necessary to ask. What I will tell you, you must not divulge to any but one person whose name I will mention presently. You give me your word of honour?' He gave it solemnly and earnestly. 'Thank you, my friend.' A little pressure on his arm rewarded him. 'Listen! You know something of the reason for which I am with these people. I was perhaps unwise to mention it even to you, but you have not betrayed my confidence, and, in that, you have shown me my judgment was good. That is why I am putting a further burden of my secrets on you. You have given your word, and I know you will not betray me.

'Captain Shannon, whom now you are getting to know very well, and who is my very good friend, is associating with me in the matter which has made me, for a little while, a lady's companion. He is of the British Secret Service, while I am of the Greek. Today men arrived who told Plasiras and Bikelas of his presence in Rome and, without doubt, proved why he was here. These men were sent, I think, to murder him. They found that he was at the Hotel Splendide. I am glad to say that they failed – Captain Shannon nearly drowned one, the other was found by the police, and taken to hospital with a broken nose and fractured skull. It will be long before he recovers, and he will not speak – that is certain. By much good fortune I heard that tonight it was proposed to put poison into Captain Shannon with the hypodermic syringe. Someone will knock into him in a crowd, he will feel a little prick, and all will be quickly over. I tried to telephone him, but was told that he had left the hotel, departing for England. It was good that he has left the hotel, but I know he is still in Rome. He told me he would communicate with me by you. When he does, please tell him the plot that is against him, and that the man who will do it is Kyprianos. You will not forget?'

'No, I will not forget,' responded Hill quietly.

'You take these matters in a manner very calm, my friend. Do they not horrify you?'

'They do, but I think Captain Shannon is well able to look after himself. It is of you I am thinking. The deadly danger that you must be in appals me. What will happen, if the people you are with discover your real identity?'

'Then, Raymond, I fear I would very quickly die.'

The thought of such a catastrophe drove all diffidence and shyness from him. In his emotion he forgot the role he was playing, forgot everything, except the fact that he loved this girl passionately, with a fervent devotion that came from his very soul.

'Thalia,' he said, 'give up this dangerous work you are doing. Live the sheltered and happy life a girl like you should live. Give me the chance of helping you enjoy that happiness. I love you with my whole soul – I worship you. Will you – will you marry me?'

It was out, much to his own astonishment. He stood awaiting her answer in a state of feverish anxiety. In the darkness he could just discern the pale oval of her face, but, of course, could not see the expression on it. He felt her arm tremble in his, however, and took heart. Presently came her words, slowly and softly, almost as though borne on the gentle breeze.

'Is it really true,' she asked, 'that you love me like that, and wish to make me your wife?'

'True!' he cried hoarsely. 'Surely you know how true it is?'

'Yes; I do know, I think, and – and I am very proud, for, oh, my Raymond, I, too, love you with a great love that seems to eat me up. No; wait please,' as, with a glad cry, he was about to take her into his arms. 'I am the daughter of a wicked, cruel man,' she went on tremulously, 'who would have been executed for many murders, if it was not that God willed him to die in prison of an illness. I also have been cruel and wicked and—'

'I know all about Stanislas Ictinos and his daughter,' interrupted Hill with impatient ardour, 'and I know that his daughter, who seemed cruel and wicked, was not then her real self. But now she is – she is just fine, noble – and wonderful.'

'But how could you know about me?' she asked in wonderment.

'Never mind that – it suffices that I do know. Thalia – sweetheart, won't you put me out of my suspense?'

'You will – will not fear me as a wife?'

'Fear you! I shall just adore you. You have told me you love me and—'

'I love you so much,' she whispered, 'that it hurts. It will be the greatest of all bliss, I think, to be your wife.'

Without further hesitation, he swept her into his arms, and their lips met in a wonderful, ecstatic kiss.

How long they remained thus, utterly oblivious to the passing of time, neither of them ever knew. At length she stirred in his embrace; her hand caressed his cheek as she pushed him gently from her.

'Raymond, my love,' she asked softly, 'why was it you spoke in English when you told me you loved me?'

He stiffened apprehensively.

'Did I?' he asked.

'Yes; as if it was natural to you. You spoke with great emotion, and I think – yes, I am sure – it was your mother tongue that came to your lips. You are not an Austrian – you are English, are you not?'

It would have been absurd under the circumstances to deny it.

'I am,' he admitted.

'Why did you deceive me?' she questioned in reproachful tones.

He sought desperately for some way out that would not betray his calling, but the more he thought the deeper became his difficulty. Then suddenly came a surprising interruption.

'I think, Hill,' drawled a quiet, attractive voice in English, 'that

Miss Ictinos has proved that she is worthy to know the truth.'

Thalia started violently, and a little cry of fear broke from her lips. Hill stood dumbfounded; then:

'Great heavens!' he exclaimed forcibly. 'It's Sir—'

'S'sh!' warned the voice from the darkness. 'Don't mention my name please. Even trees can hear sometimes.'

'Who is it?' gasped Thalia.

A slight figure stepped forward from the deeper gloom. The girl felt her hand grasped, dimly discerned the newcomer bending over it.

'Our last meeting was under rather unfortunate circumstances,' he murmured. 'It gives me immense pleasure now to make the acquaintance of the – shall I say – real Thalia Ictinos. My name is Wallace – I am afraid you will remember me without a great deal of gratification.' Her exclamation of astonishment was stifled by the hand he placed gently on her mouth. 'Forgive my taking such a liberty,' he begged, 'but it is better not to speak too loudly. Now I'm going to congratulate you, if I may.'

Thalia was the first to recover from the profound surprise Sir Leonard Wallace had given her and Hill. Her eyes flashed her pleasure.

'You approve?' she asked eagerly.

'I do,' returned Sir Leonard; 'very much so. You have guessed then that Mr – Herr Kirche is a member of my department?'

'But of course. The manner of your coming, the name by which you called Raymond, and your remark that I was worthy to know the truth – all made me guess that he also was of the British Secret Service.' She sighed, as memory of the manner in which she had introduced Hill to Shannon, and the way her lover had deceived her into believing he was an Austrian, recurred to her mind. 'It is very bitter to think,' she murmured, 'that the man who loves me so much could not trust me.'

'Thalia, I could not—' began Hill in imploring tones.

'You must not blame him, Miss Ictinos,' interposed Wallace. 'He could not do otherwise. In our job we cannot think ever of ourselves or even those we love, when we are on duty. He has only done his duty – you must not blame him for that. Without my permission he would never reveal his real identity.'

'I understand,' replied the girl impulsively. 'For a little while there was a pain in my heart, but now it is gone. I am very much happy again now.'

'You won't mind marrying an Englishman instead of an Austrian?'

She laughed softly.

'I do not mind what he is – I love him,' she replied simply.

She felt the pressure of Hill's hand on her arm, and responded gladly to it.

'I must apologise,' declared Sir Leonard, 'for being present at a very intimate event, but you will both forgive me, I hope, when I assure you that I had no idea it was about to happen.' His hearers were both very grateful at that moment for the darkness. 'To be quite frank,' he went on, 'I was not quite convinced of the wisdom of your coming out here to talk. You were watched as you met in the hall, and I rather expected you would be followed, but the man who was watching you apparently decided it was no more than a lover's meeting. He returned to his flat. I followed you, and kept my eyes and ears open, however, in order to ensure that you would not be overheard by any dangerous person.'

'Who was the man, sir?' asked Hill.

'General Radoloff, I think he is called.'

'Oh,' murmured Thalia in tones of impatience, 'he pesters me with his attentions. Now that I go so much with Raymond he is very jealous I think.'

'And, therefore, all the more to be guarded against,' commented Sir Leonard. 'A jealous man can be dangerous at even the most innocent of times.'

'When did you arrive in Rome, sir?' asked Hill who, it must be confessed, had an uneasy feeling that he had not shown up too well. He was rather afraid that Sir Leonard would consider that his lovemaking and proposal might have been delayed for a more auspicious occasion.

He need not have worried. Sir Leonard had a very great understanding of human nature. He did not expect his assistants to be mere machines, altogether devoid of feeling.

'I have been here three days,' he replied in answer to the ex-doctor's question. 'I came actually to assure myself that Miss Ictinos is in reality the very gallant lady Captain Shannon described her in a report he sent me.'

'You have been watching me,' she accused.

'I have,' he returned frankly. 'And I may add that I endorse in every way the remarks of Captain Shannon.'

'Oh, thank you,' she murmured gladly. 'I am so happy to think that, Sir – that you have now that opinion of me. It is wonderful when—'

'We have forgotten the past,' he interrupted her. 'You must forget it also.'

'It will be very, very difficult,' she sighed. 'The name Ictinos is not good, and I bear it.'

'You will soon cast it aside for ever,' whispered Hill.

'That day I will thank the good God with very much sincerity.'

'I think you had other things to tell Hill,' Sir Leonard reminded her.

'Yes. Tomorrow it is proposed that, in small parties, Messieurs Plasiras, Bikelas and the others, except Kyprianos and Michalis, creep quietly from Rome and hide somewhere in the country. Kyprianos and Michalis with Padakis, the spy, search for Captain Shannon and, when they find him, intend to murder him. You heard me tell Raymond how it is to be done?'

'I did, but I don't think we need bother about that. As a matter of fact, I saw you go to the Hotel Splendide this afternoon, and gathered you had news to give him. Afterwards I saw Shannon come out, and became aware at once that he was being followed. I, therefore, followed his trackers, ready to go to his assistance if required. I was not required,' he added drily. 'If you will tell me what it was you told Shannon in the hotel, Miss Ictinos, it will save time and bring me right up-to-date.' She was about to commence, when he added: 'Wait a minute. I will just make certain everything is all right.'

As noiselessly as a shadow, he glided away. She gave a little gasp.

'How is it he can move without sound?' she whispered to Hill. 'And for three days he has been here watching everything, especially me, and I did not know. It is wonderful. You did not know he was in Rome – no?'

'No; I did not, neither did Shannon – I don't suppose he does yet. If Sir Leonard Wallace does not want his presence to be known, you can take it from me that it won't be.'

'My father was a fool to think he could win against a man like that. When I think back, it is so—'

'You must not think back, dear,' he insisted.

'No; I must not – I will remember. Oh! What was that?'

They heard a dull thud, a low groan and, it seemed to their startled ears, the sound of a heavy body falling. Hill was about to dart in the direction from whence the sound came, when Sir Leonard's voice reached them from a short distance away.

'It's all right – don't worry! I am afraid,' he went on, and the girl jumped as she found he was by her side, 'that General Radoloff was more inquisitive than I expected. At all events I saw him approaching from the direction of the house and, as there wasn't time to warn you, I hit him on the head with the butt of a revolver. He will be quite safe where he is for the present. There is nobody else about. Now, Miss Thalia, perhaps you will go on.'

CHAPTER SEVENTEEN

The Man in the Flat

The utter unconcern in his voice did more to still her alarm than anything else could possibly have done. She suddenly felt an inclination to laugh. Everything that had previously seemed so deadly and dangerous appeared somehow almost trivial now that Sir Leonard Wallace had come on the scene. His manner was so delightfully casual, she thought; it was that which made the desperate affairs in which she was involved lose a lot of their fearsomeness.

'Can you see in the dark?' she asked curiously.

'Well, now you come to ask,' he returned, 'I suppose I can fairly well. I have never thought of it before.'

She told him in a low voice of her visit to Shannon at the Hotel Splendide and of the news she had imparted to him there. She also spoke about the report she had written at his instigation, of their discovery of the waiting Baltazzi in the corridor, and Shannon's plan, which had enabled her to get away without her presence there being suspected. Hill had, of course, heard the story from his colleague's own lips.

'What did you do with that report?' asked Wallace, when she had finished.

'I sent it by a special messenger from the English library of Miss Wilson near the Spanish stairs. I knew it would be delivered with safety, if it went from there.'

'Excellent,' approved Sir Leonard. 'Now I think I am au fait with everything.'

'You will see that Captain Shannon is warned about the plot to kill him?' she asked anxiously.

'I am going to him now,' he assured her.

'Do you know where he is?' came eagerly from her.

'No; but I rather suspect Mr Hill does.'

'Do you, Raymond?'

'Yes; it was him I dined with this evening,' was the response.

'Oh!' She suddenly realised that she, as a secret agent, must seem very much of a novice to these experts, who appeared to accomplish everything they did with such ease and celerity. 'Then, Raymond, you will tell Sir Leonard, and he will warn Captain Shannon.'

'It is very much to your credit, Miss Ictinos,' declared Wallace, 'that you are filled with so much anxiety on Captain Shannon's behalf. I am far more concerned about you.'

'About me!' she echoed. 'Why?'

'Well, the unconscious body of Radoloff lying over there has rather complicated matters, hasn't it? Whether he suspected you and Hill of conspiring against him and his companions, or merely came out after you because he was jealous does not make any difference. Either you or he must not go back. I am rather inclined to think it had better be you. We don't know if he said anything to the others about his intentions, do we?'

'But I must go back,' she insisted. 'You would not have me

neglect my duty now that danger threatens, would you?'

'No; I would not, but I suggest you have done all you can do. Won't you leave the rest to us? If I may criticise your government, I think it was unwise to give you such a task. You have done magnificently, but the time has arrived, as it was bound to arrive, when it becomes a man's job. At least you should have had a man in the background somewhere to assist you.'

'They were not to know it was so big and desperate a plot.'

'No; I suppose not. And you really feel you must go back, even though there is little you can accomplish now?'

'I must. There are things I can, perhaps, overhear, as I have overheard them today.'

'That's true. Well, I will not attempt to dissuade you further. It means that Radoloff must not go back. He won't know who hit him on the head, but he will certainly think it was Hill, I'm afraid.'

'Then will it not be better,' she asked him anxiously, 'if Raymond disappears for a little while?'

'And leave you to face his wrath and suspicions alone!' commented Hill. 'Not likely.'

Sir Leonard laughed quietly.

'You might almost have been forgiven then,' he remarked, 'if you had said that as Mrs Patrick Campbell said it in Bernard Shaw's "Pygmalion".'

Hill indulged in one of his comfortable-sounding chuckles, which Thalia had learnt to love. She did not understand what her lover and Sir Leonard were amused about, but again she reflected upon the light-hearted manner in which they seemed to take matters which appeared to her to be so deadly serious.

'May I make a suggestion, sir?' asked Hill somewhat diffidently.

'Of course. What is it?'

'I think T. will find a way of hiding Radoloff until everything is cleared up. Shall I go and ring him up and explain? He can take charge of the Bulgarian then, as soon as he recovers consciousness, force him to write a note to his companions saying that Shannon is on his track and, rather than lead him to the building where they live, has retired, for the time being, to the house of a compatriot.'

Sir Leonard considered the suggestion.

'Yes; it might do very well,' he declared presently, 'especially as today's events have made it necessary for us to act at once.' He turned to Thalia. 'You have no reason to think that they suspect Captain Shannon of knowing their address?' he asked.

'I do not think they do,' she replied.

'That settles it. Go and telephone now, Hill, but not from your flat, of course. I hope you will find T. in. It is not very late, and he goes out a good deal. See Miss Ictinos back to her flat, and continue your delightfully open method of being seen together. May I request though,' he added, 'that your goodnights are not prolonged on this occasion. Au revoir, Miss Ictinos. As soon as there is the slightest hint of danger to yourself, leave your rooms without delay, and go to Hill. I think he will accept the role of protector with a good deal of alacrity.'

'Goodnight, Sir Leonard,' she murmured, 'and I thank you very much for your kindness to me. There is just one little request I would like to make. The name Ictinos I hate more and more every day. Do I ask you too much to drop it, and call me – just Thalia?'

'Not at all. Goodnight, Thalia. Don't fall over the general, Hill.'

With another comfortable chuckle the ex-doctor escorted the girl back to the building in which they both lived. Sir Leonard walked to the place where General Radoloff still lay unconscious. He had been struck by a hard blow expertly delivered. Sir Leonard calculated that he would not recover his senses for another hour at least. Hill was gone a little more than ten minutes; came back to announce that he had been fortunate enough to find Tempest at home, had delivered the message, and received the assurance that the Rome agent of *Lalére et Cie* would be on the spot very shortly. Hill then acquainted his chief with the plans Shannon had conceived for the early hours of the morning. Wallace listened attentively. At the end he approved heartily.

'That puts a different complexion on this Radoloff business,' he added. 'It will not be necessary to make him write that note. If all goes well, they should be under lock and key tomorrow by this time. I shall not visit Shannon after all. I'll wait in your flat for his arrival.'

Hill went to the road to watch for the arrival of Tempest's car. He had not long to wait. A great eight cylinder Lancia purred to a standstill a few yards away from him.

'OK, Hill,' came a voice. 'Will it be all right to stop here?'

Hill stepped towards the driving seat, and peered within. Tempest was sitting at the wheel and, by this side, a man whom the ex-doctor recognised as a stalwart retired English soldier, who acted as general factotum to the Rome branch of *Lalére et Cie*.

'No; don't remain here,' replied Hill. 'There is too much traffic. Go on by the gardens for fifty yards or thereabouts, and you come to a private road leading to the houses behind.'

'I know it.'

'Well, drive up about twenty yards, and wait for me.'

Tempest nodded, and the big car moved quietly away. Hill returned to Sir Leonard, informed him of the arrival of the others; then went to meet them at the spot he had indicated. Within three or four minutes he was back with them. The ex-soldier was carrying a roll of strong cord and a gag. At a word from Wallace, he and Tempest, assisted by Hill, proceeded to bind the still senseless Bulgarian general, who was then conveyed to the Lancia, and placed on the floor of the tonneau.

'Where do you propose to take him?' asked Sir Leonard of Tempest.

'I have a large loft over my flat, sir,' was the reply. 'It will be an ideal place, and Merryweather and I can attend to him ourselves.'

Wallace rubbed his chin dubiously.

'He must not know where he is,' he observed, 'and it will be wiser if he does not see you. On no account must any suspicion be raised that the firm has a connection with the British Intelligence Department.'

'He won't know where he is, sir, and, when he is removed, we'll blindfold him.'

'You'd better wear masks when you attend to him. It sounds rather melodramatic I know, but I don't want him to see your faces. At all events, you will only have to keep him there for a short while. When you have put him safely in the loft, Tempest, come back with Merryweather, and wait somewhere close by. I should think this is as good a spot as any. If an emergency arises, we may want your help, but don't let yourselves be seen.'

The car drove silently away. Hill was directed to ascend to his flat, and leave the front door ajar. He obeyed instructions. Ten minutes later Sir Leonard entered quietly, closing the door behind him. He accepted the whisky and soda Hill mixed for him; then, from the depths of a comfortable armchair, regarded his assistant with a quizzical smile.

'It was not very bright of you,' he commented, 'to break out suddenly into English, when you proposed to Miss Ictinos.

However, as it was under the stress of great emotion, I must forgive the lapse, I suppose. Probably I should have done the same thing.'

Hill's face turned crimson as he stammered his apologies. He knew very well that Sir Leonard would not have committed such a blunder. They discussed Shannon's coming enterprise thoughtfully, being chiefly concerned with the question of whether General Radoloff's continued absence from his flat would be noticed and cause alarm. Two or three times Hill crept out and, ascertaining that the way was clear, listened at the door. He was unable to hear anything to indicate whether the occupants were still up or had gone to bed. The fact that neither Bikelas from the floor below, nor Plasiras and Doreff from the opposite flat, had been summoned seemed to indicate that all was well. There was a possibility, of course, that they were already with Michalis and Kyprianos but, as time went on, and the building remained as silent as the grave, except for the occasional hum of a lift as a resident returned home, the waiting men felt reassured. Soon after midnight, Hill was directed to fetch Tempest and Merryweather. Acting on instructions, he switched off the dim lights that remained burning in the corridors and hall. The two newcomers, therefore, were brought silently up the stairs in complete darkness. Afterwards, Hill again switched on the single lamps that had been alight on each floor.

Nothing now interrupted the profound silence that reigned over the whole building. Tempest and his ex-soldier assistant were provided with refreshments by the hospitable Hill, and given chairs in which they could doze if they wished. Sir Leonard sat for long periods smoking his pipe; hardly moving. For three days he had been exceedingly busy, and had had little rest, but he showed no inclination to sleep. During that time he had learnt to know each of the conspirators by sight except Kyprianos. He had even been inside the flats of Bikelas and Plasiras, when he had assured himself their occupants were out, and had searched in vain for evidence of their activities. In addition, he had had a long conference with the British ambassador that morning, handing over to the latter a document in which the conspiracy was set out in full detail. The result of the conversation was that the ambassador was ready, on notification from Sir Leonard, to place before the Italian government all particulars of the conspiracy; demanding on behalf of Great Britain the arrest of Michalis and Kyprianos for plotting against the safety of the people of Cyprus. He could not, of course, insist on the apprehension of the others, but, as Bruno's part in the activities was aimed against Italy, and the rest were conspiring against their countries on Italian soil, the capture of the whole band would naturally be the object of the authorities.

At first Wallace had considered the advisability of asking the British ambassador to inform the Italian government at once, but the risk of such a proceeding was too apparent. A representative of a foreign power could not dictate or advise a course of action to Italy, and it was certain that, directly the police were acquainted with the facts, they would proceed against the conspirators. In that case, the result might have been appalling. Like Shannon, Sir Leonard felt certain that Kyprianos – a man whose mind had conceived a scheme so diabolical – would not submit quietly to arrest. It was certain that he was prepared for eventualities. Wallace envisaged him locking himself in his room on the first sign of alarm, opening the phials containing the cultures and, by some means or other, no doubt to hand, starting them on a journey of death through Rome. A catastrophe of such a nature was to be avoided at all costs, which was the reason why the British ambassador was not to move until Kyprianos had been rendered powerless.

The time passed slowly to the men awaiting the coming of Shannon. At fifteen minutes to two, Hill again made a journey downstairs, switching off the lights. He had hardly returned, leaving the door open, when Shannon slipped into the flat, moving with astonishing noiselessness for such a big man. His surprise was great, when he became aware of Sir Leonard Wallace reclining in an armchair in the sitting room. The two men shook hands warmly, Sir Leonard's first question being a thoughtful enquiry after Shannon's wounds. The young man assured him they were practically healed. The question naturally brought up the subject of the tragic fate of Barbara Havelock and the events in Nicosia. Hill, Tempest, and Merryweather stood in the background awaiting instructions, and their hearts went out to Shannon, as they observed the sorrow which mention of Barbara had brought to his face. They realised, as Sir Leonard did, that, though he was in no way to blame for her death, nothing that could be said would prevent him from blaming himself for the tragedy. Wallace switched the conversation quickly to the affair on hand.

'You have planned the whole business in order, as far as possible, to make it foolproof, I hope?' he asked, adding, with a smile, 'I am not anxious to lose one of my most valuable men.'

Shannon flushed a little at the compliment.

'Yes, sir,' he responded, 'I think everything is as cut and dried as it can be. Few of the doors in this building possess bolts, so I think I shall be able to get into Kyprianos' room, even if it is locked, without making a sound. First I shall enter the bedrooms of Michalis and Radoloff, extract the keys, and lock them in. That done, I shall enter the laboratory – I know exactly where it is – render Kyprianos helpless, stick the hypodermic needle in him, and give him the doings. Hill tells me that in five minutes he will be helpless. Sounds simple enough.'

'Yes; it sounds simple enough,' responded Sir Leonard drily. 'I hope it works as simply and easily as it sounds. By the way, you won't have to bother about General Radoloff. He is – er – out.'

'Radoloff out!' repeated Shannon in surprise.

Sir Leonard explained, and the burly Secret Service man laughed. The latter had been rather concerned lest Sir Leonard should forbid his venture. He was now feeling very much encouraged at the realisation that he approved of it. The chief did not even take charge. He had sent Shannon out on a mission, and it was always his way to leave his men to their own resources, only interfering, or giving advice, when he felt they were in need, or knew they were in difficulties. In the present case he did not make any alterations to Shannon's plans, except to suggest that, now there were so many of them to help on the outside, there was no reason why Hill should not accompany him and administer the injection to Kyprianos. He would have gone himself, but, in that event, Shannon would automatically have come under his orders and, as it was that young man's show, he felt it would be hardly fair to him.

'We'll give you half an hour,' he declared. 'That should allow you a margin for unexpected obstacles. If you have not returned at the end of that time, I will come to see what has happened.'

Shannon, who was wearing rubber-soled shoes, waited while Hill donned a similar pair; then the two quietly left the flat. They stood listening for some minutes, but not a sound reached their ears, and presently they softly approached the door of the suite it was their intention to enter. Shannon would rather have gone alone. He was sentimental enough to desire that Hill's and Thalia's love for each other should end in complete happiness for both. If anything went wrong with the enterprise on which they were engaged, and the ex-doctor was killed, he hated to contemplate the sorrow which would overwhelm the girl. He felt he knew her well enough to realise that she had the power of bestowing love of a depth and intensity far beyond the ordinary and, in consequence, would suffer the more at the loss of her lover. The discovery of Hill's identity, too, might bring real danger upon her, for no secret had been made of her companionship with him. Hill had, in fact, been received by Madame Bikelas and, though not encouraged, tolerated by Bikelas himself. However, Sir Leonard had decreed that the ex-doctor should tackle Kyprianos with Shannon, and that was the end of it. Love, after all, could not be allowed to obtrude on duty, and the powerful Secret Service man reflected that, behind them, waited Sir Leonard himself with two others ready to render assistance if necessary. Hill, of course, had no idea of the thoughts in his companion's mind. It would never have occurred to him to put anything but the service first, despite the love which, for the first time in his thirty years of life, had come to him and taken possession of him with such force.

They stood outside the door of the flat in which Kyprianos lived, and Shannon felt for and found the keyhole. Softly, and with great care, he inserted a cleverly-fashioned steel instrument. Intent on working silently, he took so long that Hill began to feel impatient. At last, however, the door was open; was pushed inwards by slow degrees for fear that it might creak. Shannon touched his companion on the arm. A moment later they stood together in the passage. There was not a glimmer of light anywhere, the occupants apparently being wrapped in profound slumber. Shannon put his mouth close to his colleague's ear; bade him remain where he was until he returned. Silently and slowly, feeling before him for fear there were obstacles in the way – he dared not use a torch yet, though he had one in his pocket – he moved along the passage. He reached the room corresponding to that occupied by the secretary below, felt for the handle of the door, turned it, and entered. The key was in the lock on the inside as he had expected. Quietly he withdrew it to insert it in the outside. Then he stood listening, but no sound of breathing reached his ears. That occurred to him as very strange, until he remembered that Radoloff was not in the flat and that the room must be the one he had used.

Shannon took the torch from his pocket; switched it on guardedly. His surmise had been correct. He was alone in the bedchamber. As there was now no point in locking the door, he merely closed it, retracing his steps to the apartment corresponding to that used by Bikelas and his wife. There was no question about the third occupant of the flat, Paul Michalis, being absent, and Shannon, if possible, increased his precautions. After several minutes of nerve-racking caution, he had opened the door, repeating the process of transferring the key to the outside. But again he was puzzled by the fact that he could not hear the sound of breathing. There must be someone there. Surely Michalis was in bed and asleep. Or was he in bed – and not asleep? Had he been roused, despite Shannon's precautions, and was lying there now, holding his breath and listening, his finger perhaps on the trigger of a pistol? Minutes passed by, and the Secret Service man stood rigid, listening intently, hardly daring to breathe himself. At last he became convinced that there was nobody in the room. Again he warily switched on his torch. As before, the apartment was empty. What was even more astonishing was the fact that it showed no signs of occupancy. It was furnished, of course, but lacked the personal touch. There were no bags or other items of luggage; the dressing table was devoid of toilet articles; the washstand of shaving and other materials. The room, in fact, gave the impression that, if it had recently been occupied, it had been vacated. Shannon remembered now that he had not observed any signs of occupation in the other apartment. He went back to make certain. It was as he had thought. Thereupon he turned his attention to the bathroom. Except for an old toothbrush lying on the floor, that also suggested, by its emptiness, that the flat had been vacated. There was not even a towel hanging on the rail or a piece of soap in the receptacle over the marble washbasin.

Feeling, by that time, thoroughly puzzled and perturbed, Shannon rejoined Hill, and whispered to him his discoveries or rather lack of them. He sent the other, who was as astonished as he, to inspect the sitting room, while he turned his attention to the door of Kyprianos' laboratory-bedroom. This he had expected to be locked, but it opened when he turned the handle, and he stepped inside. A combined odour of several drugs caused him to screw up his nose in distaste, but it revived his drooping spirits. Whatever had happened to the occupants of the other rooms, this, he decided, was in use. He could hear someone breathing, not quietly or softly, but stertorously.

That did not cause him any wonder. The atmosphere was enough to choke anyone's breathing apparatus. How Kyprianos could exist in it was beyond him to understand. He felt a touch on his arm. Hill was back. The latter whispered that the sitting room showed as little sign of occupation as the others.

'Never mind,' breathed Shannon. 'I don't pretend to know what's happened, but the bird we want has not flown anyway. Have you the syringe ready?'

'Yes. It's in my hand.'

'Come on then!'

He was about to tiptoe forward, when Hill's hand on his arm arrested his progress.

'There's something wrong here,' muttered the ex-doctor, his lips close to Shannon's ear. 'That breathing isn't natural.'

'How can you expect it to be?' came from the other.

'I feel as though I'm suffocating already.'

'Stand ready to jump,' whispered Hill, 'I'm going to switch on the light.'

Before Shannon could stop him, he had found the switch. The room was at once brilliantly illumined by the powerful lamp hanging from the centre of the ceiling, causing them both to blink owlishly. The sight that met their dazzled eyes, however, swept all other considerations from their minds. Balanced on the balls of his feet ready to spring, Shannon froze into a state of horrified immobility; Hill, by the door, stood, his fingers on the switch, as though he had been turned into stone. Thus they remained for several seconds, the ex-doctor at last breaking the tension.

'Don't go near the bed, Hugh!' he warned.

The room, like the others they had inspected, had been stripped of personal belongings. There were no articles of wearing apparel, bags or boxes in it. Indications that it had been used as a makeshift laboratory still remained, it is true. There was a broken retort lying on a table; a couple of empty phials and a measure on the washstand, which had been pushed into a corner, and denuded of basin and ewer. A pair of rubber gloves, one of them torn, lay on the floor. The sight to which their eyes had, at once, been drawn, and which had caused them such horror, was a man lying on a divan against one of the walls. He was practically nude, and his body lay in a terribly distorted attitude, as though he were suffering intolerable agony. Yet, though his eyes were wide-open, piteous, and terror-stricken, not a sound came from his pallid lips. A bluish tinge and beads of perspiration caused his face to look ghastly. Shannon noticed that his body also looked blue.

'It's Bikelas' secretary!' he whispered. 'Good God! What have they done to him?'

'I can't tell you offhand, of course,' returned Hill, 'but, at a guess, I should imagine they have injected him with that devilish serum of Kyprianos'. So long as you don't touch him, I should imagine you are pretty safe. The very atmosphere of this room, redolent as it is with chemicals, acts as a disinfectant, a fact which I should imagine was lost sight of by Kyprianos. They've obviously fled, though why they should have treated that poor devil in such a way is more than I can understand at present.'

'What beats me is how they got away without your knowing,' grunted Shannon.

Hill drew him from the room, and closed the door.

'You tell Sir Leonard what has happened,' he suggested, 'while I see what I can do for him. It will be little enough, I'm afraid.'

'Be careful you don't catch it,' warned Shannon.

'I shan't, and I'll take jolly good care nobody else does!'

They went back to Hill's flat. Sir Leonard met them at the door; frowned a little at the expression on their faces.

'What has happened?' he began. 'Has—'

'Keep away, sir,' urged Hill. 'Wait in the sitting room. Shannon will come to you in a few minutes, and explain.' He took his big companion into the bathroom. 'Thank the Lord!' he muttered, 'that I travel prepared, though I never dreamt I should be called upon to combat anything like this.'

They were in the bathroom for close on ten minutes, and eventually emerged reeking of strong disinfectant.

'Phew!' whistled Shannon. 'How perfectly beastly! Was all this necessary?'

'No; I don't think so. Neither of us came into actual contact with the poor devil and, as I said, the air was pretty well purified by the chemical atmosphere in that room. Still, it is safer not to take risks. Now go to the chief and tell him. Keep him away from the flat though. I'm going to see if I can ease the sufferer's last moments.'

'He's dying, is he?'

'Yes; he may be dead by now. God! That fiend must have done devil's work indeed to enable him to breed bacteria that act with such appalling swiftness.'

He procured some drugs from a case, and went off to attend the dying man. Shannon joined Sir Leonard, and explained fully what had happened. The chief and Tempest listened with horror in their eyes. At the end of the recital, the former sat thoughtfully looking at the great empty fireplace for several minutes.

'It seems to me,' he observed at last, 'that this has been done with vicious inconsequence. If Hill is right, and the poor fellow has been injected with the virus, it must have been from motives of sheer, wanton vengeance. Kyprianos probably thought that his body would be found there, be handled by the finders, and thus commence an epidemic. But why should he have done such a thing? It could not be of advantage to him or his companions. I am willing to bet they were dead against it, but, like most other devils who concoct something highly injurious to fellow humans, he was passionately eager all the time to inject somebody with it, and watch it act. I should imagine he has got more or less out of hand and has become a menace to them all.'

'But if, as you told me, he and Michalis were stopping behind to murder me,' remarked Shannon, 'why has he done this now and vanished?'

'I don't think he is far away, somehow. I should watch my step very carefully, if I were you, Shannon. Somebody may bump into you in the dark.'

'Then you think he is in hiding close by, and knows that we are here?'

'I shouldn't be surprised. What puzzles me is how and when the baggage was moved out? When I saw Radoloff watching Hill and Thalia—' He broke off; was silent for several seconds. 'She was with us until ten-thirty, and obviously knew nothing of this sudden move, though she informed us they were about to go; that is, all but Kyprianos and Michalis. It seems to me, Shannon, that the rest must still be in the building. If not, then Thalia must have been spirited away. I hope no harm has come to the girl. They did not hesitate to murder the two secretaries, and she is liable to be suspected even more than they. I think I'll pay a visit to her flat, if only to see that she is safe.'

'Do you mean, go inside, sir?'

'Yes; why not. You went into the other.'

'Shall I come with you?'

'No; Hill may want you. I don't suppose I'll be long.'

'For God's sake, sir, be careful! There's something about this horrible business I don't understand. The very fact that one of the secretaries has died, and now another, is enough to cause surprise and comment, but to leave the second poor devil lying dead in a flat of some beastly disease, and disappear, seems to me sheer lunacy. The last thing these people want is to draw suspicion on themselves. Yet they seem to be going out of their way to do it.'

'That is why I think Kyprianos has got out of hand. He may even have gone mad.'

Sir Leonard was about to go out, when the door opened, and Hill entered. He passed them by without a word, his face white and set. They heard him scrubbing his hands in the bathroom; smelt again the strong disinfectant he was using. Wallace waited until he came out; then followed him to his sitting room, where he mixed himself a large brandy and soda.

'Nasty business, was it?' queried the chief sympathetically.

'Beastly, sir,' nodded Hill. 'He expired a few minutes ago – horribly. But,' he added hoarsely, 'it was what he said that has bowled me over. He spoke just before he died.'

His head sank until it was resting on his hands; a great tremor ran through his body.

'What was it?' asked Sir Leonard gently.

Hill looked up; there was agony in his eyes.

'He died warning me against Thalia.'

CHAPTER EIGHTEEN

Death in a Hypodermic Syringe

The other three men – Merryweather was waiting in another room – cast quick, startled glances at each other. At least it would be more correct to say that Shannon and Tempest did – Wallace simply frowned a little, as he glanced at his burly assistant. He looked back at Hill, and sat down.

'Tell me what he said.'

'It was very little, and difficult to hear or understand,' replied Hill quietly, 'but I gathered that he and the other secretary, who was supposed to have died of heart disease, were actually in the pay of the Greek government. First one had been discovered and murdered; then Bikelas found the other searching a private case of his. It was Kyprianos who suggested using the cultures. The others objected, but their protests were in vain. He was stripped – God knows why – and forced to drink a glass of water containing the filthy stuff this afternoon. Kyprianos said that he hoped the man called Shannon would come, try to help the fellow, and thus die of the disease himself.'

Shannon shuddered involuntarily. He reflected that, if Hill had not been with him, the chances were that he would have been infected. Impatiently he wiped away the beads of perspiration that suddenly appeared on his brow.

'What an escape!' he muttered.

'The poor fellow recognised me as – as Thalia's friend,' went on Hill in a low, colourless voice. 'He told me she was hand and glove with the others; that, although she posed as a lady's companion, she was actually very much in the confidence of Bikelas. His last words were: "Do not trust her; she will ruin you".'

Again his head sank into his hands. There was silence for a few moments.

'Is that all?' asked Shannon sharply.

Hill again looked up.

'Isn't it enough?' he asked wearily.

'Not to my mind,' insisted the other stoutly. 'Everything points to Thalia as having played a straight game with us. Why should she ask for my assistance as she has done, why should she do so much for me, put me on my guard – oh, prove in a hundred ways her loyalty? Do you think she would have allowed me to escape, after I had listened to the conference from her chimney, and found out so much? Why should she even have countenanced such a venture on my part as the attempt to install the microphone? Dash it all, man! Use your common sense.'

'How do you explain the secretary's words?' asked Hill, but there was a new light of hope in his eyes.

'He told you probably what he thought, not what he actually knew. And, after all, what do his words amount to? She was, or is, hand and glove – I presume that's your own translation – with the band; she posed as a lady's companion, and was in the confidence of Bikelas. Wasn't it her job to worm her way into the confidence of her employer's husband and that of his companions? And, as for his words that she posed as a lady's companion, he might easily have misunderstood her position, simply because he happened to know she is under no necessity to work for her living. Hang it all! You're a pretty sort of lover, Tubby, if you doubt her on such flimsy evidence.'

'I don't think I do doubt her really,' was the reply. 'I think the shock of what he said rather upset my mental equilibrium for a while. It just bowled me out.'

'I should play with a straighter bat, if I were you,' grunted Shannon drily.

Hill rose to his feet.

'You're right,' he remarked. 'I am ashamed of myself. Perhaps it's because I've lost my head over her, and anything of this nature sends a horrible fear through me that I will yet lose her. It is difficult to understand why those two secretaries, if they really were in the pay of the Greek government, didn't know that she is also.'

'You are losing sight of the fact,' Wallace reminded him, 'that while they were simply in the pay of their government, she is actually a member of the espionage service. Do you think, Hill, that, if I wanted somebody watched, and bribed his secretary to do it, I would inform the secretary, if I afterwards sent a man or woman from the Intelligence Department to investigate? But we're wasting time here. Tempest, I think you and Merryweather had better get back to the car, and wait in it. I haven't fathomed this business yet, and I don't want you to be seen with us, if we are under observation. Be careful going down the stairs. I'll come or send for you, if I want you.' He turned to Hill, as Tempest went out. 'Have you locked the door of the room where the dead man lies?' he asked.

'Yes, sir,' was the reply. 'I have the key in my pocket.'

'Good! The police and medical authorities will have to be informed – and warned, but that can wait for the present. Have you any idea what combination of diseases Kyprianos has associated in this devil's brew of his.'

'The chief are bubonic plague and cholera, but there are indications of something else. Without a thorough examination I cannot tell you that now, sir.'

'Good God!' muttered Shannon. 'What a monster he must be. Would the other malady be typhoid? I remember hearing him speaking of plagues, cholera, and typhoid when I was in the chimney.'

Hill nodded.

'I should think it very likely,' he declared.

Telling them to keep on the alert, a warning which he realised was hardly necessary, Sir Leonard left the flat. He descended the stairs noiselessly, and arrived outside the suite that had been occupied by Bikelas, his wife, and Thalia Ictinos. The corridor was in profound darkness, not a glimmer of light coming from anywhere. Neither was there a sound. Yet he experienced the uncanny feeling that he was not alone, that somewhere close by was an evil presence. Sir Leonard's instinct for danger seldom failed him. He had had too much experience of perilous situations not to recognise mentally when there was trouble about. Years of hazard and risk in the service of his country had developed in him a sixth sense, which had caused him to be intensely acute to any threatening influence around him. On many occasions he had owed his life to this. He could hear nothing, see nothing now, but he knew perfectly well there was something, not far from him, of a malevolent nature. Ability to see passably well in the darkness helped him little, for here it was thick, velvety; the murkiness of the tomb. Yet, even so, he presently thought to see something move.

He stole away from the door by which he had been standing,

keeping his eyes in the direction where he fancied he had detected the thing – whatever it was. It was aware of his presence, he believed, but, unless it were an animal, he did not believe it could see in the dark any better than he could. Before long, however, he was forced to moderate his opinion. As he moved, so the evil, uncanny creature moved after him. He presently reached the elevators; felt behind him, and experienced a sense of satisfied relief, as he became aware that the door stood open and a lift was beyond it. He backed in; drew the doors softly to. He was now in the comfortable position of being protected and, at the same time, able to look out through the glass panelling, while, if an attack was made, and the doors forced, he could ascend to the upper floor and rejoin Shannon and Hill. Nothing happened for some time, and strain his eyes as he would he could not see anything through the windows. At length, however, when he was beginning to wonder if the whole affair had been sheer imagination, he distinctly heard the doors being tried. Fortunately they possessed a strong fastening which locked on the inside. Nevertheless, his finger sought for and found the button which controlled the lift, ready to send it shooting upwards.

He had a revolver in his pocket, but did not intend using it, except as a last resource. He also possessed an electric torch; an article as small and as thin as a fountain pen, but with an amazingly brilliant light. The only reason he had not hitherto used it was to avoid drawing attention to himself, in the hope that his presence was, after all, not suspected, though the manner he had been followed, as he moved, caused that hope to appear rather wasted. Something rubbed faintly against the glass. Was the creature feeling for it with the intention of smashing it in? At once Sir Leonard's finger left the button, the torch was withdrawn from his pocket, pointed straight at the window, and switched on. A ray of brilliant light shot out, was focused immediately on a face. An indelible impression of it, as he saw it then, was impressed on his mind. Being within a few inches of the glass, every line was plainly visible under the glare of the torch. A sallow, cadaverous countenance, containing a long, pointed nose, small, thin-lipped mouth, strangely arched eyebrows, giving the eyes, magnified ludicrously by their glasses, an expression of surprise, confronted him. He had not seen Nicholas Kyprianos before, but knew he was looking at the man now. His glimpse was short, though complete. The Cypriot blinked stupidly for a moment in the glare then ducked away.

Sir Leonard kept the light on, and was thus enabled to observe the thin, bent figure hurrying towards the stairs. At once he put away the torch, and swung back the doors. This was the kind of occasion, he reflected ruefully, when the handicap of possessing only one sound arm was most apparent. Softly he ran in the direction the other had taken. He was now carrying both the torch and a revolver in his hand, having arranged them in such a manner that he could switch on the one and fire the other at the same time if necessary. He made a mental note to have similar electric flash lamps fitted to his revolvers in the future; wondered why it had not occurred to him before. He reached the stairs, and a sharp ray of illumination pierced the darkness ahead of him. Down he went, but saw nothing of the man whom he suspected of carrying a hypodermic syringe in his hand, ready to deal out a loathsome, agonising death if the opportunity offered. Sir Leonard did not wish to fire, could such an action be avoided, but he was determined to catch Kyprianos, and would not hesitate, even were the dozen or so residents roused, if no other way of rendering the Cypriot harmless presented itself.

He reached the hall, and commenced a careful search. Again came to him the feeling of danger in his proximity, and he was convinced that Kyprianos was in hiding behind one of the many lounges or great palms the place contained. He reached the switchboard which controlled the lighting of the hall and stairs. In a moment the lobby was flooded with bright illumination. He now replaced the torch in his pocket, and stood looking round him. The place appeared entirely deserted; he could see no sign of movement anywhere. Promptly he commenced a tour of examination, to return at length to his starting point convinced now that he was alone. Yet a few moments before, he would have sworn the man he was after was within a few yards of him. Had he left the building? He crossed to the door. It was standing slightly ajar, which seemed indication enough that he had gone out. Sir Leonard reluctantly decided that it would be a waste of time to attempt to follow him. There were a score of ways he might take outside, while following him with an electric torch would only serve to indicate his own position. He had inspected the porter's glass-enclosed little office, only to find it closed and locked, but he went back there again. Leaving one of the lights burning, he switched off the others, and retraced his steps to the stairs, intent now on carrying out his delayed purpose of entering the flat of Bikelas to discover if the Greek and his wife had departed like the others. He was also anxious to find out if harm had befallen Thalia, for there was a fear in his heart that such a catastrophe had very likely happened.

He was halfway up the stairs when again instinct warned him. He looked up to find a large flower pot descending from above. Skipping quickly aside, he was in time to escape its crashing on his head, but was unable altogether to avoid it. It struck his shoulder with sickening force, numbing his arm, and causing him to drop his revolver. Falling sideways, his head coming into contact with the wall as he fell, he rolled down several steps before lying partially stunned. Dimly he heard a half-suppressed, triumphant cry and, before he could recover himself, a figure approached, and launched itself on him. If ever presence of mind saved a man's life, it did at that moment. Through Sir Leonard's brain flashed the thought of the methods used by Kyprianos. He succeeded in turning on his side in such a manner that his left arm was uppermost. He had barely reached that position, when he felt a sudden, quick pressure upon that member, followed by a faint snap. As he strove to grapple with Kyprianos, the latter adroitly avoided him, was up, and stood regarding him from the safe distance of several steps below, a look of malevolence on his face that could hardly be described.

'Who you are I do not know,' he hissed, the Greek words tumbling over themselves in his fury, 'but I doubt not you are of the party of the Englishman Shannon who by now is dying. And soon you will be dead also, not of the same disease unfortunately, but one which will give you much agony first. You will—'

He darted away, as Sir Leonard rose shakily to his feet and, reaching the bottom of the stairs, ran across the hall, quickly letting himself out. The front door closed sharply, the noise echoing throughout the building. Wallace made no attempt to follow. He realised well enough that he was not in a condition to chase anyone at that moment, the blow on his shoulder and the fall having shaken him up considerably. Sitting down on a step, he worked his right arm until some of the numbness had left it; then reached out and retrieved the revolver lying a little way from him. It was a very lucky thing, he reflected, that he had not been too stunned to remember what Kyprianos would probably attempt, and had had sense enough remaining to roll over as he had done. The jab in his arm, telling him that the syringe had been made to do its work, the little snap indicating that the needle had broken, had been quite enough evidence of what would have happened to him, if the hypodermic needle had entered the right instead of the left arm. He actually chuckled softly to himself. There was no doubt an artificial arm had its uses.

He rose, giving himself a shake in an effort to clear away completely the remaining effects of his mishap. His shoulder felt bruised and sore. Curiously enough the large flower pot, a massive affair which testified to the strength Kyprianos must possess to have lifted it, was intact. Sir Leonard's shoulder had broken its fall, and it had, therefore, hit the stairs more gently than it otherwise would have done. It had rolled to the bottom, scattering earth all round it. As he contemplated it, he wondered why it had not smashed the shoulder bone; it could hardly have failed to kill him, if it had struck his skull.

Apparently the noise had not disturbed any of the residents; the building had reverted to its tomb-like silence. Sir Leonard had half expected to hear excited whispers, as people emerged from their suites to discover what had caused the crash on the stairs and banging of the door. He imagined, however, that the third storey was too high up for the sound to have reached there, though Shannon and Hill, being on the alert, might have caught it. If so, they were probably straining their ears in an effort to hear what was going on – one of them might descend to investigate. However, Sir Leonard reached the first floor, and met no one. Once again he approached the door of the Bikelas suite. From a case, extracted from the inside pocket of his jacket, he took one of the neat instruments it contained. This was inserted in the keyhole and, in very quick time, the door was unlocked.

Early in his career, as a member of the Secret Service, Wallace had made an extensive and intensive study of opening safes, locked doors, and windows, and other articles calculated to defy cracksmen and others. He had, consequently, become so expert that it is likely that, if he had possessed criminal tendencies, he could have become the most proficient cracksman in existence. His senior assistants, particularly Cousins, Shannon, Cartright, Carter, and Hill had, on his advice, studied the art until they were almost, if not quite, as expert as he. It will be gathered, therefore, that not the least of the powers, possessed by these skilled men of the British Secret Service, is their ability to open their way into the most carefully guarded and strongest receptacles – an ability that has been of inestimable service to their country on many occasions.

Stepping inside, Wallace closed the door behind him without the suspicion of a sound. The case, with its scientifically constructed little steel tools, was put away in his pocket, his hand now grasping the torch. There was a deserted air about the flat, an impression that it did not contain human beings. Why he felt that exactly, Sir Leonard was unable to tell, but it was not very long before he had assured himself that such was indeed the case. As noiselessly as a shadow, he moved from place to place, opening doors with an almost uncanny knowledge of whether they were likely to squeak or not, and taking precautions accordingly. Madame Bikelas, her husband, and Thalia were absent – the secretary, of course, he remembered, lay dead upstairs – but there was ample evidence of a hasty flight.

Unlike the flat inspected by Shannon, which the latter had described as being entirely cleared, this contained quite a conglomeration of useful and useless articles, suggesting that they had been left behind, because the boxes and bags had been too hastily packed to admit of their inclusion. There were shoes, stockings, socks, articles of underwear, toilet requisites, an overcoat, even a pair of trousers. In the room that Sir Leonard concluded must have been occupied by Thalia Ictinos, there was a wardrobe trunk containing some very beautiful and stylish dresses. She, in fact, seemed to have taken with her fewer articles than her companions. It must be admitted that Sir Leonard had entered her room with a certain amount of dread. He had felt that it was quite possible that, like the secretary above, she would be lying there dead. His relief on finding the room unoccupied was, therefore, very great. There was an elusive, altogether entrancing atmosphere about it which suggested her personality. A faint, attractive perfume scented the air; the flowers, artistically arranged in picturesque vases, the sheer daintiness of the apartment, spoke eloquently of Thalia. It seemed difficult to realise that she was not present. Wallace felt that here, if anywhere, he might pick up a clue which would lead him to the hiding place of the men he was so anxious to find.

The window was wide open, a fact that struck him as peculiar. He crossed to it, and looked out. There was nothing to be seen, of course; it was far too dark. Yet why should it have been opened in that manner? If the top sash had been down a little way, or even if the bottom had been up a few inches, he would not have taken any notice, but the fact that it was open to its widest extent suggested that it had been used as a means of exit. Had Thalia been imprisoned in the room, and made her escape that way? It rather looked like it, though, in that case, she would have had to use a rope or knot the sheets together, unless someone outside had provided a ladder. As far as he knew, she did not possess any friends likely to assist her in an escape, except Shannon, Hill, or himself, and none of them had been concerned.

He stood by the window, thoughtfully regarding the dim outline, for, after the first quick glance round, he had switched off his torch. Presently he came to the conclusion that Thalia had not been concerned in an escape by that means. In the first place, had she been made a captive, it was most unlikely that she would have been imprisoned in a room which contained a large window, not more than sixteen or eighteen feet from the ground. Secondly, there would almost certainly have been some indication that she had made her escape. The thought occurred to Wallace that possibly the articles of luggage, which the three had taken with them, had been lowered through the window, but, in that case, why had Thalia's room been used? The two windows of the apartment, that had been used by Madame Bikelas and her husband, were fast closed. Surely, if baggage had been lowered from the flat, they would have been the means of exit, considering that the greater number of articles had obviously been taken away by the two Greeks!

Wallace again looked out. Below him was a ledge on which he could faintly discern a row of flower pots. Presently, however, his keen eyes caught sight of something having the appearance of a folded piece of paper. At once he reached down; found that he could just grasp it. It had been wedged between the branches of a plant, apparently to prevent it from being blown away. It was an envelope doubled in two. He withdrew to the little passage outside the room, focused the light of his torch on it, and opened it out. A feeling of satisfaction pervaded his being. It was addressed to 'Herr Kirche' in neat though obviously hurried handwriting. Being unable for some reason to communicate with Hill direct, Thalia had written the note and, anticipating that either he or his companions would make a search when they found that everybody had disappeared, had conceived the idea of leaving the window wide open in order to attract their attention. It was quick-witted of her, decided Wallace with approval. He put the note in his pocket with the intention of handing it to Hill for perusal, as soon as he rejoined him and Shannon above. Before doing that, however, he decided to have a look at the suite of rooms belonging to Signor and Signora

Bruno on the other side of the corridor. As they were Italians and permanent residents, he wondered if the ex-diplomat had decided to stay on, trusting to the fact that, unless his confederates were caught and gave him away, there could be little evidence that he was concerned in the plot. None of them could know that Shannon had overheard perhaps their most important conference. From their point of view, in fact, Wallace saw no reason why the Brunos should depart, unless, of course, they were terrified of the disease with which the secretary of Bikelas had been inoculated.

He let himself out of the flat and, ascertaining that there was nobody about, walked quickly across to the suite of rooms opposite. The lock was quickly and silently turned, but the door would not move. It was bolted! The Brunos were in; at least, there was undoubtedly someone inside. Under the circumstances, Wallace wondered if it would be worthwhile to enter. He immediately decided that it would. Useful information was far more likely to be lying about in an occupied flat than in one from which the tenants had fled. There was not much to learn further about the conspiracy, as far as he was able to conjecture, but there was quite conceivably something, chief of which was the present whereabouts of the bottles containing the virus and incidentally the address to which all the other conspirators had fled. That, of course, might be in Thalia's letter to Hill, but Sir Leonard did not think so. If he disturbed Signor and Signora Bruno, it would not matter a great deal. In that case, he promised himself a heart-to-heart talk with the Italian.

He had noticed that the entrance door of the other flat contained a bolt at the top, another at the bottom. Presumably this would be fitted in the same way. From his case he removed two implements, one flat and curved, with a curious vice-like head, the other rounded and strong-looking. The former screwed into the latter, and it was noticeable that, according to the way it was turned, so the vice opened or closed. Wallace adjusted it to his satisfaction then worked it in between the edge of the door and the jamb. It went in easily enough. He moved it slowly up and down until his sensitive fingers told him he had reached the knob of the bolt. It was not long before he had ascertained which way it was turned. A few twists of the screw, and the tool had gripped. Less than a minute later the bolt, although stiff, had been withdrawn. The same process was repeated on the other. He had taken nearly ten minutes to accomplish the whole job, at which, owing to the fact that he merely had the use of a single hand, he was naturally not as expert as one or two of his agents, but it had been performed with scarcely a sound. All the time he had been working, he had been acutely sensible to a smell of burning, but could not make out from which direction it came. He wondered if the Brunos' flat was on fire; smiled at the thought that it would be curious, if he had arrived in time to rescue them from the flames. The pungent odour of burning wood, though not very strong, reached his nostrils, as he stepped quietly inside. He felt uneasy; decided to cut his visit to the Brunos short, and investigate.

Closing the door behind him, he sniffed, but there was no smell of burning here. Whatever it was must be in some other part of the building or, more likely, wafted in from outside through an open window. He became aware of the subdued murmur of voices and, it seemed to him, of a woman sobbing. At once he forgot the odour of burning; concentrated his attention on the new interest. Bruno and his wife were awake. He crept up to the room from which the sound appeared to come; applied his ear to the keyhole, an action he disliked doing intensely. However, it was not the time for a finical regard for the tenets of good form. He found he could hear quite plainly, and settled himself to listen. A deep sob was the first sound that reached his ears.

'I wish you would go to sleep, Maria,' sighed an exasperated male voice in Italian, obviously that of Bruno. 'I tell you there is no need for you to worry. You and I are quite safe from trouble. For three hours now have you wept and moaned, and yet I have explained over and over again that no trouble can come upon us.'

'But it is terrible, terrible,' moaned the woman. 'I did not think that you – my husband, my Pietro – could have associated himself with a scheme so wicked. Mother of God! How can you ever expect a sin so heinous to be forgiven.'

'It is over now,' grunted Bruno. 'I have finished – I have made up my mind tonight.'

'And why?' returned the signora with spirit. 'Because this Kyprianos has gone nearly mad with the feeling of power that has come to him, and now dictates to you all. Have you not tonight told me yourself that that was the reason? It is not because your conscience has told you you were committing a terrible sin. It is because you are afraid of this man; because you know that his madness has put an end to your dreams of power. You to rule Italy – I to be the wife of a great dictator! Did you think, Pietro, that I would submit to holding a position by your side that had been obtained by means so horrible? You can lie there, regretting only that the devil Kyprianos has lost his head and rendered your position impossible. There are no regrets, no sorrow for that which you aimed to do. If you dared, you would possess yourself of those bottles of poison, but you are afraid of them, afraid of him. Yet you would not have hesitated to force your poor unfortunate country people to agree to your terms, by spreading among them a disease which could not be cured.'

'Do go to sleep, Maria. I am weary.'

'Go to sleep!' she screeched. 'How do you think I can go to sleep with a tale so wicked ringing in my ears? Do you think I have no feeling?'

'If I had told you that all was well; that fame, and power, and honours were coming to me by means of the virus of Kyprianos, and that he was behaving in a sane, reasonable manner, you would not speak thus. You would have been delighted. It is only because I have told you of the scheme and its regrettable failure, which is now apparent, that you talk in this way.'

'That is a lie,' she cried vehemently, 'an unholy, wicked lie. I would have nothing to do with anything of a nature so horrible.'

'I wish I had not told you, but it was necessary to explain why we must depart from Italy tomorrow, and remain away until there is no danger. I have never known you behave in this manner.'

'Ah! You thought I had no spirit; that I was your well-tamed wife. I have always before supported you in your ambitions; I have never said anything against them. But this is too much – Mother of God! It is too much. Where is this case with the bottles now?'

'Why do you want to know?' came from him suspiciously.

'Because I want you to save the world from this fiend. I want you to blow it up, burn it – I do not mind what you do with it so long as it is destroyed. Is it still in this house?'

'Yes,' he replied in sullen tones; 'it is to be removed tomorrow.'

'Where is it?'

'I cannot tell you that, Maria. It would be unwise—'

The rest of the sentence was lost to Sir Leonard. A confused murmur of many voices raised, it seemed to him, in alarm reached his ears from the corridor outside. He turned from the bedroom and listened. At that moment came a terrific pounding on the entrance door of the flat, followed by perhaps the most startling and dreadful of all cries:

'Fire! Fire!'

CHAPTER NINETEEN

At the Mercy of a Fiend

After Sir Leonard Wallace had left them, Shannon and Hill continued to discuss the last words of the dying secretary regarding Thalia Ictinos. It is certain that Hill's sudden doubt of the loyalty of the girl he loved so intensely was caused by the peculiar complex, which seems somehow to come to all true lovers. Whether it is due to the fact that they place their inamorata upon high and insecure pedestals from which, being human, they are likely to topple at any moment, or is merely caused by the slightly unbalanced state into which love plunges them, is hard to decide. It is quite true, however, that lovers are more ready to believe reports to the discredit of their adored ones, than others, who are able to bring clear, reasonable, and balanced minds upon the subject. Not that real love will turn because it believes in that guilt. It grows stronger, if anything, possibly from a desire to help and protect. Shannon's words quickly made Hill realise how unjust he must have appeared in his attitude. It is to his credit that once he had come to his senses, as he put it, he did not attempt to defend himself, though he might, with reason, have done so, especially with regard to the previous experience British Secret Service men had had of Thalia Ictinos. On the contrary, he became so thoroughly dejected and ashamed that his companion, in his hearty manner, set about cheering him up. Shannon succeeded to a certain extent. He failed, however, to chase from Hill's mind the shadow of a fear, momentarily becoming more intensified, that harm had overtaken the girl.

Although, in the garden, they had surprisingly had the protection of Sir Leonard Wallace, it was quite possible, thought Hill, that not only had Radoloff followed them there but one or more of the others as well. Recollection of the chief's assurance, however, quickly expelled the idea from his mind. Sir Leonard seldom made mistakes, especially a mistake of that kind. The doctor's reflections then veered quickly to his own blunders – his lapse into English; his utter forgetfulness that there might possibly be someone on their trail. Quite conceivably Sir Leonard might have been one of the conspirators. What then? The chief had heard everything that had passed; so also would anybody else who might have been there in his place. On the whole Hill felt that he had hardly covered himself with glory that night. He told Shannon of the affair in the garden, which up to then the latter had not fully understood. It was the first time he had heard that Hill had proposed and been accepted, and his congratulations were hearty and sincere. He looked grave, when told of the error Hill had committed, however, and grunted. The recital of Sir Leonard's sudden appearance, though, caused him to laugh.

'At least you needn't worry about that,' he commented. 'I doubt if many people could move as silently as Sir Leonard. I'm jolly sure none of this jolly band of conspirators could.'

'That doesn't excuse my slackness,' declared Hill.

'No,' returned the other bluntly; 'but love is an exacting mistress, Tubby, old son. Perhaps you'll return to normal as soon as you're married. When this affair is done with, no doubt the chief will give you leave until after the honeymoon is over.'

'For the Lord's sake,' grunted Hill, 'don't talk as though I'm to be shelved as a punishment for my sins.'

Shannon's great laugh boomed through the flat.

'That's the first time,' he pronounced, 'that I have heard a man describe his honeymoon as "being shelved".'

As time went on, and Sir Leonard did not return, both men became anxious. They were discussing the position, and had decided to go in search of him, when there came a rap at the hall door.

'That's he!' cried Hill in great relief, and hurried out of the room.

'Wait a jiffy!' called Shannon after him. 'We'd better make sure by—'

Unfortunately Hill had already reached the door, and opened it, thus committing another mistake on that eventful night. Four men promptly crowded in, each of them holding an ugly-looking revolver. Shannon, who was standing at the door of the sitting room, quickly reached for his own weapon, but a sharp voice, speaking English, with a thick, unpleasant intonation, threatened to shoot. The muzzle of a revolver, pointed unwaveringly at a spot between one's eyes from a distance of two or three yards, is an eloquent persuader. Hugh Shannon, being a wise young man, did not argue the point. One of the intruders closed the door, but did not fasten it, while the others drove Hill and Shannon before them into the room. The Englishmen were brought up by the great ornate mantelpiece; the others stood in a line just inside the door. Hugh contemplated them calmly. The short, fat man, with the flabby face, little eyes, and broad nose, was Paul Michalis; a tall, saturnine fellow with a pair of piercing eyes was Plasiras and, next to him, dapper, almost benevolent-looking, if one missed the cruel twist of his mouth, was Bikelas. The fourth was Padakis, and, from the manner in which he glared at Shannon, it could be seen that he would have liked to have ended the Englishman's career at once, without parley.

'So,' remarked Bikelas in perfect English, regarding Hill with, it seemed, an air of reproach, 'we were mistaken in you, Herr Kirche. An Austrian gentleman in Rome studying art! Dear, dear! To deceive us in such a manner. But I admit the part was well played – you look so typical of the young men of Vienna. Also a search of your belongings revealed only letters and documents in German, and a lot of evidence that you hailed from Vienna indeed. But what is to be thought of a man who crept into the heart of an unsuspecting girl, in order to learn the secrets of her trusting companions?'

His flippant manner of addressing Hill apparently did not meet with the approval of his companions. Michalis and Padakis scowled impatiently at him. Hill's innocent-seeming blue eyes never looked more guileless than at that moment. He had the appearance of a thoroughly astonished and indignant young man.

'Of what are you speaking, Herr Bikelas?' he demanded in German. 'I do not understand English very well. Perhaps you will speak my language or Italian. What is the meaning of this display of force?'

Jeering laughter greeted him from Bikelas and Plasiras. The other two apparently did not understand German.

'You persist in the pretence?' Bikelas continued to speak English. 'It is useless, my friend. We were fooled properly, and I admit I was mostly to blame. The companion of my wife and my wife herself were at once convinced of your bona fides, and I and the gentlemen with me also allowed our suspicions to be lulled, after we had searched your rooms and all belonging to you. We even smiled at the progress of your affair with the beautiful Thalia. But tonight we learnt the truth. Thalia is heartbroken, I fear, for she truly loved you, but she is loyal to us. I am afraid we were at once suspicious of her also, but she convinced us to the contrary. We know, without doubt, that you and this big man, who breaks others like sticks, are spies of the British Secret Service. We know also that there is, or was, a third.'

In Shannon's face was an expression of dawning horror. It began to look apparent that his faith in Thalia Ictinos had been, after all, misplaced. Who, but she, could have informed the conspirators of Hill's real calling? She had learnt it in the garden. There also she had met the third man – Sir Leonard Wallace.

'You are talking nonsense,' protested Hill vigorously. He obstinately kept to German. 'Can I not have a friend who is an Englishman? And who is this third of whom you speak?'

'Enough!' snapped Plasiras harshly in his own language. 'You fool! What sense is there in attempting to keep up a pretence of this nature? The third man is dead, and you will soon follow him.' Despite a heroic attempt to refrain from showing his feelings at the news that Sir Leonard Wallace was dead, Hill started a little; his face went white to the lips. 'Ah!' sneered Plasiras. 'Who is this third, you ask, and the mention that he is dead upsets you! Bah! It is evident from your face that no mistake has been made.'

'I was upset that you threatened my death,' returned Hill.

'How is it that an Austrian, as you call yourself, can speak so many languages? German, Italian, English and now Greek! It is very surprising, is it not?'

'Not at all. What about your own knowledge?'

'I am a diplomat and statesman,' replied Plasiras. 'To me the learning of languages is a necessity.'

'You *were* a statesman,' put in Shannon, speaking for the first time, 'but you're not now. You're one of the greatest scoundrels unhung.' Plasiras roared with rage, and it looked, for a moment, as though he intended to fire. 'If I were you,' went on Shannon calmly, 'I'd put those guns away. None of you dare shoot in this building. You'd bring all the residents down on you.'

'Do you think we would mind that?' laughed Bikelas. 'My friend, we would kill you and this gentleman who likes the Austrians so much that he pretends to be one of them. Then, if anyone came, and tried to stop us, we would shoot them. There are not very many people living here. Most of the flats are vacant.'

There was no doubting that he meant what he said. Shannon and Hill were in a distinctly perilous position. Both were racking their brains for a way out; both were tormented by the dreadful fear that Sir Leonard was actually dead, though both resolutely refused to believe it. They had heard of his death before, only for him to turn up, if not unharmed, at least very much alive. The significance of his prolonged absence, however, added to their dread. Surely, if he had been alive, he would have returned to them before then. Another man suddenly appeared; stood glaring at them from between Bikelas and Plasiras, his eyes grotesquely distorted behind the thick lenses of his spectacles. Shannon at once recognised the long nose, thin lips, and emaciated, stooped form of Nicholas Kyprianos. His gaze was concentrated on the burly Englishman, and gradually it became convulsed with an expression of such ferocity that the two before him watched appalled.

'How is it?' he snarled in Greek, 'that you are not ill, in agony, dying? And you also?' He turned his eyes on Hill. 'You went to the room where lay the man dying of a disease that cannot be cured, that affects all quickly who come into contact with it. I know you went there – I watched, and I laughed – but you still live and look in health. And where is the third man?' he demanded, turning to Plasiras. 'I left him lying on the stairs. When I looked for the body, it was gone. Have you moved it?'

'No; we did not see it,' was the reply.

'Then it was you,' he grated, turning again to glare at Shannon and Hill, whose minds had become very much relieved at the announcement of the disappearance of the 'body'. It looked to them as though Sir Leonard had once again escaped his enemies. 'Where have you put him; tell me!' went on Kyprianos. 'I would see him.'

'Whom are you talking about?' asked Hill.

'You know. The man who moves so quickly and so silently. I must see him dead. Alive he is dangerous – I know it.'

'There is nobody else here,' declared Shannon. 'Why do you not search?'

Kyprianos stepped forward.

'You think,' he snapped, 'that then attention would be taken from you, but you will not escape me again.'

'Don't come too near,' warned the other sarcastically. 'We might give you the disease you think we ought to have.'

Kyprianos laughed harshly.

'We are immune – my friends and I,' he returned. 'We cannot be harmed.'

'I thought you seemed remarkably brave for devils of your kidney. Why, you little worm, if you come a step nearer, I'll break you in two.'

Kyprianos backed away somewhat hastily. He had heard too much of Shannon's doings not to fear contact with him. Hill had been studying him ever since he had entered the room, and had become convinced that he was on the verge of madness, if indeed his brain had not already gone. All remaining shreds of reason were hanging by the merest thread. Obviously he had lost a good deal of control, and it was apparent that his companions feared him now. To them he had become a deadly menace as well as a man in whom they pinned, or had pinned, their unholy ambitions.

'Tie them up, and tie them up well,' the scientist ordered his companions. 'Then you and I will consult about what is to be done with them. We will also find the other man.'

Nobody showed any particular eagerness to undertake the task of binding the two. Plasiras, particularly, eyed Shannon with misgivings. Kyprianos lashed them all with the fury of a scornful tongue. Strangely enough, although they resented his words, it did not seem to occur to them to ask him why he did not show them an example.

'We have no rope,' growled Padakis, at whom most of the Cypriot's vitriolic outburst was directed.

'Swine! Why did you not bring it? Did you think I told you of these two, and bade you make prisoners of them, in order that you could converse with them only? I said the man Shannon would come. I was right. He came. It is true I was surprised when he entered this flat, for even I had lost suspicion of the other man. Then I watched the two go to the room where lies the body reeking with my disease. I laughed. Instead of one contracting it there would be two. Yet what do I see? Somehow they have escaped. Presently they will tell me how. Then came the other man to the corridor below. He was like a mouse, so quiet, so silent – he moved without noise. But, at last, I got him, and into him I injected aconitine. It is true the needle broke in his arm, but by then the dose was inside. Where is he? These men must have moved the body, and I would see it.

Fool that I was not to watch him die. Tie them up, I say; then we can act.'

'What do you suggest we tie them with?' asked Bikelas sarcastically. 'Our handkerchiefs?'

'Are there not sheets on the beds that can be torn up into strips? They will be strong enough to hold even – him.' He pointed a long, shaking finger at Shannon.

At a word from Plasiras, Padakis went to carry out the suggestion. While he was away, Hill again made an attempt to assert himself as a supposed Austrian, without any expectation of convincing them. Actually his object was to delay whatever they contemplated doing in the hope that Sir Leonard would yet appear. They ignored him, however, Bikelas alone listening to him, though with a sneering smile on his cruel lips. Padakis returned presently with several strips torn from a sheet. He handed some to the others, retaining the rest himself, yet they still hesitated to approach the two Englishmen.

'Why not shoot them, and have done with it?' asked Michalis.

'No, no, no!' cried Kyprianos. 'They will not be shot. I have other plans.'

At that Plasiras and Bikelas, followed reluctantly by Michalis and Padakis, slowly approached Shannon and Hill, their revolvers held ready to shoot. Shannon drew himself up, and, noticing the action, with one accord they stood still. At that the burly Secret Service man laughed.

'What a pity,' he commented, 'this little scene can't be reproduced in a film! It would make a hit as a great comedy success.'

'Cowards!' screamed Kyprianos. 'I will show you.' He leapt forward, brandishing a hypodermic syringe that he had taken from a case in his pocket. 'In this little weapon is some of the virus of the disease that cannot be cured and kills agonisingly,' he snarled at the Englishmen. 'Make one little attempt at resistance and into you both will go some. Perhaps you mind not being shot, but this you will mind.'

Shannon's face paled a little under the bronze. He and Hill, who had also turned white, were forced to accept the inevitable. There was perhaps a chance, they thought, if they allowed themselves to be bound, though there did not seem a great deal of hope now. Still, if it were possible to avoid a hideous death, they preferred anything rather than that. Observing that they intended making no attempt at resistance, the four men became, all at once, very brave. Padakis and Michalis tied Shannon's hands behind him, until he found it impossible to move them, Kyprianos, Plasiras, and Bikelas standing threateningly by. He was searched, and his revolver taken away. They then made him sit in a chair, his knees and ankles being bound as tightly as his wrists. The process was repeated with Hill. When it was done, Kyprianos broke into a loud, cackling laugh. He bent over Shannon, until his face was only a few inches from the other's.

'You were fooled,' he chuckled, 'fooled by a man with a hypodermic syringe that contained nothing! Alas! I have none of my precious mixture with me, but I will fetch some now and, as you sit there, you will be injected, and I will watch it begin to act. No one will defy *me*!'

Shannon looked at Hill, and the glance was returned. Neither face contained any fear, only expressions of annoyed aggravation.

'Don't be a fool, Kyprianos!' came sharply from Plasiras. 'You must not use any more of the virus. Already we are anxious to know what is to happen about – about the body in your room. You are going insane. How can our object be attained if you do this? Even now I fear you have spoilt all.'

'Have no fear, my friend. I but rid you of your enemies. You will see how I will make all appear well. When these are dead, and I have assured myself that the other man is dead also, there will be no spies left to betray us.' He went out of the room, returning some minutes later. 'Where is that other?' he snarled at Shannon.

'I really couldn't tell you,' was the calm reply, 'and I certainly wouldn't, if I could.'

Kyprianos gave vent to a string of oaths, which stopped suddenly when Plasiras asked him what had become of General Radoloff. He stared at the other.

'I have not seen him for many hours,' he replied; 'neither have I seen Doreff or Bruno.'

Bikelas laughed.

'I think you have frightened them, my Kyprianos,' he declared. 'They talk of deserting us.'

'Then,' snarled the scientist, 'they must die for the sake of us who remain.'

'You talk too much of death,' complained Michalis. 'I think it is in your blood and brain, and is making you lose all reason. It is time we—'

'Drop your pistols, all of you,' came startlingly in a charming feminine voice, in which a note of resolute command predominated. 'Do not move, or I will shoot.'

Thalia Ictinos stood in the doorway, still clothed as Hill had last seen her. Her white face was set grimly; her great eyes gleamed fiercely. Without a tremor, she held an automatic pointed at the five conspirators, all of whom, with the exception of Bikelas, had their backs turned to her. Shannon chuckled loudly. The suspicions, which had been renewed in his mind against her by the words spoken by Bikelas, had long since been swept away by the remarks of Kyprianos concerning the manner he had been watching events. Now she had come to prove her loyalty, trustworthiness, and honour, beyond any shadow of doubt, in the most gallant manner possible. One frail girl against five desperate scoundrels. Hill's very soul was in his eyes, yet fear was there also; fear of what might happen to her. The four men holding revolvers hesitated; then obeyed orders, allowing the weapons to drop to the floor. Kyprianos turned, and started towards her with a scream of terrible fury, but the automatic, turned unflinchingly on him, brought him up dead.

'Traitress!' he spat. 'I should have disbelieved what you said. All along I have mistrusted you, with your beautiful face and glamorous personality. It was only that which convinced the others tonight that you were innocent, when I had discovered who Kirche was.'

'What is the meaning of this, Thalia?' asked Bikelas softly. 'Is it that you fear for your lover and have come for him?'

'I have come for both Captain Shannon and Mr Hill,' returned Thalia firmly.

'Ah! His name is then Hill, and you know it!'

'Of course I know it. It did not occur to you, Ivan Plasiras, and you others, that I have been working for your downfall ever since I joined you. But it is so. Now you are finished. Release those gentlemen!'

An exclamation of sheer admiration broke from Shannon. The bravery of it! Never, in all his adventurous life, had he witnessed a woman bearing herself more dauntlessly. Desperately now he and Hill were trying to loosen their bonds, but neither made any headway. The thongs had been tied fiercely, with cruel force.

'How is it you came here?' demanded Plasiras. 'How did you get from the room in which you were locked?'

'There are ways of getting from locked rooms,' came the calm reply. 'And it may interest you to know that I heard you discuss your plans; the wall is very thin. But I am not here to enter into conversation with you. Michalis, and you, Padakis, unfasten the bonds of my friends.'

It seemed as though she were about to win through. The men addressed stood hesitant a moment or two; then moved slowly towards Hill and Shannon. It was as they were leaning forward to commence on their task that the last vestige of restraint broke in the mind of Nicholas Kyprianos. Thalia, knowing him to be the most dangerous of them all, was watching him with particular attention, but she was unprepared for the cunning action he took. He suddenly threw himself forward as though diving, his outflung hand just reaching and gripping one of her ankles. She fired promptly, but his rapid descent to the floor caused her to miss and, in a moment, she was flung down as he jerked up her foot and unbalanced her. Even then, though she must have been badly shaken, she fought desperately for freedom, but they did not give her a chance. Plasiras and Bikelas, as well as Kyprianos, flung themselves on her and, before long, she was rendered helpless. Padakis was sent to tear more strips from a sheet and, a few minutes later, she was bound as firmly as the two Secret Service men, and flung into a chair. The disaster which had overtaken her caused Shannon and Hill to fight desperately to release themselves. Cries of rage broke from their lips, as they witnessed the treatment meted out to her. Shannon was a terrible sight. Exerting all his magnificent strength, he strove to burst the thongs that held him, until his eyes were swimming in blood, the veins in his temples standing out like great cords. The work had been done too well, however. He felt his shackles give a little, but could accomplish no more. Hill was equally unsuccessful; he moaned aloud at his failure and inability to go to the rescue of the girl who had dared so much for them. Kyprianos danced about in front of her, uttering cries more animal-like than human in his triumph. Bikelas, Plasiras, and the other two, who had picked up their revolvers, stood by; ugly, entirely unsympathetic smiles on their faces. At length Bikelas spoke.

'So, my beautiful Thalia,' he commented in his soft, unctuous tones, 'you were all the time working for our downfall! This is a great surprise to me. What will Madame think of the disappearance of her companion? For I am afraid you will have to disappear. It will be a matter of the most profound regret to me, my Thalia. You will never realise how I regret it.'

Thalia's eyes flashed with the utmost scorn.

'My only sorrow,' she returned with great spirit, 'is that the disappearance, of which you speak, will prevent me from seeing or, at least, reading about your execution as a traitor to your country. You fools, do you think you will be safe because you murder these English gentlemen and me? Outside is one arranging now for your apprehension. Before long the Italian police will be here. What then, my fine conspirators?'

'What is that you say?' demanded Plasiras sharply, bending forward and shaking her fiercely, while the other three, showing their alarm in their faces, looked on. 'Who is this one of whom you speak?'

She turned her glorious eyes on her two companions in misfortune.

'I hope I have not been injudicious, have I, Raymond?' she asked her lover in English.

'It won't do any harm for them to know,' he returned.

'What do you say, Hugh?'

'Not a bit,' replied Shannon. 'They won't escape, anyhow.'

Thoroughly startled, the four men commenced a hurried conference, endeavouring to include Kyprianos in the discussion, but that was, for a long time, beyond their powers. Engrossed in triumphing over the captives, threatening them with the horrible death he intended they should die, he was unable to grasp that his companions were trying to convey to his shattered mind that they themselves were in danger. At length, however, he seemed to understand the purport of their vehement and reiterated statements. He stood and stared at them, his eyebrows raised in such a manner that the permanent look of surprise was exaggerated to a ludicrous extent.

'Danger! The police here!' he repeated; became silent, as though debating the point. 'Then, my comrades, there is no time to be lost,' he decided, at last, in a shrill, excited voice. 'They will not be able to die of my virus, which is a great pity. But no matter, their deaths will be very painful and, at the same time, we will be rid of the other bodies.'

'What do you mean?' demanded Plasiras, shaking him in his agitation.

Kyprianos pushed the Greek away.

'Wait! You will see,' he cried, and darted from the room.

While he was absent, the four remaining men spoke together in uneasy whispers. Bikelas once turned to Thalia, and asked her who it was she had declared was arranging for their arrest by the police. She merely smiled enigmatically, telling him he would know soon enough. Threats, pleas, even promises of liberty failed to obtain more from her. Plasiras held a revolver to her head, and declared he would shoot her there and then, if she did not tell them all she knew.

'As well one way of dying as another, Ivan Plasiras,' she replied with amazing coolness. 'I have said quite enough; besides, I do not know more than I have told you, except that his name would terrify you if you heard it.'

At that moment Kyprianos returned to the room cackling with excited delight.

'It is done,' he told his companions 'the holocaust has commenced. Come! We will depart while there is yet time.'

They crowded round him with cries of alarm and excitement.

'What is it? What have you done?' demanded Bikelas, losing for once his smooth, silky manner of enunciation.

'What have I done!' echoed the Cypriot in a high, gleeful voice. 'I have set fire to the room where I lived. It is burning fiercely. Soon the flames will spread; the body there will be burnt to ashes; then the fire will creep, creep, creep, until this suite also is in flames, and these three people are burnt – slowly – to – death.'

CHAPTER TWENTY

From the Flames

Cries of horror rose involuntarily from the two Englishmen, who were thinking not of themselves but of Thalia. The conspirators took no heed of them. They were far too agitated to spare a thought for anybody but themselves. They upbraided Kyprianos for his madness, cursing and swearing in their terror and dismay. Plasiras abruptly gripped Bikelas by the arm.

'Come, quickly!' he cried, 'or our escape will be cut off.'

'What of the police?'

'We must risk them. You do not want to be burnt to death, do you?'

They ran together from the room, followed by the equally terrified Padakis and Michalis. Shannon roared after them fiercely to save the girl, but they did not even spare her a backward glance. Kyprianos stood to gloat over them for a few moments; then, picking up their revolvers and Thalia's automatic, he, too, followed. He closed and locked the sitting room door, and, a moment later, they heard the front door bang. A deadly silence fell on the flat. Thalia broke it.

'Please forgive me for being so foolish,' she begged. 'I should have been more on the alert for the kind of trick played by that devil.'

'Good Lord! You've nothing to reproach yourself for,' commented Shannon in tones of real admiration. 'You've been fine, wonderful!'

'Marvellous!' added Hill. 'How did you know they were here, Thalia?'

'When I left you,' she related, 'I returned to find that everyone had packed in a great hurry. I was told to do the same. No explanation was given to me, and I thought I had better not ask too much. Also I thought it would be good to go with them, so that I could afterwards let you know. I wrote a quick letter, opened wide the window that your attention would be drawn to it, if you came to search for me, and put the letter in a flower pot. The baggage was taken away down the fire escape from the bathroom window, which also goes up by the bathroom window of Kyprianos' flat. I could not take much; the hurry was too great. I think the action of Kyprianos in putting the sickness into the secretary had frightened them greatly. We went out to a little bungalow only five minutes away. There Madame Bikelas, who was weeping, and I were put into a room together. I did not go to bed; I was too much anxious. I was called after many hours, told what Kyprianos had discovered about Raymond and questioned – oh, most unmercifully. I pretended to be broken-hearted at what they told me, and convinced them that I was innocent. But they locked me in a room alone, and did not realise that I could hear through the wall the plans they were making. When they had gone, I tried to get out, but, for a long time, I could not. At last Madame Bikelas heard me. She came, and unlocked the door, not knowing that I had been shut in for a purpose. I did not wait to give her any explanation, but came quickly here. And all for nothing it seems.' Then that amazing girl smiled at Hill – a wonderful, courageous smile. 'I can, at least, die with you, my Raymond, and with you, my friend Hugh.'

Both men felt suddenly very humble in the presence of such sublime courage. There was not a trace of fear in her countenance and manner. Faced with a terrible, cruel death, she was displaying a fortitude that was beyond description. All the time she was speaking, Shannon and Hill were fighting desperately to release themselves from their bonds, but the more they struggled the tighter they seemed to become. Repeatedly they shouted for help, singly and together, but were either not heard, or the other people in the building were too concerned about their own safety to take heed.

'You are not going to die, Thalia,' vowed Hugh, 'if we can help it.'

They quickly became conscious that the fire was bearing down on them. It must have obtained a rapid hold on the other suite. Momentarily the room in which they were imprisoned grew hotter, until it was almost unbearable. It was certain that before long the wall between the two flats would crash down; then! The two men looked at each other with horrified eyes, the perspiration running in streams down their faces. Each felt they must save Thalia somehow, but second by second the hope grew fainter. If they had not been locked in that apartment, they might have hopped to the dining room, and while one held a knife between his teeth, the other could have rubbed the thongs binding his wrists to and fro on the edge, until he was free.

Despairing of breaking loose – Shannon, in his herculean efforts, knew he had opened afresh two of his wounds – the big Secret Service man shuffled across to the door, and threw himself repeatedly against it in an endeavour to burst it open. It was strongly constructed, however, and, with arms, knees, and ankles bound together, he was unable to put anything like full physical force into his exertions. Hill hopped across to his assistance, and together they tried. Shannon lost his balance and fell. It took him several precious minutes to accomplish the difficult task of regaining his feet, but he succeeded, when the others felt it was hopeless for him to try. He noticed then, with a thrill of horror, that the wall was cracking; fissures began to appear, growing larger every second. Giving one great despairing effort which seemed to be tearing the muscles of his arms to shreds, he felt the thongs round his wrists give a little, and cried out with joy. Gathering himself together for one stupendous endeavour, he put all the strength he could muster into wrenching his hands apart. A terrific strain, another; then the thongs were suddenly split asunder. Thalia gave a little cry of joy and amazement. Even in that hour of stress she was able to wonder at the mighty strength that had accomplished such a feat.

The attention of them all was drawn with consternation to the wall, part of which, at that moment, crashed in, leaving a gap, through which shot a great, hungry flame, scorching them with its savage heat. Shannon's hands were far too numbed to allow him to make an attempt at undoing either the bonds of his companions or those round his own ankles. He concentrated his attention on the door, therefore, being able to get more force into his plunges against it. It continued to withstand the repeated shocks, however, while more and more of the wall crumbled in. Volumes of smoke choked them, great crackling flames darted nearer and nearer. Part of Thalia's flimsy dress caught fire, but, with a cry of agony, Hill threw himself against her as she now crouched by the door. His action put out the flame, but they both fell over. Shannon bent, and lifted them up. Pictures, carpet, chairs were now blazing fiercely. It seemed to them the end, and their eyes looked mutely, tragically into those of each other. It was at that terrible moment that, above the roar of the flames, they heard a voice, followed by a pounding on the door.

'Anyone there?' came in Sir Leonard's well-known tones. It is impossible to describe their joy. As with one voice they cried out to denote their presence. 'Key's gone,' he shouted back. 'Stand away from the lock, I'm going to blow it in.'

Shannon drew Thalia to him, Hill crouched by his side.

'All clear,' roared the former.

There came two deafening reverberations, the second following so quickly on the first that they sounded practically as one. The door was flung open, and Sir Leonard, standing there, revolver in hand, took in the situation at a glance. He lifted Thalia in his one arm as easily as though she had been a child; carried her quickly away from the flames. Shannon and Hill hopped along after them. Placing the girl in a chair, Wallace went hurriedly in search of a knife, found one, and quickly cut away their bonds. He then hustled them from the burning flat. They only escaped just in time. Outside, they found a good deal of the corridor blazing, completely cutting off their descent by the stairs. Their only hope rested in the elevators, though the space between was already on fire. However, they got across safely, each of the men keeping a watchful eye on Thalia's dress. There a great shock awaited them. They had hardly reached the doors, when the electric system failed. Useless now to expect to escape in an elevator. It was a weird, fearsome scene; tongues of flame lighting up the darkness with a vivid, terrifying light; clouds of smoke rolling round them, choking them, causing the burning tears to run from their eyes.

'There's only one thing for it,' snapped Sir Leonard, who had examined the elevator shafts to discover that both lifts were below them, thus barring the way. 'We'll have to climb up. You first, Shannon, with Thalia. You'd better carry her over your shoulder to save time.'

'I think I can climb,' she observed quietly.

Thalia found at that moment that, when Sir Leonard gave an order, it was obeyed without question. Her remark was ignored. Shannon hoisted her on his shoulder, as though she were a kitten, passed through the doorway, and commenced to climb up the shaft. Hill was ordered to follow him, Wallace bringing up the rear. Halfway up, Thalia gave a little exclamation of horror.

'Oh, the poor Sir Leonard!' she cried. 'How can he climb with but one hand to use?'

'Don't worry,' comforted Shannon; 'he can manage with that one as well as I can with two.'

Nevertheless, she waited anxiously on the next floor when Hugh set her down; smiled gladly at the coming of Hill, but with marked relief as Sir Leonard appeared directly after him.

'I was afraid for you,' she said softly, patting the artificial arm.

The darkness hid his frown – one of Sir Leonard's few weaknesses is that he is sensitive about the false member. He hates any compassionate references to it – but he was soon smiling with admiration.

'Have you no nerves, young woman?' he asked.

'She has no thought or fear for herself, sir, at all,' put in Shannon. 'Her anxieties are all for others.'

'And to think,' commented Wallace, 'that I was once led to believe that you were cruel, heartless, and self-centred! What a fool I was! Come on! The fire hasn't broken through to this floor, but it soon will. We're not out of the wood yet by any means.'

Thalia took his arm, and they hastened together to the stairs, and up to the fourth and last floor, the others following them. The roar of the flames below was not so loud or terrifying up there. They thought to hear a faraway, confused murmur of many excited voices, the clang of bells. Apparently fire engines were on the scene.

'Have all the other people escaped?' asked Thalia, as Sir Leonard hurried her along a corridor to the end of the building.

'Yes; I think so,' he replied.

It was his intention to descend with his companions by means of a fire escape at the rear of the building, which he had noticed during his investigations. It was farthest away from the burning part of the house and, therefore, the safest. The other, running down past the bathroom of the flat that had been occupied by Kyprianos, was out of the question. A good deal of it was probably, by that time, a mass of twisted metal.

They had almost reached their objective when, from behind, came a tearing, rending, altogether terrifying sound. The faces of the three men paled; their lips set more firmly. They knew what had happened. The centre of the building had caved in. If the fire escape was impassable, their condition would have become desperate again. Shannon, at a word from Wallace, flung open the window at the end of the corridor. Outside were the iron steps descending to the ground and safety. Sir Leonard glanced down. Dawn had broken, but, under ordinary circumstances, it would have been too dark to have seen much. As it was, the fire supplied a fearsome illumination. A tongue of flame was licking hungrily from a window below.

'Hurry! You first, Thalia,' he cried.

She obeyed at once, being helped through the window on to

the escape. Hill went next; then Shannon; Sir Leonard insisted upon going last. Thalia had reached the danger spot, and Hill was guiding her by, when, with a great crack, part of the wall fell in, tilting the section of the ladder on which was the girl over at an acute angle. To the intense horror of the men following her, she was thrown through the gap down into what appeared a raging furnace. Hill gave a great cry of anguish and, at imminent peril of following her, leant inwards. Almost at once he had drawn back, was looking up, the flickering light showing an expression of hope on his face.

'She is lying across a rafter not more than six feet down,' he cried. 'I'm going after her.'

'Don't be a fool!' snapped Shannon huskily. 'She can't be alive in that – you'll go too.'

'She is, I tell you. She's lying between two separate fires. I can get her, before she's—'

He said no more, but started to climb into the very maw of the hungry flames. Shannon grasped his arm, and drew him back, whereupon he tried fiercely to shake off the grip, at the imminent risk of precipitating them all into the furnace. The fire escape swayed drunkenly.

'Let him go,' shouted Wallace. 'Hold him by his ankles. If he goes down head first, he might be able to reach.'

There took place perhaps one of the most thrilling rescues it is possible to imagine. Crowds of people were now watching below, and they were dumbfounded by the spectacle they witnessed. A man being lowered head first, literally into the heart of the flames, by another, whose mighty form, shown up luridly by the fierce flickering light below, looked more than human. One leg twined round the uneven ladder to give him a grip, he was bent inwards, holding Hill's ankles at the extreme limit of his reach. His face scorching, his hair, eyebrows, and eyelashes sizzling he saw, through the smoke and flame, Hill's hands clasp the girl. Exerting his colossal strength, Sir Leonard assisting as best he could, he commenced to raise them together from the inferno. Gradually he was able to move his grip from Hill's ankles to his thighs; then to his waist. At last, with a final great effort, he lifted them to safety. Thalia's clothing was almost burnt from her body, yet she appeared little injured herself; Hill was in a worse condition than she. Wallace quickly removed his jacket, wrapping it round her. They got her past the danger point, Shannon carrying her in his arms.

'It was a miracle,' he heard her murmur, as she fainted dead away.

Wallace assisted Hill and, at last, they reached safety. Willing hands relieved Shannon of his precious burden. Some kindly soul hurried up with a blanket, which was wrapped round the girl, Sir Leonard's jacket being returned to him. She was carried into a neighbouring house, Hill going with her, where a doctor was immediately in attendance on them. Wallace and Shannon were surrounded by an excited, applauding crowd. It was publicity of a kind they did not desire, but they could not very well avoid it. They were grateful for the fact that the police, who had arrived on the scene, were too busy to spare time just then to ask awkward questions. Eventually they escaped from their admirers – Shannon, of course, was the real object of the hero-worship – by joining Thalia and Hill in the house to which they had been taken.

They found the man and girl alone. She had long since recovered from her faint, and was now lying on a couch, one of her arms swathed in bandages. She looked little the worse otherwise for her terrible experience. Hill was sitting by her side. His head and right hand were bandaged, while his eyebrows and eyelashes had been burnt off. He rose quickly to his feet, as Sir Leonard and Shannon entered the room. Thalia greeted them with one of her glorious smiles, her lips, as scarlet as ever, parting to show the two even rows of dazzling white teeth. Shannon wondered how it was that her beautiful hair, her eyebrows, her long, curling lashes had escaped being ravaged by the flames that had licked round her, as she lay, suspended on a rafter, over the roaring furnace beneath. She held out her unbandaged hand to him. He took it very gently.

'How can I say to you all that I feel, Hugh,' she murmured softly. 'I have not the words, and my heart is so much full that it is not easy to speak. To you, and to my Raymond, I owe my life. The good God has been very kind to me to forgive me for that which is past, and to give me three such brave and wonderful friends. First Sir Leonard saved us all from the burning room; then, when I am so stupid as to fall from the ladder, Raymond comes down marvellously to grasp me. But without your wonderful strength, Hugh, he could not have saved me. Without you I would now be ashes.' Shannon began to protest in an embarrassed manner. 'No, no,' she cried, 'please do not rob me of all I can do – that is to say, "thank you" from my soul.'

Wallace smiled down at her.

'We can only thank God that it was possible for you to be rescued, Thalia,' he remarked quietly. 'Raymond is in an admirable position to tell you all he feels about you. But, speaking for Hugh and myself, I can say very sincerely – I know he feels the same – that we are honoured to possess the friendship of a very gallant and noble lady.'

Abruptly she turned away her head. Great tears had welled suddenly into her eyes. She strove to keep them back, but her emotion was too powerful to allow her to suppress them.

'I am so weak and foolish. I want to weep like the great baby. It is because – oh, I cannot say it. What is the use to try? It is not possible to tell you what this wonderful kindness means to me.'

A sob broke from her, and the three men tactfully entered into conversation with each other. In reply to the anxious enquiries of the other two, Hill told them that the burns Thalia had suffered on her arm and one of her legs were not serious. Her back had been hurt in the fall on to the beam, but, apart from being badly bruised, was not damaged severely. The doctor had declared that two or three days' complete rest would put her right again. Hill made light of his own injuries, but it transpired that the side of his head and ear had been badly scorched, while two fingers of the hand had been burnt practically to the bone. While they were talking, Wallace noticed a trickle of blood running slowly down one of Shannon's wrists.

'What's that?' he asked sharply.

'Nothing much, sir,' responded the other. 'One of those blessed wounds has opened again, I think; that's all.'

Sir Leonard insisted on his removing his jacket, and he reluctantly obeyed. Both shirt sleeves and the bandages under them were soaked with blood. Not one, but three at least of the wounds had been torn open. Wallace was about to go in search of the doctor in order to have them dressed, but Hugh begged him to wait.

'There is so much to do, sir,' he declared. 'These can be attended to later on. It seems to me we've got to start more or less all over again. By this time, the blighters are escaping from us, and, with that virus still in their possession, God only knows what will happen.'

'It isn't in their possession,' replied Sir Leonard with a smile, 'but you're right, we must prevent them from getting away, if possible. It is pretty certain that they witnessed our escape from the burning building. Of one thing we can be sure: the man we want most – Kyprianos – will not go until he can regain possession of his infernal cultures.'

Shannon and Hill asked eagerly where the case was containing the fatal bottles. Thalia, who had, by then, completely recovered from the emotion that had overcome her, listened as earnestly as the others to Sir Leonard's story. He told first of his encounter with Kyprianos, and the manner in which the latter had obtained the upper hand.

'While I was searching the hall with my torch,' he related, 'he must have dodged me, and returned up the stairs. I thought he had gone out. I am afraid I did not think a great deal of my chances, when he flung himself on me with that hypodermic syringe in his hand.'

'But how was it you escaped the poison he said he had put into you?' asked Thalia. 'I heard him tell the others that, into the mysterious third man, he injected – I think it was aconitine.'

'Well,' replied Sir Leonard drily, 'aconitine hasn't much effect if injected into an artificial arm, you know.' He did not add that it was his presence of mind alone that had prompted him to place the artificial arm in the right position. 'That reminds me, a piece of the needle must still be there – it broke. I will have a look later on.'

The three stared at him for a moment; then the humour of the mistake made by Kyprianos struck them, and they laughed. Wallace described his search of the flat rented by Bikelas and the discovery of Thalia's letter, which he handed to Hill. She had already told them what was in it, of course, but her lover insisted on keeping it; putting it away in a pocket. Sir Leonard then went on to tell of his entrance into Bruno's flat and the conversation he had heard there. He blamed himself very much for not investigating the smell of burning that had reached him.

'I thought it came from outside,' he explained. 'It certainly never occurred to me that it was anything serious, until the cry of fire and the pounding on the door of Bruno's suite. I can understand how it was your shouts for help were not heard. There was a regular stampede from above. When you were calling out, everybody had escaped down to the hall and away.'

He related that Bruno and his wife had run from their room in frantic alarm. They were both too terrified to question him concerning his presence in their flat. He had placed himself with his back to the entrance door, and refused to allow Bruno to pass until told where the case was containing the virus, for he had heard the Italian mention to his wife that it was still in the house. Bruno was far too frightened to refuse. He had confessed immediately that it had been placed in a car in a garage close to the fire escape down which it had been carried; the intention being to convey it elsewhere in the morning. The car belonged to Bruno, and he had handed over the key to the scientist, or rather thought he had. He found afterwards that he had given him the wrong one after the door had been locked.

'By his own mad act, Kyprianos has probably destroyed completely his own creation,' concluded Sir Leonard. 'I let Bruno out, and went to have a look at the garage to see if any attempt had been made to break in, though I did not know then that there was any reason for it. The door was quite intact, and, by that time, quite a lot of people had gathered, in addition to those who had escaped from the fire. It was not likely that any attempt would be made on the garage with such a crowd about. I ran into Tempest, as I returned to the front of the house. He told me he had been anxious about us when the fire started. Naturally, it had not occurred to me that you were shut in. But his remarks made me wonder where you were. Something, I reflected, might have happened to you, though I couldn't see quite what it could be. However, I told Tempest to keep his eye on the garage. You know the rest.'

He did not mention that on ascending the stairs he had met a barrage of fire near the top of the second flight, and had been compelled to fight his way through. Shannon briefly told him what had taken place, laying particular stress on the gallant attempt Thalia had made to rescue him and Hill. The girl blushed vividly, as once again, and very earnestly, his admiration showing in the steely-grey eyes, which seldom displayed emotion of any kind, Sir Leonard complimented her.

'Now,' he declared, 'we will go and see what has happened to the garage. I wouldn't mind betting that Kyprianos is not far from it.'

Begging some water and strips of clean linen from the kindly residents of the house, who also brought them wine and biscuits, Hill bathed and temporarily dressed Shannon's wounds. That done, Thalia was left to the care of her sympathetic hosts, and the three men hurried out. Sir Leonard had suggested that Hill should remain, but the ex-doctor had pleaded to be allowed to accompany them, declaring that he felt quite all right. A little smile passed quickly across the chief's face at that, but he made no comment, contenting himself with a nod of acquiescence.

The fire brigade was hard at work, but the flames had obtained too strong a hold to permit any hope being entertained now of saving the building. By this time it was broad daylight and, in consequence, the scene had lost some of the grim and grisly horror that had drawn hundreds of spectators to the spot even at that early hour, and had kept them chained there in fascinated awe. Skirting the crowd, and avoiding notice as far as possible, Wallace led his companions to the garage. It was still intact, though burning debris had fallen on and all round it. The door had been broken open by several men and, as they arrived, the car was being pushed out. Sir Leonard found Tempest close by. The agent of *Lalére et Cie* rapidly explained in an undertone that a man – the description fitted Kyprianos – had called on volunteers to help him save the car, explaining that the key of the garage door had been left in the burning building. It was rather strange that his pleas had met with such a ready response, considering the danger run in approaching the garage, but Tempest explained that he had behaved like a frantic child, making the most exaggerated promises.

'Thank goodness, we have arrived in time to stop his little game,' muttered Wallace. 'Hill, go to that police officer over there, explain yourself as the Austrian Herr Kirche, who rented a flat here, and tell him that you think an attempt at robbery is being made, as the car, you feel sure, belongs to Signor Bruno.'

Grinning broadly, Hill hurried away. Sir Leonard's sharp eyes, roving about, presently became focused on a small group of men standing secluded from the crowd, and half concealed beneath a great cypress. A little sigh, indicative of triumph, escaped from him. He did not know who was who, but he recognised them as the conspirators. Rapidly he gave orders to Shannon and Tempest, indicating the group, and warning them to be careful not to divulge their presence until the right moment. He cautiously handed his revolver to Shannon, assured himself that Tempest was armed, and the two moved quietly away. Sir Leonard guessed that it was the intention of the men to escape in the car with Kyprianos, as soon as the latter had driven it away, ostensibly to another garage. They would not dare to remain in the bungalow to which they had retreated, having probably witnessed Thalia's escape, and concluding, therefore, that she would be bound to betray the place. Madame Bikelas would doubtless have been sent to a hotel, and instructed to leave Rome as soon as possible.

Kyprianos distributed gratuities with a lavish hand to his helpers, who promptly retreated out of danger. A mass of brickwork fell on the roof of the garage, breaking a great hole in it – the car had had a lucky escape. What a pity, reflected Wallace, that it had not happened before the door had been broken open! He saw the large case lying on the seat in the open tonneau, and vowed softly to himself that, whatever happened, it would not leave his sight again until it was destroyed. A half-burnt beam, still flaming, fell with a crash against the back of the car. Kyprianos gave a high-pitched cry, and pushed it away with his bare hands. He was behaving like the madman he had become; yet nobody took a great deal of interest in him, the fire itself proving too much of a magnet. He climbed into the driving seat, but found a great deal of difficulty in starting the car. His behaviour became more frenzied than ever.

It was at that moment that three police officers hurried up and accosted him. They demanded to know if the car belonged to him. The brain of Kyprianos was too far gone to prompt him to bluff them or to assure them, as he might well have done, that Signor Bruno had lent him the car, the case, with his name on it, being pointed to as evidence. Their appearance roused the devil in him; he screamed maledictions at them in his own language and in theirs. At once they approached closer to force him to leave the car. To his warped mind that was the last straw. He sprang to his feet, at the same time dragging an automatic from his pocket, and commenced shooting wildly. People within range dashed for safety with cries of rage and alarm. One policeman was hit, but his comrades quickly drew their own weapons, returning the Cypriot's fire promptly and with far more accuracy. Hit in several fatal spots, Kyprianos swayed a little; then collapsed over the wheel – dead.

'Excellent,' observed Sir Leonard quietly, 'the onus of removing him from the world has been transferred from us to the police.'

As he spoke, there was a great cracking sound. A huge portion of the wall of the burning house fell outwards, crashing down on the garage and car. The police barely escaped death, as they pulled their wounded companion out of danger; one of them, in fact, being hit by some of the debris. The car caught fire in several places at once, and quickly was a mass of flames. Nobody dared approach to drag the body of Kyprianos from it. Sir Leonard smiled cheerfully at Hill as the latter joined him.

'That's that,' he commented. 'Only fire could adequately and completely destroy those cultures, and fire is now engaged on the job. I have never come across a more eloquent case of poetic justice than this.' He looked across at the spot where the other members of the band had been standing. They were no longer there. 'Come along!' he bade Hill. 'We'll go and find out what Shannon and Tempest have done with the rest.'

CHAPTER TWENTY-ONE

A Gallant Daughter of Greece

Obeying the instructions given to them by Sir Leonard, Shannon and Tempest had made a circuit, coming up behind the group of men standing under the cypress tree. Their approach was unnoticed, due to the great caution they exercised and the anxious watch the four men were keeping on the activities of Kyprianos. The Secret Service agents concealed themselves behind some bushes, and waited. They heard the others give expression to their alarm in various forcible ejaculations, when the police accosted Kyprianos. As he drew the automatic, however, and commenced shooting, their exclamations became more suggestive of thwarted and disappointed fury. The game was completely up, and they knew it. All that was left for them to do was to get away as quickly as possible. They turned at once to escape, stood stricken with utter dismay. Confronting them was the gigantic Englishman they had left to be burnt to death. A cynical, though amazingly good-humoured smile, considering the treatment to which he had been subjected, was on his face; the revolver, held steadily pointed at them, was eloquent proof that his intentions were not exactly friendly.

'Isn't this nice,' he observed. 'There's Plasiras, Bikelas, Michalis,

Padakis – Uncle Tom Cobbley and all. Well met, gentlemen. We'll take a little walk, if you please.'

They stood too much in awe of this man to make any attempt at resistance. It was not so much the weapon he held as their knowledge of his might which kept them subdued. Directing them to lead him to the bungalow they had occupied, he forced them to walk two by two in front of him, assuring them he would shoot, without the slightest hesitation, anyone who attempted to escape.

Tempest did not show himself, but he was following, ready to aid Shannon in case of necessity. Sir Leonard had given him strict orders to keep out of sight, unless necessity made it imperative for him to appear. It would not be wise for the Rome manager of *Lalére et Cie* to be seen taking part in matters so much at variance with the sale of perfumes and other articles dear to the feminine heart.

A short distance from the scene of his coup, Shannon glanced quickly back to observe the car on fire and the body of Kyprianos lying grotesquely over the steering wheel. He cheerfully informed his captives of the fact, but was met with sullen silence as they tramped on dejectedly before him. Their thoughts must have been distinctly unhappy ones he decided, and smiled to himself. They reached the bungalow, the door was opened, and the four entered, reminded by a further warning from Shannon of the fate that would overtake them, if they attempted what he called 'funny business'. He marshalled them into a small room, and courteously bade them to be seated.

'You may be here for some time,' he went on, as though chatting with friends, 'so you may as well make yourselves comfortable. From all accounts, Italian prisons are not the most luxurious of residences.'

Bikelas shot him a terror-stricken look. Gone was the Greek's suavity of manner, while there was no expression of benevolence now in a face that had become white and pasty-looking.

'It is not your intention to hand us over to the police?' he gasped.

'It is,' returned Shannon. 'Of course, if it had been left to me, I should probably set about the lot of you myself by way of reprisal. It's a pity I can't. It isn't that I mind so much that you left me to burn, but the fact that you treated a young girl in the same manner makes my blood boil.' His voice had lost its casual note, and had become very stern. 'You, above all, Bikelas, deserve to be hanged – indeed, hanging is far too good for you. Thalia Ictinos was, in a sense, a member of your family. Your wife, I believe, was very fond of her. Yet you could countenance the dastardly act conceived in the brain of a madman.'

'I suffered most at her hands,' retorted Bikelas, 'for she betrayed my confidence in her.'

'How did you get away?' snapped Plasiras.

'Didn't you see? We thought you'd be sure to be watching. Oh! I suppose you were too busy keeping observation on the garage, and wondering how to get the car out with its very valuable luggage.'

Exclamations of surprised consternation broke from the four men.

'How did you know about the car and – and what it contained?' asked Bikelas, almost in a tone of awe.

'You'd better ask the man who has baulked your intentions at every turn,' replied Shannon drily. 'He will be here in a moment.'

'Who is he?'

The sound of voices reached their ears.

'You are about to meet him,' returned the Englishman.

Four pairs of eyes looked towards the door, through which there presently entered a slim, upright figure. The conspirators saw before them a man with an attractive, good-humoured face, in which a pair of remarkably sharp, steel-grey eyes belied his general air of nonchalance. He stood for a moment regarding them, his left hand thrust casually into his pocket, his right holding a pipe.

'A poor looking bunch,' he commented. 'Did you have any difficulty with them, Hugh?'

'Not a bit, sir. They were most lamblike. I haven't searched them for weapons. They're probably well-armed.'

'Hill,' called Sir Leonard. The ex-doctor entered the room; looked questioningly at him. 'Relieve those fellows of any weapons they may possess,' directed the chief; 'we don't want them to get hurt, if we can help it.'

Hill commenced at once on his task, Shannon standing by very much on the alert. No resistance was attempted, the four appearing to be thoroughly cowed. Plasiras alone showed any vestige of spirit. As he was being searched, he regarded Hill's bandages with a mocking look in his eyes.

'So!' he sneered. 'The Austrian art student has been playing with fire, it seems, and has burnt his fingers.'

'Be quiet, Mr Dictator!' returned Hill. 'As a certain royal lady would have said, "We are not amused".'

The four certainly had been well armed. Six revolvers, with ammunition, and three knives were taken from them. Sir Leonard had sent Tempest to the British ambassador with a message to the effect that the diplomat could now act at once, giving the address at which the men were being held captive. Tempest also had instructions to visit Thalia, and advise her to ring up the Greek embassy, if she could; otherwise to give him a note telling her people to act immediately on her report. On his return, the manager of *Lalére et Cie* was to bring back General Radoloff.

'As far as I know,' remarked Wallace, when the conspirators had been disarmed, 'there remain only two unaccounted for. Kyprianos is dead, Baltazzi is in hospital. It will not be difficult to lay Bruno by the heels. What has happened to Doreff?' he demanded of Plasiras.

The Greek shrugged his shoulders.

'I do not know,' he replied sullenly. 'He has, I suppose, run away.'

'Well, it doesn't matter much about him. He will never dare to show his face again, if he does escape.'

It may as well be mentioned in passing that Monsieur Doreff was arrested a few days later in Brindisi, whilst attempting to escape from Italy.

Sir Leonard put a few other questions to the captives, which they refused to answer. He found out, however, rather to his relief, that Madame Bikelas had, as he expected, already been sent to a place of safety. He went on a tour of inspection, during which he came upon a good deal of evidence against the men who had conspired together to obtain power by means so diabolical. This he placed ready for the Italian authorities. It was while he was away that Michalis made a desperate bid for freedom. Now that the captives were unarmed, Shannon had put away his own revolver, knowing quite well that he could quickly draw it again if necessary, though confident that he could deal with any trouble that might arise without having recourse to a weapon. Lulled into the belief that the two Englishmen were off their guard – he can hardly have made a bigger mistake in his life – Michalis suddenly made a dash for the door. He did not reach it. An enormous hand grabbed him round the neck, another caught hold of his leg, and he was flung back across the room on top of the other three, who were about to follow him. They all went to the floor together.

'Don't be obstreperous, little man!' growled Shannon, wiping his hands as though they had touched something unclean.

Hill glanced at the four men lying on the floor, apparently too surprised at the moment to rise; then looked reprovingly at his companion.

'For goodness' sake, Hugh,' he begged, 'do give a little thought to those wounds of yours. They'll never heal, if you persist in throwing – er – things about like that.'

There was no further attempt on the part of the prisoners to be 'obstreperous'. If they had not known it before, they knew now that their chances of escape from that room were nil. Weaponless, the four of them were no match for the herculean Englishman, who threw grown men about as though they were dolls. They sat sullenly together thereafter, making no attempt to address remarks either to their captors or to each other. To judge from the expressions on their faces their thoughts were gloomy indeed. Nearly an hour went by before Tempest returned. He did not enter the bungalow, but contented himself with calling for the chief. Sir Leonard went to him; was informed that the ambassador had risen promptly from bed on receiving the message. He had gone round at once to see the Minister of Foreign Affairs, Tempest being kept waiting for his return at the embassy. Early as the hour was, the Italian minister had received his visitor and, on hearing what he had to say, called up the Minister of Justice. The result of the consultation was that the matter was immediately taken in hand. A force of police was already on its way. Thalia Ictinos had promptly telephoned the Greek ambassador from the house in which she was resting. She sent a message of congratulation that the affair had been brought to a successful termination. Tempest concluded by informing Sir Leonard that Radoloff was in the car outside. He and Merryweather brought him in blindfolded and with his hands tied behind him.

He was thrust by Wallace into the room where his confederates were incarcerated, demanding indignantly to know who dared lay hands on him; threatening all kinds of pains and penalties to those who had treated him – an important Bulgarian officer – with such violence.

'That reminds me,' observed Sir Leonard. 'I must tell the embassy to explain to the representatives of Bulgaria.'

The handkerchief was removed from the general's eyes by Shannon. Another torrent of invective suddenly ceased as he observed his companions in misfortune. Realisation of the truth dawned on him, and he grew as white and dismayed as they. Bikelas, who was nearest to him, began to whisper to him, and, as the Greek spoke, the Bulgarian's face became more and more haggard. There were no further threats or indignant remonstrances from him.

Tempest and his assistant departed, followed shortly afterwards by Shannon and Hill, whom Sir Leonard did not wish the authorities to meet. They were instructed to remain within calling until the police arrived. Armed with a revolver, the chief stood on guard himself. The prisoners grew a little hopeful when they were left alone with a man leaning so nonchalantly against the door, his left hand pushed into his jacket pocket, but the hope was soon killed. Plasiras rose to his feet; stood measuring the other with his eyes.

'Sit down!' commanded Wallace. Plasiras continued to stand, whereupon, without another word, the Englishman fired twice in rapid succession, putting a bullet through each sleeve of the Greek's coat, but not harming him. 'Let that be a lesson to you,' remarked Sir Leonard, as the other sat hastily down. 'If you move again, I won't be so kind.'

Shannon's and Hill's faces appeared at the window; grinned appreciatively as they saw Plasiras shakily examining the holes in his sleeves, and disappeared again. At last came the sound of several cars drawing up outside, the noise of many men gathering, sharp words of command. Into the room presently stalked a high officer of the police, followed by several subordinates. He glanced curiously at the prisoners; turned to Sir Leonard, and saluted him.

'I was told, signor,' he remarked in excellent English, 'that here I should meet Colonel Wallace of the British Diplomatic Service.'

'I am he,' returned Sir Leonard, putting away his revolver, and handing the other a card.

The newcomer took it with a bow, read it, and again saluted.

'I am honoured, signor,' he declared. 'My name is Pirelli. These are the prisoners?'

'They are. You will find any amount of evidence against them in this house; the rest will be provided by the British and Greek ambassadors. There is another man lying dead in a burnt-out car, which is already in the possession of the police. Two – a man called Doreff, who is a Bulgarian, and Bruno, who is a compatriot of yours, are still at liberty.'

The officer smiled.

'Bruno has been already caught,' he announced. 'We know him by sight. He passed us in a car near the Porta Pinciana, was recognised, and chased by some of my men. He is by now in custody.'

'Excellent,' murmured Sir Leonard. 'Then I will leave you to take charge. I shall be at the British embassy, when you require me.'

They shook hands, and Sir Leonard departed. Shannon and Hill joined him a short distance away, and they walked together to the house where Thalia awaited them, passing the burnt-out block of flats as they went. The fire had by that time been extinguished, though it still smouldered in places. The great house had been completely gutted, nothing but a mere shell remaining, in which enormous gaps enabled observers to get a comprehensive view of the now piteous interior. The three Englishmen approached the heap of twisted metal that had once represented a motor car. A piece of the framework, a hinge, some broken glass were all that was left of the case and phials containing the deadly cultures. The virus, with its creator, had been destroyed completely. The world was safe from a disease that might have annihilated humanity.

Thalia welcomed them with a glad little cry. Hill went straight to her and, bending over, kissed her without a trace of embarrassment. Sir Leonard and Shannon smiled at each other, and were about to leave the room again, but she bade them stop.

'Oh!' she cried. 'Would you desert me, my wonderful friends, before I have congratulated you on your so great achievement? Mr Tempest told me all that which had happened, and I am so happy. It is now all over?'

'Yes, Thalia, it is all over,' replied Sir Leonard. 'And a great deal of the success is due to you. I will take care that the Greek government is made aware of what it owes to its most gallant daughter.'

The colour rose slowly to her cheeks, her glorious eyes sparkled gladly.

'Again you are too much good to me,' she murmured. 'It is little that I have done. Those others, the poor secretaries, died, while I was lucky to have so much protection – without it I would have also died.'

'They were in the same service as you?' asked Shannon.

'Not exactly,' she replied. 'They were bribed to find out what they could about their employers. They did not know me, but I knew about them. Part of my duty was to watch them to see that they did not do the – oh, what is it – the word I want?'

'The dirty,' hazarded Shannon.

'No, no – ah! I have got it: I was to watch that they did not do the double-cross.' Shannon smiled significantly at Hill, who flushed painfully and lowered his eyes. Thalia looked from one to the other. 'What is it, my Raymond?' she asked anxiously. 'Why do you look so?'

'For a little while I doubted, Thalia,' he confessed. 'Words spoken by the secretary, when he was dying, shook my faith – a little. Shannon quickly showed me what a fool and a rotter I was. I – I'm terribly sorry, dear.'

She put her fingers gently on his lips.

'There is nothing for which to be sorry,' she declared softly. 'It is a great wonder to me any of you ever found the faith in me.'

'It would be a sign that we were lunatics if we had not,' retorted Sir Leonard. 'And now I want to beg a favour.'

'Oh!' she cried, 'I will gladly grant it, if I can. What is it?'

'I want to give you away at your wedding. May I?'

'And I'll jolly well insist on being best man,' vowed Shannon.

She gave the bandaged hand to Wallace, the other to Shannon; smiled gloriously, happily at them, though tears were in her eyes.

'You dear men, I shall love it. When that day comes, I shall feel that I am cleansed from all taint of the name Ictinos, for it will belong to me no more.'

'No,' breathed her lover, 'but there can be no taint on a name that you have glorified.'

He and she forgot their companions, as he took her into his arms. Sir Leonard Wallace and Captain Hugh Shannon quietly left the room.